Her voice when it came was very soft. "So we're going to do nothing."

"Dickie . . ." He reached out to her, but her eyes did not leave his. "It's the way things are. It's not fair, but it's the way. I'm sorry."

"*You're* sorry." Her fists grasped the black material of her dress up against her throat. "Well . . . I won't let them do this to us, Dad. Sam," she turned to him, "you're still going to fight them, aren't you?"

Sam bit his lip. "Oh, Dickie." He shook his head. "Dad's right. They'd never believe us. Mr. Redfield'd be that embarrassed he'd have to fire Dad to protect his sons. It's the way they are, blood's thicker. We'd have nothing."

"We have nothing now," she said with a voice so soft they could hardly hear her, "if we haven't our pride."

Also by Pamela Townley:

THE IMAGE

ROGAN'S MOOR

WINTER JASMINE

WOMAN IN THE WIND

Pamela Townley

Formerly entitled: *The Stone Maiden*

IVY BOOKS • NEW YORK

Ivy Books
Published by Ballantine Books
Copyright © 1987 by Pamela Townley

Originally published under the title *The Stone Maiden*.

Library of Congress Catalog Card Number: 86-30395

ISBN-0-8041-0230-9

This edition published by arrangement with G.P. Putnam's Sons, a division of The Putnam Publishing Group, Inc.

Manufactured in the United States of America

First Ballantine Books Edition: May 1988

for my little boy

and for Gavan who gave me Rogan
and to my friends who cared for him whilst I was working:
Kate, Mari-Paz, Gaylie, Mary-Ann, Mary, Stella and
Maureen,
also Mummy,
Carolyn,
Harvey Tring, Ronnie Grey,
special thanks to Michael Taylor, aviation expert,
and as always, Meepy-Mewl

BOOK ONE

1913–1929

ONE

Late October, 1913

With the touch of his prize he lost all reason. He could smell her, feel her skin. He kicked his horse into a gallop as he looked for the place he was seeking. This was a prey that he could abuse in quite a different way.

The wood opened into a copse and a bank climbed upwards thick with bracken. Sunlight streamed in rays through the trees. He reined his horse in, letting her go. She fell, jarring herself on the hard earth. He was right behind her, freeing his horse as he advanced on her.

He threw his hat to the ground. She saw his thick yellow hair; in a face washed out by its blondness, the eyes stood out unframed and cold. Hunter's eyes. She moved, her mind clearing. There was a bank behind her. Her feet scrambled for a hold in the sliding earth, her hands clawed at the bracken. His hands gripped her ankles.

At the edge of the clearing the other man brought his horse to a halt. He ordered the hounds to sit. As he watched his brother mount the girl, Frederick Redfield caught his breath. He felt the answering surge in himself. The chase had filled him too and he was a hunter. He responded to the scent of fear and finish with the hunter's instinct to capture a thing of beauty.

As the man dropped his weight upon her, the sun reflected off the back of his blond hair. She closed her eyes. She felt the press of his body, the rough material of his jacket and the sharp buttons that bit into her bared breasts. She felt the sudden awful pain.

Frederick moved out of the shadows towards them. He began to shake as her cries became an aphrodisiac. It took all his concentration to walk towards her. Suddenly Rupert was gone.

His face came into the sunlight above. She stared at him, incapable of movement. His eyes had darkened and he seemed in the grip of something beyond his control.

'Forgive me,' he breathed, and then forgot her in his need. He felt the warm body, the sun on his back and the musky smell of her in his nostrils. He clutched her breasts and shouted his emotion into the stillness.

He turned away and dressed himself. She did not move. He could feel the accusation like a knife blade in his back. He closed his eyes briefly.

His horse was standing still beneath the branches of the tree. He clasped the reins and turned back to her. She was lying there, staring up towards the break in the branches, the sun full in her eyes. It was the first time he had noticed. Underwater eyes, cool, clear and luminous. Frederick felt an emotion he could not explain. His hand lifted and he moved as if about to speak. The girl did not register him at all. She stared upwards. It was as if he did not exist.

He threw himself onto his horse turning its head roughly, and swung round through the woods, racing away to join his brother.

Behind them, the hounds sniffed briefly around the clearing, aware of the heat of their action and the smells of sweat and something new. Their scent led them to the girl. She lay still and unmoving, alone, not reacting. This time she did not kick them away.

'Jasper! Bunter! Come on!'

The hounds lifted their heads to the familiar voice of their master. Happily they bounded away, panting as they raced up through the wood towards the rest of the hunt.

After some time and when the wood was still again, Dickie lifted herself to a sitting position. She looked down and was silent. She pulled her petticoats down to her ankles and saw the stain. She felt revulsion, and then revulsion cleared and anger took its place. She lifted the hem of her black skirt up over her shoulders to cover her naked breasts, and picked herself up. She looked for the direction of the fields and took a step. Her legs were weak, but grew stronger. She started to run.

* * *

The men picked in the wake of the foreman. Jim drove his plough through the furrows where the potatoes had been grown. The soil was thrown outwards from the double-sided plough-share like the wake from a ship. The old carthorse pulled it along behind him as it split through the dried remains of the potato stems.

Sam stopped a moment and grinned, wiping the sweat and dirt of the day from his face with the back of his calloused hand.

'There's got to be twenty tons in that clamp already, Thomas.'

'Ay, I knew that extra fertiliser'd pay off.'

Dickie stumbled to the edge of the wood and looked up the field to where the two men were talking. The cool October air was filled with the musky odour of freshly turned soil. Sam's voice carried on the air, and she could hear the jingle of the harness and the creaking of the high-sided cart as it moved slowly up the field.

Sam bent down again to grasp the white potatoes from the dark, newly turned soil. He threw them into an enormous wicker basket. Thomas tipped the basket into the lurching cart.

'Sam!' She lifted her hand. 'Sam!'

He did not hear her call. The small team of men moved on slowly up the field. Her voice was faint from running, her throat too raw from the panic breathing of her fear. She held the skirt of her dress fisted against her chest, her eyes on him. 'Sam!'

As Thomas tipped the new load into the cart his eye caught sight of the small figure of the girl down at the bottom of the field at the edge of Cobbold's Wood. She lifted her hand again. There was a sense of urgency about the gesture. Thomas frowned against the light. 'Hey, Sam.' He tapped the younger man on the arm. 'Isn't that young Dickie? Look.'

Sam turned. Her face was a white moon in the distance but he could see the darkness around her eyes, the tension. She was clutching her dress against her, her petticoats showing. Something was wrong.

He dropped the potatoes he was holding into the basket.

'Dad!' he shouted. Jim turned from the plough. 'Something's up with Dickie. Hold up, would you?' He was off down the field with his long stride, running across the freshly exposed earth, as Jim called, 'Whoa, whoa, boy!' and pulled the massive beast to a halt.

As he reached her he saw the way she looked. His hands gently held her arms, his eyes first on her face and then travelling down her body. 'Dickie, love. Whatever happened to you?' His voice was tinged with alarm. Her dark hair was tangled on her shoulders, loosed from the neat coil he was used to seeing, and her clothes were crumpled and smeared with dirt. She was holding her dress against a torn bodice and her shoulders were naked. She was trembling slightly. Her face lifted to his now looked different.

'Oh, Sam!' At the sight of her brother her strength gave way. Her legs buckled and she swayed slightly. Sam caught her in his arms and she leaned gratefully against his chest. Behind them, Jim started to run down the field. In the distance, Thomas held the reins of the horse, his worried face staring down the field.

Sam held her. 'What happened, Dickie?' His voice was gentle.

She looked up at him then, her arms still pressed to her chest. The green eyes held his. 'The Redfield brothers,' she said. 'They came to the cottage while I was making lunch. Their hounds frightened Mixie,' she said, referring to the kitten he had given her for her fourteenth birthday that week. 'So I ran out. Sam, I told them to get off our land, but they didn't. Rupert Redfield barged me with his horse. He enjoyed it. He wanted to frighten me, I know, and I meant to stand up to him, but oh, Sam, I couldn't help it, I started to run. I was running to get help from you and Dad. They came after me. It was awful. He threw me across his horse and me petty over me head, and I couldn't see nothing, until he threw me down on the ground.' She stopped and looked away remembering Frederick then. She had loved him—impossibly, but none the less she had. She had seen him in the village, knew that he, Frederick, was liked by everybody. He was a decent man, the youngest one, that was what they said. And so handsome. She remembered how she had seen him watching, her heart's surge of joy when he had walked forward from the belt of trees. He had come to save her. And then, as he had come closer she had seen that abandoned look in his eyes, and she had known she was lost. Dickie closed her eyes tight against the vision that followed. The disillusionment set in. She felt its bleakness surround her like a damp, grey cloud.

Sam grasped her arms tighter. His eyes were filled with her, her face, her story. He forced her to look back at him.

He shook her slightly. 'And then? What then? What did they do to you?'

She clenched her jaw. Her eyes ran over his face and back to his eyes. They stared through him as she told him what they had done.

'Sam, they hurt me. It hurt awful.'

'Oh, God!' Sam pulled her to him. He held her tiny body close and felt the impotent rage building in him. Her dark head was pressed in against his chest. He looked over her head and down at the bottom of the woods, the farm gate, but saw nothing. His fury contained him completely. He heard the sound of his father plodding down the field behind him, his laboured breathing, but he did not turn. He fed her all his strength. For now she needed it from him for the first time. She was only a child, damn them, damn them to hell.

'What happened, lad?' The wiry figure of their father, Jim Bennett, stood beside him. Sam's thoughts raced on. His sister. They would not get away with it.

'Dickie?' Jim asked again. He laid a weathered hand on her back. His eyes jumped with shock as he touched the torn blouse. He looked down and saw the blood on her petticoat. 'My God, girl. What has happened? Tell me.'

Dickie took a deep breath. Her face was calmer now, her eyes still and bereft of all emotion. Her rage and pain had died against Sam's chest.

Sam answered for her, his arms still around her. 'The Redfields. They chased our Dickie into the woods. They raped her, Dad.'

Jim had known it the moment he saw her. He had sensed such a thing had happened. He clenched his fists and looked at Sam. 'The young Redfields? Not *both* of them?' It was all he could think of to say.

'Both of them.' He held Dickie away from him. 'I'm going up to Foxhall, Dad. Take care of Dickie.'

Jim stepped forward. He reached out and held his son's arm. 'Wait. What you going there for?'

Sam turned and looked down at his father. 'To find them and give them the beating of their lives. I'll tell the old man too. I'll take Thomas and Jack.' He lifted his hand to call Thomas down from the field.

Jim brought Sam's arm down quickly, his hand clutching his

son's sleeve. 'Stop, *stop*, Sam!' He stared into Sam's angry face. 'Let's think about this a moment,' he added more quietly.

'What's there to think about?' Sam's normally gentle blue eyes held a fierce light in them. Dickie's eyes were on him too.

'Well,' said Jim. 'Us, for one thing. All of us. Our family.' He looked at his daughter, at her dirtied clothes and white face. And yet her eyes were bold, that was half her trouble. Jim felt like a man torn in two. He was simple, hardworking and unde-manding, a man used to rules and the position he had been born into, a position of servitude that would never change. He knew the way things were. 'Think what it might do to us,' he finished unhappily.

'What does that matter?' Sam turned away again, ready to go.

Jim caught his arm once more. 'It matters a lot,' he said firmly. 'Don't you see? What can we do about it? We'll lose our jobs if you go up to the Manor now shouting for those two lads to come out and fight, sure as anything. And do you think that Mr Redfield's going to believe you . . . ? Well, do you?' His voice rose against the accusing look in their faces. He jabbed a finger against his chest. 'Our word against theirs. Who do you think they'd believe, eh?'

'What are you saying then?' Sam shouted back, Dickie for-gotten between them. 'That you're going to let them get away with this?' He thrust his arm wide. 'They ought to hang people that do what they did! A beatin's not good enough for bastards like them!'

'I know, I *know*.' Jim sighed and shook his head. His eyes searched blindly around him for an answer. 'But he won't be-lieve us! He can't, for the sake of his family he can't. So, what will happen? We'll lose our jobs. I only work here. I'd get the sack and then where would we be? The cottage is tied in to the job, like.' He shoved his hands in his pockets. 'And then again, Dickie's due to go up there as scullery-maid next week.'

Her voice burst in between them. 'I'm not going there now, Dad. You can't mean it.' Her eyes were piercing; she pulled her clothes protectively to her. 'I'll *see* them.'

'No, you won't,' he said. 'You never did before. They live in the house. You'll be in the scullery, working.'

'She can't work there *now*, Dad.' Sam put his arm around her, seeing her shiver with dread. 'Not after this.'

'She's got to.' For the moment, Jim looked over her head,

avoiding her eyes. 'We need the money. And it's all arranged. If she didn't go now, it'd look peculiar. Besides, it's a good job. Well paid. Don't look at me like that, Sam. I know what I'm talking about. Don't you think I want to avenge Dickie as much as you do? Good Lord.' He shook his head and looked at her. His eyes were full of tears as he reached for her hands and took her into his arms. He was helpless. There was nothing they could do. 'We'd lose everything,' he said. 'Our home, everything. The Redfields own not only this land we work on, but the village as well and the minds and the purses of most of the people around here. You know that.'

His words reached through Sam's anger at last. He let out a painful breath and hung his head briefly, his eyes empty. The new thought reached him at that moment. 'What if there's a child, Dad?' he murmured. 'What then?'

Jim held Dickie fast against him. He stroked her dark hair briefly. His voice was as certain as if he had already faced that thought and assessed it clearly. 'They must never know,' he said quietly. Dickie stiffened in his arms. 'That'd be it, for sure. We'd be kicked out. Out of the village.'

Dickie pushed herself out of his arms. 'You mean you wouldn't ask him to recognise his child?' She did not say who.

Jim frowned. He looked both puzzled and shocked. 'Would you *want* him to?'

Dickie ignored him. Her anger was born inside her. 'You're going to let them get away with it?' Her voice was slow and disbelieving.

Jim lifted his hands helplessly. 'You've heard what we've said, child.' He blinked as she stared at him. Her look held humiliation, accusation, disbelief. He could not face it.

They were all silent, the quiet heavy after the angry voices raised a moment before. A bird shrilled in a treetop close by. In the distance the men's voices called to each other at the top of the field.

Her voice when it came was very soft. 'So we're going to do nothing.'

'Dickie . . .' He reached out to her, but her eyes did not leave his. 'It's the way things are. It's not fair, but it's the way. I'm sorry.'

'*You're* sorry.' Her fists grasped the black material of her dress up against her throat. 'Well . . . I won't let them do this to us, Dad. Sam,' she turned to him, 'you're still going to fight them, aren't you?'

Sam bit his lip. 'Oh, Dickie.' He shook his head. 'Dad's right. They'd never believe us. Mr Redfield'd be that embarrassed he'd have to fire Dad to protect his sons. It's the way they are, blood's thicker. We'd have nothing.'

'We have nothing now,' she said with a voice so soft they could hardly hear her, 'if we haven't our pride.'

She paused, the green eyes eloquent. The two men hung their heads. They were silent.

'Well, I'll fight,' she said. For the first time she realised the vulnerability of their position. The Redfields were immune from basic laws of humanity, while they were not. The shock had coursed through her as they had spoken and she had understood what they were essentially saying. She had thought they would fight for her. They would not, or could not. She held her head higher. 'I will defeat them, Sam,' she affirmed. 'Even if you will not.' She glared at her father and brother, pulling her pathetic blouse tighter around her. Her voice was thin on the cold air but defiantly proud. 'One day I will have money to own land like this. And then no one, not even the Redfields, will be able to use me again in this way or any other.' Her voice became raw with emotion, her eyes filling with her own impotence. 'I'll fight,' she said again. 'I'll fight those damn Redfields to their graves.'

Jim stretched out a hand. 'Dickie,' he said. 'I know how you feel.' But he did not touch her. The wounded look in her eyes kept him away.

'You don't know, Dad,' she warned.

'I do,' he said sadly. He took the jacket off his back and laid it around her rigid shoulders. His hand touched the small of her back. 'We'll go home now. Tomorrow we'll go to church.' He looked into their faces as he spoke. 'Let's pray that you're not with child.'

The bells tolled gently over the fields for matins.

A few people were still moving towards the old Norman church that sat beside the bridge at the foot of the village. The soft lights from the leaded windows glowed and an icy drizzle began to fall.

They hurried then, collars up against the rain. Over the bridge

Dickie and Sam half ran towards the open door of the church. The organ music was stealing out gently and persuasively, inviting them in to the warm house of peace.

Jim followed them at a quick pace. They turned the corner of the bridge and ran down the grassy verge towards the grey flagstones at the front of the church. Beyond, the pews were full for a Sunday morning.

The music stopped as they stamped their feet lightly and went in. The Bennett family were recognised for what they were and whispered to a pew at the back of the church. All were equal in the eyes of God, some more than others.

They knelt to pray. Jim stayed bent a long time as if he was deep in thought. Dickie's prayer was brief. The anger was stronger in her now if anything. She did not believe that church was the place for her to be. She would not be a hypocrite and pretend that it was, neither would she forgive, nor forget. She would not turn the other cheek.

She sat up straight and looked ahead of her. She was dressed in her smartest clothes, a grey worsted coat and hat, and her black boots were highly polished. The music ploughed out again, this time fervently. Ahead of them the vestry door opened and the choir began to file out in twos. The parishioners stood dutifully with a brushing of clothes and a shuffling of feet against wood and stone. They opened their hymn books and began to sing.

Dickie's sense of occasion was dulled. The memory was physically with her, her body ached with it, and her mind kept returning to the scene: the terrifying dash through the woods, the mauling of her body, the stripping away of her pride—so much a part of her. She mouthed the familiar words of the hymn without thought, her mind elsewhere. The choirboys streamed out of the vestry, turned the corner and crossed before her vision. Now they were followed by the older men in slow procession, singing and praising the Lord. Sam's and Jim's heads were still bent reverently.

Dickie's hand suddenly clutched the wooden rail of the pew in front of her. She swayed with the shock. Her mouth closed and her eyes opened wide to fix on the man who now walked elegantly from the door of the vestry, following the choir. He was dressed in long black cassock and pure white surplice, a blue scarf around his neck trailing to his hem, the·medallion shining on his chest. His blond hair was smoothed back and in the light of the candles his profile was handsome and strong. Dickie's hymn book lowered slowly as if the weight of it were suddenly too much for her.

He climbed the steps to the altar and bowed reverently. Then, head slightly bent, he took his place at the head of the pew. He turned then to address the congregation. The blue eyes bore down on them, seeming to single her out from the crowd. A smile was on his face, a smile that asked them to join with him in one perfect union. His charisma was powerful. He was tall and magnificent. He held out his arms to embrace them all. His voice was resonant.

'Let us pray.'

They fell to their knees, obedient. They bent their heads. Ladies, young and old, thrilled to the aspect of their new lay reader. This would swell the congregation.

Dickie's head remained raised. Across the heads before her she stared at him, as the little church filled with the sound of his reverent voice and the willing responses. Her hate blazed. Now she knew what her father meant. The music swelled out. He began to sing. He had a beautiful voice. He had them in the palm of his hand. No one would ever believe her.

Her small body sat rigid on the edge of the hard, polished seat. God forgive me my blasphemy, she thought. I will destroy him.

TWO

July, 1914

Above a broad sweep of the river Thames, the Redfields held their annual Henley house-party at Foxhall Manor. The house was set imposingly against its backdrop of trees on a hill that overlooked the whole of the long valley for miles. Long sweeping lawns ran down to the river, today clustered with friends and family. The afternoon sun blazed down on a sea of straw boaters and shady hats, and beds of colourful roses. On the terrace stood rows of tables, their starched white cloths gently billowing in the breeze under jugs of iced lemonade, tea and home-made cakes.

It was high summer and five miles away to the north-east, the annual river regatta at Henley had started. In London, the streets sweltered in a heat wave, but here in the country it was idyllic. The long hot days had been spent idly boating on the river, playing tennis, cricket or croquet. Along with the other families, the Redfields had spent the Season at their London residence in Belgravia. One party had followed another. Now the Season was over and they were back in their country houses.

Lady Caroline Lancing stood shyly beneath the silk-trimmed brim of her white hat and listened to the young man talking to her. Frederick Redfield was nineteen, lean and handsome. His fair hair was smoothed to his head from a high forehead, his nose was long and straight, there was a sensuality to his lips and all his movements were graceful. He was tall, his shoulders slightly bowed as he bent to the small girl beside him, and his dark, sleepy, blue eyes were creased with gentleness. He was telling her about his hopes for that autumn when he was due to go up to Christchurch College, Oxford. In her hand, Caroline held the slim volume of verse that he had given her. Later, he had offered to take her boating on the river. She wondered if he would pick her some flowers to press and lay carefully in the book. The Season was over and she was supposed to have made a match. Maybe it could be Frederick. She listened with interest to his conversation and wondered if he liked her enough to ask for her hand. She smiled hopefully at the thought of what he might say.

Frederick, seeing her smile, thought how pretty she was when she relaxed. He was aware of the air of fine delicacy about her, as though she was fragile enough to break. All the Lancing girls had that air about them, even their mother. It drew all men in like a scent, making them instantly protective.

Frederick spoke gently.

'Would you care for some lemonade, Lady Caroline? It's so very hot today. Perhaps the shade of the terrace . . . ?'

'Thank you, I would. Mr Redfield . . . ?'

'Yes?'

'Could you, perhaps, could we . . . that is, would you take me to see the fireworks after dinner tonight? I've heard it's very beautiful by the river, and I've never been allowed to go before. Is it true they light the tow-path with Chinese lanterns and take all the punts out on the river?'

'They do indeed. I would be honoured if you would accompany me.' His voice was intimate and warm. 'I know this river better than anyone, Lady Caroline. I can think of nothing nicer than to share it with you.'

He touched her arm to guide her, and caught her elbow just below the edge of her ruched lace sleeve. Caroline started at the brush of his fingertips on her skin. Her eyes swiftly met his. Frederick's dark eyes showed his feelings all too clearly.

He dropped his gaze as she blushed, and stood back for her to precede him up the lawn to the terrace. Their eyes now averted, she breathed more easily, though her heart beat a little faster. Caroline was very innocent; the youngest of four girls, she had been the last to come out only three months earlier, straight from the schoolroom to the drawing-room, her black hair piled on her head for the first time and only a light dusting

of powder on her cheeks. Her dark blue eyes were now warm
with anticipation. A man's attentions were still a novelty.

They started up the lawn together.

Alexander Redfield stood in the cool darkness of his study and
looked out over the bright array on his lawn. He watched his
younger son escort the girl to the terrace in front of him with
approval.

The sound of loud laughter from the direction of the tennis
court to the side of the house distracted him. A small party
strolled through the yew hedges and onto the lawn. Rupert was
in their centre. As they walked into the sunshine, he pulled a
woman briefly towards him. She laughed up flashily into his
face, the green feathers on her hat dancing. Clare Finhaven was
notorious; a sophisticated London hostess who gathered a group
of young men around her, many of whom were her lovers. From
the way she relaxed against his son's broad chest, Alexander had
no doubt that he was one of them.

Alexander had few illusions about Rupert. People were a
commodity to him, and yet they allowed themselves to be used.

One of the Labradors bounded across the garden towards
him. Rupert bent to it almost immediately, ruffling its ears. As
he squatted on the ground, the small group waited around him.
Rupert's eyes scanned the party as he patted the dog, and came
to rest on Frederick and Caroline. Rupert was jealous of his
brother: Frederick was a Redfield with the graceful beauty of
that family, where Rupert was a Bryn-Parry like his mother's
side, headstrong and wilful, fighters all of them. They expected
to win.

Rupert straightened out to his full six feet and flexed his powerful frame. He was a big man, barrel-chested with long legs.
The group got ready to move, but he ignored them. His eyes
were on Caroline. He walked purposefully across the lawn towards her.

Alexander ran a hand over his thick white hair. 'You're lucky
to have daughters, George. Sons can be a trial.' He touched the
copy of Country Life lying on the circular polished table. 'I
worry about Rupert.' He saw Clare Finhaven watch him go, a
disappointed look on her beautiful face. 'Can't leave women
alone.'

George, Earl of Lancing, crossed the room to join his friend at the window. 'Nothing wrong in that. Healthy appetite.' He puffed at his pipe. 'I was like that. So were you, Alexander. Not so old that you've forgotten, surely!' His eyes twinkled as he tapped the other man's shoulder with his pipe. 'No,' he closed his eyes briefly and smiled. 'Not his fault. The women sense it. A certain type anyway.' He indicated Clare Finhaven. 'Just good training. He's a lad with oats to sow. And heir to all this.' He thrust his arm wide. 'Land, money and a bank to run. Eligible young fellow. Women, they sniff it out. No harm in saying yes when it's offered on a plate, so to speak. We did, same sort of women, too.' He chuckled warmly. 'Just so long as he's discreet, eh? Ah, those days. Oh, to be young again, eh, Alexander?'

'Yes, indeed.' And with the knowledge that we have now, thought Alexander.

'Marriage'd put him right,' said George.

Alexander looked at him. George winked and smiled, and drew on his pipe. Alexander knew what he meant. The Lancings were one of the most aristocratic families in the country, but they had lost their historic grip on the reins of power and much of their wealth. The weddings of George's succession of daughters had practically broken him, or at least consumed what little he had left. They needed a good match for their last and youngest unmarried daughter, Caroline.

Alexander turned again to watch Rupert. He had joined the other two now and with her face uplifted towards his, Alexander could see that Caroline was a remarkably pretty girl, small and delicate, but nervous. It was apparently Rupert who made her nervous. She appeared to retreat slightly from his presence.

He opened the leaded window on its latch. The noise of the party carried up the lawn towards them. Frederick looked uncomfortable. Alexander felt sorry for him. He was no match for Rupert when he wanted something. And Rupert now wanted Caroline. Her fragility seemed to fascinate him, and her fear. He seemed to enjoy her discomfort, pressing his attentions harder on her. George was right. Women were affected by him, one way or another. It was time he married. A woman should be mistress of Foxhall now that Mary was dead. Poor Mary, she had not lived long enough to see what it had become.

* * *

Alexander had been shrewd. Before the end of the nineteenth century the influx of cheap corn from America had led to twenty years of deep depression in the farming industry in Britain. Upper-class families who were entirely dependent on income from their land had found themselves in difficulties. A good many had had to sell up altogether, the myth of landowning was over, but the lure of the country house remained as strong as ever. Spreading cedar trees still cast their shade over green lawns and tea-tables laid with white tablecloths, the hostesses pouring tea from silver teapots. Nothing, it seemed, had changed, but in fact a great deal had. The families that survived the agricultural slump were those with rents from property in London, or money from a family business.

Alexander had both. He was a banker as his father had been before him. Redfield-Strauss dealt in cotton and gold bullion and by the end of the nineteenth century they had won their place in the City and were accepted.

Alexander did not consider himself a new man from the City. He was a banker and bankers were so essential to the upper classes that they stood in a special position all their own. Previously they had had no hope of getting a peerage until the 1830s. By the year 1900 the situation was different. The new rich were being given titles and taking the train up to their London offices to deal in trade and industry. However, at a time when trade was edging its way into acceptability with the upper classes, there were still guidelines to adhere to; necessities, if one was to become totally integrated into that world.

Alexander was ahead of the game. A country estate was essential to underline their relatively new position. Foxhall Manor had been crumbling when he bought it. It had once been a vast estate, taking in the whole village of Foxhall Green and the thousands of acres of outlying farms. To invest in that much land was now socially, politically and financially unwise. He was unwilling to lumber himself, anyway, with too much land. He was not a farmer. He kept enough to provide adequate shooting, fishing, hunting, four tenanted farms, a home farm with a pedigree herd and some village properties. He sold off the thousands of acres, investing the money in shares, but still maintained a beautiful country house set in acres of tranquil parkland.

He had engaged Sir Edwin Lutyens to restore Foxhall to its original magnificence. The house was of medieval design, built of stone and weathered wood with mullioned, leaded windows and a large central drawing-room surrounded by a beautifully carved minstrel's gallery. It was protected from the worst of winter weather by a thick beech wood to the north and east. In the summer it was dignified and mellow, bathed in perpetual sunshine.

Lutyens had equipped the house with central heating, electric light and eight bathrooms. A south-facing terrace was designed for afternoon tea; the bedrooms were modernised. However romantic he might have been about the past, Alexander wanted to be comfortable. A grass tennis court was laid down, and the stables rebuilt as was the crumbling stone balcony that ran the length of the house. From the front of the house there was the most magnificent view over the river, the valley and the hills beyond.

And then Mary, his wife, had died in a hunting accident. He had never even considered remarriage: theirs had been a great love not to be defiled by a replacement. She had been so much younger and destined for a very different marriage. They had met on a day such as this one and fallen in love. Mary was like all the Bryn-Parrys: headstrong. She would do only what she wanted and not what others wished. She was a strong woman. Marrying for love was frowned upon, dynastic considerations far more important, but she had refused to comply. Their love affair was already beyond stopping, but their plans for elopement never materialised. Her parents gave their consent.

His eyes were warm with memory as he looked out over the lawn. She had been his strength and consolation, and half his age. He wondered if they would have eloped in the end. The thought made him smile. The garden was shaded now as the sun moved round. The air was heavy with the scent of roses. The river sparkled in the sunlight under the weeping willows. It was an idyllic spot, a home for people who loved each other. He had been in a strong enough position to marry the girl he loved. He wanted his sons to be strong too.

'Pity Mary's not here, Alex. She'd have enjoyed today.'

'Yes, she would.' It was as if the other man had read his thoughts. 'She'd have gone riding . . . remember the way she used to do that? Great parties, and then she'd always take off suddenly in the middle.'

'She was very spirited, your Mary.'

'Yes, she was.' He smiled, remembering. 'And I try to keep things the way she would have wanted them—relaxed and informal, a home full of laughter and light. Impossible though to recreate what Mary brought us all. My ideas were always of a different ilk, more traditional. My father always taught us respect for our elders and betters. Keep them in line with what's important in life. One has to with sons. But they need a mother. Children need to be given a balance of right and wrong. Mary knew that.' He sighed. 'Do you know, George, without her I'm lost. She was everything to me. I needed her.'

'The boys need you, too. And Foxhall needs a mistress again, Alexander. Thank the Lord you don't have all these girls to marry off. I'm going to be a pauper by the time I've finished. Still, there's only Caroline left now.' He caught his bottom lip with his teeth, his eyes straying towards his daughter standing between Alexander's sons and back to the older man again. 'You'll find willing brides. They're handsome boys.'

Alexander watched Rupert break away and for an instant Caroline's eyes followed him. There was apprehension there but perhaps something else. Frederick offered Caroline his arm and they walked away and down to the river. Rupert strode off across the lawn heading in the opposite direction, towards the stables. Alexander frowned as he saw a woman detach herself and follow casually at a distance.

George noticed too. He smiled and raised an eyebrow. He picked up the jug of iced lemonade from the silver salver on the corner table. A bowl of crimson roses stood beside it. The smile stayed on his face as he poured.

'I wouldn't hold back my consent, Alexander. I think they'd be good for each other. What do you say?'

'You mean Frederick?' Alexander took the proffered glass.

'I mean Rupert.' His eyes held Alexander's as he drank.

'I see.' Alexander turned his head. In the distance Frederick helped Caroline into the punt at the river's edge. Alexander worried for a moment remembering his own love. 'Shall we see how your daughter feels after the ball tonight?' He put his hand in his pocket, and straightened. 'It's a little early to see the way things are really going between them.'

George returned to the fireplace, his drink in his hand.

'Matilda will direct her as to the way I wish her to feel. I'm sure she likes Rupert well enough. He's a fine young man. And he is your heir.' He turned towards Alexander. 'I will make my feelings known to my daughter.' The bonhomie was overlaid now with an ingrained discipline. 'Girls have been known to be married on the strength of a few dances at a ball. She'll get to know young Rupert tonight. I think she will prefer your elder son by the end of the evening.'

'Very well. If that is what she wishes. No one would be happier than me to have Caroline in the family. You and Matilda are, after all, two of my dearest friends.'

George beamed. 'It will be a perfect match.'

'There is Rupert to consider.' Alexander looked up from under his eyebrows. His voice warned slightly. 'He has a mind of his own.'

George looked unruffled. 'He is the kind of man to want my daughter.' His blue eyes were very knowing in the chubby face. 'All the girls in my family are, shall we say, very feminine, with that shy delicacy that needs to be cherished, their confidence won.' His hand described something transient in the air. 'It's like trying to catch gossamer.' He lifted his chin. 'I *know*. It took me the devil of a while to catch Matilda's heart, but I did. Whets your appetite. From what I've seen of Rupert, that's the quality that will entice him.'

'Perhaps.'

'You'll see. You're too fine a man, Alexander. I'm more a cavalier, like your son. Or was. It took that kind of a woman to tame me. He'll stop breathing fire before long, and start knuckling down.'

'Yes,' agreed Alexander. 'You're probably right. Frederick's like me. We need women to bring us out. Women who are our strength. A stronger sort of woman, courageous.'

George put down his glass. 'He'll find one,' he said, matter-of-factly. George had no time for sentiment. 'Boy's young yet. Plenty of time.'

'Well,' Alexander clasped his hands together. 'That's settled then. Shall we go down and join the party again? I believe Lady Armitage has some delightful stories to tell about the Season!' They walked towards the door. 'By the way, did I tell you I've bought the new Daimler motor? It's in the garage. Fine instrument, George, you should get one.'

'By God, have you? I should like to have a look at it.'

'We'll slip away in an hour or so. Take you for a spin.'

'Look forward to it.'

As they walked out onto the lawn, Alexander saw the slender figure of the woman he had noticed earlier. She had made her way to the croquet lawn and now with a swift glance over her shoulder she slipped through the privet hedge and headed for the stables. George was right. It was high time Rupert was married.

Rupert strode down the cobbled yard towards the stables. The noise of the party receded into the distance. His shoes echoed in the silence.

A small man appeared from the stable door of the furthest stall. At the end of the yard the fields stretched away into the distance beyond the wooden perimeter fence. The open land was tempting. Rupert looked forward to his ride.

The man was polishing a leather bridle, the rag in his hand still moving as he squinted up the yard. The frown disappeared and a ready smile took its place, the eyes smoothed with respect. 'Afternoon, sir, Mr Rupert.' He tipped a well-worn cap.

'Afternoon, Arthur. How is he today?'

'Raring to go, sir. You taking him out?' He stepped back as Rupert approached the stall and whistled. An answering whinny came from beyond the door and a huge chestnut moved forward, its fine head nodding its greeting.

'I am indeed. Had enough of a party full of silly women.' The head groom grinned at Rupert's caustic tone. Rupert stroked the chestnut's nose affectionately. 'Rather be here with Perryman, wouldn't I, boy?'

Arthur nodded approvingly. They spoke the same language. Arthur was from out of town. He had been hired especially by Alexander to take charge of the stables, and as such he thought himself a cut above the other stable lads and the staff in general at the Manor. He was small and wiry with a thoroughness about him that he gave to any undertaking. He had the confidence of being in charge that horses sensed and responded to, as did women. His rough charm and easy ways worked as well on both; he knew how to handle the mettlesome, skittish ones. Those were the ones he preferred, the challenges. Then his brown eyes would twinkle, and his voice with its soft country burr would become soothing. Arthur had already run through many of the housemaids up at Foxhall, as well as in the village. His reputation glittered in the eyes of many of those women. As for Rupert, to Arthur they were of the same mind. Though he was ostensibly Alexander's servant, it was to Rupert he gave his loyalty. He knew of all his affairs, yet would not think of betraying him to the master as he ought. He would no more betray himself. The son was like his mother, and Arthur had been very fond of Mrs Redfield. It had been a tragedy when she had died, on her favourite hunter too. Like his mother, Rupert's affection for his animals was his password. In the stables he was treated with tolerant respect. Perryman whinnied and tossed his head. He was ready for exercise.

'Saddle him up, Arthur.' He stood away from the horse.

'You going now, sir?' The groom caught the stallion's head between his hands to steady him. A hand absently stroked the muzzle. He looked pointedly at Rupert's clothes.

Rupert caught his look. His mind had been on the ride. He had forgotten he had been dressed for the party. He looked down at the tennis whites. 'I'll change in his stall.'

'Very good, sir. Come on, boy.' He unlocked the stable door and shouldered the animal aside. 'Move yourself there, you great fellow.'

Rupert went in to the musty darkness of the stall. The small windows high up in the stable let in very little light, and were dressed with ancient cobwebs. Straw was thick on the floor of the stall, flattened in the centre by the trampling of the horses. On the wall an iron rack half full of hay was cemented into the open brickwork. Beside it on a hook hung an old pair of jodhpurs, a shirt and a tweed jacket. Rupert went over and lifted them down, laying them over the edge of the stall at chest height. Rupert was a man of impulsive action. The old clothes were left here for precisely such a need. He pulled the tennis shirt over his shoulders and threw it into the corner. He undid the waist button of his trousers.

A slight cough from Arthur made him lift his head. The groom inclined his head towards the stable door. Rupert looked.

The woman stood there, a slightly uncomfortable look on her face. She put out her hand and made as if to touch Perryman and then withdrew it, her hands clasping a small bag held against her breasts.

'Oh, I so love horses,' she said quickly. 'I just couldn't resist . . . when I saw you come down. I . . . I hope you don't mind that I, er . . .' She glanced towards Arthur and swiftly back to Rupert.

She looked ridiculous standing there, her long dress tapering towards her feet so that she had difficulty in managing anything but a hobble. The sleeves were buttoned and the pale grey silk

was full over an ample bust, above which a froth of lace climbed
to her throat. She wore a hat piled high with pale and dark grey
feathers, and long gloves. She had felt brave, but now she felt
awkward and embarrassed. The small wiry man said nothing,
he just raised an eyebrow at her, and Rupert. Rupert was half
naked. She said nothing, but she wore her desire in her eyes as
blatantly as if she had spoken.

'It's all right, Arthur,' he said slowly, his eyes on her. 'You
can go. I'll manage on my own.'

'Very good, sir.' He moved to pass the woman.

'Oh, and take Perryman. You can finish saddling him outside.'

'Yes, sir.' The man was in a hurry to be gone now, all emotion wiped from his face, his expression a perfect blank. He was
in the way. 'Come along, boy.' He tugged the big horse behind
him, and Perryman slowly clopped from the stable and out into
the yard.

Rupert inclined his head towards the interior of the stable.
He picked up a towel from the door. It had been used to rub the
horse down. Rupert did not care. He slung it around his neck
as the woman gave a quick smile and lifting her skirt stepped
into the closeness of the stable.

She tripped slightly as she came in and stretched a hand to
steady herself. Rupert did nothing to help her. He merely
watched her and smiled, aware of her discomfort. Righting herself, she looked up at him.

Now she could see him more clearly. His long yellow hair
was combed back away from his high forehead. He had the air
of breeding but also of lechery. His teeth were widely spaced
and the blue eyes fringed by white lashes were hooded and up-
tilted. Satanic. They were observant, missing little of importance to himself. He had a redhead's albino look which made
his eyes appear cold and alien. That coldness told women that
he held them in scant regard, yet taunted the masochistic sexuality in them.

Her eyes faltered under his observation of her. She dropped
them downwards, taking in the broad shoulders and barrel chest,
the smattering of saffron-yellow hair there and the pallor of his
nipples. In the shadows of the stable his skin was pale but slightly
iridescent with sweat from the heat of the day. His presence
coiled around her like a snake. The silence built. Suddenly she
wished that she had not come. She averted her eyes. Her mouth

was tight and dry. Her eyes drew back to the safety of the square of light beyond the stable door.

Rupert saw the change in her and acted swiftly. He knew when to stop. He reached out and grasped her wrist. He turned and headed for the furthest stall.

She tripped rapidly along behind him, the feathers bobbing on her hat.

'Stop. What are you doing?'

'What you want.' His eyes caught hers briefly.

He led her into the stall, turned and pulled her quickly to him. He bent his head to hers.

Her gloved fists came up and pushed at his chest. 'Leave me alone. What do you think? Oh, that I came here for . . . !' Her eyes were round with outrage.

His eyes half closed. 'I know what you came here for.' He started to pull off his trousers. 'You can undress in the corner, if you wish.'

Suddenly she became angry. 'I think you're the most rude, presumptuous and boorish man. I just came to tell you that. And to tell you to stay away from Caroline Lancing. She's not for you. She's totally innocent and weak. You'd destroy her. She's my cousin. I won't have you inflicting your brutality on a sweet girl like her,' she said, her eyes darting with anger and . . . jealousy? Rupert looked interested. He stepped coolly out of his trousers and stood there, a demanding figure, his shoulders blocking the light. *Caroline*, he thought. Well, a challenge perhaps. 'Stay away from us all,' the woman trailed to a finish. Rupert moved quickly. She gasped and turned to get away from him. His hand caught the back of her arm.

'If you want me so badly,' he said softly, 'why don't you just go ahead and say so?' He moved up behind her so that his body touched hers. He held both her arms now. Tight.

'Oh!' She struggled in his grip. 'Let me go!'

He was bored with playing games. 'Come on.' He slid his hands from her arms and grabbed her hand firmly. He dragged her towards the corner and the bed of straw.

She stumbled behind him. Her hat fell off. 'I'll scream.'

'I hope so.'

She was still fighting as he grabbed her and she smelled the sweat on him. He threw her on the straw, and came down on her, his mouth rough and his hands hard and swift to find her. She struggled and fought beneath him. She was half dressed and he was harsh with her, not relenting for one moment, but soon her struggles became a clinging to him, her gasps of outrage those of pleasure.

Downstairs in Foxhall Manor, Dickie sweltered in the hot kitchen with its glowing range. She was corseted and laced in tightly. Had they known she was pregnant she would have been thrown out immediately. On top of the boned corset she wore a liberty bodice, cambric knickers, a petticoat and thick stockings she had knitted herself. Only the gentry got sun on their skins. Down in the kitchen they never saw it.

She was a scullery-maid. She worked fourteen hours a day and sleep came as soon as she crawled between the sheets in her attic room. Each morning that summer she had been up as soon as it was light, to clean the range as she was doing now. She knelt on the floor, smothered the range with black lead and then rubbed as hard as she could. There was a brass fender in front. When it was dry it was polished until it gleamed.

Dickie climbed to her feet. Her back was aching, and the baby dragged its weight down inside her. She felt that any day it would come. It was due in a month. She crossed the steaming kitchen and set to work on the long scrubbed table with a lump of salt, then poured a kettle of boiling water over it to take the grease out. She leaned down and scrubbed as hard as she could.

The cook, Mrs Maitland, bustled to and fro. She was distracted by the party. She had to prepare food for upstairs, downstairs, *and* the children's food for the day. She was in a bad humour.

'Dickie. Hurry up with that table. I want you to do all that washing up, and then peel the potatoes and prepare the cooking pots. How can I get organised if you're so slow? What's the matter with you, girl? You should have been finished an hour ago. Come along now.' She waved an impatient arm at her.

'Sorry, Mrs Maitland.'

'Go into the larder and fetch me that fish we got in this morning.'

'Yes, ma'am.'

Dickie hurried into the larder. The fish was packed in blocks of ice delivered by the fishmonger to keep it fresh. The room was cool and welcome. Slate slabs and mesh on the windows kept it like that. Dickie laid her wrists against the ice and leaned against the cool white bricks of the wall. She closed her eyes and drank in the sensation. Her pulses throbbed and her ankles were swollen from the hard work and the heat. Her feet cried out to be released from the thick stockings and the heavy shoes.

'Dickie!'

Her eyes flew open. She had been so tired she was almost asleep. Quickly, she broke off some small chunks of ice with a knife, and twisting them into her handkerchief, pushed them deep into her apron pocket. At least she could take them out when possible and press them to the insides of her wrists to still the aching throb from the heat. She lifted the fish from its nest and carried it out to the table.

'Bring it over here!' the cook called, indicating the space before her. Out of the corner of her eye Dickie saw that Bessie had arrived in the kitchen. She was straightening her uniform and glancing at the chauffeur who had just entered through the back door. She was inordinately vain, and men figured strongly in her scheme of things.

Bessie was a house maid. She wore a black dress, white apron, and a white cap with streamers on it. She had blonde curls and baby-blue eyes. Her figure curved substantially within the confines of the uniform. She made the beds, tidied the rooms and emptied the chamber-pots from upstairs.

Dickie placed the fish in front of Mrs Maitland, who wrung her hands impatiently.

'Mr Rupert's asked for a hip bath. Goodness knows why now we've got bathrooms upstairs, but ours not to reason. Bessie, get upstairs with the water jug and fill his bath. Go on, now. He's out riding, he'll be back in half an hour. Groom said so.'

Dickie caught frantic signalling from behind Mrs Maitland's back. She looked at Bessie. Bessie winked meaningfully. Then suddenly she clutched her stomach.

'Oooh!' she said. 'Oooh, me stomach. Oooh, it's something awful. Oooh, I'm sick, I am, I'm dying.' She rolled her eyes heavenwards, and sat down heavily on a stool.

Mrs Maitland, distracted from her stream of panic, looked at her quite coolly. 'Whatever is the matter with you, Bessie?'

'I'm sick, Mrs Maitland. I can't do it by myself. Could Dickie help me with the bath?'

Dickie's eyes signalled a frantic 'No'. She did not want to be upstairs near Rupert, but Bessie did not know that. She continued with her pantomime.

Mrs Maitland gave a cluck of exasperation. 'Oh, all right then. Dickie's not supposed to be upstairs, but just you don't be seen by Mrs Merriman or you'll both be dismissed. Hurry up then.'

They carried the jug up the stairs together. As soon as they were out of earshot, Bessie grabbed Dickie's hand at the foot of the back stairs. Her voice was excited. 'I'm not sick, Dickie pet. I just had to show you these clothes upstairs in my lady's trunk. You'll never believe what she's brought. She's rich, richer than I've ever seen. And the jewels, oooh! Wait till you see!'

'Bessie, I've got work to do. I'll have to do it and be late home.' She hung back.

'Come on. I'll help you later. You've got to see this.' She dragged an unwilling Dickie up the stairs.

'You're not sick then?' Dickie asked as she climbed behind her, carrying the jug beside her.

Bessie stopped and turned towards her. 'No,' she said more slowly. 'I'm not sick, but I'm that tired. When do you get time to yourself? To rest?'

Bessie had only been working a few weeks. She was a village girl, still young and eager, but the work was hard.

'When you're in bed,' said Dickie drily.

Bessie sat down on the step. 'I daren't tell my pa, Dickie. I'm so scared. He says I have to look after my character. He says I'll lose it. Do you think I'll lose it? Mrs Maitland handed me a bit of darning at half-past nine last night. Dickie, I'm that scared I'm going to die here and never see nothing of the world.'

Dickie patted her knee. 'You'll see the world, Bessie, don't worry. It'll wait for you,' she said, her own voice strained with tiredness. She felt the cool ice in her pocket, pulled it out and pressed it to the insides of her wrists, and then the back of her neck.

'And do you think your brother Sam will too?' Bessie perked up, grinning.

'I don't know.' She looked at her. 'Are you sweet on him, then?'

'Maybe!' said Bessie coyly. 'And maybe not. Tell me, Dickie, whose is it? Whose is the baby?' She pointed at Dickie's stomach. She was one of the few who knew.

Dickie's face closed up. 'I'm not telling you.' She picked up her jug.

'One of the village lads?' she persisted eagerly.

'I'm not telling you, Bessie. Now there's an end of it. Let's get up and see these dresses, then, before we're both dismissed. We've taken too long as it is.'

Bessie's train of thought was short-lived. Now she scampered up the stairs, and led Dickie along the quiet carpeted corridor to the third door on the left, Lady Finhaven's room.

There was a step down into it. Beyond, three long leaded windows looked out over the lawns. The sun streamed in on patterned carpets. A four-poster, dark and carved, hung with burgundy velvet and brocade, stood to the right of the room, and to the left was an open fireplace. The room was silent and gracious.

Dickie took a long breath as she stood on the threshold. She had never seen anything like it. She had never been upstairs in the main house before. Since the redesigning of Foxhall the servants never crossed paths with the family unless essential. In the last months, Dickie's only thought had been to drag herself through the day until the climb up the back stairs to bed in the servants' quarters, and blissful sleep to her racked and cumbersome body. Hands on her stomach to feel the baby's feeble kicking, she would fall instantly asleep to wake in darkness before the dawn and begin another day.

Now her curiosity came alive. Slowly she walked across the room to look down out of the windows. Her small hand rested against the cool stone as she gazed out on a sea of colour.

The party was gathered mostly on the terrace, seated on wicker chairs, the men in their flannels and straw boaters, the girls in muslin or linen frocks. In the distance, the rhythmic sound of ball against racket drifted over from the tennis court. Laughter lilted easily on the air. It was a different life.

'Look, Dickie, look at this.' Bessie was holding up an evening dress of pale pink taffeta belted in saxe-blue *moiré*, with sleeves of *écru* lace, roses on the shoulder and a *diamanté* buckle. It was a confection.

Dickie's eyes widened. She was awestruck at the size of the room, the heavy tapestries on the walls, the woven rugs, chintzes and silks. She crossed to the dressing-table. Spread out were the silver-backed hairbrush and comb, the tortoiseshell and silver mirror. A leather jewel-box was half open, trailing a string of pearls; brooches of emeralds and diamonds; rings, one after the other, lined up: rubies, diamonds, aquamarines; necklaces to match.

'I'm to be Lady Finhaven's maid for the ball tonight. She hasn't brought a ladies' maid, you see,' sighed Bessie. 'Oh, it's going to be splendid. Fancy being a lady, Dickie.' She whirled about the room, the dress pressed to her bosom.

Dickie crossed to the bed. She fingered the tea-gowns, the petticoats, the shawls, scarves and ornamental combs, the evening-dresses laid out unpacked to be put away.

She heard a loud burst of chatter from the terrace below. 'We'd better be getting on with the bath, Bessie. We don't want to be caught up here.'

'Oh yes, we'd better.'

'Where is his room?' she asked quietly.

'His room?' asked Bessie. 'Oh, you mean Mr Rupert. Why, next door!' She giggled. 'I think Lady Finhaven wanted it that way!'

She pushed open a heavy oak door, lifted the jug from the floor and carried it through into Rupert's room. 'We'll have to get more water. You're going to help me, aren't you, Dickie?'

'I don't know.' She came in and looked around. So this was his room. Ahead of her, Bessie pulled the hip-bath into the centre of the room. She splashed her jug of water into it.

'Your turn,' she said. 'We're going to be at this all day. I don't see why he has to have a bath like this, I really don't.'

Because it causes us more trouble, people like us who don't matter a damn to him, thought Dickie. Just as long as he gets his way, the bastard.

She poured her jug into the bath, and imagined him in it. Not a care in the world, scrubbing his back, taking it easy. She felt the anger build in her.

Footsteps sounded in the corridor outside.

'Oh lor', it's her, Mrs Merriman, oooh, heck.' Bessie grabbed Dickie's uniform by the shoulder. 'You're out of bounds. We'll be dismissed on the spot if we're caught. Oh, lor', what are we going to do?'

'In here, quick.' Dickie pulled her back into Clare Finhaven's bedroom, leaving the door to Rupert's room wide open. They hid in the deep, folded curtains of the four-poster bed.

The footsteps approached the door to the passageway, and stopped. The handle of Lady Finhaven's door turned. The imposing figure of Mrs Merriman appeared, white-capped and dressed in black, wielding the keys that were the symbol of her authority. The girls held their breath as she looked around and came into the room. She then went across to the dressing-table and she too looked at the jewel-box. Slowly, she lifted a brooch, gazed at it, and then held it against her ample chest. She turned this way and that. Behind the curtain, Bessie could hardly contain herself. It seemed an age before she replaced the brooch, turned and walked from the room, closing the door behind her.

Bessie burst from behind the curtain, her hand clasped to her mouth. 'Did you see that!' She primped this way and that, holding an imaginary brooch to her breast. 'Old Mrs Merriman! I never did!'

But Dickie was not laughing. She had heard another pair of footsteps, coming up the main stairs two at a time. A man's heavy feet, and they were coming fast.

'Ssh, *Bessie*!'

They both listened. The man came down the passageway towards them. Dickie froze. The door opened and in he came. She watched him saunter into the room. He yawned and stretched and pulled off his boots. His eye caught sight of the partly filled hip-bath. He gave an angry curse and turned to press the bell beside the fireplace.

Dickie remembered that impatience all too well. Her hate was rekindled with all the old intensity. She could not move with the pressure of it. She thought he must feel it directed at him through the crack in the door.

An urgent tugging on her back made her start. And then suddenly she felt the pain in her. She bent over double.

'Dickie!' gasped Bessie. 'What is it? Are you all right? The baby's not coming now, is it?' she cried in alarm.

Dickie had paled with the shock. She clutched her stomach. Had the strength of her hate caused this driving pain that twisted inside her? 'No,' she whispered. 'I'll be fine in a minute.'

'Not long now,' Bessie sympathised. She picked at her sleeve. 'Come on, I'd better get you downstairs quick.'

Dickie was still. The hate surged through her. She could not take her eyes off him. Her memory was rekindled by the animal smell of him.

'Dickie! What are you staring at? Come along! We've got to get downstairs before Mrs Merriman!'

She dragged at her friend and hauled her away, breaking her transfixion. The two of them ran lightly across the room and away down the back stairs to the kitchen. As Dickie ran down the stone stairs every jarring step drove the memory of him farther into her brain. She had to get out of this oppressive house as soon as she possibly could. As she reached the bottom of the stairs she felt the sweat pouring down her, seeping into her heavy clothes. Her legs ached and her back felt as though it would break if she did not rest it. She had to get fresh air, or she would fall in a dead faint and then they would all know the truth.

She crossed the room towards Mrs Maitland and steadied herself on the table. Mrs Maitland's damp and rosy face swam before her.

'Mrs Maitland,' she said, the dizziness slowing her voice. 'Please. Can I go outside for five minutes? I've come over all faint.' She held a steadying hand to her forehead.

'What? You, now, as well!' the woman started. She stopped rolling her pastry ready to give the girl a firm talking to, but it was true, she did not look well. Her eyes were glazed, and her face had a grey pallor to it. Mrs Maitland was not a bullying woman, she had daughters the same age as Dickie Bennett. 'All right,' she said. 'Five minutes, then, and no longer. We've got a lot to do today,' and then she added more gently, 'Sit on the bench out there and loosen your clothes, girl. That'll help. Bessie,' she said to the other girl now standing and staring, the fear in her eyes with her own knowledge of Dickie's predicament, 'stop staring at her like that and help her outside, then get back upstairs sharpish. You've got to get that bath filled yet. Well, go along, then.' She waved her rolling pin at them both, as Bessie hurried to Dickie to give her the support of her arm. They headed for the back door together as Mrs Maitland, muttering under her breath, rolled her pastry again with renewed vigour.

Bessie led her to the bench. 'You all right, Dickie? Is it the baby?'

Dickie sat down. 'Yes,' she breathed. 'But I'm fine now.'

'I've got to go, then, love.' Bessie touched her on the shoulder and was gone, back through the kitchen door.

Once she was alone Dickie closed her eyes and wrapped her arms around her stomach, hugging the ache to her. She breathed out heavily, and then lifted her face to feel the breeze on her skin. It felt so good, so welcome. She was so unhappy. Eyes still closed, she felt the tears well up inside her and burn the insides of her eyelids with a prickling heat. They squeezed out of her eyes and coursed down her cheeks. She could not stop them. She rubbed at the base of her stomach with both hands.

The baby began to kick, and Dickie let herself go, crying uncontrollably. Her tears held the vulnerability of a mother who was little more than a child herself and the emotional exhaustion that went with pregnancy. It was the baby's kicking that had done it. She wanted it to live, and yet it was *his*. She had to live under his roof now she was working at the Manor, away from home for the first time and with the baby growing and tiring her more each day. The work was back-breaking and almost beyond her endurance, yet she had to keep at it, somehow pushing herself through each day until its end.

Dickie took another deep breath. Her five minutes were almost over. She wiped the tears from her cheeks with the back of her hand, and stretched behind her back to loosen her stays. The relief was indescribable. She took what remained of the ice from her pocket and rubbed it across her wrists, the heat of the day turning it to water within the minute. She dropped it to the ground, tucked her handkerchief back in the pocket and stood up, pulling her clothes down around her. Luckily, she carried the child high and small. She had managed to conceal it from everybody in a busy household.

She took a few steps across the gravelled path towards the side of the house, taking in her last breaths of fresh air. She could now see the party guests enjoying themselves at the far side of the lawn. She moved back into the shadows of the wall so that they would not see her. Her eyes followed the path down to the river. Vaguely they travelled over the statue that stood at the side of the path. She returned to it. It was a stone maiden, the lines long and graceful, her expression serene as she poured water from a stone jug held in her arms. She looks like me, thought Dickie. It would be easier to be made of stone, never to feel pain, or be weakened by emotion or fatigue as she was now. She leaned against the wall. If she was like that she would never be hurt again, she would be resolute, untouchable. Dickie's eyes changed, the pride and strength coming back into them as she came to a realisation. That's what I will be, she thought, a stone maiden. I will have no emotion and nothing will ever hurt me again, never another moment's weakness such as this. She drew herself up, her eyes clear now, a colder light in their depths as they focused on some far distant point, a future where she would destroy him, as he had destroyed her.

'Dickie!' The voice called from the back door.

Head high, she took one more look at the statue. She even

managed a smile. Nothing would touch her now. She turned and went back into the house.

The house was never more beautiful than at dusk. On the high paved terrace outside the drawing-room windows, fireflies could be seen across the lawn. It was a balmy summer night, warm and luminous.

The ball had started.

In the side garden a vast marquee had been erected, its ceiling hung with dark blue silk to imitate the night sky. A black-and-white chequered dance-floor had been laid across the lawns and flowerbeds, in its centre a miniature lake on which floated waterlilies lit by coloured lights. Around the sides banks of flowers between white columns formed a passageway for those of the three hundred guests who wished to sit out the dancing.

Foxhall itself was magnificent. Gilded and flower-decked and open to the night, the gardens dotted with fairy lights along the winding paths. The supper tables were heavily laid with rich food, exotic fruits and ices. Champagne stood in rows upon the sideboards. Baskets of gardenias and sweet peas, huge bowls of orchids and roses were everywhere.

The guests were dancing to two bands, while electric fans whirled above enormous blocks of ice buried in the banks of flowers to keep them cool. The chaperones sat on upright chairs around the room and kept an eye on their charges as they danced happily by in delicate shoes of pink or white satin, their gloved hands resting lightly on their partners' broad shoulders.

Alexander and George strolled down the flagged stone terrace in the early moonlight. Music from the band lilted out onto the air. They were both mellow with brandy taken in the library well away from the noise of the party.

George stopped by the french windows as the music came to an end. The girls gathered by the door, the young men surrounding them. It was like a slave market. The girls held dance cards and the most popular arranged their partners to their own satisfaction.

'Caroline!' George signalled his daughter as the young unknown man bent towards her.

She lifted her head and looked for him. An uncertain smile crossed her face, she excused herself and came over. 'Yes, Father? Good evening, Mr Redfield.'

'Good evening, Lady Caroline.' He inclined his head and smiled at her. He would have loved to have had a daughter. 'Are you enjoying yourself, my dear?'

'Yes, thank you. It's a splendid party.' She sensed his interest and was grateful. Her dark hair was coiled around her head, and she wore a billowing white dress with a blue satin sash around her waist. It matched the deep blue of her eyes. She looked very pretty. Alexander smiled approvingly.

George held out his hand. 'Let me see your dance card.'

She held it out to him. George studied it carefully. He nodded as his eyes travelled down the list. She was behaving. Most of the dances were taken by Rupert, a couple by Frederick, and one by Lord Beatley's son.

'Good,' he said. 'You're getting to know Rupert. Do you like him?'

She looked a little pale. 'Yes, Father.' She could say nothing. She knew that Rupert had been told to single her out. She knew because as he had held her tight, too tight for etiquette, on the dance-floor, he had made a point of telling her so. She did not know what to say.

The deep voice from behind her made her jump. The music had started almost at the same moment.

'My dance, I believe.'

She whirled round to see Rupert, towering over her, a charming smile on his cold face.

Once again she had that sensation of wanting to retreat. Rupert simply moved forward and caught her by the waist. Clearly her fragility and evasiveness intrigued him, apart from the fact that she was of extremely high pedigree and his brother's fancy. In sibling rivalry there were no known barriers.

She hesitated as his gloved hand encircled her tiny waist. And then he remembered, stood back and offered her his arm. She was different, after all. Caroline succumbed, with a quick look at her father, and laying her own gloved hand lightly on the proffered sleeve as if it might bite her, she stood ready to be led onto the dance floor. Rupert raised an eyebrow and looked back at his father, almost insolently, his blue eyes bright with interest, and dawning desire. He wanted her now; the more she held him at bay the more she gained his interest. And this was a girl he could not throw in the hay. He would have to marry this one, and soon. Rupert did not like to wait.

George beamed paternally from the side of the floor as the

dance started again. Rupert and Caroline made a handsome pair, and he cherished his daughter. He wanted her to marry a man of consequence. He lifted a champagne glass to them and drank. Marrying off one's daughters was a prime consideration and now they were all almost taken care of. It was very satisfactory.

'I believe your son will approach me for my daughter's hand before the month is out. I know that look in a young man's eye.' He sighed and pushed out his ample, beribboned chest. 'And I will happily give my consent. I think she likes him well enough.'

Alexander's eyes sought them on the dance floor. Among the sea of tulle and uniforms, Rupert swirled her round the floor. He seemed to clasp her very close, and Caroline's small head was tipped back showing a mixture of emotions. She seemed as unable to resist as a rabbit in a trap. Rupert had decided on her now and she was his.

The first of the fireworks exploded beyond the garden's edge. It lit up the river in a crackle of yellow light. The party guests turned to see and swarmed out onto the balcony. Rupert led Caroline down the lawn towards the punts.

Frederick hunted through the mêlée for the sight of Caroline in her white dress. He could not find her. He started down the lawn in the darkness and came to the river's edge. Punts swung out across the river in the punctured darkness. In the jumble of boats there was laughter and shadows. He could not see her. She was gone.

THREE

August, 1914

Dickie screamed in the bed. The flannel sheets were crumpled and stained with damp grey patches of sweat. The August night was hot and still and her labour had started during the day. Now the night wore on and the pains tore at her, clutching like a giant's malevolent hands. Dickie moaned again and flung her head against the pillow. Her black hair was plastered to her skull and her pale green eyes stood out like luminous moons in the semi-darkness of the room. Her small oval face was white with pain.

A candle guttered on the window-ledge and another at the foot of the bed. The midwife sat squarely on the side of the small truckle bed and pushed her legs upwards and away. Her hand reached up inside the girl and pulled.

'It's got to come, lass, now *push.*'

'I can't, oh!' Silently, she cursed the Redfield family.

'You must, *push*. There's no time for the doctor now. Come on, when I say. Now, *push. Push!*'

Dickie pushed with all her might.

'Scream if it helps, lass.'

She screamed again, and pushed and pushed. The midwife's lips tightened in worry. The baby was not coming well. The child was large and the girl's pelvis was small. There was no one else to help, just the two of them in this empty room: the young girl streaming with sweat on the bed and herself with her bowl of hot water and towels. She had delivered many babies, and some had been dead. It was a way of life. She thought now that this one would be too if they did not hurry.

She looked desperately towards the wooden staircase that led down from the bedroom to the front kitchen of the cottage. If only the men would come back soon, but, then, what could they do anyway? It was up to her.

She turned back to the girl and dampened her forehead with the towel. Dickie's eyes were wild and staring, extraordinary eyes, as light as a cat. They were unseeing now in her exhaustion. She would die, too, if they were not quick about it.

The woman saw the next contraction coming as Dickie closed her eyes against it. She reached in, twisted the child and pulled as the girl pushed desperately to be free of the infant that was forcing its way into the world.

Now she could see the head. At last! Once more. The next time would be better.

The window was open and a tiny breeze curled round the frame and into the room. With it came the sweet smell of flowers, cloying on the night air, and the distant sound of revelry from beyond Cobbold's Wood.

'Push, lovey,' the woman said softly. There had been no care for this girl, no hospital. This was a child born of shame, out of wedlock. These girls, they never understood, yet this one seemed different. She was so contained. She had hardly said a word, did not even scream until she had told her it would be better to relax the tension that had built in her. The woman felt sorry for her, and more than anything now she wanted her to have this child. 'That's it,' she said, encouraging, 'that's it. Just a bit more and we'll make it, pet.'

The child's head was dark, emerging, coming, coming and with a final groan it slid wetly onto the bed. He was born bawling, loud and indignant. 'You've got a boy, pet.'

The midwife went to work quickly to clean him, checking him thoroughly. 'He's perfect, love,' she said. 'What a beauty!'

Dickie sighed and closed her eyes. Her legs fell limply to the wet sheets. Her breasts rose and fell gently as she let the pain flow out of her, and rested at long last.

'Let me see him,' she said.

The midwife wrapped the baby in a blanket and handed him to her. Dickie cradled him against her chest in wonder.

'There!' said the woman. 'Didn't I say he was a beauty?'

'Yes,' she said slowly. She stroked the blanket away from his cheek and felt his skin with the brush of her finger. He was very soft.

'What you going to call him?'

'Maxwell—after Ma's family name. Maxwell Bennett.' She held him close and felt the stirrings of a new emotion.

Frederick awoke and listened to the milk train puffing away from Foxhall Green station. He dressed quickly and crept downstairs. The grandfather clock in the hall ticked heavily within the sleeping house. The high window on the main landing showed a soft eastern light through the leaded panes.

He stood on the doorstep outside the house and breathed in the freshness of a new day. A light dew still stood on the grass where there was heavy shade under the chestnut trees. He crossed the still garden to his studio, a white wooden treehouse on stilts that had been built for him as a boy. Now roses spilled over the arches and ivy had twined all round the short staircase to the door. White pigeons cooed in the loft alongside. It was his book-room, his own special place where he could go to be alone. He climbed the stairs.

From the window inside he could see out across the terraced part of the garden to the west of the house. The gardens sloped down towards distant parkland and beyond the fields stretched for miles. Behind him alongside the pathway that ran at the side of the house was the walled kitchen garden and to the east the Italian garden and on its periphery, the stone maiden. He could see her now, a delicate sculpture of a woman's form, high-breasted, small and slender. The early lemon light of morning bathed the stone in a pool of delicate light as the sun rose behind the trees at the edge of the river. Frederick felt himself drawn to it suddenly, something stirring in him, something familiar about the way the light fell on the curves of the body, something he did not want to face.

He tensed, remembering. He heard once again her cries, saw the writhing of that pale, succulent flesh, saw her face dash before him, the wild green eyes in that white oval, the black hair strewn against the burned autumn leaves. He caught his breath. He held the vision of his brother in his hunting clothes, a brute against her fragility, mounting her. He remembered himself walking forward as if in a trance, led by those eyes, her beauty like something out of a myth, a legend, a wood nymph ravished by a man. He groaned at the memory, his head in his hands. He saw again how her body lay beneath him, unmoving, felt himself fall downwards onto her, his eyes on hers, felt again that exquisite pleasure. He closed his eyes, expelling a long moan, the palm of his hand rubbing across his face as if to shut out the sights as he shook his head in despair—and pleasure. He had never known anything like the way he had given himself at that moment, yet when it was over, the guilt had absorbed him totally. How could he face the enormity of what he had done? He had tried to suppress it until now. Frederick looked up once again to see the statue now flooded with morning light, and was surprised to find that the light blurred and danced before his eyes. His face was wet. She had been the first awakening of his sensuality, and how she must hate him now. She would never forgive him, he had seen that with certainty in that last look before he had turned and run for his horse. What a coward he was. He ran his hand slowly through his hair. He had to forget, the mixture of pleasure and guilt in him were impossible to digest.

He let his mind wander, away from the statue and onto the lawns. Once again he saw the summer party they had held the month before. He saw Caroline in his mind's eye, beautiful, delicate in stature also, and allowed. Very different, with a spirituality about her that was far more palatable. He looked up at the stone maiden again. She had changed now. The rays of light no longer pinpointed her, but integrated her into the sunny light of day, a beautiful part of the whole picture of the garden. She did have a look of Caroline about her. Caroline. He filled his head with her, her soft voice and her deep blue eyes, darker and more translucent than the sharp Redfield blue. She was very feminine, very gracious. She would look perfect here at Foxhall Manor; he could imagine her floating through the rooms. He could hear the sound of her laughter, smell her perfume. He remembered the softness of her skin as he had touched her elbow to guide her up the lawn. Caroline. He smiled to himself. He let the image of her take over, transferring his feelings as he gave himself to what was now to be a lifelong obsession. He ignored the chord that had been awoken in him, like a distant strain of music that he loved. He pushed it far to the back of his mind. He blinded himself with thoughts of Lady Caroline Lancing.

He opened his book and looked at the poetry he had written

in careful script on cream and vellum paper. He ran his finger down the crease to flatten it. He smelt the sweet odour of the pages, clean and ready for him to compose on in his flowing italics. He would make her immortal. The window was open in front of him, and the scent of roses filled the room. The first birds were singing hesitantly outside as the dawn rose. No one would be stirring yet.

He thought for a while and then started to write.

In the cottage on the other side of the wood, Dickie looked wearily at the child asleep in her arms. The hate she had expected to feel was not there. Instead, she felt love. She carried him and tucked him gently into the wooden crib that Sam had made for him. Then she slept soundly for the first time in months.

Alexander Redfield entered the bank. The City office of Redfield-Strauss was a fine old brick building just off Threadneedle Street. The heavy wooden double doors were open to the day. Alexander was intolerably hot.

He climbed the stairs to his office. Windows on two walls afforded a view over the Thames and the waterside buildings on the opposite bank. Books were ranged from floor to ceiling and a Rembrandt hung on one panelled wall. A large mahogany desk with green leather top dominated the far side of the room, and a soft green carpet ran from wall to wall. Flowers stood on a table by the window. A cooling breeze blew in from the river.

Alexander placed his cane and hat on the table and crossed to the desk. Here, his business was done more on a gentleman's handshake than the hard sell. Many of his clients were friends. They would have luncheon at the bank or in his club, and after an excellent meal, during which they would discuss anything *but* business, they would get to know each other. It was only after coffee and brandy that business would begin.

He went behind his desk and sat down. A sheet of paper lay on the blotter before him. The price of gold bullion had risen as it always did before a potential major catastrophe. War was brewing just around the corner. In wartime banknotes would be useless, gold was always a better form of bargaining power. He pressed the bell on his desk to call Herbert in for his daily meeting.

The door at the far end of the room through which he had just come opened and Rupert walked in. Alexander frowned and looked at him.

'Sorry, Father.' Rupert was unperturbed. He closed the door behind him and walked arrogantly across the room. 'I have some news I thought you would want to hear immediately.' He drew off his gloves and placed them on the edge of Alexander's desk. He sat back in the chair, and waited.

Alexander looked expectantly at him. 'Well?'

'I've talked to Caroline's father. I've asked Caroline to marry me.' He paused, and then continued, his eyes on his father. His voice was smooth. 'She's accepted.'

Alexander's expression changed immediately. 'That *is* good news.' He came round the desk and took his son's hand in his own. 'I'm delighted.'

'Yes. And you sound so surprised, Father,' he said. 'As if you did not engineer the whole thing.' He smiled wryly.

'Well,' Alexander conceded. 'Maybe a little, but one has to in matters of this sort. Steer you in the right direction, anyway. Right sort of girl for you, Rupert.' He rounded the desk again.

'Oh, I know that. And I'm delighted to co-operate. She's going to be quite something to have when I finally catch her.' He raised an eyebrow. 'And then, of course, there's all that blue blood to add to the Redfield line, eh, Father?'

'Not such a bad thing. Your mother would be pleased. She wanted you to marry Caroline, I seem to remember.'

Rupert's expression changed. He seemed to withdraw for a moment, as if thinking of something.

'Father,' he said slowly, looking at his hands, 'I . . .'

There was a discreet knock at the door.

Alexander laid his hands on the desk before him. 'Come in.'

His secretary looked around the corner of the door. 'You're wanted in the board room straight away, Mr Redfield. They're waiting for you.'

Alexander lifted his hands in acceptance. 'Coming now.' He stood up, pulled down his waistcoat and looked down at Rupert as if in afterthought.

'What was it, Rupert?' He crossed to the mirror over the fireplace. He stroked his moustache briefly, brushed his eyebrows with his fingers, altered his stock. 'Can it wait? Can't talk now. Got a meeting.'

He turned, his face already businesslike. The moment was

lost. Rupert's face had its arrogant guard back in place. He stood up.

'It doesn't matter. I'll see you back at the house this evening. The Lancings will probably come to dinner.' His voice was brusque.

Alexander frowned. Somehow he had missed something of import. 'I've got a moment, Rupert. What did you want to say?'

'Nothing, Father. Nothing at all.'

Alexander nodded. He crossed to the door. He faced Rupert. They were silent for a moment. Alexander looked into his son's face. There was nothing there for him, only the light blue eyes looking back, their expression unreadable.

'Rupert . . . ?' Alexander laid his hand on the brass door-knob. 'I wish that maybe now you are getting married we could somehow get to know each other a little better.'

Rupert looked surprised. 'We know each other very well.'

'Maybe. Maybe not. Frankly, I often feel that we don't know each other at all. I even feel that perhaps you resent me for something. Am I right?'

'You're quite wrong.' Rupert opened the door and looked briefly at him. 'I'll see you at dinner.' He walked from the room.

'Frederick? Frederick?'

The soft voice called out from the garden. Frederick put down his pen, coming swiftly out of his reverie. It was very still.

He crossed to the doorway. He was still wearing the casual clothes of that morning: old flannel trousers and open-necked shirt. His dark blond hair was ruffled. He smoothed it back with both hands as he recognised the voice.

Caroline stood beneath the light wooden balcony. He clasped his hands to the rail. 'Caroline!' he said in surprise. 'What brings you here to Foxhall? Not that I'm not delighted to see you, but . . .'

'Are you alone?' she interrupted.

'Yes.'

Her face in the soft light was warm and beautiful. She wore a wide straw hat heavy with silk roses and a long, soft lilac dress caught with an oriental silk tassel at her waist. Her dainty feet were clad in satin shoes and she wore a velvet ribbon around her long throat, also in pale lilac. Frederick's heart caught with the sight of her.

'Can I come up?' she asked. 'I've something to tell you.'

Frederick stood back. 'Of course.'

She came around to the steps and climbed them. As she passed him she did not catch his eye, but he was aware of the slight delicate perfume that lingered around her, and the brushing of her dress against him.

He came into the room behind her. He was suffused with feeling and sensation. She had come to him, not Rupert.

'I said I have something to tell you,' she said. 'But I don't really know how to say it.'

'Can I help you?' he said. 'I have something to tell you, my love.'

She blushed. Her hand flew to her throat. The blue eyes darkened. 'Don't call me that, Frederick.'

He rustled through his papers. And picked up the book. He opened it to the page. 'This is for you.'

She opened her mouth to say something and then, out of politeness, she bent her head to the page. She read it in silence, and when she had finished she made no comment. She closed the book and replaced it slowly on the desk. 'Frederick . . .'

'Do you like it?'

'It's beautiful, but . . .'

'As you are.'

'. . . I can't accept it, you see . . .'

The words were never finished. The footsteps bounded up the stairs behind them. Rupert's overbearing presence filled the room. His hair seemed white in the late afternoon sunlight, his skin darker, and the eyes too brilliant a blue.

'Ah, so this is where you went.' He reached out and drew Caroline towards him. 'We've been looking for you.'

We?

'We have something to tell you, haven't we, darling Caroline? Do you want to tell him?'

He waited, pulling her to him. Her eyes lifted, deep with feeling, to hold Frederick's. 'Rupert has asked me to marry him,' she said clearly. 'We hope you will give us your blessing.'

Frederick recovered fast. He could not bear the gleam in Rupert's eye a moment longer. 'Of course.' He bowed formally over her hand. 'I hope with all my heart that you will be happy together. I shall be delighted to welcome you to the family as my very own dear sister.'

'Well said, Frederick,' said Rupert. 'The poet as ever. Now come and join the party. Caroline's going to play the piano to us. I hear she's quite an accomplished musician . . .'

Alexander rode home in the Daimler. He leaned back in the leather comfort. It had been a long day. He looked forward to celebrating Rupert's engagement that night at Foxhall.

He heard the newsboy's cry, and in his contentment hardly registered the words. When he did, he sat up with a start, thrusting his papers to the seat beside him.

He leaned forward to the chauffeur. 'Stop here.'

The gleaming black car pulled to a stop at the pavement. The newsboy's face looked in. He drew a newspaper from his bag. Alexander paid the boy and took the newspaper.

He sat back in his seat and opened it. The headlines proclaimed the news he had dreaded seeing. 'Drive on. To Whitehall,' he said.

On August 3rd, the King of the Belgians had telegraphed from Brussels to his fellow monarch King George V asking him to intervene on behalf of their friendship to safeguard Belgium's neutrality, but the appeal came too late. Germany had declared war on Russia, the German army was ready to march on France, and their quickest route to victory lay through Belgium.

In the crowds in Trafalgar Square and all over the West End and Whitehall the excitement intensified as the deadline grew nearer. As Alexander drove through he looked up at the lights of the Foreign Office and the Admiralty, still bright at this late hour.

It had been imminent for so long but they all thought it would never happen. Having received no reply to her ultimatum that German invasion troops be recalled from Belgium, Britain had acted as she had promised.

On the night of August 4th, 1914, she went to war with Germany.

FOUR

The poster of Lord Kitchener stared down at her from the wall of the post office. Dickie stopped to look. The fierce moustachioed face glared outwards, finger pointing: 'Your Country Needs YOU.'

The sun was warm on her back, the village street wide and empty of all but a few passers-by. Above all it was quiet. It all seemed so unlikely.

There was an excited little group around the post office chattering about the news. At the far end of the village a car suddenly came into sight. Dickie watched the local magistrate drive by in the uniform of the Territorial Army, his wife at the wheel dressed in VAD uniform. They stopped outside the post office.

The vicar's wife, Mrs Caversham, stopped them. 'How are you today, Mrs Baldock?'

'Joining in with the war effort. I'm off to bandaging classes at Longbarrow. Lord Lancing has lent it for the Red Cross classes. Are you coming along?'

'Of course. As soon as I am able. I'm organising sock-knitting at the church hall.' She smiled complacently.

Mrs Baldock's smile was equal to hers. Bandaging classes were the new social event.

Dickie watched the interchange with vague interest. She pushed Max to and fro in his pram. He was half asleep, a good baby, thank heavens, not waking her constantly as some did. War did not truly affect her as yet. Her hands were quite full with the minding of the house for her father and Sam, and tending her new child.

A finger tapped her on the shoulder. She turned, frowning slightly in the sun, to see Bessie. She was grinning from ear to ear and dressed in a new dress under her old cardigan. The blonde curls now released from her housemaid's cap sprang up like a halo.

'Guess what, Dickie?' she said gleefully. 'I'm off to work in the munitions factory. You like my dress?' She turned round for approval.

'You're leaving Foxhall Green? What's happened to your job?'

'Oh, that!' Bessie waved a hand. 'My sweetheart's off to the war. Didn't I tell you? Thomas Green who used to work the fields with your dad. He's asked me to marry him when he comes home. I asked Mr Redfield for a week off and he said no. Well, it was Thomas's last chance before he went off to become a soldier, so I thought, that's it, I'm going.' She tossed her head. 'So up I got and gave a month's notice. It was worth it just to see Mrs Maitland's face!' she giggled. 'I'm not going into domestic service no more. I've got a job in a factory up near London building the first aeroplanes.' Her baby-blue eyes rounded. 'Oh, Dickie. It's ever so exciting. I'm getting five pound a week!'

'Thomas has left the Manor to go to war?' Dickie said slowly. She looked up at the poster again. 'I thought it was only for the gentry.'

'Oh, no! Anyone can join. Isn't war exciting? Arthur, the groom in the stables that I was sweet on last year,' she explained for Dickie's memory, 'he says he's going too. He says Mr Redfield told Mr Rupert that he had to sell all his polo ponies. They had ever such a row. Oh, do you hear that? Those are the bells for the wedding! Are you coming?'

'Whose wedding?' Dickie looked down the street to the far end. The church bells were pealing out now.

'Why, Mr Rupert, of course. Didn't you hear?' Bessie clicked her tongue. 'He's marrying Lady Caroline Lancing from Long-barrow way. I'm going down to watch. You coming?'

'No.' Dickie's eyes looked down the street. She did not turn for a moment. She gazed down into the pram. 'I have to get Max home for his tea.' There was more on her mind now. *Sam.*

'All right, then. I'll come and see you before I go away. 'Bye, Dickie.'

' 'Bye,' she said. And turned to wheel Max for home.

* * *

Alexander's guest left as quickly as she had come. As the front door closed Alexander was already marching into the hall, his face tight with outrage.

He arrived in the hall just as Rupert started to come down the stairs. He was in a good humour. It was his wedding day, the sun was shining and tonight he would have Caroline in his bed. He smiled pleasurably at the thought, pulling at his cuffs with his long fingers as he made his way down the staircase. He would enjoy that.

'*Rupert!*' The voice was as he had never heard it. He looked down into the hall with some surprise. His father stood there, his face pale with anger, his blue eyes boring into his son. 'Come down here this instant.'

Rupert shrugged disdainfully, neither quickening nor slowing his pace; he was already on his way down. The sensual light in his eye was dimmed and the lids now half closed with the old arrogance. This was his wedding day. What could possibly have angered the old man?

He reached the bottom of the stairs and looked levelly at him. 'What is it, Father?' he asked matter-of-factly.

'Get into my study.' There were white lines around Alexander's mouth and he was breathing heavily.

Rupert gave him a nonchalant look and strolled into the study ahead of him. The door closed behind him with a thud. Alexander strode across the room to stand before him.

Rupert waited.

His father looked into his face for a moment as if seeing him truly for the first time. When he spoke at last his voice was low-pitched and vibrating with suppressed fury. And shame? Rupert thought he had detected that too, and wondered at it. He did not have to wonder long.

'A woman has just been to see me, Rupert,' he said, keeping his voice even. 'A woman whom I believe you know. She once had a tryst with you, apparently, in the stables, to which Arthur was a witness.' Rupert stiffened, remembering. Surely this could not be about something as plebeian as that. 'Apparently, although it seems unbelievable, she then had a liaison with the man . . .'

'With *Arthur*?' The laughter crept into Rupert's voice. The muscles in his face tightened into an amused smile. 'Why, the old devil . . .'

'Be quiet, Rupert.' Alexander's voice was like a whip. 'I'm talking.'

Rupert's smile was wiped from his face. His father was more angry than he had ever seen him.

'This woman,' he went on, making his distaste for her patently obvious, 'took the trouble to come up here, to Foxhall Manor, our home,' he added, his voice quavering with the humiliation of it, 'to tell me a most virulent and appalling story. One which I hope against hope is not true, but which already holds the ghastly ring of truth about it. It concerns you, Rupert.'

'Me?' Rupert's eyebrow lifted. 'In what way?'

'You were riding in the woods to hounds last October, were you not?'

'I often do.' Rupert felt the gnawing of knowledge begin inside him. 'Any particular day?'

Alexander ignored him. 'Arthur was riding with you and you left the hunt and went in the direction of one of our tied cottages. Some time after that Arthur came after you. He caught up with you at the edge of the wood and rode in to find you.'

Rupert was silent as he looked at his father. The cold blue eyes stared him down. For once, Rupert faltered briefly and dropped his eyes from his father's.

'He told this woman, Rupert,' he went on harshly, 'that he saw you . . . chasing after a girl, on horseback, and that just as he was about to call out, you picked her up, threw her across your saddle and rode with her to the clearing by the brook. He then said,' Alexander continued, the frown darkening over his eyes as their expression became at once disbelieving and accusing, 'that you threw the girl to the ground and—he believes— *you raped her*!'

'Did he see me?'

'No!' Alexander roared. 'He did not! *Did you*?'

Rupert was equally angry at being accused. 'I run my life as I please, Father. I don't have to answer that.'

'Good God! You insolent bastard!' Alexander advanced a step towards him, his face purple with rage.

Rupert's eyes warned his father. He was the bigger of the two men. Alexander stopped in front of him.

'You don't deny it?' Alexander stared at his eldest son. 'The girl has a child. Did you know that?' He saw that Rupert did not. 'What do you intend to do about it?'

Rupert shook his head. 'Nothing. Why should I?'

Alexander's voice was hushed with fury. 'You shame the whole family, Rupert, the Redfield name, with your disgraceful behaviour, and now this attitude. You'd better pull yourself together, young man, and start answering some questions. I could cut you off without a single penny.' He shook his finger at him. 'I could stop your wedding.'

'You won't do that.' Rupert's voice was disrespectful. 'I'm your eldest son. Your heir. I'm marrying the girl you picked for me. Today. Now, in fact,' he said, looking at the carriage clock on the mantelpiece behind his father. 'If we don't go we'll be late. That wouldn't do, would it?'

His pale, heavy eyelids drooped over the mocking expression in his eyes. He knew precisely how much his father's tenuous position as a new member of the upper classes mattered to him. He was much too much of a snob to stop a society wedding with the news that his son and heir was about to be displaced and was therefore unworthy of the match agreed upon.

Alexander's silence confirmed it. Rupert smiled. His look told him that he had his father where he wanted him. He was absolutely confident of being his heir, as well he should be. Ground rules did not change that easily. It crossed his mind at that moment to tell him about Frederick, but the thought disappeared just as quickly. It would mean further argument on this his wedding day, a day he did not wish spoiled any longer, and would serve no purpose except to implicate himself in this affair.

'May I go now, sir?' he said.

Alexander hardly heard him. He paced across the room. 'I was going to let you have the reins of this estate after you were married, Rupert. That was to be my gift to you. I now withdraw it. I see you are not fit and ready. You will have to convince me over the next few years under my jurisdiction that you are a reformed character before I change my mind back again,' he threatened.

Rupert shrugged. 'I'll outlive you, Father.'

'How dare you!' Alexander swung round, his face reddening.

'Frankly, I have no desire to run the family estate, anyway.' Rupert's voice was contemptuous. 'Frederick is far more suited to that than me. And as for my future plans, well, I've already made them.' He touched the collar of his uniform and straightened. 'I'm going to war in two days.' He smiled. 'Once I've enjoyed my new wife, that is.'

It was a body blow. By assumption, the more dispensable younger sons were going to war; the eldest son always stayed at home to continue the line and run the estate.

Alexander drew in a breath. 'Go then, and be damned!'

'Thank you, Father.' Rupert inclined his head. 'I'll see you at the church.' He turned and walked from the room. He had the old man beaten.

Frederick pulled on his gloves. He went across to the mirror and adjusted his top hat to the right angle. Rupert was marrying Caroline. *May the better man win.* Well, what could he do? He knew. Soon he would be a better man too. His romantic nature had been redirected with a passionate desire to take part in the war. Since the advent of it all a few weeks previously he had absorbed everything he could that had been written by statesmen, ministers and the press. They were fighting for king and country and all the principles of justice and freedom that were important to an Englishman. He had decided to fight too with valour and pride.

That very morning, he remembered with a proud smile as he brushed at his immaculate lapels, he had lined up outside the headquarters of the local battalion. He did not want to use his connections, he wanted to be a regular soldier. It would be a wonderful war full of heroism and glory. It was an ordered world, and things would right themselves ultimately. Frederick had been shielded by the basic innocence of an idealistic society. He was unworldly and had never even read a newspaper properly, but he was nineteen, and just old enough to join up for an exciting chance of travel and adventure. It was a welcome diversion from the marriage that was taking place today and having to live under the same roof as Caroline. Rupert, too, was going to war. The army life would be nothing new to him, of course. He had joined the 11th Hussars some years previously and Frederick had never understood the pleasure of fighting and an army life, as Rupert had. Now he did. He would return in time for a family Christmas. But before that . . . He gave himself a last look in the mirror, imagining his uniform. He could picture himself leading the men against the fleeing enemy across the fields of France in crisp, autumnal weather.

He ran lightly down the stairs to join the family in the hall. Alexander was crossing the floor as Frederick turned the corner on to the landing.

'Father!' he called, as he came down the last stretch of the wide stairs that opened out onto the chequerboard hall. 'Wait! I have something to tell you!'

The smile lit his young face as he came down towards his father. Alexander turned with slow dignity. He looked up at Frederick. The expression on his face was awful; he looked haggard and lifeless, his eyes bereft of emotion as if from some great shock. He seemed hardly to see him.

Frederick stopped. 'Father? Are you all right?'

Alexander's eyes cleared. He frowned. 'Yes,' he said tersely. 'Of course I am. What is it, Frederick?'

'Well, Father,' he went on then, his dark blue eyes warming to his subject. 'I know how pleased you're going to be about this . . . I've joined up! At the local battalion headquarters this morning. They said I might have to go to the front for a bit, asked me if I was fit, and of course I said ''yes'' to it all!' He took his father's silence for approval. 'I'm going to be fighting for all of us. There in the thick of it!'

Alexander was perfectly still. His blue eyes flickered down over Frederick's body and then up again to hold his eyes with his own. 'You're not going, Frederick.'

'What?' Frederick's healthy glow fled from his face. He looked crestfallen. 'But why not? I don't understand.'

Alexander tapped the mahogany newel post of the stairs. He appeared to give his answer some thought. 'Your desire to go away and fight for your country is very commendable, Frederick, but it is no longer possible. Rupert has informed me that he intends to join up, within the next few days in fact, so you see . . .'

'Rupert's going away to fight?'

'Yes.'

'But surely he's to stay here, Father! To run the estate for you.' He tapped his chest. 'I'm the one who should be going off to war.'

Alexander sighed. 'Yes, that's perfectly true, Frederick, but Rupert is going. And you are staying.' His mouth was set in a firm line. 'Now don't argue with me, my boy. Caroline will be here at the house, and she cannot be left entirely alone. I will be up at the bank, of course, and there is also the matter of staff

. . . they're all off to work in the munitions factories. I need help, Frederick. It has to be you, you're going to have to run the estate single-handed, I'm afraid. You're going to be the farmer you always wanted to be. You must resign. I'll speak to the colonel. He's an old friend of mine.' He pulled on his gloves. 'There won't be any trouble about it.'

'No trouble?' Frederick could not believe it. He had set his heart on this. 'What do you mean, "no trouble", Father? I want to join up. It's the only thing to do.' Especially now with Caroline in the house, alone. It would be torture. 'I need to go,' he said forcefully. 'All our friends are joining up. I can't be the only one left at home!'

Alexander turned and looked at his son. His face was strained, the anger still lying there beneath the surface. 'Frederick. There is more than one way to help a cause.' He tried not to let the fury that was in him affect his judgement as he dealt with the awkward hurt that Frederick was now feeling, yet he was not going to have any more opposition. 'I understand that you would like to be out there fighting for our salvation along with the rest of your friends. So would I at your age. Even now I want to, God knows, feelings don't change because you age.' His eyes dwelt on his son. 'But I have to consider our home and the fact that we have been asked to use the land for food and crops for the war effort. This year we'll have to plant more crops than ever. The army is sending in some young fellows to help. Without someone in charge, the scheme could fall apart, Frederick. This is your way of fighting, my boy. Try to understand that. No one's going to think less of you. On the contrary,' he said, turning away from Frederick's empty face, 'they'll think well of you for holding back your natural urge to fight and staying behind to run things at home.'

He walked away towards the half-open front door. Chalmers brought him his top hat and cane. He acknowledged them as the man moved to open the door wide. He had regained his air of natural elegance but the anger still pulsed in his heart, more so now as across the lawns he saw Rupert, resplendent in his regimentals, wandering back across the drive. He was appalled at Rupert's behaviour, at his absolute belief that he, Alexander, would do nothing to punish him. He remembered his insulting manner, his insolence and lack of regret, and he felt a wave of total dislike for his son. He braced himself, his blue eyes hardening.

Frederick appeared alongside him. His voice was hushed so that the waiting Chalmers could not hear.

'Father,' he said. 'I'm sorry, I've just got to go. I can't stay here. Not now.' His mind was on Caroline, her constant presence here in the house, with him. It was impossible.

Alexander gave him a swift look. Frederick saw how his eyes had changed, the understanding gone. 'My mind is made up, Frederick.' The eyes flashed at him, and Frederick was startled by the ferocity in his voice. 'Collect yourself! We will go to your brother's wedding.'

He walked on through the open door. Frederick had no choice but to follow him. Outside, the Daimler stood on the gravel. It was a cool day, with an autumnal clarity, the colours bright. Rupert strode across the circular lawn in the centre of the drive. He signalled them to join him. His regimentals made him seem flamboyant and larger than life, his long legs encased in the cherry-coloured trousers and polished black boots, his brass buttons shining. Frederick felt an overwhelming sense of defeat as he looked at him.

The chauffeur opened the door and stood back smartly. Rupert climbed into the car, his sword at his side, and his helmet in his lap. Frederick climbed in beside him. He looked at his brother and held out his hand. 'Good luck, Rupert.'

Rupert took his hand in his own. He had fully recovered from the episode with his father; he did not give it enough credence even to discuss it. Behind them, Alexander climbed alone into his Daimler. 'Thanks, Freddie,' said Rupert. 'May the best man win, eh?'

The cars started down the road. It was a joke from childhood. 'May the best man win.'

Sam crossed the room and turned again, his hands thrust deep into his pockets. 'But Dad, I want to go and join up.'

Dickie pushed the front door closed behind her and looked quickly from one to the other. She said nothing. They did not look at her. Jim was bent over the table, his arms leaning on the wooden surface, his hands clasped together. 'Not now, Sam,' he said. 'Look, Dickie's got the child.' He swept an arm briefly to indicate her as she lifted Max silently from his pram and Max gave a little hiccuping cry of hunger. 'She's not bringing in any money.' He reclasped his hands and stared ahead of him into the fire.

There was a small oak stool beside the fireplace, crudely made with the legs worked into the seat. Dickie pulled it forward and sat on it, the baby on her lap. She lifted her blouse and shushed the baby as he began to smell the milk. She held him to her breast and rocked him gently as he suckled.

Sam looked down at her for a moment. He did not really see her. His mind was on argument. 'There's more money in being a soldier than working on the land, Dad.'

'That's as may be. But we need you here.' Jim's hands tapped the table emphasising the point. 'It's harvesting time for us. The war'll be over soon. It's not for the likes of us, it's for the gentry with their money and all. We're just farm folk, and that's the way we should stay. Not get ideas above our station.'

Dickie turned her head then. She hated her father to talk like that. 'We're not just farm folk, Dad. And that's no way to think. That Kitchener wants all of us for his army. He says he needs one hundred thousand men.'

'Wonder where he's going to get them all,' Jim muttered. 'One hundred thousand. That's a lot.'

'Through men like Sam,' she said. 'That's what I'm trying to tell you . . . Sam's got to go if he wants to.' She rocked Max again gently in her lap.

'And leave me single-handed? Threshing's within two months. Jack's the only one we've got out there. And Thomas.'

'Thomas is going to the war. Bessie told me.' She looked down at Max's dark head.

'Well, there!' He dipped his head, his eyes adamant. 'There'll be help needed in the dairy. Sam, lad,' he said persuasively, 'at least think of Dickie and the baby. We need you here. Wait a while. Don't be so hasty. It'll all be over before you know't. Stay, lad. I can't manage on my own.'

Sam drew in a breath, and his eyes looked trapped. He was bursting to go. He wanted to fight.

At the mention of Max, Dickie became colder.

'I can work on the land beside you, Dad. Just as soon as I've weaned the baby.'

'What? You? You're not strong enough.' Jim looked at her. 'The top fence needs mending, the field needs ploughing. Think you could do all that, and hedging and ditching?' He snorted. 'That's men's work, love.'

'I can learn,' she said with hauteur, her bold eyes turned on him. 'I can carry Max on my back. Do some picking. Work in the dairy. Mrs Canter'll mind him. Once I've learned Sam will be free.'

She looked up at her brother, leaning against the fireplace. She had that fierce look on her face, the one that made him smile. His eyes softened. She had always been a scrapper, their Dickie. It was he who had given her her nickname: Dickie. Her real name, Josephine, didn't suit the tomboy. She was like a little dickie-bird, always standing up for herself.

Jim shook his head wearily. He was no match for his girl when she fought back. 'And who do you think is going to allow you to work on the land? Better you work in the house, in the Manor.'

'I'm not going back there, Dad,' she said steadily. She lifted Max onto her shoulder to burp him, patting his back as she spoke. 'There we are, lovey . . . Ask the master, Dad. He might say yes. Nothing's lost by trying.'

'I can't ask him.' Jim screwed round in his chair. He braced his legs and leaned his elbows on his knees, his hands dangling between. 'If anyone, I'll ask Mr Frederick. He's easier to talk to. And he has an interest in the land.'

'Ask who you wish.' Dickie's face became guarded at the mention of his name. The light eyes were bleak. She looked back at her child as she held him to the other breast. 'Only do it.' Her heart hardened. Would they always be under the thumb of the Redfields? She looked at the baby in her arms, contentedly suckling and wondered why she did not hate him; he was a Redfield, poor little thing.

'Pity Mrs Redfield isn't still alive,' muttered Jim. 'She was a good woman. Women understand a better way of doing things sometimes.'

Dickie's head lifted, the words on her lips. Sam saw the fire light her eyes and stopped her quickly with a look. Dickie saw and stopped. Jim was bent over the table. He had not forgotten. She had been about to mention their mother, who had died of tuberculosis at about the same time as the mistress had fallen from her horse and broken her neck. Sam was right. They should never talk about Ma at a time of argument, only in a time of peace. She held her tongue and looked back at the baby. There was silence in the small cottage.

'Well,' she said at last. 'Baby's done. Sam, you want to change him and put him to bed while I make the tea?'

Sam took the child in his arms with no hesitation. Dickie was always working for them and he would do anything for her even though some may have thought it unseemly for a man to take care of a baby. Sam had never been one to care what people thought anyway. Dickie stood up, brushed down her skirts and crossed the room. Over the fire were a hook and a kettle. Dickie took it outside to fill it with rainwater, brought it back and fastened it up again. She knelt on the brick hearth and stoked up the fire.

Sam had laid Max on the rag rug beside the fire to change him. Max kicked gently and gurgled. Dickie gave him a quick smile before she went to the back room. Jim sat silent and filled his pipe thoughtfully. A twisting wind blew up outside and he leaned over and pulled the long hook closed, shutting the window.

From the back room, Dickie called out. 'Sam, carry him upstairs, would you?'

There was a bread oven in the wall. She opened it. The fire she had built earlier with faggots was now dying down as she wanted it. She raked out the red-hot ashes, swabbed it with damp rags and then put the fresh dough for their bread onto the hot stones.

She took a handful of gypsy pegs and hung Max's washing across the kitchen. With the storm coming, they would have to dry inside. She skimmed the rich yellow cream off the pail of milk to make butter later, and carried a jug of milk and yesterday's bread through to the table.

'There's a keg of cider in the pantry, lass. Bring it to us, would you?' Jim hardly turned. It was the first thing he had said. He had watched Sam handle the baby with disapproval. Jim was of the opinion that there was woman's work and man's work, and never the twain should meet.

'Dad,' she said gently, laying a hand on his shoulder. 'If I'm going to be working on the land and Sam's going to be away, you're going to have to learn to get your own cider.' She kissed his cheek. 'Go along, now.'

Sam came down the stairs as they stood there. He stopped, one foot still on the step. He looked at the two of them, so different yet strong in their love, and Dickie was so like her mother in that moment. 'Baby's asleep, Dickie.'

'Thank you, Sam.'

He looked into her eyes. She was strong and capable, but their dad was right. Her pride had made her say what she did, but he knew he would also have to make a sacrifice to help the family stand together. 'I'm decided. I'm not going yet, Dad. Not until Dickie's free of the child and she's learned how to work on the land.' It was a promise to her. He saw the flicker of gratitude in her eyes. She squeezed her father's shoulders briefly. 'There we are, Dad. A compromise.'

Jim smiled with relief. 'That is good news, lad. The way things are you'll never have to go at all.'

'Maybe. Still, Dickie may as well learn. After tea we'll go out to the dairy. She can start there.'

Dickie grinned. 'And Dad can sit with Max!'

Jim grunted and turned back to the table. 'You can get Mrs Canter, I'm not becoming some wet nurse. Fetch me some cider, Sam.'

Sam and Dickie exchanged a look of humour as he opened the pantry door. A feeling of pride filled the little room. They were a family. She laughed lightly and went to the fire to boil the kettle for their tea.

He reached for her again in the bed. Caroline's eyes flew open. He turned her over. At the sight of her pale slender buttocks, his need of her overcame him. He was brutal. Caroline's fingers clutched the pillow; she closed her eyes and bore it. She was his and she knew her duty. A wife never said no to her husband's desires.

When it was all over she lay silently. His hand ran roughly over her small breasts and then he laughed and kissed her briefly before turning his back to her. He pushed the pillow more comfortably beneath his head, settled himself and fell quickly into a deep sleep. The novelty of her was gone and it was rather disappointing; once their clothes were off they were all the same.

The room was dark. She was still, hardly daring to breathe in case he should wake and take her again. She probably could not have moved anyway—Caroline was in a state of shock. She had been innocent of whom to love. She had sensed something with Frederick, but before it had had a chance to take shape she had been swept off her feet by Rupert. She had dreamed of this moment as something beautiful. Now her legs felt as if she could not stand on them, there was a weakness in her, and a pain where he had ravished her as though she had been torn and broken beyond healing. She was terrified to touch herself and find out; between her legs she felt the stickiness of fresh blood. Tears filled her beautiful eyes. She remembered a look her mother had given her as they had kissed goodbye; she had not understood it. Now she did. Was this what a woman had to bear? The silent tears coursed down her cheeks. Rupert started to snore. Still she dared not move or cry aloud. She bit her lips and held it in. Suddenly the girlish dreams had faded; her lessons in adulthood had been drastic and swift, smashing her gentle and cosseted past from her. A first seed was born, to build on. She was at least the lady of Foxhall Manor. If she could not have the love she had fantasised, she would have the money, the gowns and the prestige.

Everybody was joining up. At Foxhall Green station the train was standing waiting as they loaded suitcases and boxes on board. Smoke curled into the grey sky above and there was a cold wind blowing across the draughty platform.

There was tremendous excitement all around, heads sticking out of windows and people pushing food hampers in. The doors stood open and the guard was blowing his whistle.

Alexander, Frederick and Caroline stood beside the train as Rupert pushed his cases onto the rack in the first-class carriage. Further down the platform George Lancing and his daughter Edwina were saying farewell to her husband James.

Rupert closed the door with a bang and pushed the window down, leaning out. Caroline handed him a New Testament in red leather with gold embossing on the outside.

He laughed, took the book and leaned down towards her, lifting her under the arms to him. He kissed her full on the mouth. Caroline was released to the ground, her cheeks warm, and her eyes cast down.

Frederick moved forward and shook his hand. 'Good luck, old fellow.'

'I'll need it. Goodbye, Father.'

'Goodbye, Rupert. My regards to General Haig when you see him!' Despite their recent differences, his voice was proud. Not every man's son had been personally invited to work on Sir Douglas Haig's personal staff. The fact that it was not Haig himself but a senior officer, an old polo partner of Rupert's, who had requested the transfer, was irrelevant. What was relevant was that Haig had approved it; Rupert was a cavalryman. Alexander's voice carried, and Rupert gave his cynical smile.

With a jolt and a squeak, the train slowly edged forward as the last doors slammed. The whistle blew again. Women cried and waved. The crowd cheered. The smoke began to billow out rhythmically as the train gathered speed. Rupert waved. Caroline lifted her hand. Her eyes never left him. He gave her one brief look and then disappeared inside.

Further down the platform Bessie Jones cried loudly as her desperate fingers lost their hold on handsome Thomas Green.

'Oh, he'll never come back,' she wailed. Thomas blew her a kiss and smiled for the benefit of all the others on the platform, waving. He was a soldier off to war and he had never had so much attention in all his life. He was on the crest of a wave.

The band struck up:

> God save our gracious king,
> Long live our noble king,
> God save our king.
> Send him victorious,
> Happy and glorious,
> Long to—

The voices that had joined in were drowned by the blast of the trumpets and the whistle of the train. The soldiers cheered as the small band of family and friends faded in the distance. They were off to glorious war.

Bessie pushed past the crowd of well-dressed people and ran out through the station to the lane beyond. Behind her, the Redfields and Lancings walked slowly through together.

'I can't believe it, can you, Caroline?' her eldest sister Edwina was saying. 'We were all staying with Aunt Katie for the Farringdon dance only five weeks ago. It all seems such a short time ago. And now you're married, and he's gone. It seems too tragic.'

The party opened out onto the lane. Bessie went past pushing her bicycle, handkerchief pressed to her face. Edwina gave her a cursory glance. 'We went to the Hippodrome last night and took a box,' she was saying. 'We found it so difficult to keep off the subject of war. James has been longing to go and now it's come at last.' Her voice slipped. 'Oh, Caroline,' she said suddenly, 'it's the last time I'll see him, I just know it's true. It's all so awful.'

She burst into tears. Her father, George, put his arm around her and led her to their car. Behind them there was silence as the small group felt the weight of her words.

Frederick opened the door of their car. 'I'm sorry, Caroline. Don't worry about Rupert. He'll be home soon.'

'I'm not worried, Frederick. I know Rupert will return.'

She bent her head as she climbed into the back of the car, and Frederick cast his eyes over her. It was not her words but a sense of something else that made him know the truth. She was carrying Rupert's child.

Christmas came and went and then it was winter. The war had not finished at all. The first convoys of wounded were arriving at hospitals all over the country.

Caroline had asked if she could help. She walked down the length of the ward. Fourteen beds, and all of the men terribly wounded. A stretcher brought a new patient in from the front. The man was moaning with pain as they carried him to the bed. It was night-time and should have been silent, but the ward was full of the groans of men trying to be brave and unable to hold back their shock and pain. They were frightened, damaged men with amputations, terrible wounds, tetanus and gangrene, totally unprepared for the horrors of war, and now handed into the care of young girls totally unready for anything like this. Girls such as Caroline had had no one to train or guide them.

It was a baptism of blood. The VADs had done little more than practise their bandaging in classes at homes like Longbarrow. Now all their friends were dying or dead.

Caroline felt faint. She had wanted to help, but now it was no longer possible. She let her face drop into her hands at the desk and remembered Edwina's words. Such a short time ago they were all dancing and gay and now those days were gone.

The sister came over.

'Go home, Lady Caroline. You've done more than enough to help. You need your strength,' she said. 'It'll all be over soon.'

Gratefully, Caroline took her coat and left the hospital. Very soon she would have a new life to care for.

The baby squalled in the bed beside her. He was red and demanding. The nanny bustled over and took him away. Caroline longed to hold him and nurse him herself, but it was not done. Her breasts were bound against the milk. She felt lonely.

It was July 1915, and the war still raged in Europe. The boy was Charles Alexander Redfield.

FIVE

October, 1915

Dickie was in the stable rubbing down the horses with a handful of straw to wipe away the sweat and dirt of the day's work. Her back still ached from the previous day's strenuous bending to lift the potatoes into baskets. Her hands were chafed and worn from groping in the rough soil.

In normal years the low land by the river would be under pasture to provide winter hay and summer grazing for the dairy herd and the young stock and most of the higher land would be ploughed and sown in a rotation of crops: barley for the cows, oats for the horses and turnips for the cows in winter, before being sown in grass again.

However, potatoes grew well and the high land was now planted with this crop. They stored well and could be eaten immediately. Foxhall had expanded their acreage this year to help in Britain's food production drive.

Dickie had been up milking at dawn and she would still be working as the sun set. Cows would calve in the middle of the night and she had to be there. She had learned to mend the fences, plough the fields and drive the horse-team with the sea-gulls flying inland behind her. She had learned to farm beside the men. She had worked harder than any of them, against their scepticism.

The bumper wartime harvest had led to prosperity for the Redfields and she had contributed to it. But at the back of her mind she put their gain down to her gain also. She was learning all the time.

It was a day like that other. Once again, on a cool October day two years later, she had tramped up the field beside the high-sided cart and listened to the jingle of the harness, the groaning of the cart as it lurched across the field.

This time it was she who took the potatoes in their baskets up to the clamp site on the high land at the top of the field to ensure good drainage in winter. Some soldiers had been helping them out. She took little notice of them, and their taunts had soon died. They had learned to respect Dickie. That afternoon she had helped to carpet the clamp with straw and then the potatoes had been tipped in and built into a high mound. Then they had been covered with a thick cladding of straw to protect them from the frost and the clamp itself sealed with soil. It was the first time Dickie had had the responsibility and it suited her.

Entering the stable, Sam was silent for a moment watching her. Instead of exhaustion, she glowed with purpose. The stable was permeated with the smell of the linseed oil that she had put into the steaming hot tonic mash for the horses.

Jack came in and saw him. He took the fork that he had come to fetch. 'Won't need you no more with that young sister of yours. She's a fine farmer!' he cracked. He went out again.

Dickie turned to look at him. She knew what was coming. She turned away again silently and brushed at the sweating flanks of the horse.

She was exhausted, but she would let no-one see, particularly Sam. She wanted him to be free to make his decision. Now she knew she had done her best all too well. She had had precious little time to herself and Max, but the bonus of freedom and working the land in the open air was worth it, and not being tied to the kitchen at Foxhall. She had steeled herself for this mo-ment, and now it had come.

Sam touched her shoulder gently.

'I'm going, Dickie.'

'Yes.' She brushed vigorously.

'Kitchener's New Army are going to mount an offensive on the Somme. I'm going to be a part of it. At last.'

He grinned. His face was evangelistic. He was in his cloth cap and jacket and high white collar and tie, his belongings stashed away in the bag over his shoulder. He looked so proud and she was proud of him.

'It's the Big Show, Dickie. I'm ready to volunteer now, and I've watched you. You're doing fine. You don't need me no more. All the other lads have gone. I've looked at those posters long enough.' He hefted the bag higher. 'I can't stand back no more. I've stayed for the boy and you, but you're all right, aren't you? You're strong. You'll help Dad, and old Mrs Canter in the village'll take care of Max like she has been, won't she?' He came to a halt in his flow of words, wanting her confirmation.

'I'll be fine, Sam. Don't worry.'

'I know, Dickie. I know you. You'll always be fine. That's what you're made of. I'm proud of you, I am that.'

'Oh, Sam. I'll miss you.'

She stopped brushing the horse, struck by the knowledge that he was going at last.

She could not stop him. She wanted to, yet she understood. If she'd been a man she'd have gone too. But she was saddled with a child, and her dad. Yes, she understood only too well. She could do her bit for the war effort, making things in her spare time when she wasn't working.

'I'll miss you too, love, but I've got to be a part of it, now haven't I?'

'Yes, Sam, you have. Even though it's an army commanded by men like that Redfield. I hear they never even see action. They're too busy drinking and eating while the men do all the fighting. And the killing,' she finished.

'Now, Dickie, that's not true. You've been listening to village gossip. Shame on you. I thought you were above all that,' he teased. 'No, everybody fights for their country, officers too. It's a fine time to be British and out there fighting all together, every man shoulder to shoulder, despite his background. We'll be joined in one goal, every man pulling his weight for king and country.'

She looked up poignantly at her handsome brother, blond and decent, and a little too naïve. She felt too wise for her years, with a vision far beyond her experience to date. He was obsessed with words like 'new' and 'big', and full of valour. She could not destroy that, though in her young heart she felt the village gossips might be right, and it was not the way he saw it at all. She would miss him. Apart from Max he was the light in her life. She said none of this, nor how she needed him.

She looked at him with her queer light eyes, bold eyes that

looked right through you, thought Sam. You never knew what she was thinking, just like Ma.

'You're right, Sam,' she said. She had to help him hold to his beliefs, other wise there was nothing. 'You'll all be after the same end, I don't doubt it.' She laid a hand on his arm. 'God be with you, Sam.'

'Oh, Dickie.' And then his resolve left him and he clasped her in his arms. His eyes squeezed tight shut as she held him too. 'I'll be back before you know,' he whispered over her head.

And then abruptly he had left her, striding away down the cobbled yard. She watched him go, so brave and tall, his bag over his shoulder. He turned the corner of the stableyard without looking back and was gone.

Dickie dropped her hand to her side. She turned slowly back to the horse and automatically lifted the brush to start again. She could not. Ridiculously, her eyes were filled with tears. She was trembling. She leaned against the horse's sleek neck and gave a little cough of pain. She remembered Sam's pride, his face all aglow. *Oh, Sam*, she thought, will I ever see you again?

It was three in the morning. Caroline woke from a nightmare and lay still, hardly daring to breathe. The evening breeze rattled the tiny panes of the window. It was an unseasonably mild night. There was a heavy moon and the room was still. The breeze rattled the window again. The noise had woken her. Now she would not sleep again.

She threw back the covers, swung herself out of bed, and crossed to the window to close the catch. Her hand stayed on the iron bar as she looked down.

On a bench in the garden sat a man; he appeared motionless. Caroline tried to see more clearly. By the light of the moon everything was bright, the stones of the path pale as they stretched down to the river, and the ornamental pond beside him like soft silver, against the shadowed grass. She was sure it was Alexander.

She put on a warm dressing-gown and crept down the stairs, letting herself out of the front door, and wondering where she found the courage except that it was that sort of night. A night in the past when she and her sisters would have gone on a moonlight picnic in the grounds of Longbarrow, jumping and clutching each other with delighted fright every time they heard the hoot of an owl.

She made her way towards him. It was Alexander. He looked up, startled from his dreams.

'I'm sorry. Would you rather I went away?' she said in an apologetic voice.

'No, no, of course not,' he said, recovering, and patted the seat beside him. 'I would be glad of company. Your company,' he encouraged.

She sat down beside him and sighed. The garden was beautiful, stretched out before them in the moonlight. There was no need of words. They were two of a kind. She had known that on the night of the dance.

'I would have loved a big family,' he said at last. 'A daughter or two.' He smiled wistfully. 'We would have if she had lived. Mary always loved the house full of people.'

'Mrs Redfield?' she said.

He turned to her. 'Of course. You didn't know her!' he said, sounding brighter. 'You were too young.' There was a smile in his voice. He had wanted to talk to someone about her, someone who didn't know her, someone understanding. Someone to whom he could tell all the wonderful things about Mary, all the pain since their parting. Night after night he came out here, as they had used to do, together.

'What was Mrs Redfield like?' said Caroline.

'Like a ray of sunshine, she really was. She was my life. I loved her too much, I think. She made me so strong . . . That's what you need in life. Strength in a partner.'

She lifted a slender shoulder. 'But you're strong. On your own. Without her. And you've got your sons.'

'Yes,' he said slowly. 'But, you know, Mary was special. Everybody loved her. At parties, do you know what she'd do . . . ?'

'No, what?'

'. . . She'd get up and sing. Or dance. She was a great dancer. She'd throw impromptu parties and have all the servants rush around to bring the food out. And then she'd lay big cushions out on the terrace and tables of food and champagne and then she'd just invite everybody over. The boys would go out on horseback with the grooms and round up everybody in the neighbourhood.' He laughed indulgently. 'It wasn't quite the done thing, I suppose you might say, but they all loved it. To a boring old banker like me it was like coming home to a house full of light. She'd open up those double doors and run out to greet me. We'd walk in the sunshine and we'd talk about our day. Hers was always more interesting,' he said in an aside.

'Maybe she was just a good story-teller,' she said. 'Some people are better than others.'

Alexander smiled quickly at her. 'Maybe.' She *did* understand. 'She'd always dress up for the children's birthdays. They adored her. Especially Rupert.' His voice trailed thoughtfully.

Caroline's mind spun from the picture he had painted to that of Rupert. She opened her mouth to ask about her husband.

'. . . Yes, the house was always full of laughter then,' he went on before she had a chance to speak. 'Full of people. Our love was one of those rare ones. Do you know what I mean?' Against her silence he looked at her. 'You're happy, aren't you? I don't mean to pry, but I hoped my son would make you welcome, and he would love you. He does, doesn't he?'

'Yes, of course he does. And I'm very happy.'

His eyes searched her face for a moment. 'War,' he said softly. 'It's a terrible thing. Splits families, but it doesn't last.' He shook his head, drifting in a thoughtful silence. 'All our sons.' His head dropped a little. 'I'm sorry, my dear. I think I'm very tired. I'm falling asleep. I must go in.' He twisted round to look at her. 'I'm glad to know you're happy with us. You're like a real daughter to me, Caroline.'

She nodded, her smile tight as she looked down at her hands.

'Well, now,' he said, patting her hand. 'It's too damp out here. Are you coming in?'

'No,' she said. 'I think I'll stay here a while.'

'I'll see you at breakfast. Good night, my dear . . .'

'Good night.'

He stood up. 'Thank you for listening to me.' He turned and went away towards the house.

She sat on the bench and wondered. The garden was soothing, the breeze gentle. She leaned her head against her shoulder and closed her eyes. She thought of Rupert, and wondered what he would say when he heard she was pregnant again.

June, 1916

At a château in Montreuil, fifty miles behind the line, was the
headquarters of Sir Douglas Haig, commander-in-chief of the
British Expeditionary Force. The leaders on the Western Front
all lived well behind the lines and throughout the war had continued to make their plans without any first-hand knowledge of
what went on in the No Man's Land between the ordinary fighting soldier and the Germans on the other side of that strip of
ground.

Haig never visited the front line and neither did his staff.
There was therefore no liaison between staff and fighting-man.
All too often the staff officers, on whom so much depended, had
been selected more for their social connections than for their
worth as strategists of war.

Rupert and David Stratton-Holt came down the corridor into
the drawing-room. They had just had a very good dinner with
fine local wines. David laughed as he strolled into the room and
took up a stance beside the fireplace. A young soldier brought
them their brandy and cigars. They did not notice him at all. He
quietly withdrew.

Rupert sat down, lit his cigar, stretched out his long legs and
relaxed, blowing a plume of smoke into the air. The wine had
warmed him, and the food had been excellent. The front was
only a word to him. The war would soon be over and they would
be welcomed home as heroes, decorated probably. Everyone
would want to know what they had been through. There was
nothing wrong with war. It was really quite a pleasant diversion.
He ate well, exercised his horses and mixed with fellows of his
own type. David was a good sort. It was his influence that had
brought him here.

'Well, the plan's set now, old boy,' said David. 'We'll blast
those bloody Huns off the face of the earth.'

'I hope you're right.' Rupert's voice was cool, his eyes half-
closed against the stream of smoke. His manner was lazy and
relaxed. 'Better them than us.'

David laughed. 'Oh, we'll do it. The old man knows what
he's doing.'

'The old man's a fool.'

David's laughter left his face. He looked swiftly around.
'Great Scott, man. Don't talk like that.' Across the room a few
officers lounged in chairs talking quietly after dinner. 'And be-

sides,' he turned back and felt his way to a chair, 'I don't know if you're right. Oh, I know there's been argument, but how did he get where he is unless he is an excellent commander?' He sat down.

'By being in the right place at the right time, as we all have been. Don't tell me, David, that you don't know what they say about him. At Sandhurst he was just about the most unpopular fellow there with his contemporaries. The reason he's where he is, is typical of the whole system . . . he looks good in his uniform.' Rupert drew on his cigar, exhaling slowly.

'Oh, come now,' David expostulated. 'You've got to do better than that if you want to put up a serious argument.'

'All right.' Rupert blew smoke at the ceiling. 'He's handsome, well connected, studious in military matters, religious and patriotic. And, as I said, immaculately dressed. He's everybody's idea of the perfect general, but you and I well know, David, he's intolerant and only likes to hear what he wants to hear. And I, for one, am not a toady. By the way,' he said, looking across at his friend. 'How did the briefing go?'

David was silent a moment, remembering those same toadies at the briefing that morning. 'Oh, pretty straightforward stuff really,' he murmured. Rupert was right in a way, though he would not confirm it. He frowned as he tried to recall the exact details. 'It seems a diversionary attack by two divisions of Allenby's Third Army will draw away the German reserves at Gommecourt to the north, while Rawlinson's lot—and of course our chums, the French—are to smash open the whole German trench system in the south along a twenty-mile front.' He drew on his cigar, running his middle finger thoughtfully over the separate bars of his blond moustache. 'Once the breach is made, the attacking forces will turn northwards pushing back the exposed flanks of the enemy and Gough's cavalry are to charge through the gap and deep into the enemy's territory. They're bound to counter-attack, of course, but everybody seems pretty confident that it'll all be achieved on the first day—starting at first light, the men'll go in and wreak the first damage. Well, what d'you think, eh? Good plan?'

'Can you think of a better?'

'Maybe! But it's not up to us, is it? Ours not to reason why, my dear Rupert.' He drew on the cigar again. 'Old Haig believes that the artillery barrage will smash the enemy's line so that the infantry will be able to make their first blow at full force. You remember the failures in Flanders in 1915 when there was not enough shelling before attacks? Or when reserves had not been brought up in time or the break in the enemy's lines had not been extensive enough? Well this time, I feel, we will overcome all those separate difficulties. And, after all, Haig did say that if it doesn't succeed at once, it will be broken off.'

'I don't think that will happen,' said Rupert, placing his brandy on the table beside him. He pulled himself up in the chair, and leaned forward to emphasise his point. 'Why, we're going in after first light when we'll be sitting ducks . . .'

'Well, to be fair now, that was not what the old man wanted.'

'Even so. He's an ambitious, vain man, who is obsessed with a belief in cavalry, to the exclusion of all else. He believes, I do think, that a war of this magnitude could actually be fought with cavalry alone. He covers it all up with that olde-worlde charm that totally fools men like you, David. But I know the sort.'

He held his cigar over the fireplace, his mouth now pursed in thought. Haig reminded him too much of his father. He could see right through the old man. He was consumed with his own single-minded righteousness. He was totally unimaginative and set in his ways. Rupert held no respect for him. His mind slipped back to that day at the bank. He had been about to confide in his father for the first time, and his father had cut him off to go to one of his meetings. He had never had time for him, always expected him to be like himself. That was partly what had driven Rupert to take up the position of lay reader in church. To show his father that he could do something entirely of his own creation, and achieve some standing in the community. He had achieved that. He gave an inner smile as he remembered that first day, all the faces lifted to his. It had been a marvellous feeling, the feeling of power that he needed. There was also the ceremony and the robes. He loved to be in a position of control, to hold people in the palm of his hand, to think their thoughts for them. Lead them his way. Thank God, he hadn't weakened that day and shown his father that he really did want to communicate. They would always talk at cross purposes now. His eyebrow lifted as he saw the man himself, Sir Douglas Haig, enter the room with his fellow officers around him. Sycophants. Rupert's eyes narrowed. Something he would never be. He was destined to lead, bowing to no one.

'Old Rawlinson's dead against it, of course,' said David suddenly.

'What?' Rupert brought himself back to the present.

'This plan.' David lifted his glass. 'He says it's based on false premises and too-great optimism. There's no sign of German morale weakening and until that happens he thinks a decisive success is out of the question. Says the idea of hurling attack after attack at the enemy frequently exhausts the attacker first.'

'He's probably right,' said Rupert. 'Still, it won't affect us either way, David. It's the men who'll do the fighting.' Out of the corner of his eye he saw Patrick Broughton-Smith heading towards them. Inwardly he groaned. The man was a crashing bore. 'When's it to be?' he asked.

'The 28th.'

'I say, you chaps, have you heard?' Patrick had threaded his way through the chairs and arrived ashen-faced at their sides. 'Kitchener's been killed.'

The room went silent. Heads turned. David looked aghast. 'How, by God?'

'Seems he was on some errand or other to Russia in the cruiser, *Hampshire*. It was struck by a mine off the Orkneys on the 5th and sank in heavy seas. There were practically no survivors.'

'Good God, Kitchener.'

There was hardly a sound. The famous figurehead was gone, the hero who had masterminded strategy and enthusiasm, killed. He at least had seemed invincible. Even Rupert was quietly thoughtful. It did not seem such a good omen.

Rawlinson's troops were landing in France. A few had served in Flanders and were not new to the game of war. They had marched south with the guns through the dry heat of the summer. The new recruits out from England were different: untested and excited, war to them was still an adventure.

Sam Bennett marched along, more able than some to carry the weight of the kit on his back. He was dressed in flat cap and jacket buttoned to the neck, heavy boots with socks to the knees over his breeches, and his rifle over his shoulder. He also sported a blond moustache to suit his new status. Years of labour had made him strong and the pack strapped to his body was little trouble. He marched side by side, as he had expected, with factory hands, clerks and ploughmen, but of the officers there was little sign. The ones that were in sight drove in comfort. It did not matter. They were united in a common cause. His young voice sang out with the others: 'It's a long way to Tipperary, it's a long way to go . . . !'

The song carried them along. They had left the rolling plains and were entering Picardy, the fields bright with the ardent colours of poppies and mustard under a wide, blue sky. Rows of dark green poplars speared the sky above their route. The earth was damp and warm with the smells of summer, and wild fowl cried by the water's edge. As they tramped they approached the area of the Somme and the look of prosperity gave way to empty desolation, cottages and farmhouses smashed and broken. Every field was jammed with thousands of men, wagons, guns and vehicles. Square-nosed brass-bonneted Crossley ASC lorries jostled with ordinary pack mules, their backs and legs encrusted with the white cloying chalk of the trenches. The soldiers marched in rows of four, the crunch of their boots echoing as they passed through tiny ghost-like villages, with poverty-stricken houses overgrown with wild flowers; daisies and scabious fluttering gently in the breeze on the tops of old stone walls where iron crucifixes rusted in the sun.

Their backs were scored by their equipment, their khaki uniforms were stained with sweat but they pressed on, sure of purpose, their voices lifted to the whining of mouth-organs. They tramped on through the night, and then it was that they began to see the flashes of light in the dark sky ahead and hear the ominous rumble of distant gunfire. It was a new sound that quivered at the edges of their youthful enthusiasm. At long last they were approaching the war.

Sam entered the vast network of trenches along with the other men. They seemed to be moving along a muddy path that slipped lower and lower until it reached the bowels of the earth. He was issued with his bowl-shaped steel helmet by a silent old soldier whose face showed no emotion except utter exhaustion and disillusion.

Sam's spirits remained high, despite the appalling conditions. He was buoyed up by a feeling of duty and patriotism such as he could never have imagined. The preceding days had all been leading up to this event, and now he was here. He sat in his scraped-out niche, a roof of corrugated iron over his head and gratefully pulled off his boots. Then he scooped his food hungrily from his can, hunched over it, his face lined with the white muddy chalk that had clung to him, his feet braced wide apart. It was not until he had filled his stomach with a few quick mouthfuls of food that he stopped eating to rub his blistered, aching feet. It was then he noticed the smell of mud, sweat, manure and something else. He did not yet know it was the smell of death.

He took out a piece of paper and started to write home to Dickie. He told her how proud he was, and how weary. He asked her to read the letter to Dad and to tell him he had been right to be a part of Kitchener's Big Show.

And then darkness fell and he could write no more. He put away his paper and curled into uncomfortable sleep. Around him the summer night was warm and close, the inevitable mouth-organs whining sad and sweet upon the air. Men did not speak. There was nothing to say.

Away in the countryside in the woods behind them, squirrels darted through the undergrowth around the camps near Thiepval, and at Martinsart the nightingales sang so loudly they kept the encamped men awake. The summer was rich with warmth and abundant with wildlife and flowers and the countryside was at its best.

The bombardment that opened on June 24th filled every man with awe. The tremendous roar of guns blasted and rattled over the hot air, rolling all the way along the front line from north to south. It reverberated through the camps and the valleys and cast away any doubts or fears that might have lingered in the minds of the men.

It thumped and thudded through the night of the 27th, as men sat up late by thousands of small fires, writing their last letters home, singing softly or playing cards, dreaming of their loved ones. On the 28th, they rose and began their slow march forward to attack. Each man was in full 'fighting order', sixty-six pounds of equipment strapped to his back and unable to progress at anything faster than a slow walk.

The rain began to pour down in torrents. It was sudden and the men were drenched in a moment. The surface of the roads turned to white slime and in confusion the men were ordered off the roads to take cover wherever they could, under groundsheets, in disused farms and houses. The attack was postponed for forty-eight hours.

Tired, hungry and miserable, the edge was taken off the men's fervour that had been building up for days. Now they waited under dripping trees at the sides of the road, nervous and disorderly, trying to eat when they could and soaked through as the rain continued to teem down upon them. They longed for zero hour.

July 1st dawned. It was a beautiful day, the mist lying in the hollows so that even the battlefield looked as it might once have done, a meadow full of flowers and insects basking in the summer warmth.

Men assembled their kit and said their last prayers. They thought of their loved ones with hollow hearts. Sam stood quietly cleaning his rifle and thinking of home. He felt lonely and disillusioned for the first time, his gut twisted with fear of the unknown and his mouth unaccountably dry now that the moment had come.

He looked up into the sky as it softened with promise of the day. The sun would soon be up.

Twenty miles behind the line, Rupert and his brother officers slept soundly in their beds after a good dinner and fine French wines. Sir Douglas Haig was also still asleep.

In the hour before bed he had written to his wife: 'I feel that every step in my plan has been taken with divine help.' And to his diary he had penned the notation: 'The weather report is favourable for tomorrow. With God's help, I feel hopeful. The wire has never been so well cut.'

SIX

Alexander stood at the sideboard and lifted the lid of the silver chafing-dish. The sharp aroma of the bacon filled his nostrils. He lifted out two of the rashers and laid them on his plate beside a mound of creamy yellow scrambled egg and two sausages. Despite the war, conditions at Foxhall had altered little. The country may have been rationed, but Foxhall, though contributing with milk, cream and crops, always held enough back for the family.

The dining-room was long and mellow with deeply polished oak, a refectory table and twelve tall carved chairs ranged along it. Rays of summer sun flooded the oak floor and touched the sombre oil paintings that hung on the panelled walls. It would be a hot day. The french windows stood open to the day and the stone-flagged terrace and balcony beyond. There was not a breath of air.

On the table a bowl of fruit stood next to a vase of sweet peas, roses and clematis. The scent filled the air, coupling with the deep perfume of beeswax. The servants had been up for at least four hours before the family drifted down to breakfast, and had now gone to leave them to serve themselves and eat in peace, as if the staff did not exist.

Alexander carried his food back to his place. The newspaper lay unopened to the left of his plate. He had instituted a rule: no newspapers until after breakfast. The first list had come through after the Battle of Mons and after that it had gone on and on, all of their friends killed, wounded or missing. He could no longer bear to read it.

75

Frederick walked into the room. 'Morning, Father.' He lifted the lid of the dish and replaced it.

'Got to eat.' Alexander motioned his fork towards him as he took a mouthful of food. 'Go on. Plenty there.'

'No. Just some toast.' He came towards the table. 'Have you seen Caroline?'

Alexander looked briefly at him as he chewed. 'In the morning room. *Frederick,*' he said, stopping him as he turned to go. 'Yes?'

'Take her some tea. She refused breakfast again.'

Frederick caught his look. Alexander was worried. Caroline had become like a daughter to him. She was as beautiful as Mary, and must in some ways have reminded him of his wife. She had the same colouring. Anyway, whatever it was, Alexander had taken her welfare under his jurisdiction. The baby was due any day, and Caroline was far too thin. She simply would not eat. She was morose and silent and spent hours gazing away into the distance. There was definitely something wrong, but so far she had not confided in them.

Frederick poured the tea and went through into the morning room.

She sat in a corner on a wicker chair, her feet up on a stool and a light shawl thrown over her legs. The sun fell on the side of her head, striking blue-black lights into her hair. Her pale face was shadowed and the blue eyes as dark as midnight as she looked up. She looked more fragile than ever, and by being so, even more beautiful. 'I've brought you some tea,' he said.

The soft smile crossed her face.

'Frederick, you're so kind. Thank you. Come and sit with me, will you? It's such a beautiful day. Do you see all those roses I planted last year are already coming out?' She talked nervously, her eyes averted, and her fingers plucked at the shawl.

Frederick sat down slowly and handed her the tea. 'Here,' he said, his voice very soft.

She put her hands around the saucer and took it from him, placing it on her lap in front of the swell of her pregnancy. 'Thank you.' The corners of her mouth trembled.

'Caroline,' he said. 'What is it?'

And then he saw the opened telegram beside her.

Frederick touched her wrist in alarm. As he did so he noticed how narrow the bones were. 'The telegram, Caroline? What news is there? Not bad, is it?'

Caroline's eyes flew to his face. Her hand reached out and took the paper between her fingers. 'No,' she murmured, 'not bad news.'

'What is it then? Will you tell me?'

'Rupert's coming home,' she said.

'Oh!' He sat back. 'Well, that should make you happy.'

'Yes, on leave,' she said. 'It does. It's a special dispensation,' she said. 'From General Haig himself.' She looked at the telegram in her hands, but her voice was colourless. She spoke the words in a monotone. 'Isn't that marvellous?' she asked him. 'I told him that I was not well, and that I needed him here, in case . . . in case . . . well,' she licked her lips. 'Anyway, it's not the time for him to have leave, but he was given it anyway. The perks of being on the general's personal staff, I suppose!' she said lightly. And then, to his horror, burst into tears.

'Caroline, my dear. Whatever is the matter?' He wanted to touch her, but did not dare. His arm started to go round her bent back and then stopped.

She took a deep breath, said, 'Oh!' very tragically, and swallowed her sobs. 'Frederick,' she said. 'You're the only one I can confide in.' She looked desperately at him. 'Dr Biddy says after this . . . I can't have any more children. It's too dangerous. He says it could kill me.' She looked down, her voice fading as she said the words.

'Oh, my poor dear,' he said.

'No, no,' she said. 'It's not me. I don't mind. Two is enough. But Rupert. He practically commanded me on the night we married. I was to provide him with a big family, at least seven children, that was what he said. I'm so dreading telling him. I've failed him, Frederick. Already.'

'Oh, no,' he reassured her. 'I'm sure he'll understand. Rupert loves you.' She did not look convinced as he spoke these words to her. 'Caroline, for all of Rupert's . . . ways, he has compassion. He would not have taken up his post in the church if he had not. What will be much more important to him is that you're alive, and with him.'

'Do you think so?'

'I know so,' he said, though he was not sure. Rupert was very unpredictable.

'I hardly know him. Sometimes he's so difficult to understand.'

'Well, you haven't had much of a chance, have you?' he smiled. 'With this war starting the way it did.'

'No, I suppose not.' She gazed out of the window. Clouds passed over the absolute blue of the sky. The shadow of them drifted across the glass of the morning room and shaded her face briefly. 'Tell me about him, Frederick. Help me get to know him.'

'Rupert?' he said. 'Well, now, let me see . . .'

And so he started. A small part of him laughed at the rich irony of it. Here he was, telling Caroline what a grand chap her husband was, when years before he had thought he would be the one to love her. Since her presence in the house he had effectively turned his raw adoration into a brotherly devotion, though there were still times when her beauty affected him as it did today. And yet he had to do it. In a time of war, the families that were left behind of necessity drew closer and shielded each other from pain. The strong unity was of increased importance as they held each other spiritually and waited.

'. . . You should have known our mother. She was beautiful, rather like you in fact. Rupert adored her. And he was there when she died, that was the tragedy of it. We never talk about it now. She took him out on one of her wild sprees, riding together. She was a superb horsewoman, crazy, always impetuous. Rupert was just the same. They were full of fire and verve together. She was always challenging us to grab life by the throat, I suppose you might say. She did. And never let it go! Rupert thought her every word was law. He can never let a challenge go now, though. He's never buried his memory of her. I think somehow he felt responsible, though of course that's ridiculous. He was only ten at the time. He took on her persona, but somehow . . . never got it right. It affected us all,' he said. And now the therapy was beginning to work on him too. They had buried it all unspoken for so long, the three men. He needed to talk about her too. His voice went on, remembering, and Caroline listened, staring away across the lawns in silence as the clouds drifted away from the sun and the shadows left her face.

Out in the field Dickie was haymaking. It was a time of year when all available hands were put to work. With pitchforks and rakes they gathered in the hay and threw it onto the high cart. All the female help on the farm joined in, the children too.

Without exception they all wore headgear and white overalls, while the men wore their flat caps and were in their shirtsleeves and braces. Kegs of cider stood ready to quench their thirst.

Mrs Canter came lumbering across the field with Max's hand in hers. His sharp eyes had already found his mother and were pinned on her as he lifted his sturdy legs over the sharp stalks. He was two years old with dark curly hair and his mother's direct look, though his eyes were deep blue.

Dickie straightened as she saw them, a hand to her back. She narrowed her eyes against the sun, shielding them with a slim brown hand. Max came running. As he reached her he flung himself into her arms.

Mrs Canter puffed up behind him. 'I couldn't hold him back, not once he saw you. There's a letter from Sam.'

'From Sam!' Her arms around Max she tore open the letter. 'Dad!' she called. 'Dad, come on! A letter from Sam!'

A hand lifted from the top of the hay cart. Jim was climbing down already and making his way up the field towards her. Dickie read on, a frown creasing her forehead and then another easier look.

Milly Canter watched her. Sam had been like her own son. She had watched over the two of them since their mother died. Sam was a good boy but Dickie had always been the strong one. Strong, like her mother, but like her mother she always took on too much. And Elsie Bennett had died young. Milly Canter frowned.

'Dickie, love. You look all done in. News not bad, is it?'

'No.' But her voice was slow as she said it, still reading. 'He says that when I get this he'll be a part of something grand that he'll tell me all about when he gets home inside the month. Something he's that proud of.'

'He can't say what?'

'No. But you've heard the talk.' She hoisted Max a little higher on her hip. 'It's that big war in France on the Somme. The whole of Kitchener's Army have gone there. It's a plan to break the Germans once and for all.'

'And they will that.'

'I hope so. I truly do, Milly.'

As she read the letter, Max held on. He felt that she was about to put him down. The little boy had a desperate need to stay with her. It was exciting in the fields and his mother's arms were familiar. It was rare that she held him and it felt good. Old

Mrs Canter left him in a corner of the kitchen while she worked. He knew that an outburst would send him back there. In the absence of a solution he clung on tighter. He patted her face, touching the freckles on her smooth cheek. Dickie smiled and stroked his back. She looked into his face and understood. They shared a common need at that moment.

'It's all right, Max,' she said. 'You can stay.'

The little face split with a smile.

'You can help though,' she said. 'Be grown up. Go and lift the hay onto that pile like May's doing. Go on now.' She put him down and patted him away.

He was gone, his child's interest already distracted. The pile of hay looked good.

Jim smiled at the child as he passed him, and ruffled his hair. He took his cap off as he approached Mrs Canter.

'Afternoon, Milly. Nice day, isn't it?'

'Oh, it is, Jim. Very nice.'

'What is it then, lass?' he asked, holding his cap in his fingers as he stroked back his damp hair. 'Good news?'

'I'll read it you, Dad.' The family had understood their father's problem; he had never mastered the ability to read. Once they had learned, they always did it for him. The wind blew dark wisps of her hair across her face, snagging loose from her cap. She brushed them away deftly, and began to read.

It was dawn on July 1st. A great hush seemed to fall over No Man's Land and then suddenly the crashing of the guns swelled to a cacophony of sound, rattling across it. It was ten minutes to zero hour.

The smoke curled and twisted, blotting everything from view, and from the distance came the steady beat of the German machine guns. The air was full of bursting sound that shook the trenches beneath them with frightening violence. Sam was held in a grip of shock as though by an unseen hand that rattled him as if he were a toy. Around him the men started to laugh from nervous tension and the sudden vastness of noise. They were drunk from the din. He adjusted his pack, gripped his sandbag and all of his 'fighting kit' and got ready.

The counter bombardment increased. Salvoes split through the air. The banging of the shells burst their eardrums, raining earth and stones upon them. The men threw themselves to the bottom of their trenches, weighed down by fear and the ghastly weight of their equipment piled awkwardly upon them.

It was almost zero hour. The mortars joined in. The order was given: 'Fix bayonets.'

All along the line came the clattering of preparation. Men shook hands, swallowed nervously and stood ready.

It was seven thirty. The whistles blew.

The sun blistered down as one hundred thousand men threw themselves up the ladders and into the open, forming into perfect lines as they had been told, an equal distance apart from each other, their rifles gleaming in the harsh sunlight.

Heads up as though on parade they started their slow march forward.

It was a perfect day, fine and hot, and they were clearly visible. From the opposite side the German barrage gained momentum as the soldiers moved inexorably forward, unable to manage anything more than a slow tramp under the weight of their equipment.

To Sam, the truth was suddenly all too clear. The German line was by no means damaged. In his view through the smoke, the men around him began to just melt away, simply falling forward slowly to lie on their faces, their knees bent under them as if in prayer. His eyes drilled ahead as he went forward as he had been ordered, and then he saw it. The wire had not been cut at all. They were caught like flies in a trap, as instinctively they drew together in protection. The cracking shells covered them with dirt and the spattered blood of their friends who fell against the lethal barbs of the wire never to stand again.

Around him they were falling like corn under a scythe, some still moving horribly, trying desperately to clamber back to safety.

Sam was driven forward, the sweat pouring from under his helmet, in rivers down his body. He was still alive. Please, God, he said, save me. I'll never be bad again. The wire came closer and closer. He could see the evil barbs twisted towards him.

He threw himself at the wire as the first cut of the machine gun blasted into him. He gasped with the shock of it as he fell to the ground, his rifle loosed from his hold. The pain from his bloodied chest raged through him and down his shattered leg. Whimpering aloud, he dragged himself away, a few yards across the ground. He saw the welcoming edges of a muddy shell-hole, pulled himself over the edge and felt himself slide into its slippery depths. The mud sucked at his legs. It was cool and heavy. The blood poured from his side. Sam tried to pull himself free, but it was too late. He was sinking lower. The pain ripped through him as if he was being torn apart by iron hands. He cried out, his life flashing before his eyes. He looked up. The sky was very blue. On a day of blazing beauty, was he to die like this? It would be hot summer in England, and they would be haymaking. He heard again the sound of the cart lurching along, the chatter of the women, he smelt the scent of the hay, his own sweat, and tasted the blood in his mouth. He felt the hot sun on his back and heard Dickie's voice as she called them in for lunch, saw her strange green eyes full of laughter. Brave Dickie. He cried for his pain and his inability to save her. England would be so beautiful now. He remembered their hill and how she had coaxed him to run through the woods in the early beauty of a summer morning, to catch the sunrise. She was the strong one, but he was the poet. He had recited to her. Let me see, he thought, how did it go?

> . . . and, when he shall die,
> Take him and cut him out in little stars,
> And he will make the face of heaven so fine,
> That all the world will be in love with night,
> And pay no worship to the garish sun.

The mud sucked him down. He could not fight it. He closed his eyes.

SEVEN

The baby let out a wail as it announced its arrival in the world. There was a murmur of approval from those gathered in the room.

'Congratulations, Caroline,' said Dr Biddy. 'A fine baby girl.' Dr Biddy was an old family friend, his familiarity allowed.

Caroline wearily lifted her head from the pillow and gazed upon her daughter. She was wrinkled and red and a tuft of dark hair was plastered to her head. The nurse took the child and bundled her away as Caroline sank gratefully back into the pillows. She closed her eyes briefly and let herself relax. The darkness seemed to hum around her.

The doctor was back in a moment, gently touching her arm. 'The baby is beautiful, my dear. Perfect. Sister's just cleaning her up and then you can show her off. Shall I call Rupert when she's ready?'

She touched his shoulder. 'Yes, please. And thank you, Dr Biddy. If you hadn't been here . . . I know how busy you are.'

'Never too busy for you,' he said fondly. 'But don't forget what I said. This is the last one. Your blood pressure was much too high. Have you told Rupert yet?'

Her hand slipped back to the bed. 'No.' She looked at the still-closed door. 'I thought I'd tell him now.'

'Good.' He patted her arm. 'You do that. Before he gets any more ideas!'

* * *

Rupert stood in front of the fireplace downstairs in the main drawing-room. His eyes lifted briefly to the landing as he heard the cry. And stayed there, wondering, as he waited for the doctor to finish with her.

Dr Biddy had hinted that Caroline was not very strong, and the baby was also weak. He had counselled Rupert to stay downstairs with the family until it was all over for fear of upsetting her.

Now, at the sound of the cry, his impatience was impossible to contain. The family were gathered around him, the atmosphere hushed, but his eyes went to Matilda, Caroline's mother.

She was an elegant middle-aged woman with fine features and hardly a wrinkle on her aristocratic face. She wore a pale grey silk dress that fell almost to the floor. Matilda, Lady Lancing, looked at home here in Foxhall as she stood in the bay window of the drawing-room waiting for the news.

At the sound of the cry she had turned and now her crystal blue eyes met those of Rupert. For a moment a feeling of empathy ran between them. It was interrupted by the sound of the door opening and closing up on the landing. Dr Biddy's face peered over the oak balcony of the minstrels' gallery and down into the room.

'Mr Redfield. Would you like to come up now?'

His eyes caught those of the older man.

'A baby girl,' answered the doctor without waiting for the question. 'Congratulations.'

A stiff smile caught at Rupert's face, as if he were afraid to betray his emotions. The congratulations echoed round the room as the Redfields and Lancings stood to shake his hand.

Caroline's maid, Lucy, eyed the bell beside the bed as she tidied up her mistress ready for presentation. She straightened the white lace bedspread and puffed up her pillows. She held the mirror as Caroline brushed her hair.

Downstairs in the servants' hall it was a flurry of expectation. Mrs Maitland bustled from one place to another, cursing the housemaids as she fell over them. Her eyes kept darting to the bell system on the wall. When the baby was born the little tag would flip down on the glass orb marked Master's Bedroom. Lucy, the maid, had her instructions. One flip for a boy, two flips for a girl.

The red tags remained annoyingly still.

The door opened and he walked in. Caroline lifted her eyes away from the baby in her arms and looked towards him. She looked more frail than ever, but there was rose in her cheeks and her blue eyes were deep with exhaustion and yet happiness. There was a new tranquillity about her that he had never seen before.

He approached her and looked down into the face of his daughter.

Awkwardly, she was trying to interpret her new way of life. Her small mouth worked as she sought to fulfil an instinctive need to feed.

Rupert lifted her into his arms. 'Pretty,' he said. 'I knew she would be. She's going to look just like my mother. A dark beauty. At last.'

Caroline heard the words and remembered her conversation with Frederick. 'You're pleased, Rupert?'

'I am.' He lifted her hand and kissed it tenderly. 'You've given me what I wanted. A daughter.'

Caroline held him with her eyes. Now was the moment to tell him, now, when he was so obviously happy. She did not question why he would want a daughter. Most men wanted sons. She thought she knew the answer now and silently blessed Frederick. 'Rupert,' she said softly. 'Would you listen to me for a moment? I have something . . .'

The baby suddenly gave a little hiccuping cry. And then started to wail. The nurse came swiftly over. She took the baby instantly into her arms. 'Baby's hungry, Mr Redfield. Better go now, sir. I'll call you when Lady Caroline is ready again.'

Caroline took a deep breath, her eyes slightly desperate as she saw she had missed her moment, but now the baby needed her. It was her choice. With Charles she had dutifully been bound against the milk; now she had a mind of her own. This time, she had decided to breastfeed her child. Rupert turned away.

The nurse went round the other side of the bed. 'Has the wee one got a name?' She wrapped the swaddling blanket more neatly around her charge. Her eyes looked only at the child.

Caroline forgot her problem for a moment. Her eyes caught those of Rupert as he turned from the door.

'Jessamy,' he said. 'My mother's name. Father called her Mary, but her name was Jessamy. Jessamy Anne.'

The door closed behind him. Caroline took the baby to her breast. 'Jessamy Anne,' she murmured.

'Do you still need me, my lady?' said Lucy, coming forward from her position by the foot of the bed.

'Yes, Lucy.' The baby started to suckle. 'I'd like you to stay with me.'

Now she could not get away. 'Very good, my lady.' She moved round to the right of the bed. The bell was within her reach now. 'I'll stay here until you need me.' She moved forward so that her back was against the wall and she was looking down on the serene picture of mother and child. Behind her, her fingers felt for the bell. She pressed twice.

Downstairs in the servants' hall, the red flap dropped. And then again. A cry went up all around.

They all gathered round the table for Chalmers, the butler, to pour them a small glass of port. They raised their glasses. A baby girl was born at last to the Redfields.

The two brothers sat by the fireplace in the blue drawing-room, a small, more intimate room off the main drawing-room which ran the length of the minstrels' gallery overlooking the lawns.

Each of them was deep in thought, drinking his brandy.

The intimacy of the room brought them together. Frederick finally broke the silence, his voice mellow in keeping with the room.

'How is it out there, Rupert? The war?'

'Not all you imagine.'

Frederick nodded. 'I wanted to join up too. Father wouldn't let me. Said I had to run the estate.'

'You're not missing anything.' Rupert seemed far away, distracted. He put down his glass and stood up, pulling at his waistcoat. He stretched slightly. 'Think I'll go up to town.' He looked at the carriage clock on the mantelpiece. It was three o'clock. 'I'll be back in time for dinner.'

Frederick glanced up at him. 'You're not staying? What if Caroline asks for you?'

'Caroline won't need me for a while. She's got all her family upstairs and Father. By the time they've finished with her she'll feel like sleeping it off. Tell her I'll see her later if you go up.'

'Rupert, I don't think . . .'

'Tell her I've gone riding or something.' His voice was marked by a slight exasperation now. He wanted to be away.

'Well, where will you be?' Frederick looked faintly alarmed. 'If I should want to contact you?'

Rupert lifted his chin and paused. He pursed his lips briefly. 'At Lily's house.' He raised an eyebrow as he looked back at Frederick.

'At *Lily's house*!' Frederick jumped to his feet. 'Rupert, how *can* you? Your second child's just been born!'

Rupert surveyed him coolly through half closed eyes. 'It's easy.'

They faced each other. Rupert stared him down.

'You'll reap what you sow, Rupert. Mark my words.' Frederick shook his head. 'I cannot believe you would do this.'

'Many do,' said Rupert casually. 'I've been at war, don't forget, and Caroline hasn't been, how shall we say . . . available, for quite a while.' He stared at Frederick, the cold blue eyes hooded. 'A man has needs, you know,' he said facetiously.

Frederick's anger made him careless. 'Is that all that concerns you? And what about now, then? Now that she cannot have any more . . .'

And then he saw his mistake, the swift cloud that was passing over Rupert's eyes as he heard Frederick's words. She had not told him. Frederick stopped himself just in time. She had sworn she would tell him the minute he came home.

'Cannot have any more what, Frederick?' Rupert faced him like an aggressive bull. His dominance was forceful. He would drain the information from him by mere will-power as he always had done when they were children. It was hard to stand up to Rupert in one of these moods. 'Tell me.'

The cry of alarm broke in between them like the cut of a knife. Both of them turned towards the door. Frederick was first. He ran to the door, opened it and went out into the main drawing-room.

'What's happened?'

George Lancing looked over the balcony. His hands were clasped desperately to the rail. 'Up here, Frederick, quickly. Your father's had a seizure.'

Frederick took the stairs two at a time. Stretched out on the landing Alexander lay gasping, his face turning blue.

Frederick fell to his knees beside him. 'Father, calm yourself. Please. Don't fight it.'

He took his hand. He wished he knew what to do, but he didn't.

Alexander's hand clutched his with a grip of steel. Frederick reacted in kind. For once he started to issue orders. Turning wildly around, he saw Chalmers, the butler, crossing the hall at a half-trot. He stared upwards.

'Chalmers. Run to the kitchen and get Albert to go after Biddy with the car. Quickly, man, quickly.'

The butler stared for an instant with blind shock. Then he turned quickly to go.

'Stop.' Rupert's voice commanded from half-way up the stairs. 'I'll go on Perryman. We can cut across the fields and head him off.'

He raced down the curve of the stairs and across the hall swinging the great doors open and leaving them that way so that the cool air rushed in in a swirl, its icy fingers touching them as they all gathered round the body at the top of the stairs. Chalmers was already on his way to close them as Rupert's feet could be heard racing off across the crunch of gravel.

The slaughter went on and the days were long. The newspapers at home were hailing the battle of the Somme as a major breakthrough. The press reports bore no relation whatsoever to the facts.

Dickie saw the poster outside the post office. GREAT BRITISH OFFENSIVE BEGINS. The first reporting of the attack came within a few hours. Much was made of the unimportant villages that were captured, but little was said of the tragic and increasing death toll. The press were fed restricted information by GHQ. They knew nothing and fabricated reports in the absence of hard news.

She bought a copy of the paper and made her way home, taking a short cut over the fields towards the cottage in the valley.

She was absorbed in reading and did not notice the figure of her father immediately. He came over the rise on the other side of the valley, and started down the slope of the cornfield towards her. He saw her long before she saw him. He started to run.

Dickie idled, the paper in her hand, the sun warming her back. She wanted to read everything she could. Maybe there would be a clue to what was happening to Sam, how soon he would be home. The shopping basket on her arm hung heavy and reminded her that she had to get home. There was nothing particular to read today. She pushed the paper into her basket and quickened her pace.

It was then that she saw him. By now he had reached the valley and was starting up the field towards her. In his hand he held something aloft. Even from this distance she could see the look of terror on his face. Then she recognised the buff colour of the telegram form.

Oh, God. Her hand flew to her mouth. She knew by the way he was clambering up the field at a half-run exactly what he was thinking.

'Dickie. Dickie!' he called. The wind caught at his voice; it sounded as if it came from some distance under water.

She clasped the basket in her arms and started to run down the field, the weight hampering her movements. Without another thought she dropped it and was running as fast as she could go, the feeling of fear clutching at her heart again as his figure drew nearer to her. Breathless, she reached him and pulled herself to a halt. 'It's Sam, Dickie. I know it,' he said desperately. 'Read it quickly. I can't stand it.'

His eyes were already full of tears. She grabbed the envelope and drew out the form. Her hand held her father's shoulder. Her eyes scanned the lines.

'Oh, God!' she said. 'Oh, God, Dad. It is Sam.' Her fingers clutched his shoulder, her eyes blurring.

Jim gave a terrible wail and fell to his knees. 'No . . . !'

His body shook with sobs. 'Tell me it isn't true!' He clasped his head in his hands.

She went to her knees beside him, her hand to his shoulder.

'It's true, Dad.'

Her empty eyes sought restoration in the beauty of the day around them. Oh, God, her eyes closed tight, oh, Sam. Her heart was squeezed dry by the grip of fate.

Jim grasped the telegram from her as if it was his lifeline. It was a part of his son. He stared at the lines that he could not read as if he would force a lie from them. Then with a terrible cry he crumpled the paper in his fist and buried his head in her lap. Her hands gently touched his shoulders. 'Dickie, love,' he cried, his voice choked with tears. 'My lad! My boy! Now what will we do?'

'We'll go on, Dad.' Her voice quavered slightly, but she held it firm. 'I'll help you. We'll go on as we have been doing. Together.' Her hand rubbed his bent back, feeling the dampness through his shirt.

'You're not strong enough.'

'I am that. I've done my share all along. So don't say I'm not strong enough, Dad.'

Now it was the time, the time she could say it. She lifted up his face. 'Look at me, Dad. Ma would have wanted it. Think of that. You remember what she used to say? Do you?'

He looked blearily at his daughter. She was beautiful as she spoke so forcibly, the tears making her green eyes glassy, the strength shining out of her face. The lines of tiredness were etched beside his mouth. His eyes were those of a simple man, a man who took orders. She had her mother's eyes, out of her station, too bold, but they hypnotised him.

'Dad,' she said. 'You *cannot* fall apart over Sam's death. You owe it to him not to. He lost his life for us. For our country. We've got to make sure . . .' she paused, the pain tight in her throat. She took a deep breath. 'We've got to make sure he didn't do it all for nothing.'

Her mother had known how weak her husband was. She had worried how he would make it without her strength. Innocently, Dickie echoed her words.

'We will not be defeated, Dad.'

Neither of them noticed the horseman who galloped

swiftly over the crest of the hill behind them heading back to the village the way Dickie had come.

Jim was quiet now. She took a firm grip on his hand and drew him to his feet. Her back was strong and straight, and a dignity was born in her.

He would hand the responsibility to her.

'One must never be defeated,' she said again.

He was just too tired.

Frederick turned back to his father. And knew it was already too late. In the urgency of the moment he had not realised that the clench of their grip was now solely his own. His father's face lay white and still against the blood-red carpet. Frederick looked at him and then slowly uncurled his hand as if in disbelief. Alexander's limp hand slid from his own.

'He's gone, Frederick,' said George. 'My dear, dear friend.'

Frederick said nothing. He was looking down into the face he had had no idea how much he had loved. His face was noble and lifeless and free from pain in its peacefulness. Frederick mouthed silently: 'Father.' And then he bent slowly to kiss the cool forehead. He took Alexander's hands and laid them crossed over his chest, surprised despite himself at their weight and texture. He had not felt his father's hands since he was a child of eight. Another day like this. Warm and summery. He laid his head against the still chest and wept.

In the early hours of the morning Dickie left the cottage. She went to the ridge of the high field and sat on the hillock beside the silver birch that grew alone there. From there she could see right down into the sweep of the Thames valley. Mist lay deep in the bowl of the valley as the sun came up with its promise of a hot hazy day ahead. The sun gilded her face and she felt its warmth. She imagined what it had been like for Sam who would feel warmth no more. She imagined the tramp of their feet marching towards death, their terror as the war rained down around them taking the place of the pride that had sustained them from the first.

She saw his face. Poor, gentle Sam. When they had been children she had pulled him protesting from his bed in the early hours to run through the wet woods and the grass to this beautiful spot to watch the sun come up. Sam had always been scared in the dark woods, even though he was older, and she had always held his hand tight and told him not to be silly. Sniffing back his fright he would come alive when they reached the sunny knoll and felt the sun's glow on their faces. The richness and the beauty all around them had been magnificent. They would forget their hardship and poverty and dream of what it would be like when they grew up. Dickie would have brought a piece of bread and they would chew it, knees up, talking energetically about what they would do, what they would become. Dreams. Sam would never grow up now. She would have to do the growing for both of them. Dickie held her knees and bent her head. The sun gilded the crown of dark hair and the nape of her delicate neck. She sat still, unmoving, her eyes closed in a silent vow to Sam.

EIGHT

Frederick put down the telephone in his father's study. He ran his finger over the edge of the huge leather-topped mahogany desk. It was slightly worn as if his father had done the same thing many times over the years.

The room was dark and close, with a smell of sweet tobacco, furniture polish and the mints that Alexander used to keep in a jar on the desk. There was a faded blue Chinese rug on the floor and in the corner by the bay window, a wide-seated, tapestried Gainsborough chair where Alexander used to sit and look out over the lawns which led down to the river.

Frederick did the same. He missed his father dreadfully. The whole house seemed so strange without him. He expected him at any moment to come through the door and everything would be all right again. The seizure had been so unexpected. The doctor told them he had been under some pressure. Naturally he had kept all his feelings hidden. As a parent, especially one of his generation, he did not confide easily in his children. He had been a rather remote and apparently humourless man, and since the death of his wife, somewhat severe. Like most bankers he was serious and lived by the rules of the book, and, like most fathers, he applied these equally and rigorously to his sons. But to Frederick he had always seemed fair and consistent. Frederick felt the ache of his loss more than he had ever known he would.

He gave himself to memory. It had been another day like this, warm and still. He had been a child and Alexander had pulled him onto his knee. There had been a sudden summer storm and thunder and Frederick had been frightened, running away from his nanny into his father's study to disturb him at his work. Alexander had broken one of his own rules and allowed him to remain in the quiet of the study behind closed doors and had allayed his fears. He had told him to be brave and strong, because one day he would be a man with responsibilities. He had started to explain the workings of an estate and a business which one day Frederick would share with his brother, Rupert.

Even in those early days it seemed that Alexander had known that Frederick would be the one with interest in the land and Rupert, with his wildness, would be the one to want the army life and to play his polo and be constantly on the move. Maybe he had understood them better than they knew, after all. Why was it that one was always so wise after the event? It was too late now to share any of the things they might have shared, to get to know each other better.

Footsteps approached the study door. Frederick quickly recovered himself as if guilty and turned back towards the desk again. The heavy door opened wide and Rupert came into the room.

As always he carried with him that strong presence that made it impossible to ignore him. He was wearing his riding clothes, his cream breeches stained with the sweat of the horse's flanks. It crossed Frederick's mind that he must have been riding the animal too hard.

Rupert sauntered into the centre of the room, made his way to the fireplace, picked up a china ornament, examined it, and put it down again. He had an air of expectancy about him.

'Did you have a telephone call from Mr Renfrew, Freddie?'

'Yes.' Frederick inclined his head towards the phone. He laid his hands on the desk top. 'Just now. Says he wants to meet us here and talk about Father's wishes.'

Rupert nodded in agreement. He reached into the silver cigarbox on the mantelpiece, and took out one of his father's expensive cigars. Frederick watched every movement, wanting him to stop. Alexander only smoked the Havanas on special occasions. At this time it seemed like sacrilege.

Rupert ignored him as he came across and sat down in the leather chair opposite, struck a match and held the flame to the tip of the cigar. He balanced one leg on the other knee and leaned back in contemplation, holding the smoke momentarily in his mouth. Finally, he let it go with satisfaction.

'The old man knew about cigars.'

Frederick ignored him. 'Is it just us, do you know?'

'Just us?' Rupert surveyed the end of the cigar. He shrugged.
'I don't know. I imagine so, wouldn't you? And the trustees.
There's not much to squabble over after all. I inherit the estate,
chairmanship of the board, and probably the shares will be split
between us. You can stay here, of course.'

Frederick looked at him with surprise. 'I don't know if it will
be as cut and dried as all that.'

'Oh, I think so, don't you?' Rupert leaned back. 'Father was
a banker after all, no imagination at all. Just like old Haig. Hope
Renfrew doesn't take too long. I've got to pack. Leave's nearly
up.' He drew on the cigar, and stood up, dropping it into the
ashtray. He looked around him, his air proprietorial. 'Call me
when he gets here, would you, Freddie. I think I've just time to
take Perryman round the bottom field before he arrives. Get this
thing settled before I get back to the front.'

He left the room. Frederick sat silently. *You can stay here, of
course.* The words ran over and over in his head. He had never,
ever thought otherwise, but now Rupert's words had chilled him
as he realised the position he was in. Rupert was right. As the
eldest son and heir he stood to inherit everything, even and
especially the family seat, this lovely old house that Frederick
adored and cherished, the lands that he knew inch by inch. He
in turn would become his brother's chattel, his underdog. Knowing Rupert, it would be exactly that and nothing more. Frederick
had too much pride to ask that things should be different. But
even to entertain the thought of leaving this house. Frederick
knew his position all too clearly. His brother would be his
keeper.

The old family firm of solicitors, Renfrew, Renfrew and Pon-
sonby, had looked after the affairs of large ducal and landowning
estates for generations. Everything was always organised and
properly done. This time, old Mr Renfrew had taken the meeting upon himself, though he was practically retired due to his
bad rheumatism and gout. Too many years of a sedentary life,
rich food and cold draughty chambers had damaged his system
beyond repair. Today, however, it was a difficult case, to be
handled only by someone with his experience.

The journey from London in the hansom cab had not been

comfortable. He much preferred his clients to come to him, but with families such as the Redfields, the journey was worth it in terms of goodwill.

As he was shown into the inner drawing-room, he looked at the two men with whom from now on he was to do business.

One stood quietly by the window, and the other sat, half in the shadows thrown by the fire lit now for the cool of the evening.

He came straight to the point.

'Which one of you is Mr Rupert Redfield?'

Rupert stirred slightly in his chair. His yellow hair caught the light. 'I am.'

'Mr Redfield,' he said, 'obviously you realise I wish to talk to you about your father's estate.' A long sofa faced the fire. A table stood behind it. Renfrew placed his briefcase upon it, and opened the catch.

Rupert nodded. Renfrew observed the man. He was dressed as though he had just come in from hard riding. His clothes were still stained with horse sweat. His yellow hair was damp with exertion. He was handsome and contained and there was something else about him too. Something that said he would not be a good man to cross.

Renfrew drew in a breath and tucked his fingers into his waistcoat pockets, a habit he enlisted when nervous. It stopped his hands betraying him, and gave the client confidence.

'The will is unusual,' he began. He saw that he immediately had their attention. He paused. 'Er, would you mind if I sat down. My rheumatism. A long journey.' He took his case as Frederick indicated the sofa and went and sat down with a sigh of relief. He opened the case on his knee, took out the sheaf of papers, and set the case beside him on the floral cushions. 'I've asked you two alone to be here today, gentlemen, as you are the main beneficiaries. There are others, but,' he shrugged, 'their allowance is minimal. Besides, I have the feeling that what I am about to read is better for your ears alone.' He looked up briefly as Frederick crossed the room towards him and sat on the arm of a chair. Beside the fire, Rupert remained motionless. Mr Renfrew fitted a pair of glasses to his broad nose, looked down at the will, and sniffed. He held his bad leg out in front of him, his hand braced against the pain in his knees. 'I'll begin, if you're ready . . .' He cleared his throat. 'The will is dated September 20th, 1914 . . .' Once again, his eyes took them both in over the rim of his spectacles. He could see from their interest that the date was significant to them. '. . . I, Alexander Sebastian Redfield, being of sound mind and body do hereby . . .' the voice droned on over the legal paraphernalia.

Rupert closed his eyes momentarily. He knew what the will contained. He felt lazy and warm beside the fire. Now it would all be his. He opened his eyes, their expression bored, and gazed about him with a proprietorial air.

'. . . I hereby leave the estate of Foxhall Manor, with all of its lands, its rights, including the four tenanted farms, the village properties as listed within the deeds attached hereto, and all their appurtenances, incomes et cetera, to my son, Frederick . . .'

'*What?*' Rupert sat bolt upright. He stared from one man to the other. Frederick looked shocked.

'. . . also the furnishings and contents of said properties, my majority shares in Redfield-Strauss bank, plus three hundred thousand pounds in cash and bonds,' the voice went purposefully on. 'To my grandchildren, Jessamy and Charles, I leave fifty thousand pounds each in trust until their twenty-first birthdays. To my sister, Agnes, with the understanding that it is a Redfield family residence to be used as such during her lifetime, I leave the London house at . . .'

'Wait!' Rupert thrust out a hand to stop him. He was half out of his chair, his blue eyes blazing against the softening dusk. 'What is this ridiculous nonsense? Where is my inheritance?'

The old man pursed his lips and looked gravely at him. He did not like being stopped half-way through a will, but he had foreseen that this might happen.

'Yes . . .' Frederick looked to him for an explanation, his expression totally bewildered. 'I don't understand either. Foxhall should have been Rupert's. He's the elder brother . . .'

'There must be a mistake.' Rupert reached out his hand towards the papers. 'Let me see . . .'

'Gentlemen, gentlemen . . .' Renfrew held the papers to him, then placing them safely upon his knee. He raised a hand. 'I think it's time to explain.' He took a breath and looked from one to the other. 'I saw that you were both aware of the significance of the date of the will. That is why I read it to you, to prepare you in some small way.' He stretched out his leg. 'Your father, Alexander,' he went on slowly, 'came to our offices the day after your wedding, Mr Redfield,' he said, addressing Rupert. 'He was in a state, shall we say, of some displeasure. The utmost displeasure,' he repeated, more gravely. 'It seems that he had made a discovery with which he confronted you, and to which you reacted in a most offensive and unseemly manner, to which he took extreme exception. He came straightaway to London and changed the will at the height of his anger. He never changed it back again. There is in fact, a provision made for you later in the will, whereby your brother, Frederick, is to make allowance for you as he sees fit, as trustee of—'

'Never mind about that,' Rupert barked. He stared fiercely into the flames. 'The old bastard,' he muttered furiously.

'Rupert?' Frederick's eyes were on him. 'What on earth was it about?'

Rupert did not answer. His anger was absolute. It raged with no direction inside him, his eyes unseeing.

'It must have been something dreadful,' Frederick pressed. 'Father wouldn't change a will for nothing. What was it?'

Rupert's rage found direction. He turned his face to his brother, the hate stamped lividly upon his countenance. 'That wretched girl,' he hissed. 'That farm girl that we took into the woods. *You too, Frederick,*' he said darkly and with menace. His eyes accused him.

Frederick paled. So that was it. He remembered now his father's ferocity as they had left the house to go to Rupert's wedding, but it had not been directed at him. Rupert had not implicated him, despite his father's accusations. Frederick felt both a flood of shame and of gratitude towards Rupert, who now had to suffer for a crime committed by them both. No matter that Rupert had obviously angered Alexander further by his attitude; he had kept his counsel. Frederick did not realise that he was giving his brother more than his due—Rupert would certainly have told Alexander, only his own arrogance had stopped him. He had never believed that he would be disinherited.

The two brothers were momentarily silenced. Renfrew spoke again. 'It is my belief,' he said, his voice sounding awkward against the tension in the room, 'that your father might have intended to change the will again once he had recovered from this . . . episode. He was not an unreasonable man.' Neither of them even glanced in his direction. 'But . . . I'm afraid, it is as it stands. Perhaps none of us expect to die as young as we do . . .' He tried a smile, and let it die again. He sighed. 'Would you like me to read the rest of the will?'

'No.' Rupert breathed heavily. He rubbed the back of his neck roughly. 'What I want to know is, what can be done to change this?' His eyes held Renfrew's as he turned. Now he could see the dangerous element surface in Rupert.

'You could contest it,' he suggested, and shook his head. 'But I'm afraid it would bring it all out into the open.' He watched Rupert's face as he spoke. 'It would be public knowledge. And,' he paused, 'it does seem to me from what I gather, that you would rather the source of this argument were kept quiet.' His voice lowered slightly. 'I do have some idea of what went on, you see. Your father had a habit of confiding in me.'

'I see,' said Rupert slowly. Now his eyes had lost the hard inflexible anger and were more aware, more calculating. 'And is there any other way?' His eyes flickered over his brother as he spoke. Frederick, shaken by the news, had left them to cross the room alone, absorbed by his thoughts as he switched on the lights and warmed the room against the dark.

Renfrew followed his gaze. 'Yes,' he said, nodding his head. 'There is. If, as the will states,' he suggested, tapping the papers gathered in his hands, 'your brother were to see fit to hand the estate back to you of his own free will. Then it would be yours.'

His eyes met those of the other man. Frederick came back across the room. Rupert knew his brother's love for the land.

'Thank you,' he said.

Frederick had a moment to survey Caroline as she lay dozing on the silk pillows of her bed. Her skin was milk white and her black hair now lay unpinned and strewn across the pillow. He felt like an intruder, though it was she who had called him to her. She was as beautiful a woman as he had ever seen.

He was about to leave when she stirred. His presence must have been sensed by her, for her eyelids fluttered and she appeared to wake up from a light sleep. She saw him there immediately and looked directly at him, a slow smile warming her face.

'Frederick, please excuse me.' She pulled herself upwards in the bed. 'I must have been more tired than I knew. Thank-you for coming to see me.'

Frederick took one of the gilded chairs from the bay window

Pamela Townley

and brought it to place beside the bed. He sat down. 'What can I do for you, Caroline?'

'I wanted to thank you for these.' She lifted the heavy, creamy pearls between her fingers. 'It was so good of you, Frederick.'

His eyes travelled to her breast where they lay. 'It's not every day I'm asked to be a godfather.'

Her eyes were on his face. She let the pearls slide through her fingers. 'No, but they were your mother's. Rupert told me. And yours to give . . . though won't you want them for your own wife? One day you'll be married too and you might regret your generosity then, Frederick.'

'They could never look more beautiful than they do on you.' He looked up slowly. 'You wear them as graciously as she did. It was the least I could do for you.'

'Under the circumstances,' she added as his eyes met hers. 'I know, you see.'

Frederick looked surprised. 'Rupert told you?' he said softly. It seemed incredible that Rupert should admit it to her.

'Yes.' Her voice was soft. 'Poor Rupert. He's been badly affected by the news. Thank goodness you told me a little about him, his closeness to your mother. It's helped me to understand him.' Her eyes looked wistful. 'I told him about the children in the end and do you know what he said . . . ?'

'No, what?'

'He said that as long as I was healthy and with him, nothing else mattered.'

'Rupert said that?'

'Yes.'

'Well.' He let out a quick breath and nodded in thought. 'Well. That *is* good.'

'Yes,' she said again. Her smile was slow and exotic. Gone was the glassy fragility that he had seen of late, the distancing of herself from everything around her. She slid a little lower in the bed and pulled the sheets gently with her fingers. This Caroline was stronger, a direct candour in the blue eyes that looked at him now as if she was about to impart some revelation. Her pale eyelids fluttered. 'I think the death of your father has hit all of us hard. Rupert wants to be a father now, in place of your own.'

'Does he?' asked Frederick. 'Where is he now?'

'Taking evensong.' Her voice was light. 'Apparently he preached a sermon this morning. Were you there?'

Frederick shifted on the hard seat. 'No, actually. I was down at the dairy. They went short on one of the hands. A death in the family.' His voice was vague. He was still trying to adjust to this new Caroline.

'Oh!' she said. 'How sad. Well, Dr Biddy came in and said he preached a marvellous sermon. Everyone was so impressed that he took the time, especially with such a short leave. He preached about the horrors of war. You know, he told me a little about it, the front line. As much as he could anyway, knowing how they're sworn to secrecy. So many of his friends have been killed or maimed. It can't be easy for him.' The dark blue eyes lifted to hold his, a sense of tragedy in their look. He saw her hand almost reach out to touch him, but it stopped beside the curve of her hip. 'I think it's bound to affect his attitude,' she said. 'Try to sympathise with him, would you, Frederick? For me? Help us.' Her voice was wistful. 'I think he kept so much to himself until the death of your father. He didn't mean to tell me about the will, and I told him it didn't matter in any event. That we should all be together and stay together in these terrible times is so much more important. But I sensed something was wrong, and so I made him tell me.'

Frederick could not imagine anyone making Rupert do anything but he was hypnotised by her persuasion. Perhaps indeed *she* could.

'He needs you now, Frederick,' she added. 'Will you try to understand him? I had so wanted this to be a happy home with all of us here together at the end of the war. I imagined we would be one big happy family. Will you? Please? It's up to you to make it that way.' She looked at him directly. 'He needs your good sense and your strength, Freddie. I'm worried about him. I think the loss of his inheritance might be too much for him to bear. He might go back to the front and feel he has nothing to live for.'

'How could he feel that with you and the children to come back to?' Frederick simply could not imagine such a thing.

'Well, I don't know. He is so . . . unpredictable.'

'Yes.' Frederick stretched his fingers and looked down at them in thought.

'So you will try to convince him that all is not as black as it seems?' Her hand stretched out again across the bed.

'Of course. How can I refuse you when you ask me like that? I'll do all I can to help.' He reached forward and took her hand.

'Thank you. I knew you would. You're such a good man, dear.' She lay back on her pillows, the shadow of exhaustion now under her eyes. He wondered why the compliment jarred on him.

'You're tired,' he said quickly, and slipped his hand away from hers. 'I'll leave you now to sleep.'

'I am, rather,' she said. 'Leave the curtains, would you? Just switch out the lights. I'll lie here in the dusk. It's lovely at this time of night.' Her voice was already fading into sleep.

Gently, Frederick stole away switching out the soft shaded lamps in the room. The leaded windows were open to the evening. Dusk settled into the room. Frederick heard her soft breathing. He slipped out of the room, closing the door softly behind him.

Caroline smiled.

The sun was breaking through and the air outside was crisp. It was a perfect morning for a canter out with the dogs. There was a fresh wind and the horses would give a good ride on the downs. It was Rupert's favourite way of working up an appetite for breakfast. Then he would stride into the dining-room, the dogs wet and happy at his heels.

Frederick found him at the long polished table alone. He was studying the paper. He looked up as Frederick came in.

'Morning. Going back to the front today, Freddie. Just got my orders.'

'So soon?' Frederick helped himself to a good breakfast and joined his brother at the table. 'What's happening over there now? Papers say the bombardment on the Somme was a spectacular success.' He spread a linen napkin over his knee, picked up his knife and fork. 'Think we're winning?'

'Who can say?' Rupert looked weary. Frederick remembered Caroline's words. 'We try hard enough. But the best plans don't always work out the way one might expect.' He laid down the newspaper, and tapped it with a blunt finger. 'This news is rubbish, though. Don't believe that. Tailored to fit, that's all. Not the truth.'

'What is the truth?'

Rupert ran a thumbnail between his teeth. 'The truth is, Freddie that there are enormous casualties. Men in the thousands getting slaughtered, needlessly, every day. Just because of a few narrow-minded generals. I could run a better war. But it's got to be done, I suppose. If we're not to fall under the sword of the Germans.'

He fell into an uneasy silence. 'Let's talk about something else.'

'Not going riding this morning?' Frederick forked up a mouthful of haddock, dripping with butter. 'It's a fine day.'

Rupert looked out of the window, his finger in the handle of his coffee cup. 'No,' he said. 'My last day. I promised Caroline and Charles that I'd spend it with them.'

Frederick chewed thoughtfully. 'You're going to really miss home, aren't you, Rupert?'

'It's what war does to you.'

Frederick paused against the new silence.

'Rupert, I've been thinking . . .'

Rupert drank his coffee slowly.

'Before you go, I'd like to get this thing settled.' Rupert's eyes lifted. 'The business of the will.' He pushed the fish around his plate. It had suddenly struck him with the force of a hammer blow that Rupert might not come back. That was what must be in his brother's mind. He wanted to capture as much as he could of a new family life now that their rock, their father, Alexander, was gone. It was a devastating shock for him to go back with. Maybe Caroline was right, maybe he did need encouragement. Whatever, the inheritance was his by right. Frederick would not hold it from him. He had to do it. For Caroline, Rupert, the family. He wanted to give Rupert something to hang on to in case he did something crazy out there. Something to make him want to come back. He knew, in that moment, what he could do for all of them. What he must do. Maybe Rupert *had* changed. Maybe war made a man different. Maybe the circumstances lately had shattered his morale. Whatever it was, he had to re-store it to his brother. He took a deep breath inside before com-mitting himself. He had held the reins for so short a time. Foxhall, his beloved Foxhall. Had he the strength to give it away?

'Rupert,' he began. 'I've been thinking. God knows, I'd love to have owned Foxhall, but it's yours by right. I know yesterday's news must have come as a huge shock to you. I know it did to me.' He bit his lip and looked at his plate. 'I'd like to give you something to come back to. Foxhall is yours. I can't keep it from you because Father never changed the will before his death.

If he had, I'm certain he would have given it to you as the first born, and the money to maintain it and your family.'

A dim spark was born at the back of Rupert's watching blue eyes.

'I'll speak to Renfrew this morning. Have him draw up a set of papers in keeping with what should have been yours as heir to the Redfield estate, and what should have been mine. By the time you come back for your next leave, it will all be yours.'

Rupert had maintained an absolute silence throughout. Now the blue eyes absorbed his brother, though their inner guard was still in place. 'Freddie,' he said, reaching for his hand. 'I don't know what to say. You don't have to do this, you know, old chap.'

'I know that. It was entirely my choice.' Rupert had never asked for a thing after Renfrew had left, nor had he made any mention of fighting for what was his by right. He had just seemed to acquiesce. That was what had alarmed Frederick more than anything. He put his hand out, his dark blue eyes warm with emotion. He knew he'd done the right thing, despite his own love for the estate. 'Let's shake on it, brother.'

Rupert's hand gripped his. His eyes were febrile, but steady. The blue blazed beneath his white brows in the softness of the room. 'I misjudged you, Freddie,' he said. 'You're a brother to be proud of.'

'No more than you,' said Frederick, slightly embarrassed. 'You'll come back a hero, decorated for your country. What more can one do than that? Let's say no more about it.'

He bent awkwardly to his food. His momentary feeling of power had stimulated him, made the adrenalin rush. He had burned with the pleasure of being able to give his brother something he really wanted, of seeing his gratitude. Pride filled him as his brother released his hand.

He leaned his arms briefly on the table, a sense of exhaustion in him. For a moment his mind drifted in the gloved silence.

'There is one thing though . . .'

Frederick started at the sudden sound of Rupert's voice.

'What's that?'

'Could you have the papers drawn up this morning? Before I leave?' Rupert opened the paper again with one hand. 'I'd be easier knowing it was settled.'

Frederick paused for a half-beat. 'Well, yes, of course. If you wish,' he added.

'Yes.'

'I'll do that then.'

'Well.' Rupert caught him with another look. He smiled and tapped him on the shoulder with the newspaper. 'Think I'll just go and see Caroline. Tell her the good news!'

He strode from the room, whistling, and climbed the stairs two at a time.

Behind him, Frederick returned to his breakfast, but he had no appetite. He laid down his knife and fork, rested his chin on the knuckles of his hand and ran his teeth idly along his finger. He gazed outside to the soft slope of the lawns running down to the river, gently green and contented under the early summer sun. Foxhall. And he had given it away.

NINE

November, 1918

The war was over at last and the Battle of the Somme had died
an unredeemed defeat, the Armistice signed by Germany on
November 11th. All that came out of it was the sense of loyalty
that had endured between comrades, brave helpless soldiers disillusioned and misled, with nothing to show for the thousands
of lives that had been lost, only a churned-up wasteland and a
few demolished farm villages. Yet nothing had been too much
to ask of the weary men. And now they were back in their home
villages and looking eagerly for work.

Dickie looked up from the fence and stared down the field.
The man had Sam's walk. She was motionless. The man came
closer, pushing his way up the steep slope. Dusk was falling
and there was a damp fog in the air.

It was not Sam. Of course she had known that. The tension
dropped out of her shoulders.

'Hello, Dickie. Remember me?'

He looked so different: lines beside his mouth though he was
barely twenty, his eyes strange and disillusioned, though soft as
they rested on her. 'Of course, I remember you, Ted. Max,' she
brought her son forward gently with the tips of her fingers, 'this
is Ted Latham. A friend of your Uncle Sam's. This is my son,
Max.'

Ted put out his hand. 'Hello, Max.'

'You're a friend of Uncle Sam?'

'Yes.'

Max looked seriously at the newcomer, with blue Redfield eyes. 'I'm four,' he announced.

'Are you?' Ted braced his hands on his knees and bent to Max. 'Well, then, I must remember to get you a present. I know,' he bent his head and pulled a shiny brass button from his tunic 'will this do? It's been in the war. It's a pretty special button, that, all right.'

'Thank you, sir.'

Ted laughed and patted him on the head as Max gazed, absorbed by the shiny button. 'Formal! He speaks up, doesn't he? Like his mother, if I recall!'

'Max is a clever boy,' she said. 'He learns fast.'

She looked down at him, away, and back to Ted. It was a blustery day, autumn in the air, cold mists riding the valleys in the morning and chill fogs early in the evening before the night came down. There was still a fair amount of work to do before winter set in.

'Can I talk to you, Dickie?'

'Yes, but it'll have to be quick. Night's drawing in.'

She looked over to the other field. She raised her hand to her mouth and shouted at the figure driving the cows towards the far gate. Jim was taking the herd in for milking. 'Dad!' she called. 'I'm just going down the field with Ted. I'll see you in the dairy!' The figure lifted its hand and waved.

'Come on, Max,' she said. She held out her hand to him and they started down the field.

Ted was silent for a moment. It felt good to be walking beside her again like in the old days. The child was a surprise though. He stole another look at him. He was good-looking, quiet and dignified, with a formality strange in a village child. He was almost like gentry. He did not know it but Max had inherited the atavistic grace of a true Redfield.

'Thomas Green died, you know,' he said.

'Yes, I know. Bessie went up to London.'

Sam's death hung in the air between them. He could have cut his tongue out. He tried again.

'You married then, Dickie?' he asked her.

'No.'

'Oh, I see.' The cold wind tore at his eyes.

'No, you don't see,' she said. 'But it doesn't matter. Max is going to have the opportunities I never had. I'm going to make sure of that.'

Below them the field curved down into the valley. At the bottom of the slope there was a thick hedge which ran the length of the field towards Cobbold's Wood, and then beyond the field started to rise again, intersected with neat hedging. The fields were a patchwork of colour, the hedges russet and yellow with autumn. A small cottage stood on the hill, smoke rising from its chimney. From somewhere there came the smell of an autumn bonfire.

'And how you going to do that, Dickie?' he asked her. Her boots clomped down the field beside him, the small boy hanging onto her hand. 'In your position?' he said significantly. He almost laughed at her seriousness. 'Why, you know that's not possible. We can't change the way we are.'

She stopped then, and looked him firmly in the eyes. The light eyes were arresting in the sharpness of the day. 'There *are* ways, Ted. You've just got to believe. Ways if you know where to look. Ways if you know where to find them. You can change anything if you believe you can. You talk like the rest of them. Have you no spirit? You always used to. Not like them. Did the war knock it out of you too?'

Ted set his jaw. 'No, it did not,' he said fiercely, 'and there's no need for that kind of talk. There's no chance for us now, though, Dickie. The war saw to that. Do you know how many of us died out there in that unspeakable place, and in agony?' He threw his arm wide, his face contorted with anger and memory. 'Six hundred thousand were killed or wounded. And for what? A few miles of flat land. Each time we captured a stretch we'd move down into a valley and into a mire of mud, and so any advantage we got, the Germans soon got back.' His eyes tore away from his memories and back to her. 'And you know why?' He jabbed a finger at her. Dickie was still. 'Because we were under the control of blundering, obstinate officers. It was systematic slaughter, and they didn't care. Oh, no, why should they? They just sat on their fat backsides and gave orders. ''Capture that wood. No, not *that* wood. *That* wood. Or perhaps, that hillock.'' And who got the decorations? Not the men, not the men who laid down their lives for England, but the officers behind the lines who never saw no action. Officers like that Redfield up at the manor.' His eyes fired with anger as she watched silently, hearing that name in her head. Suddenly he quietened, looking beaten. 'I have a right to think there's no chance, Dickie, girl.' He looked away down the valley to the bleakness of the day, the fog building now, the distant hill obscured. Cobbold's Wood to their right was dark and thick. 'We fought for nothing,' he said. 'We're not thanked. We're not heroes. It was a pointless waste of good lives, and now we're back and desperate for jobs, pleading and begging where once we were proud to be English and fighting for our country. Our country, huh? What does it do for us now?' He pushed his hands into his pockets, and kicked at the soil. 'So don't tell me about *spirit.*'

He had a right to be bitter. Dickie had seen his reaction in others. The returning men, many of them boys like Ted, held the whole world in contempt. They had been led like lambs to the slaughter, and by men who now received decorations for planning a war without regard to actual conditions and without ever experiencing a fraction of what the men were enduring. Her bitterness had been due to the fact that it was Ted here and not Sam.

'I'm sorry, Ted.' Her eyes were cool and steady. 'But that's still no reason to give up. Surely it's a reason to fight on? To make sure it never happens again. To make sure that next time you're strong enough not to be in that position. God knows, Ted, you're alive. Doesn't that count for something?'

The wind lifted her hair away from her face. She caught at a strand and tucked it back in the bun that she now wore at the nape of her neck, under her cap. The gesture made him look at her. She was proud, and she was high and mighty too. He admired that in her. He always had. She would be a strength for a man. Her figure was trim despite the child. She had the figure of a woman now; she was nineteen and strong and brown from working on the land. She would make a good wife.

'It counts for something, Dickie,' he agreed. 'Sure it does. But now I need a job, and that's the most important thing. I came to ask your dad. Is there room for another hand?'

Max swung his leg. She looked down at him, felt his warm hand in hers. 'It's a slack time of year, Ted,' she said, regretfully. 'All the crops are in. Potatoes are already in the clamp for winter. All we got left now is hedging and ditching and the cows to take care of.'

She looked at his haggard face, too old for a young man. She saw his need. She laid a hand on his arm. 'Let me ask Dad. Maybe he'll take you on in the dairy.'

Her jaw tightened as she looked into his face and saw the

hope there. He was so dependent it frightened her. She thought of Sam. She turned, and they started back. She had to ask one thing. 'Ted?' He stopped and looked at her. 'Did you see Sam before he was killed?' Her voice was small.

He paused, started to speak, and paused again. He didn't want to hurt her. 'I didn't, Dickie. There were a lot of us out there, you see,' he said gently. 'I never knew what happened to him. Early on we were in the same billet, but then we were split up. We were that dirty you'd hardly recognise your best friend, anyway, passing you in the trenches. And if he were wounded, well . . .'

'Never mind.' So Sam had died alone. 'Come on. Let's go and ask Dad.' She turned away and started to walk. Max trotted along beside her, clutching her hand.

Ted stayed her for a moment with his hand. He seemed suddenly awkward. 'Dickie? There's something else . . .'

'Yes?' Max looked up at him too. His hand was firmly clasped around the button. Two pairs of eyes looked at Ted directly with the same look.

'I wanted to know . . . That is—' he looked at the child and back at her, 'Could I court you?'

She hardly paused. 'No man will be courting me, Ted Latham, but thank you all the same.'

He looked down into Max's face. His expression was strangely disconcerting. He had that same intangible quality as Dickie.

'The boy needs a father,' he argued.

'The boy needs no one but himself and me.' She grasped his hand tighter. 'Come along, Max.' She turned and went up the field.

Ted followed her, trudging along behind them. She had been working all day and it was cold now and growing dark, but her feet were still as light on the soil as if she had just started out. He shook his head. Maybe he had been let off lightly. As a wife she would never have known her place.

It was darker now, the edge of a cold crisp night closing in around them when she and Max finally walked back to the cottage together. She had him wrapped in a shawl and held his tired body close to hers. His head lolled against her shoulder.

They enjoyed these moments alone. The day was ended and it was time to get into the warm cottage and cook supper, the smells good at the end of a hard day before she tucked him into bed. Their bond was close and sometimes it was even hard for her to leave him in his bed, however tired she was herself. She loved him with a fierce mother-love and missed his company when they were apart. He was a part of her. He took a lot of her time but she valued it. She was certain she would find a way out of this place. What worried her was losing their home. Rupert Redfield would soon be back and she was certain once he found out the unusual arrangements of her working the land he would be bound to put a stop to it. She knew the man. She had thought about it a lot lately; it was her abiding anxiety. Frederick knew of their situation—it was he who had allowed it. Obviously he felt some guilt towards her. It did not make her feel any more kindly towards him. Now she hated all Redfields equally. She just wondered how she could use his guilt to her advantage.

Ted was wrong. There was always a way. It was just a question of finding it.

She wrapped the shawl tighter against the frosty night. Max was heavy in her arms but she could not put him down. He had been helping with the milking. With his small hands he could already milk the old cow, Susie, the most patient, and now he was tired, his dark head nestled drowsily against her chin.

The moon was up. As they passed the old duckpond she stopped a moment. By day it was a hollow filled with dirty water in the midst of a track of mud churned and trammelled by horses and farm machinery. Now, with the reflection of the moon, it took on a new beauty. The reeds were reflected in its glassy surface, and the early frost glittered in the cobwebs and the debris at its edges.

'Look, Max,' she said. 'Isn't that pretty? See the moon.' She wanted to instil some of the magic into him, but he was too tired. He moaned sleepily against her. Dickie took one more moment to look into the inky depths, dreaming alone for a while in the night before returning to the brightness of the cottage, her dad and the pots and pans.

The sound of the plane startled her. She had never heard anything like it before. Max started too and looked up.

High above the biplane stuttered through the sky. It traversed the path of the moon and headed east towards Cobbold's Wood, tracking across the streaked evening sky.

It passed overhead and disappeared over the trees. She listened but the puttering faded away into the distance. Dickie felt an absolute sense of wonder as she shifted Max higher into her arms and made for the lighted door of the cottage.

Jim was sitting inside, cutting a slice of bread from the loaf. He buttered it thickly.

'Did you see the plane, Dad?' she asked excitedly, as she put Max to the ground and hung up her shawl and coat.

Jim swivelled round in his seat. 'Plane? No. Where've you been, lass?'

'Just on our way home.' She crossed to the table and cut a piece of bread for Max and buttered it. She handed it to the boy whose eyes devoured it long before he did. 'There you are. Now go and sit by the fire and get warm till tea's ready.'

'It was flying just overhead.' She knelt at the fireplace to take the kettle from its hook over the fire. 'Beautiful sight, it was.'

Jim wasn't listening. 'My back's fair broke from all that hedging and ditching.' He sucked a splinter from his finger. 'Get the tea on, lass, I'm starving.'

Dickie threw him a look. 'You know your trouble, Dad. You've got no sense of adventure.'

'Huh!' he said. 'Sense of adventure. All it does is get you into trouble. You mark my words.'

She stood up, the big black kettle poised between her hands. 'Well, we'll see about that, won't we?'

Dickie drove the cows slowly back to the field. She kept a stick to hurry along the strays at the back. Dawn was streaking through the sky and the ditches and fields were dazzling softly under the rays of the early morning sun as it touched the crisp layer of frost that covered the countryside. The world was silent and sleeping still and there was only the noise of the cows snorting and clopping down the lane and Dickie's voice urging them on.

Dickie drove them to the field and shooed them all in. She bent to lift the iron bar and lock the old five-barred gate into place. A spider's web was spun across one corner. The sun was well out now and it was a crystal-clear day, the sound carrying far. It was the best time of day, as a farmer would say. Now she would go home and cook breakfast for her father, Max and herself, and they would discuss what needed to be done that day.

She bent to lock the gate. The coating of frost on the wood was cold, biting into her fingers. The voice came from behind.

'Excuse me.'

She turned quickly.

The man was tall and handsome and moved with an ease born of athleticism and freedom. He did not move like a farm worker. He was dressed in leather with a fur collar and breeches tucked into long boots. Dickie stared.

'Yes?'

The man smiled hesitantly. He had strong white teeth. He did not look threatening, but his words set her on her mettle.

'Are you the only one here?'

And at her silence he added:

'. . . I mean, are there any men around?'

No matter what happened, she would never run again. She stood straight, her manner defensive. 'No.'

'Then, perhaps you could help me?' he tried. His voice was friendly against her hostility. He was amused by it, she thought, and suddenly realised that she had no need to fear him. 'Mind telling me where we are now?'

She wondered at his accent. It was not local. 'Foxhall Green,' she said. 'Henley-on-Thames is just down the road. Where are you from?'

'America!' He grinned.

'America!'

He laughed at that. 'Well, not right now. Right now I'm on my way to Booker airfield. My name's Joe O'Rourke. I'm an American.' He held out his hand, pulling off the gauntlet-sized gloves. 'Of Irish descent!' he added. His eyes were blue and they had a straight and decided expression. His smile was humorous.

'Josephine Bennett. Dickie,' she said and held out her hand.

'Well, Miss Dickie Bennett. Nice to meet you. Mind helping me with my plane?'

'Your plane . . .' She looked around at the empty fields and up towards the sky, and back to him. 'Was it you last night then? Very late? I saw a plane flying over that way.' She pointed behind her.

'Yep. That was me! It was getting dark pretty damn fast so I just hauled her over and brought her down in one of your fields over there.' He pointed over the brow of the hill and slapped his gloves together with the sound of heavy leather. He nodded and looked around. 'Pretty country!'

'Yes,' she said. 'I suppose it is.' She looked in the same

direction as him and tried to see it with new eyes. 'Where's the plane?'

'Right over that rise. You coming?'

'You've got nobody else!'

The man laughed and patted her shoulder with his glove. 'Come on, then.'

She walked up the field beside him. 'You slept in the field, then?'

'Sure. We all sleep out back home, though it's a fair bit warmer than here. It's great to lie under the stars on a warm summer's night. You should try it some time.'

'I have done,' she said, turning to him as she strove to keep up with his long stride. 'Last summer, when I was working the land for my dad. A couple of nights when we were late home from harvesting. My son and I. I lay down in the side of the field one night to take a quick nap. The next thing I knew the dawn came up. Max loved it. He thought it was an adventure.'

'You're a farmer's daughter, then,' he said. 'I might have known.'

'Why?'

'They're always the strong ones. America's the land of farmers. Here we are . . . !'

They had reached the brow of the hill and her face had been turned to his. Swiftly she looked, her curiosity alive.

It lay in the valley, resting like some giant green insect, darker than the green of the grass, and marked with stars on its wings and stripes on its tail. It basked in the early sun like a huge dragonfly.

It took her breath away like nothing before in her life. She could only stare, drawn to it as if it were the most splendid creature she had ever seen.

'What is it?' she said at last. Her face glowed as she looked first at the plane and then back at him.

He was pleased at her admiration. 'She's a Curtiss JN–4,' he said proudly. 'Popularly known as a Curtiss Jenny. American made. We brought 'em over to use as trainers for the Allied pilots. Great little plane. I was taking her back to the field, gonna meet up with some of the guys again. Say, you got pretty eyes. Anyone ever tell you that?' He smiled disarmingly at her and started down the steep bank towards his craft.

'No,' said Dickie behind him and ran lightly down, bracing herself sideways against the slope.

The American strode ahead towards the plane, and slapped her affectionately on the fuselage. He called to Dickie, 'Here she is! You wanna ride?'

'In that?'

'Sure. Just help me get her started. I'll take you up.'

She was intrigued by the airman's affable manner and the novelty of him. No one had ever treated her like that before, as if she had known him all her life. She ran the last bit of the slope and then came towards the plane, aware now of its size. She studied it from end to end and back again. And then approached, a little cautiously, as if in awe. Her eyes were huge. She laid a tentative hand on the warm curve of the wing, seeing the thick green paint. She ran her hand along, suddenly aware of its fragility. It looked so heavy and yet it was nothing much more than paper.

'It's made of nothing,' she said.

'Oh, a little more than that,' he said. The structure was wooden, braced with taut piano wire, and then covered in doped translucent fabric.

'How does it fly?'

He ran his hand over the top of the wing. 'Curve of the wing. Flat underneath. Air lifts it. Simple as that. What we call aerodynamics, but I won't bother your head with that.' He touched the plane with affection. 'Not a lot to her, but she goes like a bird,' he said fondly.

She remembered suddenly. 'You were in the war?'

'Sure. I was a Dominion man, a fighter pilot. The RFC couldn't have managed without us,' he said, referring to the Royal Flying Corps. He reached into the cockpit and touched the controls, his voice stretching as he leaned over and into the machine. 'I had this mate, he drank too much. He wore side-whiskers and a dirty stock, but the Brits said he was a splendid fellow. Snooty ones didn't care for him much, he used to pull their legs a bit, but he would have done anything for anyone. Some of your countrymen treat us like we got two heads, you know that?'

He grinned back at her as he went round to the nose of the plane. He made Dickie want to smile. He opened up the cowling. 'Yeah,' he said, 'we were a great crowd. A bit rough, but we had spirit. See,' he leaned into the engine, 'we got no social preconceptions. Some guys reckoned it was our open-air life, or cold baths in the morning. We're a tougher breed. Something like that. I reckon it's because we're free in America. Everybody's equal. We've all got the same chance. We don't believe, for example, that you have to be officer class to have anything unique, like fighting qualities or the ability to lead. All men got that. In America we don't have no class system. There,' he adjusted something in the engine. 'Bit of a dirty carb there,' he said to himself. 'The British, now, they kept up the class system, and you know what happened, Dickie?' He waved a rag at her.

'What?'

'Many of those lads were just dumb as officer material. Good families, but dumb. That was their mistake. *We*,' he tapped his chest, 'now, we were all crack fighter pilots, and we all came from very different homes. You never know who's going to be a good fighter pilot,' he said, replacing the cowling securely. 'You sure can't tell by appearances. It's "seat of the pants", that's what it is; an instinct for flying. Any sound man with sound nerves. Or woman.' He came round to her again and leaned against the plane. 'You, for instance.' He wiped his hands on the rag. 'You might make a very good pilot. You could do it in America.'

'Me?'

'Sure.' He threw the rag in the cockpit and leaned his arms on the plane and looked out across the field. 'In the States anything's possible.'

'America sounds wonderful the way you talk about it. You must miss it very much.'

'Yeah, I reckon.' His eyes were thoughtful. 'All those cookouts, warm nights by the beach, barbecues, and riding country as far as your eye can see. There's nothing like it. It's a *big* country. The land of opportunity,' he said, making it sound like an advertisement as he spread his hands, 'where anybody can make it, provided they've got the guts and the determination. I'm going back to be a barnstormer.'

'What's that?'

'A barnstormer? Gee, you know nothing, do you?' he teased. 'They're aerial gypsies. They go to the county fairs and rodeos and holiday picnics with their beat-up old planes, much like this Jenny here,' he said, patting it again. 'And they take you up for a ride. Then some of them spin and loop and dive and do spirals in the sky, and others bomb you with flour-bags or dive through bridges or barns!' He painted the scene with his hand as he spoke. Dickie did not move. Her mind saw the picture he portrayed. It sounded wonderful. A land where anybody could make it, rich or poor, where your future was in your own hands. How she would love a land like that, and what she could do with it! He had said she could fly too! She imagined herself at the controls of a plane, she heard the roar of the crowd as she dived down towards them, she sensed the freedom of a totally new and different life. She saw little Max's face coming back from a decent school, new clothes on his back. She imagined money to buy things, money to build a future upon. She did not know where the thought suddenly stopped being a dream and took hold in her fertile brain. The seed flowered. She would need money for the journey, and a bit put away to start. That is, until she started earning. Could she, too, become a pilot? If there were other girls out there doing it, then yes, why not? She definitely could. She was strong; she was willing. She felt the tingle of excitement run through her. She stood separate from him and his machine, watching. 'Mebbe they tour with a flying circus,' he went on, 'that's what I want to do. Gerry Oswald's Flying Circus. He's an old mate of mine. An ex-flyer, same as me. He set up last year just outside New York. He's got stunt-flying, wing-walking, exhibition pilots, parachuting, you name it. He wrote and asked me to join him. And that's where I'm going, just as soon as I deliver this baby.' He stood back and surveyed the plane. 'You need your own plane, though. Got to have something behind you. I'm lucky. I've got a bit of ready cash. M' family'll help too.'

'How much is a Jenny?' Her voice was contained.

'Few hundred dollars, about three hundred pounds.' He smiled. 'Why? You thinking of taking it on?'

'Maybe.' She would think about it. It was a crucial decision. She would be leaving behind everything she had ever known, yet she was surprised at how fast the decision came to her once she had thought it through. 'That is . . . yes,' she said, suddenly certain. 'Yes. I am.'

He laughed. 'Good for you. Knew you were a plucky girl.' He drew a piece of paper from his pocket. She watched him as he wrote, the blond hairs on the backs of his strong brown hands. 'Here's an address. It's a little airfield in upstate New York. Somebody there'll pretty much know where I am. Should you get over,' he added as he finished writing. He handed the scrap of paper to her. She liked the fact that he didn't question where she, a farm girl, would get the money. He just accepted it. In fact, she liked everything about Joe O'Rourke.

'You got the right attitude,' he said. 'We'll make a Yankee out of you yet. Let's go with the first lesson.' Without any warning he leaned forward and bodily lifted her onto the wing. 'Here we go. Mind the wing now, it's nothing but cloth under your feet. Stay on the inside, nearest the plane. That's right. Climb in.' He indicated the first of the two cockpit seats.

His hands were still on her waist and now Dickie had her balance. She lifted her skirt and stepped over into the bucket seat and slid down. Ahead of her was a panel of dials and between her knees a well-worn lever. The seat was hard and not particularly comfortable. She looked out to her left and between the two wings braced with wire and struts. The green pasture and the distant cows grazing on the top of the hill looked like another world to her. She was sitting in a plane for the first time, and it struck her that she had not once questioned what she was doing. She had put herself into his hands. He had won her with his constant, easy chatter.

'Now, what I want you to do is this, sweetheart. I'm going to turn over the prop. Propeller,' he explained. 'This,' he said pointing in, 'is the throttle. You keep that closed and the switches all off.' He ran his finger across them, indicating his meaning. 'This is the stick.' He tapped the lever between her knees. 'This is what controls your direction. It lifts the nose and drops it. You keep this well back. I'm going to put the chocks under the wheels and when I tell you "contact" I want you to turn these, magnetos, on. OK? Think you can do that?'

'Yes.' Her eyes were alert to the instrument panel.

'OK.' He ran around the wing to the front of the plane. 'Here goes,' he shouted. 'Now here's your first flying lesson. Once we get her started I'll come back and take your place. I'll just pull her through to get the juice flowing, and then when I say "contact" you open that throttle and switch on. Another pull and she should start right up. OK?'

'OK,' she echoed him.

Both his hands gripped the propeller and swung it smoothly. 'Contact!' he shouted.

Dickie's hand reached for the throttle and pulled it. She held the stick right back. She turned the switch.

'Contact,' she shouted back, her voice thin with excitement. He pulled the propeller through again. Suddenly with a great roar the plane burst into life. Dickie was filled with it, and with an exhilaration that she had never known. Her whole body reverberated. She felt as if she was really *doing something* for the first time in her life. She knew how right the feeling was. She was almost giddy and wanting to laugh. She sat there as the little plane roared steadily beneath her, and the excitement was infectious.

Her face showed it as he came running round the wing. 'OK,' he shouted as he climbed up onto the wing. 'You out!'

Dickie started to climb out and down onto the wing.

'No! Not down. In there!' He put his arm under her and swung her into the back of the plane. Dickie's legs slid down into the seat. 'Here, put these on!' he shouted.

He thrust a pair of goggles at her and pulled off his leather jacket. He passed it to her. Dickie struggled into it, smelling his smell, and the oil and the carbon, and tried to close it at the front. Joe leaned over, the enthusiasm matched on his sunburned face. He pushed her hands aside, fastened the jacket with deft fingers and pulled the safety harness around her, tying it tight. He pulled the goggles down over her eyes. Her heart beat rapidly with excitement.

'You're not afraid, are you?' he called. His face was grinning at her through the goggles.

'No! Should I be?'

He made a thumbs-up at her. 'OK, baby, let's go!' He slid down swiftly into his seat, his manner changed from that of before into a smooth air of control. His ebullience was only a front. At the helm of his machine he became a part of it. Joe had been one of the best fighter pilots of the war.

The engine ran for a moment, the roar building up and up, and the plane shuddered as if it wanted to hurl itself down the field but was being held back by invisible ropes. It died for a moment as he idled the engine again, before rapidly roaring up once more.

Suddenly the feeling was torn away and they hurtled down the field. Dickie was too shocked to react. The field flew by, the wind streamed into her hair and cheeks. She saw the fence that she had been mending the day she met Ted again. She saw it coming closer. Her hands were pressed to her thighs.

The nose lifted and skimmed sweetly over the fence, the hedge, the trees. They were airborne.

Dickie's breath was torn from her in a cry of pleasure and

surprise. The smile stayed wide on her face. There was the old barn with grass growing on the roof. Foxhall, away to their left, a massive house, but strangely unchallenging from up here. The plane banked to the right and she felt an uncontrollable urge to laugh. Her green eyes were wide with delight.

Joe lifted his thumb as they flew back over Cobbold's Wood. She lifted hers in turn. There was the cottage, the smoke pluming from its chimney. If only Dad could see her now. He'd have a seizure. It was glorious. No one could touch her up here. The sense of freedom was almost impossible to contain. The world held a different perspective.

The plane dipped from side to side as it skimmed the trees. The blue sky tilted all around her. Beyond the trees, the land opened out to the fields like a patchwork beneath her, dotted with cows. The wind buffeted her face and tossed the little plane around like a leaf. Yet she had never felt so safe. She had complete faith in the airman. No one had ever treated her like he did before. He treated her like a friend.

The surge and fall of the plane lit her inside, licking up the bones of her spine like a hot tongue. The pleasure was intense. She had never believed such a world existed, so far away from anything she had ever known.

The field was familiar. They were flying low, skimming the hedge again as if they would hit, too close. Dickie tensed for the first time in apprehension. And then they were landing, racing along the grass to come to an unsteady halt.

Joe kept the engine running. 'If you ever come to the States, look me up.' He kissed her cheek. 'Thanks for the help.'

'I will. Thanks, Joe.'

'Sure. Keep smiling.'

And, with a wave, he was firing the little plane down the field again.

He had filled her head with dreams. 'America is the land of opportunity.' She felt an affinity with the little machine that now took off over the hedges, soaring quickly up into the blue of the mid-morning Berkshire sky. One could call it a sense of destiny. Whatever it was, it was there, seeded in her.

America was the land of opportunity.

The plane cut through the wide blue sky. She watched it until it was just a speck in the distance.

America was the land for her.

* * *

Dickie smiled to herself as she lay awake in the dark. Beside her in his bed lay Max, sleeping soundly with the soft snore of a child. She held the scrap of paper to her, feeling it against the palm of her hand. *America.* The word shone like gold in the darkness. She would get there. She would find Joe and he would help her get started. She and Max would have a new life, the life she had dreamed of. She would wait until Max was a little older. Next summer he would be five. That would be the time.

She knew at last she had found the way. The way to her freedom. And the one who would help her now was Frederick Redfield.

TEN

June, 1919

Frederick strolled out of Cobbold's Wood onto the lower lawn, his gun under his arm and his black Labrador at his heels.

The house was mellow and creeper-clad, bathed in sunshine, the doors open to the summer day. He was alone and he loved it. He wandered around the acres, feeling that sense of belonging. The garden was rich with flowers, burgeoning with scent and colour. The summer was long and perfect. The war had been over and forgotten, everything restored to normal. He was at peace.

Since the end of the war the previous year Rupert had spent little time at home. The children were growing and Caroline was with him for the season at their Belgravia mansion. They would return at the end of the summer. Frederick had opted to stay down, enjoying the idea of some time alone at Foxhall. It had been perfect.

He looked up at the sky feeling the wind on his neck. It was picking up. The humid weather had been bound to break sooner or later. A storm was coming. He could see the front over against the skyline. Clouds scurried forward from the horizon, dark and heavy.

Maybe tonight he would ask the servants to build him a fire as the night drew in. He would sit with his dog at his feet and breathe in the atmosphere of woodsmoke, dog and lamp. There was an odour about a country house that he loved better than any scent in the world. Once the servants had all gone to bed and he was alone for the evening, he would relax with his glass of port and perhaps a pipe of sweet tobacco, the windows open to the night air, and he would listen to the creaking of the old house, each sound he knew so well. And he would dream.

As he walked up the lawns towards his house he was content.

Mrs Merriman appeared on the balcony, her long, black skirts sweeping across the stone.

'Mr Redfield.'

'Yes, Mrs Merriman. What is it?' He placed one foot on the shallow steps that led up to the terrace. He looked up at her. She seemed agitated.

'The farm foreman's daughter, Dickie Bennett, wants a word with you, sir.' Her face was grim with disapproval. 'I told her no, but she insists. I'm sorry, sir, to bother you with this. Shall I send her away?'

Frederick's happy dream came to an end. The dog came and sat exhaustedly at his feet. He stroked its domed head thoughtfully. 'No,' he said. 'Tell her I will see her. Take her to the estate office. I will be down in half an hour.'

The storm buffeted the window in a flurry of punches, rattling the panes. The gale started outside. The high sycamore trees bent and bowed in the wind.

Dickie felt the pressure build, compressing her inside this house, in a feeling that was intimate, dark and musty. Everything seemed living, and old. The books, the dark furniture, seemed to pause and wait along with her. There was a magnetic and tactile sense in the room as if damp fingers were pressed to her bare neck. The nerves under her skin were on edge. She felt exposed and alien.

She was afraid, it was true, or rather fearful, but more determined than she had ever been. It was her resolve that had brought her up here, past Mrs Merriman, and to this room. The fearfulness was conditioned into her: servants were supposed to stay in their place, not order the gentry to them. She told herself that she was superior to these men who could do the things they did and not be ashamed.

She took a deep breath and turned back into the room, so that she was framed in the window. There was a portrait of Rupert Redfield on the panelled wall above the fireplace, a coat of arms beneath. She could feel his live sexuality from the portrait. She

remembered his hands, his laugh, and suddenly Sam. *Sam.*
Dead, while Rupert Redfield lived. There was no God. Help
me, Sam. Help me to defeat them. She held her head high with
a new strength. If ever she might have wavered she would not
now. She owed it to his death and to her family's lives not to fail
them.

The strange stormy light suddenly filled the midday room and
made it squeeze dark as if the light had been sucked from the
room in a rush, as if an underwater anemone had suddenly
closed in danger, swiftly contracting. Dickie's eyes though, still
held the light, and so for a moment she was unfocused, yet her
emotions still blazed in her eyes. Her hate, her need, her pain.

Frederick, coming into the darkened library at that moment,
saw her quite differently. He stopped and caught his breath. In
her best green cotton dress, black stockings, her dark hair piled
up onto the back of her head, the starched white collar framing
her face, he saw her as she had never been seen. He held his
breath and stayed at the door, unseen by her.

She was beautiful. She stood, framed by the long window,
her eyes glistening bright with unshed tears of anger, her dark
hair twisted on her damp forehead. He could see the texture of
her skin and he remembered how she had affected him. That
knowledge was in the air between them as she turned, suddenly
aware of him.

She said nothing. Frederick composed himself swiftly, muttering something inane about the storm and the light, and lit the
lamp. The fire still burned in her, and she had that aura, the
quality that one could sense in someone powerful. And then
Frederick understood. She and Rupert. No wonder he had felt
himself enticed to do what he had done. They were alike in that
power. He did not possess it, and as anyone weaker would do
he had wanted to stand near that fire and warm himself by it,
take strength from it. He had taken from her, unable to help
himself.

She did not speak for a while, as if she could not trust herself.
Her condemnation of him burned steadily in her eyes, and Frederick tried not to flinch from that awful gaze.

He waited for her to speak as he lit the lamp.

'I want your help.'

Her voice, though quiet, filled the room. He realised he had
never really heard her speak.

'How?'

'I'm leaving the village. I'll no longer be helping my father in the fields and on the farm. I want your assurance that if I leave my father will not be thrown out of his home.'

Her voice was low and only lightly accented. There was a distorted intimacy between them as if they knew each other, yet did not. She had great bearing, not like a village girl. All those things crossed his mind before he answered her.

'I see. Well, you have my word.'

'And what about your brother?'

'My brother's too. I run the estate.' His voice was calm. 'Your father will stay.' He walked slowly to the fireplace. 'May I ask why you are leaving your home?' He turned to look back at her. She had not moved since he had entered the room. Only her eyes, those underwater eyes that surveyed him now so coolly, as if she controlled this interview.

'I am going to America with my child. I intend to make my fortune. And then I will return.' The words hung in the air like a threat, but Frederick heard the earlier words with a sharp thrust to his temples.

'Your child? I didn't know you . . .'

'I am not married, Mr Redfield.'

He lowered his eyes. He asked the question he now could not avoid. 'How old is the child?'

'Five.'

The silence was a strain. He wanted to turn and apologise. He felt a mixture of emotions and was suddenly desperate for her to be gone so she would not look at him like that, so he could be alone, yet he did not want her to leave. Is it mine? he wanted to say. Or is it his? What does it look like? A girl or a boy? He could not ask. It would resurrect something too dreadful. They would have to admit to what had gone before, and that was impossible. It was best to pretend it was not there.

'Is there anything else I can do for you?' he said at last.

'Yes. I need money,' she said. 'Five hundred pounds.'

'It's a large sum.'

'Yes.'

'May I ask what you need it for?'

'No. You may not.'

He took tobacco from the jar and took his time filling his pipe, pushing the twist down into the bowl.

'Very well, Miss Bennett. I'll give it to you.'

He walked away towards the desk at the far end of the room.

She watched him go, seeing his walk and the lean, easy body, remembering how he had once looked at her as if overcome, how he still looked at her now.

The storm passed in a moment, the rain lashing down hard into the dry earth. As he opened the drawer of the desk at the gloomy end of the room, the sunshine returned, unfolding smoothly across the dark. The room no longer seemed so forbidding. The wind was still up and the sunlight was as crystal on the rain-wet leaves that thrashed within the wind's grasp. The sound was like rushing water in the trees outside the window behind her. It relaxed her. She was tempted to turn round and enjoy it, but knew that for as long as she was in this house she could do no such thing.

He returned with a thick wad of banknotes in his hand. In front of her he counted them out carefully. Seven hundred pounds: money that Rupert kept in the house at all times. Holding the money in his hand, he stepped into the light before her. He looked down into her face. It was smooth and lovely, the strength and pride held in her, although he knew it must have taken a great deal for her to come here at all. He admired that, and knew that even now he wanted her. He weakened.

'Miss Bennett . . . If only I could turn back the clock, I would never . . .'

'Please. I'd like to be going.'

She looked up at him, the green eyes accusing and absorbing him.

He held out the money. 'Here. There's seven hundred.'

'Five,' she said. 'It's what I need. No more.'

He gazed at her, his dark blue eyes naked with his need. Her expression was closed against him. He could not buy his freedom from her. He peeled off two hundred from the sheaf and passed the rest to her.

She would not touch him. He looked down at her motionless hands, rough from work, on *his* farm. He understood. He placed the money on the table beside them.

Dickie took it, opening a bag that he had not noticed before. She placed the money inside and closed it.

Her eyes lifted briefly to his. They spoke volumes, yet he did not know what they said. He was lanced by that look.

And then she was moving towards the door. She spoke not another word. Their business was at an end.

* * *

'Child, you cannot go across to America. You and the boy. Whatever are you thinking of? Have you lost your mind? What about his future?'

'That's what I've been thinking of, Dad. I've already planned for his future.' She opened her bag and took out the money. She passed it across the table for his inspection.

Jim forgot his tea. He pushed his plate aside and touched the money tentatively. 'Wherever did you get all this money?' His blue eyes were bright with alarm.

'It's all right, Dad. I didn't steal it! Keep your voice down, you'll wake Max.' She took it back from him, her face grim. 'I asked Redfield for it.'

'You never did!' he gasped. 'You went up to Foxhall and asked Mr Frederick to pay you off?'

'I did indeed.' Her eyes flashed at him. 'And he gave it to me, soon as you please. Conscience as long as your arm. One day it'll be more than money that I'll be taking from the Redfields.'

'Why, I'm ashamed of you, girl.' His voice condemned her as if she was a leper, his tone hushed with shock. 'That's no better than a common criminal. That's blackmail, that is . . . !

'And what they did to me is not a crime?' She leaned fervently across the table at him. 'An eye for an eye, Dad,' she said. 'Only I'll be taking more in time. When I'm back.'

She stuffed the money back into a small leather purse and hung it behind her petticoat in the swirl of her skirts. She stood.

'Oh, Dickie, you'll not leave me. By God, I'll miss you. First your mother, then Sam, and now you.' He shook his head.

'I know, Dad,' she said softly, stopping to look at him. 'But I'll be back. Mrs Canter'll look in on you. I already asked her. And when I'm back I'll have enough for all of us. You'll never want again.'

She went across to the fire, lifting the iron pot of stew from the hook. She ladled out two bowls of the hot meaty stew and carried them back to the table. 'I'll give you fifty pounds before I leave,' she said matter-of-factly. 'It's more than a whole year's wages . . .'

'Ah, Dickie, I can't take that money. It's bad that's what it is.'

'. . . You don't want it?' She set the bowl before him.

'It's not that.' He sighed and laid his fists on the table each side of his plate. 'It just feels wrong, that's all.'

'It's not wrong, Dad.' She lifted the knife and cut the bread. 'You might be needing it. I don't trust the word of any Redfield though he promised me he'd not be putting you off, and nor would his evil brother.'

'He's a man of the church, Dickie,' he said quickly.

'Man of the church.' Her voice was scornful. She buttered the bread quickly and put it on the table beside his place.

Jim looked at it absently and then back up at her.

'Dickie, why do you need so much? What are you going to do over there?'

Now her face lit with a smile. 'I'm going to buy an aeroplane,' she said. She lifted the kettle and poured the tea. 'I'm going to be a barnstormer.'

ELEVEN

Spring, 1920

Dickie held Max close to her, his small body wrapped in their shared blanket. She had bought it before leaving, along with a heavy coat that reached to her ankles and a coat and tweed cap for the boy. A large cloche hat was pulled down over her head to protect her from the cold and secured with a shawl. Her face stung with the sea spray and her eyes were misted from the wind. She had never believed that the sea could be so immense or so threatening.

On reaching the docks in Southampton they had been enthralled by the size of the boat that would carry them. The sea had swirled grey and deep as they climbed aboard. Nothing had prepared her for these mountainous waves and the conditions they were facing. They were huddled on deck, their belongings stowed away behind them. She was using them now to lean against as she tucked the blanket up around his face and held him close to her while he slept.

She looked out over the sea. It was endless, dipping and cresting in gulleys of lacy foam and huge black swells. The day was like night and a sharp wind blew over them. The sky was bigger than she had ever seen it, even out in the country. Max struggled in his sleep and woke.

'Mama?'

'Yes, Max?'

'I'm hungry.'

She dug in her bag and found him a biscuit. He took it and

129

ate it, his expression serious. He looked round at the sea and the deck but he wasn't scared; he had her. Her heart went out to him in gratitude. He relied on her. And though she might have her times when she feared the unknown, he trusted her to make things work out, because she was his mother. She loved him deeply at that moment. This was more than she had ever anticipated; she had never even left the village before. She would not have done it without Max. He was her motivation. It was for him and because of him that they were here. Together. She was not alone. The small boy, earnestly eating his biscuit, relied on her to get it right. She stroked his dark curls and smiled for the first time since they had left home. For him, she would do it. He made her strong.

As he fell back against her breast and sighed himself to sleep, her mind rode back over the past and how it had been. The ship dipped and rose, and with the rhythm her mind drifted. They were on their way to America.

The parting had been sad and hard for her. Her papers had finally come through in the spring of 1920, and her father, after much deliberation, had understood and accompanied her to the railway station. But then he had broken down in tears, and she had had to take her suitcase and her papers and Max's hand in her own and climb on board with more resolve than she had ever known she had.

At the dock she had waited in line, clutching their belongings. Her papers were checked and they were given a medical examination before being shown to their sleeping quarters in steerage. They were to sleep on thin straw mattresses on iron-tiered berths. The storm had come almost before they were out of the harbour. All passengers were confined below decks and the smell soon became nauseating. As soon as possible she escaped to the deck, fighting her way round the crowded gangway to find a space to settle down with Max, thankful for the fresh air. When they all retired below later she had stayed up there, dreaming of the country and those fresh cool evenings, the smells of the harvest and the good cooking smells in her kitchen. She wondered what they would find in the promised land.

Various immigrant men approached her but Dickie kept herself to herself, not speaking to them. There was nothing she needed to know, and nothing she wanted to ask. Conversation for its own sake had never been important to her; she was used to managing alone. Soon they left the high and mighty dark-haired girl alone with her child in the blanket. She knew all that was necessary about America from the airman; the past she did not care to discuss.

She was up on deck at sunrise and so was one of the first to catch sight of the land. The early-morning sun gilded the buildings on New York's waterfront, making it seem like a magical city. The tugs guided them in, hooting their way to the brick buildings of Ellis Island, the immigration centre.

They were given numbers to hang round their necks and remained with their belongings until called. Dickie sat on the knotted bag with their clothes and held Max in her lap. She was content to wait while all the bustling and officialdom took place. She was here.

They climbed down the ladder and into the barge that was to take them to the shore. The sea swelled dangerously, the small craft bobbing in the water. Max clung to her skirts as they made their way down. The clutch of her hand reassured him. They were on board and chugging their way towards the shore, the New York clammy sea mist as tactile as skin. They arrived at the island.

Two examiners were seated in front of them in the shed.

'What is your name?'

'Josephine Bennett,' she said. She handed them her papers. 'And this is my son, Max.'

The older one was busily writing.

'No father?'

'No.' She had rehearsed this moment. The semi-hostile eyes met hers. 'My husband was killed in the war.'

Somehow she knew unmarried was wrong, widowed would be all right.

'Do you have a place to go to?'

'Yes.' She reached into her bag and brought out the address of the airman.

The second man stopped writing and glanced up. He reached out for the slip of paper with Joe's address on it, studied it, and then her. His eyes were kinder, a warm brown and rather tired, but the look was still direct, an official's eyes. 'Do you have work here in the United States, Mrs Bennett?'

'I do, yes. The same man,' she said, indicating the fragile piece of paper which she desperately wanted back. 'He has promised me work.'

'I see.' Slowly he handed it back to her. She tucked it safely in the pocket of her bag. 'And are you willing to abide by the laws of the United States?'

'Yes, I am.' She held her head straight and looked him in the eye. Max was very still beside her.

Then came the question she had been dreading. 'Have you any money?'

Were there laws about how much? She could not start on the wrong foot. She lifted her bag from the belt at her waist and opened it. Her father had made the belt for her before they had left home, the wallet sewn to the inside. She laid the four hundred remaining pounds on the table. Three hundred for the Curtiss Jenny, one hundred for food, clothes, lodging . . . *time.*

The brown eyes were warier now. 'That's a lot of money, Mrs Bennett. Where did you get it?'

'From my employer, Mr Frederick Redfield of Foxhall.'

He nodded, referring back to her form. 'Thank you. You may put the money away now.'

He scribbled something on a sheet, leaned over and whispered to his associate and then handed her a card. The card said, Admittance.

'Show this to the immigration officer. Give him your full name and address. And change your money. If you do not commit a crime for five years and have satisfied us that you would make a good American citizen, you will be permitted to apply for full United States citizenship. Thank you, Mrs Bennett, and welcome to the United States.'

'Thank you. Come along, Max.'

They walked out into the crisp spring day. New York. She looked up all around her at the tall buildings, hearing the hum of traffic, the people, the noise. Now they would find Joe and see his surprise. She found a telephone kiosk and went in. Max sat on the bags at her feet. It took her a while to understand the workings of the thing and which coin to use but soon she had mastered it. She spread the crumpled paper open in front of her and telephoned the number of the airfield in upstate New York.

'I'm sorry, ma'am. Who did you say?'

'Joe O'Rourke. He gave me this address.'

'Uh-uh. There's no Joe O'Rourke here.'

'But there must be. I've come all the way from England!' She clasped the phone tighter, her mind searching the distant voice for an answer.

'Wait a moment.' The voice went away, mumbled something, and came back. 'Well, lady. You're in luck. Seems there was a Joe O'Rourke here . . .'

'Yes . . . ?'

'. . . but he's gone now. Been gone a year. Last address we've got is this . . . you got a pen?'

'Wait.' She fumbled for a pencil, dropping her bag to the ground.

'Mama, I'm tired,' muttered Max, his huge blue eyes gazing up at her.

'Just a moment, Max. Yes? I'm ready.' She listened. '128 Apartment 2B, yes . . . Brooklyn . . . yes, thank you.'

She put down the phone and gathered her bags up again. She put out her hand for Max. He clambered to his feet and held it. 'Come on,' she said. 'Let's go and find Brooklyn.'

Max was tired and dragging his feet.

'Not far now,' she said, looking up at the street to check the name. The area was derelict, tall, redbrick buildings and wide-open disused spaces. She did not like the look of it at all. She lifted Max into her arms. It was growing dark now. They had been walking since the morning.

At last she found the address and rang the bell.

He was no longer there. No, they did not know where he had gone. A woman and a child in early evening with no ring on her finger, and chasing an American airman half-way round the world. They knew what she was. They slammed the door in her face.

'Mama?'

Dickie turned on the doorstep. Max's hand lay trustingly in hers. For a moment she was unable to think what to do. This was an eventuality she had never even considered. In her haste and certainty she had never doubted that he would be here.

Max's face looked up at her.

'Mama, can we go to sleep now?'

'Yes, Max. In a little while.'

* * *

There was a sign in the window: ROOMS.

The window was dirty and the curtain grey, but she had no choice.

'You're not married. I don't know what my wife will say.'

It was dusk. She stood on the doorstep, her bags on the step and Max holding her left hand. The fat, brutish man filled the doorway. The stench of cabbage floated out onto the street. His hair was sparse and greasy and his face was grey with lack of diet and air. His stomach hung over his trousers, so that the waistband was suspended underneath it by his braces. He scratched at his chest and shook his head.

'But I *am* married,' she said. 'My husband was killed in the war.'

He looked pointedly at her finger. She wished she had thought of it earlier and bought a ring. Never had she imagined that her lack of marital status would count for so much in such a big city.

'I sold it to buy my passage to America. I've got friends here. I'll soon be moving out of New York. It's only for a few days.'

'I don't know.'

Max started to tug at her hand. 'Please,' she said, hating the position she was in, 'we're both so tired.'

'What if you run out in the night without paying? Some do, you know.' He picked his teeth and examined his nails. 'You gotta pay for your food and lodging in advance.'

She turned to look up the street in desperation. Across it two youths were watching her from behind a parked car. She could go no further than this, but she did not want him to see where she kept her money, nor how much she had. She did not trust the fat man. The passage beyond him was narrow, dank and dirty. She did not want to stay for more than a night, but they had nowhere else and it was already late. She had to think of Max.

'I can get you the money in the morning,' she said. 'You can see we're both exhausted. We're not going to run out tonight.'

He looked down at the child. 'All right then,' he said. 'You can come in.'

She gave a sigh of relief as she lifted her bags, and persuaded Max to move on ahead of her down the passageway. It was worse than it appeared. The cooking smells were heavy and stale, the stairs that led upwards steep and bare. The fat man's ascent was laborious and punctuated by his heavy breathing. Dickie's stomach heaved at the rancid air around her. After the bad food on the ship and the lack of sleep, she needed a good meal before they slept, and so did Max.

The corridor at the head of the stairs was narrow, covered in yellowed lino. He arrived at a door, and inserted a key.

'Here you are, best in the house.'

She went in. The room was small and dark, a tiny window thick with dirt in the centre at the far end. It had a broken sash. There was a wash-basin in the corner and a sagging bed with a worn green cover. The brown curtains over the window were pinned into place and held back with string.

She looked around, her heart weighing heavily. She remembered her sparse but spotlessly clean room at home in the cottage.

'Could we have some food?'

The fat man's tongue explored his tooth. 'No food. Supper's at seven. Too late now. Thought you said you were tired, anyway.' He picked at the tooth. He had obviously eaten.

'We are tired,' she said firmly. 'But we could do with something. My son hasn't eaten since breakfast. Could I perhaps speak to your wife?' She looked towards the doorway.

The fat man's face became hostile. 'Look, lady, do you want the room or not? You take what you can get. Don't start making your demands with me right now. I'll just throw you right out where you came from.' He moved forward. 'What you trying to imply? I haven't got a wife?'

'No. Nothing of the sort.' She held Max's shoulders between her hands. 'That'll be all then, thank you.' She moved Max away, and took off her hat to put it on the hook on the wall.

The man did not move out of the room. He could see her now. Without that hat pulled down over her face, there was something about her. Those pale eyes and the dark hair. Quite a contrast. He grinned, his little eyes disappearing in the fat rolls of his cheeks.

'Well, there again, maybe I could rustle up a little something for you. That is if you were to come down to the kitchen once the boy's asleep. Might see my way clear to that. How does that sound?' he guffawed. 'Seeing's you're alone and in need of a bit of help.'

Dickie looked up, pleased. And saw the leer on his face. She straightened, and the light eyes fixed him with the stare of a cat.

'I need no one's help. You'd better understand that.' She stared right through him. 'Excuse me. This is our room, I believe.'

The man gave a grunt of anger. 'Goddamn women,' he said, as he shuffled to the door. 'Try to do 'em a favour.'

She heard the lock from outside.

'Hey! What are you doing?' she said, running to the door and trying the handle.

'Just making sure you don't pull no tricks,' he said through the panel of the door. 'I don't reckon you been telling me the truth. I reckon you're a girl on the run. You pay me in the morning. Then I'll let you go.'

Summer, 1920

New York was a city of immigrants all hustling for jobs. The streets were wide and dusty, the buildings tall and braced with iron fire-escapes into alleyways littered with garbage. The shops were garish and cheap. Cardboard boxes were tossed on the sidewalk outside the dingy restaurants. Cats yowled on rooftops and in back alleys at night. Brooklyn was ugly to Dickie and alien. There was no sky to see, no view, only building after building, red brick and grey, the concrete streets, and an assortment of people hunting for work, all strangers.

Dickie took what work she could get. She got odd jobs as a waitress downtown. Max would sit in a room off the kitchen waiting for her. She would not leave him alone in the new room she had found them. She worked hard, but soon the presence of a small boy would irritate the manager. It always happened. There were others who needed a job, others with no responsibilities. Dickie was told to quit time after time. She did not regret it as they walked out on the street hand in hand, looking once again for a new job—it was no life for a small boy—but it meant she was without work.

In the end, she had found a job as a night cleaner in a club with the understanding that he could come too. She wrapped him in a blanket on one of the plastic banquettes while she cleaned. Then she would carry him home at three in the morning. Men treated her like a whore. She was a woman alone with a child. She bought a cheap brass ring for her finger but it made little difference. New York was a big bad city, not a place where a girl would go unless she had to.

She had known it would be hard, but not *so* hard. She had never considered the sheer size of New York. It had been just a name to her, a future. The city was endless, and though she scanned the papers and the billboards there was no mention of a county fair starring Gerry Oswald's Flying Circus.

At the end of the summer her luck changed. Sitting in a café one hot afternoon with Max having a soda, the proprietress had started chatting to the boy. It was not long before the two of them were dropping in each day for a soda and a chat with Mrs Tomczak. She wanted to talk. She had no children of her own, and her husband had died the previous year. She was a kind though curious woman, who soon discovered that the pretty young English girl needed a good home. She invited them to take a room with her.

Dickie walked home in the early hours of the morning from the club. At last things were brighter. She could leave Max sleeping in his bed, safe in the knowledge that Mrs Tomczak could be trusted. At first he had protested. He had found their night-time existence an adventure of a sort. Soon, she realised, his enquiring mind would need further stimulation. It was time Max went to school.

She was deep in thought as she crossed the road, and did not see the dark shadows following her along the street. As she turned under the street light and crossed to the opposite corner, they jumped.

The first one felled her with a blow to the head. The second rifled quickly through her clothes. Once again, Dickie knew the humiliation of being defenceless. She looked up into the Puerto Rican face and saw the warning in the black eyes. She did not scream. He slit the purse from her waist and she heard the rapid exchange of chatter as they found her precious nest egg. Then she cried out as she reached for it. The heavy boot caught her in the side of the head and everything went dark.

TWELVE

Rupert walked into the chairman's office. He crossed to the desk at which his father had held the power for so many years. He went round behind it and sat down. For a moment he surveyed the elegant room as his father might have seen it. He leaned forward and pressed the bell set into the desk.

There was an instant response. The immaculate man who entered the room had been his father's private secretary, a man Alexander had trusted implicitly, a man to whom Rupert was about to give the same trust.

'Mr Redfield,' he said. 'May I say what a pleasure it is that you have decided to join us? What can I do for you?'

Rupert leaned back. 'For a start, you can get me membership of my father's club. I hear the food is excellent.'

'I have already done so.' Guy Prudham came across the room and stood beside the table. He pointed to the right-hand drawer. 'You will find the details in there. I arranged it as soon as your father died.'

Rupert looked at him with interest. 'And have you booked me for lunch there today?'

'I took the liberty, sir. Perhaps I could recommend the game pie. It is excellent.'

'I'll remember,' Rupert said slowly. 'Now, what I want is this: a complete list of who is who in this bank, what their duties are, how long they have been here, and how close they were to my father,' he finished carefully. He looked into the man's eyes and saw he understood quite clearly. 'All right so far?'

'Yes, sir.'

'I want it by noon. Also, a very short report on the state of the bank at the moment, our financial ties, and our own particular standing in the market. And,' he ran a finger up the side of a gold-embossed blotter, 'I want to know how a bank works.' A smile lit the depths of his eyes. 'In simplest terms, of course. I'm only a layman. Can you manage that?'

'Of course, sir.' It was obvious he knew that Rupert was not the layman he professed to be. There was an intensity about Alexander's son that his father had lacked. It set Guy Prudham on his mettle, but it did not sit awkwardly with him. He thought he might enjoy the challenge. He sensed a quick rise in responsibility were he to play his cards exactly right with this one. 'You want to know who to trust and who not, is that right?'

'Precisely.' He scratched his name on the cheque book opened before him. 'Cash this money for me before luncheon, and set up a full board meeting in the board room for three o'clock. I want all board members there without fail, and seated according to a seating-plan which you will put before my place.' He handed him the cheque.

Guy turned to go.

Rupert raised his finger. 'One more thing . . .'

Guy turned, a quizzical look on his narrow face.

'I want the keys to all the cupboards that hold files. I would like to study the business we do at my convenience.'

Guy nodded and left the room.

Outside the board room there was a sign saying, Meeting in Progress. The uniformed commissionaire stood to attention and saluted. Rupert hardly noticed him. The man hurried to open the door.

Rupert's stride did not falter a fraction. He strode through the opened door and into the board room. Twenty heads turned as Rupert crossed the room towards them. There was a glimmer of a smile on his lips, but his eyes remained cold. They all began to stand.

'Good afternoon, gentlemen,' Rupert's voice was affable. He went round to the head of the table. The huge armchair was vacant. Rupert stood in front of it. 'Please,' he opened his hands to them, 'be seated.'

The oak-panelled board room was directly below his own on the corner of the building, and overlooking the grey waters of

the Thames below. The table was curved in a U shape beneath
a massive chandelier, softly glowing now in the dim light of the
afternoon. Behind Rupert an original oil painting of the bank's
premises in the early pioneer days dominated the room.

'Gentlemen,' he said at last. 'I lay myself at your mercy. I
know next to nothing about banking. And . . . I do not intend
to start learning.' He looked casually at the seating-plan as he
spoke, marrying names up with faces, and recalling the excellent report that Guy Prudham had brought him before lunch. He
saw the interest in some, the greed in others, the respect in a
few. 'My father always told me,' he went on, 'just how well you
all ran the place when he was out of town. And I feel that you
can be relied upon to continue to do just that. I, and my family,
will continue to hold majority stock, that's all.' He had their
attention, they were breathing easier now. Their lives were not
going to change. Rupert knew that complacent men were off
guard. 'My brother, Frederick,' he went on, 'is only interested
in running the family estates, both in the country and our property up here in town. I, for myself—well!' He gave them a disarming smile. 'I will visit the bank from time to time. Draw a
little petty cash!'

There were polite ripples of laughter round the table. A few
of the board members started to relax, leaning back in their
seats.

'Apart from that,' he continued, 'I shan't bother you very
much. The day-to-day running can carry on as it is, and I shall
continue to be chairman . . . in pretty much name only. You
can report anything you wish to tell me to my secretary, Guy
Prudham. Well,' he placed his hands on the table, 'I think that's
all.' He smiled blandly. 'Any questions?'

Faces turned to look at each other, and back to Rupert. There
were none.

A large, well-fed man at the foot of the table raised his hand
lightly. Rupert glanced quickly at his seating-plan. Robert Hewdon-Vassar, not to be trusted. Very old family, pompous and
opinionated, very manipulative.

'Yes?'

'I'd just like to say, Rupert, on behalf of all of us, welcome
to your father's bank . . . however little you visit us!' He smiled.
There was a murmur of agreement from around the room.

Rupert returned the bow. 'Thank you.' He gave a half-pause.
'But it's not my father's bank any more.' He smiled easily.

Robert Hewdon-Vassar coughed lightly, as if to excuse himself. He did not see the slight gleam that appeared in Rupert's cold blue eyes which disappeared again almost as quickly. He had already summed up Alexander's son. The man was a sop and a fool; he would not give them any trouble.

Rupert returned to the house in Belgravia. The woman was waiting for him in the drawing-room. She whirled round as he entered, the black veil still draped to her shoulders.

Rupert went straight over and put his arms around her. He lifted the veil and looked down into the exquisite face of the Countess of Thamesdene, once a dancer with the whole of London at her feet. Emma had married the old earl and gained the stature essential to her. The dancing days were forgotten as society fawned.

'I don't want to meet you here like this, Rupert,' she pouted at him, as her arms went round his waist. The huge, brown eyes looked up into his.

'My dear Emma. It's not like you to be shy!'

'It's not shyness, Rupert. What if Lancelot were to find out?' Rupert bent and put his lips to her throat. Her head tipped back with pleasure. 'What if he did?' he said. 'Shall we just say I like it this way. It adds . . . spice,' he went on softly.

She laughed. Her drowsy eyes met his, their expression now erotic. It was her position she could not bear to lose, not her husband. 'You understand me better than any man I've ever known. We're two of a kind, you and I.' Her eyelids lowered over her eyes, and the full lips pulled into a smile of promise.

Rupert's hands tugged at the dress she wore. 'I hate this fashion. I like women to be women. I want to see you. Take it off.'

The dress was cut in the latest mode, the bustless look with draped top and long skirt and a waistline at the hips. Her delicate ankles shimmered under silk stockings and she wore a band round her forehead, glittering with sequins.

Emma laughed and moved away, swaying slightly. She undid the dress and it slid to the floor. Her movements were sinuous.

'More,' he said, moving to the sofa, his eyes deep with sensuality. She loosened her petticoat and dropped it to her hips. 'Now, dance for me, Emma,' he said.

'Rupert, I don't want to.' Suddenly she looked hurt. She did not want to remember those days.

'I said, *dance.*' He took a handful of coins from his pocket and threw them to the floor. 'You're one of the few women to whom I come back for more. I want you, Emma,' he said, his eyes closing like a snake. 'So, dance. And then,' he added softly, 'then I'll take you the way you like it.'

Her eyes on him, she began to move.

It was hours later that Dickie staggered home, her handkerchief pressed to the wound on her head. She almost fell against the bell.

The window opened above her head. Mrs Tomczak leaned out in curlers and a hairnet. 'Whatever time do you . . . my goodness, Mrs Bennett, whatever happened to you?'

Dickie looked up. She could not speak for the thumping in her head. Blood coursed down over one temple.

'Never mind. I'll be right down. Just wait there.'

The window slammed shut. Soon after, footsteps thumped down the stairs and along the hall. Dickie leaned against the brick wall and closed her eyes.

The door opened. The big full-bosomed woman stood there. She lifted her hands in horror and gathered her into her arms, pulling her in. Dickie acquiesced with relief.

'Ah, my poor darlink. Come along in, now. Let's see what they've done to you. Thieves, was it? Did they take your money? Ah, poor darlink . . .'

Mrs Tomczak did not give her time to speak. Dickie was grateful. The kindness and maternal bustle of the Polish woman was like soothing balm. Dickie missed the comfort of a mother. She had to be so strong for Max, and it took it out of her. She let herself go as Mrs Tomczak drew her into her own private front room while she did all the talking for both of them.

'There, there.' Mrs Tomczak smoothed her hair away from the cut. 'A nasty bruise we will have there. Still, I will fix it. Ah, you're all done in, aren't you? I'll get you something to make you feel better, just you rest yourself. Here, sit, and put your feet up.' She sat Dickie in her best chair beside the fireplace and pulled a velvet footstool under her feet. She puffed with exertion as she bustled to and fro. 'There,' she said as Dickie lay back, 'now just you rest, and I'll take care of you, poor child.'

For the first time since she had been in New York Dickie felt as if she were coming home. Mrs Tomczak's kindness so soon after the attack broke what reserve she had. She closed her eyes and tried not to think about the effect this would have on her future plans. For the moment she just felt weak and tired and more than anything she wanted to rest and be taken care of.

When she opened her eyes again, Mrs Tomczak had crossed to an old dresser. She was taking a crystal decanter off a round silver tray. There were two on the tray, one of sherry and one of brandy. Mrs Tomczak chose the brandy. She bent to take two glasses from the dresser cupboard beneath.

Her room was furnished like a Victorian parlour. Dickie had never been in there before. As she recovered she looked around. The room was full of dark, heavy furniture, ornately carved. Monstrous palms grew in china pots about the fireplace and beside the small baby-grand piano that sat in the corner. The fireplace was of black iron, and rugs, deep red and patterned, were spread on a dark green carpet. The lace hanging at the windows was intricately woven and heavy. The furniture was lovingly polished to a high shine and the lamps threw a mellow glow over the spotless furnishings. It was not cosy, but it was homely.

'There,' said Mrs Tomczak, returning to her. 'Put this down you.'

She handed her the small tumbler of brandy and parked her ample backside on the stool beside Dickie's feet. 'Now, dear, drink it down.'

Dickie coughed on the first sip. It burned her throat like fire.

'Medicinal, you know,' said Mrs Tomczak. She took some cotton wool from a bowl beside her and placed it on Dickie's forehead. 'A nasty bruise, but the cut will heal.' She pulled Dickie's dark fringe forward. 'There, even the boy will not know. And now,' she said, her hands clutching Dickie's, 'you tell me what happened.'

Dickie related the story. Mrs Tomczak listened as she spoke. She was very fond of the girl: she was strong, never showing her fear or worry, always looking out for the boy, and she worked with a fierce unwavering determination, never missing time or taking a day off. Mrs Tomczak wished she had not already been over-staffed in the café before she met Dickie. She was the sort of employee any employer would wish for. Mrs Tomczak was, in truth, a little in awe of Dickie. She was only twenty-one and yet she had her destiny all mapped out. She had told Mrs Tomczak about the Flying Circus and Mrs Tomczak had kept her eyes and ears open for the girl, hoping. Most girls of her age were getting married or dressing up in flapper dresses and going down to the dancehall to meet young men. Not Dickie. She was always tidy and neat with her white blouses, black skirts and her cloche hat pulled down over her hair as if she wanted to hide rather than show herself off. She was a nice-looking girl if only she'd come out of herself. She only did it for the child, Mrs Tomczak knew that. She would look at the boy as if he were life itself. She had to admit that she had fallen for the serious little thing with her strange ways. That she should have travelled so far from home in pursuit of her goal was astonishing. What was also astonishing was that despite Mrs Tomczak's gentle persuasion, she still felt she knew next to nothing about her young tenant.

Dickie was finishing her story. '. . . and then they took my purse. My dad made it for me. It had all the money I was saving for our future. The future I'd planned for Max and me. Now . . . well,' she turned the glass in her fingers, watching the light catch it. 'I'll just have to wait a little longer, work a little harder.'

'It's a terrible thing, darlink,' said Mrs Tomczak. 'But maybe not so terrible as you think . . .'

Dickie looked at her enquiringly.

'Every cloud has a silver lining, you know what they say,' she teased in her broken English. 'Your silver lining has come!' She leaned forward and tapped Dickie on the arm. 'We have found Gerry Oswald's Flying Circus . . . !'

'You have?' Dickie sat up quickly. 'Where?'

'My sister,' said Mrs Tomczak excitedly. 'When you told me about it I telephoned her and asked her to watch out for it in the paper. Last night while you were out, she called me.' Her brown eyes were alive with her news. 'It's on in Pittsburgh. Or just outside it. That's in the state right alongside us here in New York. To the west.' She took a breath. 'What do you say we go down all together this weekend? You, me and the boy, on the train. We could have lunch. She's got a big family. You and the boy might like to meet them. How about it?'

Her eyes were shining with her news. Dickie felt her own eyes responding. 'Oh, Mrs Tomczak. How can I thank you?' She leaned over and touched her hand holding it in her own. 'This means so much to me. It's my whole reason for being here.'

'I know, darlink, I know.' Mrs Tomczak was touched by Dickie's obvious pleasure. She was gratified to see the first real smile cross Dickie's features. Why, the girl was quite beautiful. She patted Dickie's hand.

'We'll go on the train,' said Mrs Tomczak, patently moved. 'The boy'd like that, wouldn't he?'

The fair. At last. Would Joe be there?

'Max would love it!' she said, her heart lifting. The tragedy of the money would be overcome. All problems could be overcome. One must never be defeated. Mrs Tomczak's gloomy front room was suddenly brighter.

The bell on the shop door tinkled as the door opened. Out on the high street it was dusty and warm already.

Jim Bennett came into the shop and started to shut the door behind him.

Mrs Canter came out of the back room fastening her apron to her waist. 'That's all right, Jim. Leave it open. Let's have a little air in here.'

He left the door and came across to the counter. He looked distraught.

Mrs Canter eyed him. She tied her strings more slowly into their bow. 'You all right, love? Down here early, aren't you? I've only just opened. Nothing wrong, is there?'

Her son, Albert, slunk into the doorway behind her, still eating a piece of bread from his breakfast. He had heard the tone in her voice. He was always waiting on the periphery of village gossip like a vulture. He gathered it silently to himself, a hoarder by nature.

Jim did not see him. He dug into his shopping-bag. 'Oh, not really, Milly. It's just Dickie. I miss her. And I know she still resents me for what I did. Or didn't do,' he muttered half to himself. 'Not helping her. She didn't understand the way things are. The way they've always been. She's that contradictory, she is.'

'Ah, well,' Mrs Canter spread her hands on the counter. 'Now don't you go worrying now she's gone, pet, and imagining all sorts of things. Dickie loves you. She told me before she went to take care of you. She'll forgive you, love, whatever it was. Children do.' Her tone softened. 'She probably already has!'

Jim looked doubtful. In the shadows of the door Albert came

alert. Forgive him for what? He was instantly curious. What had the old man done to Dickie then? He was as interested as the rest of the village as to why she had suddenly taken off. No one left Foxhall Green. They all married either locally or into neighbouring towns and carried on as before. But Dickie had always been a law unto herself. His eyes narrowed. He had never liked her, ever since he had tried to touch her at harvesting time and she had slapped him. Hard. All the boys and girls did it, fooling around in the hay, but not Miss High and Mighty Bennett. More than anything now he was eager to find out what it was.

'It's hard without her, Milly,' Jim said, opening the shopping-bag onto the counter.

'She had to go, Jim. You know that.' Mrs Canter was a sensible woman and fond of Dickie. She understood her, had watched her grow. 'Well as I do,' she added. 'Just like your Elsie, she is. Headstrong. Nothing you can do about that, except accept it. She'll find her way back. Don't you fret. Now, what can I do for you today?' She waited.

Albert moved around the counter, looking the old man up and down. It had to be to do with the child, her son, Max. That's what it was. He pushed his hands into his pockets and came round towards his mother.

'There, lovey.' Mrs Canter smiled warmly at her lanky son. She brushed his hair fondly with the palm of her hand. She saw the thin, stooping frame and the long-nosed face as perfect. She had no idea of the inner workings of her son's mind. 'Sort out the post for me, would you, son,' she said. He passed behind her and picked up the bundle of letters. He cut the string.

Jim looked over at Albert. 'Any for me?' His voice was raised in hope.

'Have a look for Mr Bennett, Albert,' she said. 'It'll be one from abroad he'll be wanting. That's right, isn't it, pet?' she said. Jim nodded. He watched the boy's hands run through the mail.

'Here's one.' He held up the envelope. Turned it over in his hands.

'Well, there we are,' said Milly Canter. 'She's written to you, see. What did I tell you? It's from Dickie.' She handed it across to Jim.

He took it, opened the flap and pulled out the two sheets covered in neat handwriting. He felt the texture of the paper between his fingers, turned it over, stared at the writing, and then looked back at Mrs Canter. 'Read it for us, would you, Milly?'

'Oh, of course,' she said quickly. 'I forgot. She did tell me. Mind if Albert does though, love? I've got the shop to open up. There we are.' She handed the letter to Albert. He took it slowly, avariciously. Held it briefly across the tip of his nose. He smelt no perfume. Still, it was her letter. And he could read it.

'Would you come round the back of the counter, Mr Bennett? 'Spect you'd like it to be private. I'll read it to you in the parlour.'

Jim gathered up his shopping-bag, and went through the wooden door between the counters. He followed Albert into the back room.

Mrs Canter hummed to herself as she went outside to put up the blinds against the heat of the day.

THIRTEEN

It was a perfect day. It had been raining earlier and now it was clearing, a fresh wind cleaning away the staleness of New York, the hot sun striking out, and the blue sky rapidly spreading as the clouds billowed away.

> GERRY OSWALD'S FLYING CIRCUS. THRILLS, SPILLS AND GLAMOUR! GET MARRIED IN THE AIR! DOLLAR A RIDE! SEE 'THE DAREDEVIL DIVER' AND 'THE QUEEN OF THE WINGS'!

As they drove in under the banner that proclaimed the county fair, Dickie held her new hat on her head, her other arm round Max. They bounced over the uneven grass in Mrs Tomczak's sister's new car.

Overhead a small biplane was looping the loop. As they parked the car the plane went into a spin. The crowds, craning their necks, gasped with delight. The pilot brought it swooping low, down over the parked cars and away again, curving up and over in the blue sky. A girl crawled along the fuselage. She stood up, holding on to the struts between the wings. Her dress was pressed to her body by the wind. Suddenly she cried out in fright. She lost her grip and appeared to fall.

The onlookers' hearts beat in excited terror. They had not seen the rope, invisible from the ground, that now pulled her back. High above, the girl crawled back along the fuselage towards the body of the plane.

'What are they called?' Dickie asked, her eyes straining to see and take in every aspect of it.

Mrs Tomczak's sister's husband, a portly Polish man by the name of Kovak, half turned his head to answer her as he parked the car. 'Wing walkers. Flying circuses were the rage. Now it's stunt shows.' He brought the car to a shuddering halt, the engine dying with a splutter.

'They're magnificent,' said Mrs Tomczak.

'Gerry Oswald knows what the public wants!' Mr Kovak took off his hat, and swept his hand over his bald head.

'You know him?' Dickie leaned forward.

'Met him, yes.' Mr Kovak was pleased with all the attention he was getting.

'Huh!' His wife suddenly joined in, a thinner version of her sister. 'You don't know him, you only met him at the gate when he came yesterday.'

Mr Kovak looked embarrassed. Dickie felt sorry for him. She climbed over the seat and out of the car as he held her hand to help her down. She thanked him, and turned to Mrs Tomczak.

'I'm going to look for Joe.'

'All right, darlink.' She waved a hand at Dickie from the other side of the car. She came waddling round, holding Max by the hand. 'You mind if I take the boy with me to the picnic table?'

'No! OK, Max?'

' 'K.' He was already away, drawing Mrs Tomczak along behind him in his wake. She hurried along over the grass, laughing as she went.

Dickie watched them, and then turned, her eyes scanning the crowd. The sun was hot and there was the warm, sweet smell of grass in her nostrils, and the good sound of laughter and people enjoying themselves. At last she was in the country again. She had had no idea how much she had missed it.

In the distance she saw a group of people standing near the nose of a small yellow biplane. She made her way over.

Captain Bill Latimer eased himself out of his Curtiss Jenny. He was the best flyer on the team, an ex-fighter pilot. Like many of his friends back from the battle-skies of the Western Front he was trying to make a living from his new-found skills. With his government-surplus Jenny he toured the country with Gerry Oswald, giving Americans their first taste of flying at a dollar a head. He was one of the growing band of barnstormers who were to be found at every county fair.

'My friend's looking for a fellow who flies with the circus. Perhaps you know him?'

Bill Latimer turned to the sound of the voice. The jolly looking white-haired woman was gazing earnestly at him. She held the hand of a small boy.

Bill wiped his hands on a rag taken from the cockpit. 'What's the name of her friend?'

'Joe,' said Mrs Tomczak. 'Joe O'Rourke.'

Bill's smile faded. He shook his head. 'Well, I have to tell you . . . Joe's dead. He was a crazy guy.' He looked absently at the rag in his hands. 'Always flew his planes too hard. He took one chance too many one day. He didn't make it. I'm sorry for your friend. Did he mean much to her?'

'Oh yes,' said Mrs Tomczak slowly, her eyes going now to look for Dickie's small figure in the crowd. 'A lot . . .' Her voice trailed. Dickie's dreams had led her here to nothing. 'She'll be so disappointed,' she said vaguely. 'How can I tell her . . . ?'

Bill looked into the kind face. He changed his weight to the other leg. 'Look, perhaps I could talk to her? I knew Joe well. Do you want me to?'

'Oh, would you?' She laid a hand on his arm. 'That would be so kind. You could explain more easily than I could.'

'Sure.' He nodded, threw the rag back into the plane. He bent his head slightly. 'Point her out. Which one is she?'

'Um . . . um . . .' Mrs Tomczak's fingers touched her lips. She was short and could not see over the heads of the crowd. She looked across the rough grass, this way and that, and into the groups of people that mingled around the stationary planes, but she could not see Dickie. She lifted her fingers away from her lips and back again. Her brow was creased with consternation. 'I don't see her, but perhaps . . .' Bill waited patiently. She seemed a little eccentric: her long dress festooned with lace insets and the quivering hat perched on her head were twenty years out of date. 'The boy,' she said at last. 'He'll find her for you. This is Max, her son.'

She gave him a little push forward.

Max looked up at the handsome flyer. He admired him instantly. 'I'll take you,' he said.

'OK, fella. You point out your ma to me.'

* * *

Dickie stood alone. She was waiting for the small biplane to come to a stop ahead of her. Maybe the pilot was Joe.

'Mama!'

She turned to the sound of Max's voice. He ran up to her. Behind him came a tall American. He had long legs, and his shirt-sleeves were rolled up to the elbow. His fair hair was short and roughly cut.

She waited, wondering what he was doing with Max.

'Your friend asked me to come and talk to you,' he said. His voice was soft with the drawl of a Midwest rancher. He had a firm mouth, clear eyes and a refined, likeable face. 'I'm afraid I've got bad news.'

'Joe,' she said at once understanding his meaning.

'I'm sorry,' he said kindly, 'Joe was a fine guy.'

'Oh no.' Her eyes looked strained and hurt.

'Did he mean a lot to you?' His eyes looked at her, then down at Max. She followed his gaze. He was looking for a similarity.

'No,' she said, putting out a hand of explanation. 'You don't understand. Joe and I were not . . . sweethearts. I met him in England. He landed his plane near where I live. He was on his way to an airfield. He told me about flying,' she explained, 'and this circus.' She glanced around her at all the milling people. The sun was hot on her face. 'He told me to look him up if I was serious about wanting to fly.' She turned back at him, the curious light green eyes now trained on his. 'I was,' she said with certainty, her look very steady. 'And so I came.'

'You came all this way for that?'

'Yes.'

'Phew.' He ran his fingers across his forehead. 'That's enter-prising.'

'Not a lot of use right now, though. Being enterprising.'

'Well . . .'

They were quiet for a moment.

'Look,' he said. 'I'd like to do something for you. Would you like a free ride?'

She looked up at him, the interest in her face. Her eyes nar-rowed slightly against the light. His hair was very blond, his skin brown from an outdoor life. 'Were you the one flying with the girl just now?'

'Yep.' In the distance Mrs Tomczak hurried towards them,

the lace on her costume fluttering around her like the feathers on a windswept bird. Her small face was wreathed in worry and concern.

'I'd like to do some aerobatics,' said Dickie.

Bill surveyed her. 'I don't do aerobatics with someone who hasn't flown before.'

'I've flown before.'

'Well, OK. If you think you can handle it.'

'I can.'

'Darlink? Are you all right?' Mrs Tomczak was out of breath. Her double chins quivered slightly, and her brown eyes showed sympathy.

'Yes, Mrs Tomczak, I'm fine. Would you mind holding on to Max for a moment? I'm going up flying with . . .'

'Bill Latimer,' he filled in.

'Josephine Bennett. I'm called Dickie.'

'OK, Dickie, but that's going to cost you. Aerobatics don't come cheap. Twenty dollars is the price.'

It was as much as she had left in her bag. Her chin lifted. 'That's all right,' she said.

'OK then, let's go.'

Mrs Tomczak looked from one to the other. She had expected to find Dickie inconsolable. It showed how little she knew her. As Mrs Tomczak stood with Max, waving frantically, Dickie followed the young man off across the grass towards his plane.

'My mama's going to fly, Mrs Tomczak.'

'Yes, dear.' She held his hand. 'Your mama's quite a girl.'

She climbed straight into the seat. There was no coyness or hesitation about her. Bill climbed in. Now they would see what she was really made of.

As Dickie clung on for her life the barnstormer put the Jenny through its paces. For most it would have been a terrifying experience but for Dickie the thrill was unforgettable, the sense of freedom exquisite. She did not seem to care about the danger. The dips and dives and loops freed her from the humdrum of her life, the blue sky topsy-turvy all around her was where she wanted to be. Only she wanted to be in control. The plane felt right to her, second time round. The wind in her face cleansed all the past from her, filling her with the novelty and possibilities of the future. Down below, the dotted and colourful crowd spun by, pale orbs of faces staring upwards. Up here she was free and alive, not tied to the ground. Every stunt he performed shook the hidden emotion in her and brought it to the surface.

By the time he brought the small craft down again her face was transformed with exhilaration. She stepped from the machine a different girl.

Dickie pulled off her helmet and shook her hair free. From behind, the sun shone on the crisp new bob, a dark cap of shining hair lit with red summer lights, the small face now thrown into shadow. Bill looked at her a second time. Her face was striking, and her head was held a little higher now as she had gained confidence. The bold eyes lifted to his, revealing their luminous quality, so startling in an otherwise merely pretty face. She was smiling broadly as she greeted the little boy who ran towards her. Bill watched the scene and stood quietly, pursing his lips slowly in thought.

Dickie let the boy down. She took her purse from Mrs Tomczak.

'I owe you twenty dollars and my thanks, Mr Latimer.'

'Bill. And you can have it free. Because you're a friend of Joe's,' he added, 'and because you've gotta have something going for you to come all this way, and . . .' He forgot what the third thing might be. 'I'll see you around.'

She held the bag in her hand. Her smile was still in her eyes. 'There's one other thing I'd like though, Bill.'

Bill was turning away, going back to work.

'What?'

'Could I meet Mr Oswald? Would you introduce me?'

He paused a moment. 'OK. Come along. You too, Max. I'm just going over there myself.'

Gerry Oswald was a showman. He stood almost as tall as Bill, about six foot, though not so rangy. He was broadshouldered and muscular, and he wore a ten-gallon hat and a wide smile. His checked shirt was open at the neck, and he wore country-boy overalls, but there was nothing country boy about Gerry Oswald. He was an operator.

He cast his eyes over Dickie as he was introduced and gave her the benefit of his grin. He even bent to shake hands with Max, and surreptitiously palmed him a piece of gum. Max's eyes were huge and pleased. Gerry roared with delight. He liked children, too.

Dickie took in the big man and decided she would come

straight to the point, the decision she had made when she had come down from her ride with Bill.

'Mr Oswald. Do you have a job for me?' The group around her fell silent at her words. Max chewed his gum and stared upwards at his mother. 'Anything would do,' she went on. 'Just as long as it's with aeroplanes. I used to work on a farm. I can mend anything from a sewing-machine to a harvester. I'm strong and I'm willing to learn.'

Gerry Oswald's smile faded slightly. He had met a score of bright-eyed young things at every show, hunting for a job with the circus. He turned them all down. She was no exception. He picked his smile up again.

'Well, little lady, I can't say that you're not forthright, but'm sorry . . .' He shook his big head, 'Ah'm just not open to hire anybody right now. I dare say there are plenty of jobs in town if you're looking for a job in the area, but not with the circus. We got all we need. And more. I'm sorry, sweetheart. Perhaps next time we're back, huh?'

Dickie gave a quick nod. 'Thank you, anyway.'

'Sure, honey. Stick around and watch the show.' He lifted his arms to them. 'Have fun, now.' He turned away to greet another group.

'Don't be too upset, Dickie.' Bill was standing beside her. 'If I'd known you were going to do that, I'd have warned you. He absolutely never takes on anyone at a show. It's a house rule.' His smile was kind. 'It's been nice knowing you. You too, Max.'

' 'Bye, sir.'

' 'Bye. I gotta get ready for the Daredevil Diver. Stay and watch. It's a parachute jump.'

He moved away across the grass. Dickie watched him go. Mrs Tomczak stood beside her, sensing her dejection. 'Never mind. You know what they say, darlink. Never be disappointed. Fate has something else in mind for you, you just don't know what it is yet.' Dickie smiled at yet another of Mrs Tomczak's homespun adages.

'I'm not disappointed, Mrs Tomczak. I'll find a way.'

The day went on with spectacular flying displays. Dickie joined Mrs Tomczak and her family at a small table for tea. She passed a plate of sandwiches to Max, nose high at the table. He took one.

The loudspeaker blared out. '. . . and the parachuting display has been cancelled. Unfortunately, our Daredevil Diver, Chuck, was injured on his last jump. He's OK, but we gotta say sorry, folks, no more parachuting today . . .'

Dickie paused, her sandwich half-way to her mouth. She put it back on the plate.

'Excuse me,' she said.

She pushed back her chair and walked, started to half run, looking for the burly frame of Gerry Oswald. She saw him in heated conversation over by the guy-ropes of a tent. He was gesticulating wildly and pointing a stubby finger at the man's leg. The other man bent down and rubbed the joint. A third man was kneeling on the grass. He tried the leg, straightening and bending it. He shook his head. Bill Latimer was approaching them across the grass.

Dickie went quickly towards them. The three men turned to look at her.

'Now, Mr Oswald,' she said. 'You need someone to do that jump. How about me?' It was a dangerous gamble but worth it if it led to a job in aviation. 'I can do it,' she insisted. 'I don't want any pay. Just give me a chance,' she pleaded with the astonished man.

Gerry Oswald looked at her. He saw her now as a possibility. Pretty, petite, determined and courageous; a great body underneath the loose dress. He saw something of what Bill had seen earlier, but in a different vein. Still he shook his head. Beside him, Bill Latimer looked aghast. He did not want the girl to do it.

'I don't know,' said Gerry slowly. 'I don't know . . .'

'You need somebody. Look, the crowd are disappointed. Maybe some of them will go home.' Indeed, a small number were already filtering out through the gates. The parachute event was one of the highlights of mid-afternoon. Gerry had spaced his events evenly and cleverly over the day. The girl was right. It was a bad time to lose them. 'I've done it before,' she lied as she saw him waver.

Bill chipped in. 'You can't let her, Gerry. You don't know how much experience she's had. Wing-walking's dangerous enough, but parachuting . . . It's crazy. You'd be risking her life.' His voice had grown stronger as he spoke. Dickie threw him a warning look.

But her words and the argument had suddenly appealed to Gerry Oswald. 'OK,' he said. 'You're on.' He signalled a man standing over by a trestle table, the loudhailer resting on the surface in front of him. 'Larry,' he shouted. 'Get 'em back,' he said, referring to the small groups heading for the exit. 'Make an announcement. We got a new parachutist, a girl. Jumping for the first time ever . . .'

The man turned away. 'Ladies and gentlemen,' the loudhailer echoed across the field, 'only at Gerry Oswald's Flying Circus do you get a first! A young lady will now take on the terrifying leap from an airborne plane for the first time . . . !'

Ten minutes later she was climbing into the passenger seat of Bill Latimer's Curtiss Jenny once again. He was protesting mightily, but to no avail. Oswald was indeed a commercial man and the girl was just right, the sort that became a favourite with the crowds. If she worked out, they would all benefit. Chuck Bailey, the Daredevil Diver, helped her don the parachute and briefed her on how to pull the ripcord.

'Don't forget,' he said. 'Count to three before you pull on the release ring.'

Bill took them up to two thousand feet, then throttled back. Dickie clambered to the edge of the cockpit, her hands braced to take her weight. The wind streamed into her face. She looked down. It was now or never. She held her breath.

Then she jumped as though she had done it all her life.

FOURTEEN

Late summer, 1920

Frederick reined his horse in under the tree.

'It's such a beautiful spot, Frederick. You should be proud to own such an estate.'

Katherine Haslett smiled at him. She was a good deal older than Frederick and the wife of one Sir Henry Haslett. They were family friends of the Redfields, but with a smaller estate, Menderley, just outside the boundaries of the adjoining village. Katherine had long been a keen horsewoman, and she had found a willing riding partner in the younger, and to her by far the more handsome, of the two Redfield brothers.

Frederick agreed. They gazed out over the river Thames and over to the flat meadow lands beyond. The summer sun was warm and the cows munched lazily in the field. Ducks swam on the water, butterflies darted over the banks and a kingfisher sat on the branch of a tree downstream. So much had happened here. He looked up to the lawns of Foxhall, the stone maiden that he had so often admired, bending her head as she poured from her jug. The stone maiden, her body the perfect woman's body. He had always been an aesthete, a lover of beauty, human or otherwise. He had put most of his soul into poetry and books and the beauty of the land, and of course his care of Caroline's children. The family had returned, and Rupert had gone to Scotland grouse-shooting. Rupert had left the army, decorated for his role in the Battle of the Somme. He was a hero of sorts, and popular in London. He vastly preferred the glittering social life

and Caroline preferred the country. Frederick had become sur-
rogate father, a role that pleased him. No woman as yet figured
in his life. He was happy in other ways, and Caroline's presence
filled him with spiritual joy. He would walk around the gardens
with her or take the children round the farm. Soon though, that
would change.

Katherine seemed to read his thoughts.

'Where are the children today?'

'With the governess. Caroline was worried about them not
learning enough before Rupert returned. He's coming back from
London this weekend. The hunting season'll be starting soon. I
imagine he wants to get in a bit of practice.' He rubbed his
horse's rough mane. 'She's worried that he's going to be hard
on them.'

'How do the children feel about Rupert?'

Frederick turned his horse's head and they rode along the
riverbank together. 'I think Charles is a strong little fellow, but
Jessamy's like her mother. Sensitive and easily hurt. But Rupert
adores her. It's just as well. He could easily damage her,' he
said, his thoughts going to Caroline. She had returned from
London, the sparkle gone from her. She was withdrawn again.
He thought of his god-daughter, Jessamy. She was only four,
but even more fragile than Caroline. 'Do you know,' he said
proudly, 'she drew the most beautiful picture for him. I told her
how lovely it was. I only hope he tells her the same.'

'The atmosphere is not the same, though, when Rupert re-
turns,' she said, regarding him with understanding eyes. 'You're
the reason those children are so happy, Frederick. And Caroline, she seems to be off in her own little world, beyond the
reach of us poor ordinary mortals. I cannot imagine being married to your brother,' she added.

'Why?' He looked over at her. 'Has he upset you somehow?'

She smiled wryly. 'Not exactly. But he loves women too
much. Do you know, he even approached me!'

Frederick looked more closely at her. He could see why Rupert might. She was a strong and elegant woman, striking in her
dark riding-habit, the froth of lace at her throat and the dark hair
scraped back with only a trace of silver at the temples. She had
a fine figure and yet she was the mother of three children. Katherine was in her thirties, a sensual time for a woman. She had a
wide generous mouth and warm brown eyes that rested gently
on him as she spoke.

'I can see why, Katherine,' he said at last. 'You're a very beautiful woman.'

Her eyes sparkled. 'Do you think so, Frederick?'

'I do. I always have. Henry's a very lucky man. You're like a girl of twenty. You're one of those women who will never grow old.'

Her smile held but something deepened in her eyes. The horse picked its way along the track and the sun drew behind a cloud and threw her face into shadow under the trees.

'You're a good man, Frederick,' she said. Her voice was lower. 'Why have you never married?'

'I still may,' he said. 'I'm only twenty-six. And, then again, maybe I've just loved the wrong women. The ones I could not have.'

'Maybe you haven't seen the ones who want you.'

'Perhaps you're right. It's not something I look for.'

'Not like Rupert.'

'No.'

They were very different, she thought. Frederick so like his father, Alexander, kind and caring. Just like the children and their mother that he felt so protective towards. Katherine wondered if the woman he loved could be her and if that was part of it. Her feminine intuition told her it had to be Caroline.

She looked over towards the wood.

'Let's go home through Cobbold's Wood. I've had enough riding for one day, haven't you? It's far too hot, and it'll be cool in there. Doesn't the stream run through it?'

'Yes, it does.' He was hesitant.

Katherine turned her horse's head. 'Come on, then. I'll race you.' With a laugh she dug her heels into the horse's flanks and the big chestnut leaped forward. Frederick had no choice but to follow.

It *was* cool in the woods. And quiet. Frederick did not remember it being so quiet. He did not avoid the woods necessarily but he could never enter without remembering her cries, the sun streaming through on her face, those underwater eyes. And she had never screamed or fought him; she had just lain there, accusing. He felt so ashamed. He thought of her face when she had asked him for the money and wondered what had happened to her in America. He remembered everything. So clearly.

Katherine rode remorselessly on towards the centre of the

wood. The summer sun found entry and poured down in shafts of brilliant light. The foliage was lustrous and green and the leaves high above were glittering pale green and diaphanous, making a leafy temple for the soft mossy floor of the wood. It was dappled with sunlight on the green ferns and shadowy and dark on the brown carpet of fallen acorns and tiny twigs. The horses' hooves softly moved across. They reached the stream. It was silvery and cool, idling over the shiny stones.

'Oh, what a pity,' she said. 'I expected to find a rushing brook. I forgot in summer how low it gets. Still, I think it's pretty, don't you?'

Frederick drew alongside. His thigh brushed hers. He was aware of her now. She was sending him signals, and it was like electricity. The brown eyes were smoky, and she smiled at him.

'Help me down, Frederick. I'd like to feel the water.'

She put out her arms for him.

Frederick dismounted, tied up his horse and came for her. He lifted his arms and she came down into them. Her body was slight as a girl's as it slid through his arms and down to the ground. Her face looked up at him. He could smell her perfume and she did not move away. Her breasts touched his waist and she only just reached his chest in height. He had never fully realised how tiny she was.

Just as he was beginning to feel uncomfortable, she took her hands from his arms. She gave him one last deep look and turned away. She wandered over to the stream and sat down, bending forward to touch the water.

'Oh, isn't it lovely?' She looked up at him, and patted the bank beside her. 'Join me, Frederick,' she said. 'When I was a girl I would have taken off my stockings and paddled in this stream to cool my toes. What do you think? Should I now?' she teased. She started to take off her bowler hat and unpin the net that held her dark hair. She wore it unfashionably long and it tumbled glossy and rich to her shoulders. 'Well?' she asked again against his silence.

In the dappled wood she was a splendid sight, her face dusky and glowing.

'If you want to,' he whispered.

'I want to.' Her eyes held his.

'Katherine . . .' He moved closer, and bent on one knee before her. 'There's something I have to tell you. I need to tell someone. Will you listen?'

Her sensual expression immediately changed to one of concern. 'Of course. I'd be happy to. Tell me.'

He sat down slowly beside her. 'It happened when I was nineteen. Here in this wood,' he said, lifting his hand. He drew his knees up and looped his arms around them. 'I was out hunting with Rupert . . .'

She listened as he told the story. Her eyes watched the ripples of water glissading over the stones in the stream. She felt the warmth of the sun as the wind lifted the leaves of the tall trees and the sun's hot rays broke through and touched her back. She heard Frederick's voice tell the story, slowly and in a low monotone as though it was something he had heard, not done. She knew he was not the man to have instigated such a thing. She was not shocked, more sorry for him, sorry for the guilt that had embraced him all of these years, sorry for the innocence of the girl who had confronted Rupert and paid the penalty.

'I don't know why I did it,' he said. 'Except that Rupert led it, and somehow she did too by challenging him. I don't know how, but suddenly it was all happening. She was running and we were chasing. We were up for the hunt, you see, and so chase was in the air.' His eyes held some distant point ahead of him as he spoke, lancing the wound. 'It was when I saw her, lying in that glade, not so far from here.' He half turned but did not look round. 'And Rupert taunted me with her. I hardly heard him, but, you know, Rupert makes things happen. He has that power. Oh, I'm not blaming him. It was entirely my fault. She looked so lovely,' he said, his voice trailing softly as he recalled her lying in that patch of sunlight, spread out before him. He knew then that he'd seen her before in the village and felt something. Their eyes had met on one occasion before she had ducked into the village shop. It was only now that he remembered that as he spoke of it. His voice was slow as the memory patched itself into his consciousness. 'I thought maybe she did want me,' he said. 'She didn't stir or run away. I couldn't help myself.' His words brought it alive.

'Maybe she did. Want you.'

'No. She didn't. I'm sure of that. Not that way . . .'

'But perhaps there was something there . . .'

'Perhaps . . .' He drifted in wonder. Perhaps that was right. No. He dismissed it. 'No. It was my fantasy. She was like the stone maiden in the garden, her body was quite, quite beautiful. I'd always loved that statue all my life. To see the same lines there—for me. And I *am* a hunter. I couldn't stop myself. It seemed . . . inevitable,' he said, lifting his hands heavily, his face dropped as he looked down. 'She didn't scream, she didn't fight. If only she had. I would have stopped, but she didn't.'

'Almost as if she wanted it?'

'No. I think now, looking back, that she was probably terrified, and simply could not move.' He sighed deeply with his admission.

Katherine leaned on one arm, her eyes taking him in. She knew the stone maiden he spoke of. Her body was like that, too, small and boyish. Katherine was a kind woman, and a wise one. She tried to sense what had happened that day, and also to alleviate Frederick's suffering. If he could see things differently, perhaps she could help to strengthen him. Frederick seemed so under his brother's influence. Katherine understood. She knew all too well the compelling and competitive power of a man like Rupert. Her husband, Henry, was similar. They had a firm belief in their rights as ancestral landowners—their feudal dues. She knew how very charming they could be, and yet so cruel on the other hand. She imagined how it had been for Frederick, being as sensitive as he was and Rupert's younger brother. She stretched out her hand, but stopped just short of his, her fingers brushing against the soil.

'Where is the girl now?'

'She worked on the land during the war. I allowed it because Rupert was away. And her brother had died. Her father asked me, and I agreed. I avoided the areas where she was working,' he said, shamefaced. He too put his hand down and started to pick at the twigs and acorns on the ground between his spread knees. 'I couldn't chance meeting her face to face. And now. Now I know she has a child.'

Katherine felt her heart catch. She took a quick breath. 'Yours?' Her eyes flew towards him.

He gave a short laugh. 'I doubt it,' he said self-deprecatingly. He remembered his all-too-brief performance. 'It's a boy. I found out in the village. I saw him once. Dark, sturdy, strong blue eyes. Rupert's eyes.' Rupert's son would be bold and strong as he was. It was Rupert's child, he had known it before he had seen the boy at all. 'I'm sure it's his,' he finished.

'Frederick . . . Can I do anything? Go and see her? Offer her help? That way you aren't committed either way, you don't have to admit any possibilities. I could go as a neutral party. Just give her some money, perhaps.'

He turned to her, a gentle smile on his mouth, though his dark blue eyes were still hurting. 'You don't know how good it is to hear you being so understanding, Katherine,' he said, taking her hand quite naturally, without fully realising it. 'But . . . I've already given her money. She came to my study, and asked for money, five hundred pounds . . .'

Katherine's eyes flew open. Her hand she kept warmly imprisoned in his. 'That's a frightful amount of money for a village girl.'

'. . . to go to America,' he said.

'Did she go?'

'Apparently. She made me promise not to turn her father out. I gave her that promise, but I don't know what Rupert's going to say when he finds out.'

'Well, it won't matter if he does,' she said. 'Not if you promised.'

'Oh, it will!' Frederick's mouth tightened in a rueful smile. 'Once Rupert knows it. That's the day I'm not looking forward to.' He shook his head. He picked at the knee of his trouser-leg. 'I didn't know what I was doing. I was so young. So easily led. I hardly knew. When she came to my room, I wanted to say something, to apologise. Even then I didn't know what to say,' he said, lifting his shoulders helplessly. 'What could I say . . . ? Sorry I raped you six years ago . . . ? Excuse me, Katherine,' he said swiftly, 'I didn't mean to offend you.'

She squeezed his hand. 'Don't apologise, I've heard worse from Henry. And, speaking of Henry, you know he wouldn't see what the fuss was all about. Like Rupert, he believes in the old feudal system where men take what belongs to them and that includes every available woman, *especially* those working on his family's land. I know it's wrong, but the girl didn't stand a chance. Not once she provoked Rupert by telling him to get off *her* land, and then challenging him with this bold look you say she has. I can see how it happened. And how you were pulled into it. And I might say how easily excited you must have been. A voyeuristic thrill is often a very strong one,' she said, her voice quite low as she spoke. 'You weren't truly to blame, Frederick. You were wrong, but . . . sometimes we are in youth.' Her voice was very soft, her eyes on his profile unmoving as they studied his handsome face. 'It's over now,' she said. 'She's gone. You must forget it.' Her nostrils flared. She lay back on her arm. 'Frederick . . . ?'

He turned at the note in her voice. Her eyes were dark.

'*I* am willing . . .'

Her eyes locked with his, the dawn of comprehension in his own building as he realised what she meant. She reached up then, and touched his face. She let her fingers trail down his neck to his shoulder and pulled him gently. Slowly he lay down alongside her. The stream rushed gently at their feet. His hands touched her body, long, sensitive fingers that knew just how to touch a woman. The Redfield touch. *There* was his power.

Katherine had sensed how good it would be. As he undressed her against the brushing of the wind in the trees, he was silent. The wood was silent too. The water licked over the stones, slapping slightly against them; the wind rushed again, way overhead and all around them. He was so slow, taking his time in wonder at her. Katherine closed her eyes, feeling the sun in her hair, and the sensations stealing over her. Her skin was bared to the breeze and his mouth touched her breast and she cried out with the thrill of it. Frederick was unhurried and loving. Katherine's head tipped back against the earth, her long hair catching the acorns and slivers of wood as she turned her head to and fro, her sighs of joy filling the air.

The sun burned his back. He smelled the warmth in her hair. The pleasure harnessed him to her. He cried out as he neared the end and his eyes squeezed tight as the feelings burst through him, exploding to all his nerve ends. He held her smooth, white shoulders in his hands beneath him. He looked down into her face as he was released and through the haze as the blood pounded in his temples, he saw the underwater eyes again. This time they were hazy and loving. The girl forgave him.

He fell back to her, his lips against her throat. 'Forgive me,' he said echoing the past. 'I need you. Don't leave me.'

'I won't leave you,' Katherine said softly. She cupped his head in her hands and stroked the thick fair hair. 'I'll be there when you need me.'

When Dickie and Bill returned to the ground it was a very different man who greeted them. Gerry Oswald was standing waiting out on the field. He called her over to him as Bill paused to talk to one of the engineers.

'I can see it already,' he said. He spread his hands wide as if pulling open a banner. 'The Sweetheart of the Skies.'

Mrs Tomczak bustled up in his wake. Her round face was pink and wreathed in excitement. 'I was so scared, it was wonderful, darlink, just wonderful. If I'd been twenty years younger I'd have been just like you.'

Dickie pulled off the straps. She bent to lift Max from the ground. 'And what did you think about it all, partner?'

'I want to fly too, Mama.'

'You will, darling, as soon as I have learned. Mr Oswald,' she said, turning to him, 'Do I have a job?'

'After that?' The big man laughed aloud. 'I'd be crazy not to hire you. The crowd went wild. You carry on like that, we'll have you wing-walking too. In a flimsy dress out on that wing, wind blowing. You'll be perfect. Start right away if you want. We're here for the summer season. What do you say?'

'How much?'

'Fifty dollars a week. How's that sound?'

Fifty dollars! She remembered what Joe had said. She would need her own plane. Her money had gone. She needed three hundred dollars. She would have it by the end of the year if she was careful.

'Yes,' she said. 'That sounds about right.'

'Sounds about right!' Gerry Oswald swayed in his mirth. 'You hear that?' He addressed those around them. Bill climbed out of his plane and started to walk towards them, pulling off his helmet. He tucked his gloves inside. 'That's a king's ransom, hereabouts, little lady,' said the showman. 'You oughta be grateful.'

'It is a good deal,' she said carefully. 'But I'm sure you pay only what the job's worth, Mr Oswald.' Her voice was steady.

He eyed her speculatively. 'You're damn right about that! OK, now we'd better get you fitted out with some suitable outfits for your initiation. Get some posters made.'

'Can I learn to fly?' she asked.

'Learn to fly,' he repeated. 'It's expensive. Five hundred dollars for ten lessons.' He saw Bill walking towards them. 'Bill!' he shouted. 'We're signing her up!'

Five hundred dollars. One lesson a week and her money would be gone. And what about the price of the Jenny? She would need a place to live and food and clothes and schooling for Max, money for her dad. It would be a long time before she was on her own.

Gerry Oswald walked over to greet Bill. He threw his arm around the pilot's shoulders and walked away with him, outlining his plans. He could already see the billboards. She was fearless as well as being so pretty. She had proved that already. In America all was possible if you had determination and guts.

Albert Canter waited for the mail each day. When the letter finally came he was filled with an uncontrollable urge to open it. He looked around quickly for his mother, and put the letter in his jacket for later.

Up by the old well at lunchtime he opened it. The money fell out onto his lap. He picked it up very slowly and studied it. He held it in his hand as he scanned the pages. Nothing, no clue to that secret, but things were going hard for her in New York. It served her right. She thought she was too pretty and too smart for him. Well, he would see who was smarter. He would take her money. She'd never be back. He crumpled up the letter and threw it into the well, put the money in his pocket and headed for the pub.

FIFTEEN

Early autumn, 1921

The candlelight was soft and pure in the chancel, the cloth of white and gold an altar of sacrifice to God. Rupert left his place in the choirstalls and crossed the red carpet towards the altar. Around him the choir sang their aria, and behind him a packed congregation bent their knees in unison and bowed their heads to God.

He reached the altar and inclined his head. Lifting his cassock from the ground, he stepped up and then knelt down himself. The choir sang sweetly. And now he was God's messenger. The bishop had trained him to convey the message of the scriptures, to instil faith into the people of Foxhall Green, through his messenger, Rupert Redfield. In Rupert he had seen the power, the charisma of a man born to lead, an orator, the resonance of whose voice would sway a crowd to follow him.

Rupert stood and slowly returned towards his flock. The heads were still bent as he approached them; he felt his long robes undulating against him. Once again he bowed to the cross and climbed the stairs to the pulpit. The choir sang to the end of their aria as he stood there, gazing down upon the assembled crowd below. Who was in the church? Who had dared to stay at home?

The choir singing came to a close.

'I am Alpha and Omega, the beginning and the end, the first and the last. Blessed are they that do His commandments, that

167

they may have right to the tree of life and may enter in through the gates into the city . . .'

Rupert's voice rang through the church.

'For without are dogs, and sorcerers, and whoremongers, and murderers, and idolaters, and whosoever loveth and maketh a lie, I, Jesus, have sent mine angel to testify unto you these things in the churches. I am the root and the offspring of David, and the bright and morning star. And the Spirit and the bride say, Come.' He paused, his hands braced on the carved wood of the pulpit. His blue eyes raked across the faces of the people beneath, strong blue eyes that pierced into their souls and knew their innermost secrets and their guilt; eyes as blue as the cloth that was draped around his neck. His voice softened, but lost none of its resonance. 'And let him that heareth say, Come . . .' He bewitched them, seduced them with his words. '. . . And let him that is thirsty come.' He looked around him. He paused and watched them. He was in total control of them. They were his to do with as he wished, his to command. 'And whosoever will, let him take the water of life freely . . .' His voice trailed to silence.

There was a hush in the church. He paused again. There was not a sound. The church was waiting, cool and beautiful. Everything here was purity and power. And Rupert was an actor, desiring that power over people.

'I say unto you, good people,' he whispered, 'God says, Come . . . and when God says come, will you obey? Will you partake of the waters of life without price?' His blue eyes flashed. 'Or are you sinners, all of you? And do you dare not, because you are sinners? Show me a man who says he has not sinned, and I will show you a man who is a liar!'

In the front row they shrank back. They knew now that Rupert Redfield knew they had lied, knew what they had done last week, knew what they were thinking now. None of them had any secrets from him. The men tried to keep their eyes on him to show they had no fear. The women shivered inwardly and tried to look pious and yet not too pious, a hard combination to achieve. He was so very handsome, and he wore his vestments so very well.

'We are all sinners, every one of us, every man, woman and child. Don't be afraid. I am too,' he confided. 'But together we can fight the devil. We can be brothers in the praise of our Lord, and love each other . . . I will help you . . . You can turn to me at any time to give you strength . . . but don't think you can sin and He will not know . . . He has sent me as His messenger to say: "The Lord is watching you" . . . He knows. It's no good just to come here and be seen in church, and then think that everybody knows you as a Christian. Do you then go home and sin and think He is not watching you . . . ?'

In the front rows they cowered and wished they had not wanted it to be so apparent that they were in church. They felt that his words were beamed directly at them. They tried not to look guilty.

Rupert rained wrath upon them from the pulpit. He was evangelistic. He roared at them, and then seduced them softly, till they did not know whether they were coming or going, only that he was going to lead them.

'He is a cruel God and a jealous God.' The blue eyes flashed with fervour. 'But He loves you . . .' His words scored the hearts and minds of the rapt villagers.

They believed every word he said, they believed in him. They longed for the moment when they would leave church and shake his hand, come into that aura for a moment and let him see they were his; they had been there.

They clung to every word of his sermon. Until the final words. 'And now to God the Father, God the Son, God the Holy Ghost . . .'

They felt an emptiness, a pouring out of themselves as he turned from them. They wanted those burning eyes on them again, charging them with hellfire and damnation. They *wanted* to shiver with fear.

The bishop had been right. Rupert had them in the palm of his hand.

A line of oaks shadowed the park. Beyond in the sunlight the cows grazed in the meadow in the early morning.

Frederick came out of the cowshed. He closed the door behind him and latched it. He picked up a pail and walked back across the cobbled yard that had been swilled down with water.

There was something very therapeutic about farming, working with the soil, the actual manual labour. He liked to get up early, hearing the milk train puffing away from Foxhall Green station. He would put on old clothes, a soft shirt and loose trousers and go downstairs while the house was sleeping. He would pull on his wellingtons and clump down the drive to the fields, cutting through the stables. At this hour of the day the air was so fresh it was invigorating. Frederick would see the cows in, milk them before they were taken back to the field, and muck out the yard afterwards. There was no need for him to be so involved but he found he enjoyed it, being in touch with the whole thing.

He was absorbed in his thoughts and so did not notice Rupert immediately. The morning was still crisp and cool, the grass wet. He had not expected to see his brother.

Rupert was standing at the stable door. He was dressed for a ride.

'Rupert!' His tone was one of surprise. 'I didn't expect to see you up this early.' He was pleased. 'Decided to keep farming hours?'

Rupert leaned his elbows on the door. He raised an eyebrow and surveyed his brother, the mud-stained boots and open-necked shirt, the tweed cap pulled onto his fair hair.

'Thought I'd take Perryman out early. Like I used to.' Frederick nodded. 'I wanted to talk to you, though.' He straightened up. 'Now's as good a time as any. How is the estate?'

'Well, we're all right,' said Frederick. 'But many farms are finding things hard this year. The endless wet weather's turned the harvest into a nightmare.' He put the pail down on the ground. 'The men have been working from dawn to dusk to save the crops, and we're still nearly a month behind. Normally we expect to finish by the end of August and then start planting for next year.' Foxhall had three hundred acres, most of it put down to crops. Only sixty acres had been harvested so far, leaving them way behind schedule.

Rupert frowned. 'It's sunny now. What's the forecast?'

'Wet.' Frederick grimaced. 'The main problem we have is just getting the wheat off the field. At the moment it's down on the ground, flattened by the rain and lying in water. The wetter it is, the worse are our problems.' He looked up at the sky. 'If we could just have a week or ten days of this weather, we'd be able to save some.'

'How's it going to affect us financially?' He started to walk towards the fence, looking out over the fields. Frederick kept pace with him.

'Oh, we will survive, because our farming interests are well structured. With the beef cattle, we'll be able to make up some of the difference.' They reached the fence. He pointed over to the far fields and the rain-sodden wheat. 'In a good year we could expect a few hundred tons. We'll probably lose a quarter of our crop this year. And get a few quid a ton less for the remainder. There aren't too many smiling faces around, I can tell you.'

Rupert placed his hand on the fence post. He stared across the rain-soaked fields. 'We need to cut corners, I can see that. Which brings me to another point. I want to make some changes to Foxhall. Perhaps we should sell off some of the land to drum up a bit of money.'

Frederick stared at his brother, 'Changes to Foxhall? Whatever do you mean, Rupert?'

Rupert's look was indecipherable. 'Conversion. I plan to convert the old stables, the coachhouse and the barn. Perhaps take on one of the farm cottages too.' He looked directly at Frederick. 'If we cut down on land we don't need so many employees. Perhaps one farming family with a tied cottage. One's enough, don't you think? Especially now you're mucking in so well, Frederick.'

Frederick could not believe it. To change Foxhall. And did he already know about Jim Bennett? Was this his way of saying it?

'Yes,' said Rupert. 'It's so hard to get good servants since the war,' Rupert went on, 'They've all run off to offices and factories. They want more money. They have to be tempted now by easy-to-run houses. That's why I thought I'd modernise Foxhall. Sell off some of the property, a couple of farms, and cottages in the village perhaps, and we'd have more in our pocket. I thought of improving the gardens too. I've already engaged the architect, Sir Edwin Lutyens. He originally saved this place from ruin for Father. I've asked him to add a new wing. He's a brilliant man. You'll hardly notice the difference.'

'Rupert. You amaze me. You just announce that this will be done. Have you not taken into consideration that I might disagree?' He spread his hands wide.

Rupert thrust his own hands into his pockets. His eyes narrowed. He did not like to be thwarted. 'Forgive me, Frederick, but I thought Foxhall was now mine.'

Frederick's eyes went cold as he stared at his brother. 'It is yours, yes.'

'Then.'

'Rupert, I wrote Foxhall over to you because it was rightfully yours and would have been yours under the terms of Father's will. I did not mean for you to run roughshod over my feelings, or those of Caroline for that matter. Don't you think you should consider our attitudes, as I considered yours at the time? Foxhall is mine too, admittedly in spirit. I don't want to see it changed, for God's sake.' His eyes were angry.

Rupert clicked his tongue and smiled. 'Freddie . . . Freddie!' He touched him patronisingly on the shoulder. 'Did I ever say I wouldn't consider you? It's you I'm considering!' He stood back. 'You want to farm, but look what's happening!' He pointed out to the fields. 'You've as good as told me that it's uneconomical this year. If we just keep some of the land, it'll be enough to interest you, won't it, Freddie? And adding to the house, well, it only adds to the value.'

'I don't want to let any of the land go, Rupert. It's all part of Foxhall,' he argued.

'Not even if it's best for the family?'

'I don't think it is,' he argued.

'Well, Caroline wants it.'

'Caroline does?'

'Yes.'

Frederick said nothing.

Rupert gave him a long look. He moved away. 'I'm going up to the house. You coming? We can finish this conversation on the way.'

Frederick felt the seed of regret germinate in him at the thought that he had indeed written Foxhall over to Rupert. It was rightfully and completely his, as it always would have been. He did not have to consult Frederick, as he was doing, at all, if he did not want to. Maybe they could reach a compromise.

'Why do you want to add to the house?' he asked as they walked up the cobbled yard together.

Rupert shrugged. 'We could house guests there more easily.' Frederick gave him a quick look. Was he planning to bring all his social crowd down from London? 'And the other thing I thought was that as the children grow, the extra quarters will be perfect for them to live in. I'd like the family to be together under one roof, so to speak,' he explained as they came out of the yard and crossed the lawn that led up to the house. 'My theory was that we should all meet at least once a day. I want a big family around me,' he said, persuasively. 'Meeting up perhaps once a day at dinner will ensure that we all stay together. That's all I'm aiming for. Keeping the family here at Foxhall.' His voice was hypnotic, lulling Frederick's fears.

'Children often want to leave home,' he tried.

'Of course,' Rupert agreed. 'If they were under one roof in the main house, but not if it's part of their inheritance. The new houses will be theirs. That'll encourage them to stay. I don't want a dispersed family. The strength of a family is through unity, and that's how I mean it to be.'

'And until they're grown up?' They crossed the gravel to the front door.

'Until then, the new buildings will be for our guests.'

'I don't know, Rupert. You may be wrong. I know Charles, he's a pretty independent boy. I don't think he'll be staying at Foxhall when he grows up.'

Rupert turned towards him, his eyes colder. Frederick regretted bringing Charles into it. Rupert might have been one for family unity, but within the family he was a hard father, especially with his son. 'They're my children, Freddie. I think I know them rather better than you do.' His voice was hard. 'And as for Charles, I think that independent streak you mention needs curbing. I intend to send him away to prep school next year. They'll lick him into shape. Too many women around here.'

He mounted the steps to the front door. Frederick followed.

'He'll hate it. He adores Jessamy and his mother.'

'Frederick, in an argument you do very badly. You keep emphasising my point.' He pushed open the doors and strode into the hall. 'Caroline!' he called.

Frederick followed him in.

Behind them, Chalmers appeared from nowhere and moved silently to close the door against the wind. Rupert handed him his hat and riding crop.

Up on the landing the door opened. Caroline appeared. Her slender body was now too thin. In a short dress of cream *foulard* silk, the waist dropped to the hips, and her hair cut in a shingle to set off her jaw and face, she looked far too fragile. A fox-fur coat was draped over her shoulders, the collar high, framing her face.

Rupert looked up at her. 'Where are you going?'

'Out with the children. I'm taking them to the Haslett children's party.' Frederick's heart lurched as he thought of their mother, Katherine, with whom he spent so many wonderful days. Her children, playing with his niece and nephew.

'You'll have to go another day. I have something of importance to tell you. Come into the big drawing-room with them.'

Caroline's fingers clutched the oak balustrade. She was diminished by the great sweeping staircase that curved up to meet her. Behind her the nanny appeared with the children, Charles neatly dressed with short trousers, silk shirt and bow-tie, Jessamy in a plum velvet dress with pretty lace collar. They made a charming picture.

'But, Rupert, the children are so seldom with me. Couldn't it wait?'

'No.' His eyes warned her. He would not brook argument in front of the children. The appearance of unity must be preserved.

After only a moment's pause she came down the stairs, holding the hands of the children. Rupert went ahead into the drawing-room. Charles let go of his mother's hand and let himself down, his hand sliding on the banister.

Caroline stopped him gently. 'Charles!' she warned softly.

Frederick looked up at her. He regretted having shown his hand, especially in mentioning Charles. His closeness to Rupert's children somehow irritated his brother. Rupert would now be more obstinate.

He followed the family into the drawing-room and closed the door.

Rupert stood at the far end beside the stone fireplace. The sun tilted in through the delicate stained glass of the three mullioned bay windows that lined the south side of the room. Large sofas filled the window alcoves and the floor was strewn with animal skins. A Broadwood piano stood in a corner with family photographs in silver frames. A portrait of Alexander stood upstairs on the landing above the minstrel's gallery, and below and beside the fireplace another was placed of their mother, Mary, reclining in those beautiful pearls that Caroline now wore so graciously.

Frederick thought how perfect Rupert looked as lord of the manor, and yet how wrong. His undeniable power was tainted with a need for it, for more.

Rupert came forward.

'I've called the family in today to discuss the future. Namely Charles's education.' Frederick saw Charles stiffen, though the small boy stood straight, his hands behind his back. 'I have arranged for you, Charles, to start at your prep school next year.'

She held Charles's hand. 'But he's far too young. He's only six, Rupert.'

'He'll be seven next year. And a young man. It's time he grew up. And let go of his hand, Caroline. You don't need to hold your mother's hand, do you, Charles?'

'No, sir.' He removed his hand.

'Are you ready to attend prep school, Charles?'

'If you say so, sir.'

Charles's lips were tight. Knowing him as well as he did, Frederick's heart went out to the child. The curve of his boyish profile lifted and he regarded his father without showing a hint of what he was feeling. Charles was a quiet and serious boy, studious, altruistic and kind, with a strong body—he had not inherited the grace of the Redfields—a thoughtful, interested face and floppy brown hair. He was unprepossessing, but his thoughts now were for his sister, Jessamy. She would miss him, and so would his mother. It was part of the system, being taken suddenly away from the bosom of a mother to spend two-thirds of the year at a lonely, severe and sometimes cruel establishment far away from home. It was called character building.

Caroline said nothing. She looked down at the small boy beside her. His face looked dead ahead. Rupert's words had somehow managed to sever the last strands of the umbilical cord that held mother and son together. From now on they would be separate entitites. Charles was already learning.

Charles looked at his father calmly. 'When will I be going, Father?'

'Next autumn. Turner, the headmaster, has already agreed to take you.' He turned to the mantelpiece to fill his pipe. 'Time you had some real discipline. I enjoyed my prep school.'

'Yes, Father.'

There was a small gasp from the other side of Caroline. Jessamy suddenly started sobbing pitifully.

Caroline swiftly bent to her.

'Leave her.' Rupert's voice called out. 'Jessamy, come here.'

The little girl did not obey at once.

'Jessamy, I'm waiting.'

Catching at her sobs now, she went forward and stood in front of him.

'Now, stop crying, and tell me what is wrong.'

Jessamy sniffed and stared at the floor. She was hypersensitive and terrified of the big, loud father she hardly ever saw. She and Charles spent most of their time with the nanny, and occasionally their mother. The only man who paid them much attention was their uncle, Frederick, and he was funny and gentle. Jessamy was as dark as her mother, as delicate, and equally as captivating. Everybody was entranced by her beauty. 'What is it?' he said. His voice was gentler.

'I don't want Charles to go away,' she said. 'I don't want to be left alone.'

'You'll be with your governess, Miss Ingram, Nanny and us. That's not alone, Jessamy.'

She swayed slightly. 'I want to go too.'

Rupert lit his pipe. 'Girls do not go to prep school.'

'Please, Daddy. I don't want Charles to go.' She looked up tearfully.

Rupert ran out of patience. 'Charles is going, and you are staying. Miss Ingram will teach you. Charles will be at home in the holidays. Now, both of you go to the nursery.'

Frederick watched Charles. He had suffered more as his sister ran forward, but he was not intimidated by his father. He had a sense that his sister needed protection, and whereas school held no real problems for him, the separation would be hard to bear. He loved his family as Frederick did. He was an independent boy, but could not stand his sister to be in any sort of pain. Frederick looked at his grim little face and gritted his teeth against Rupert's insensitivity. There were, surely, ways and ways of doing things. He could have handled this more tactfully.

Charles suddenly saw that Jessamy was about to throw one of her tantrums. He was the only person she would listen to at such times. Quickly, he moved forward. He took her hand.

'Come on, Jessamy. I'll show you my new stamp collection.'

Jessamy turned, and looked up into her brother's face, her smile suddenly lifting into her eyes. 'Would you, Charles?'

'Yes. Come on.'

He took her hand. Jessamy let go and ran ahead of him from the room. Charles followed.

Caroline, aware of their disappointment at not going to the party, and of the confrontation that had so narrowly been avoided, looked quickly towards Frederick. Their look was exchanged, but not missed by Rupert. Frederick saw him flare with annoyance. Caroline did not.

'Would you mind if I took them to the Hasletts' now, Rupert? There's still time to get there if we hurry.'

Rupert studied her deeply. His voice altered. 'Is that what you would like, Caroline?'

She looked at him. It was another of Rupert's strange changes of mood. 'Yes,' she said.

'Then that is what you shall do.' He left the fireplace and came across to her. He put his arm round her waist. Caroline seemed to tense, her hands lifted as if in protection. They fluttered at his chest as he pulled her into his arms.

'Rupert . . . !'

'What is it, darling?'

'Nothing, just I . . .' She tried to free herself from his hold.

Rupert bent and kissed her. Frederick wanted to look away. He half turned in embarrassment. Love between a man and a woman was a private affair.

Caroline's cheeks flushed. Her hands pushed on his chest and Rupert still held her. 'Beautiful, isn't she, Frederick?' he said, forcing his brother to turn and look at them.

He looked into the two faces.

'You make a very handsome couple,' he said.

'Don't we? A wife is something every man should have,' he said, the cold eyes raking over her white face. 'Especially a beautiful one.' There was no mistaking his desire for her.

Frederick took a deep breath. He cast his eyes to the back of the chair in front of him. He placed his hand on it.

'Rupert, I think I should be going . . . get the children . . .' Her eyes wavered, dark blue pools in her face. '. . . We'll be late . . . it's so rude . . .'

Abruptly he released her. 'Of course. Off you go.'

Caroline regained her balance. She hesitated for a moment, recovering, then turned on her heel and swiftly left the room patting her dark hair.

Frederick turned to leave also.

Rupert smiled as if deep in thought. He lifted his head as Frederick moved towards the door. 'Hold on a minute, Freddie. There's something I wanted to talk to you about.'

'I thought we'd finished. You're going to add to Foxhall. We're going to hang on to the land. Isn't that all?'

'Not quite.'

He crossed the room to the table beside the fireplace. 'I wanted to go over the books with you. Just checking on our . . . property down here,' he said, absorbed in turning the pages. 'Ah, yes, here it is.' He stretched his neck from his collar, as his fingers undid the top button of his shirt. 'That's better. These shirts, too damn tight.' He took a short breath. 'Who have we got living in these farm cottages now?'

He did know. Frederick tapped the back of the seat, and moved to the sofa beside the window.

'We've got three families, Rupert. All working on the estate.' He crossed his legs. 'The Smiths, the Baileys, and the Bennetts.'

Rupert nodded. 'All working well?' He walked towards the light from the window. It caught the edge of his thick, yellow hair and the strong profile. His eyes lifted, startlingly blue as he reached Frederick. 'All working hard?'

'Yes.' Frederick looked at him. 'They've all been with us for years, you know that, Rupert.'

Rupert held his look. 'Good. How many altogether? For instance, Bennett . . . Now, what's his family situation?'

'Family?'

'Yes.'

'His son was killed in the war. He has a daughter. As a matter of fact I allowed her to work on the land during the last years of the war.' He looked meaningfully at Rupert. 'They live in Oak Cottage. You remember . . .'

'Oh, that girl . . .' Rupert's eyes hardened. A touch of hatred lit their depths. 'Of *course* I remember.' His eyes reached some distant point. It was she who had caused him so much trouble, brought his father's attention to him to the extent of losing him his inheritance. 'And you let her work the land!' he said. He rested himself on the back of the chair in front of his brother. 'Was that guilt, Freddie?'

'In a way, yes. But she was actually a very hard worker too. Just as good as the men,' he said defensively.

'Really.' He sucked his lip and nodded, his eyes unkind. 'Did she affect you *that* much?'

Frederick uncrossed his legs and started to stand up. 'Rupert, have you finished? I really want to get back to—'

Rupert stayed him with his hand. 'No, I haven't,' he said, his unpleasant tone intensifying. 'Is she still here?'

'No. As a matter of fact she went to America.'

'*America?*' He looked astounded. 'When?'

'Eighteen months ago.'

Rupert looked incredulous. 'And you call that managing the

estate! You mean some old man's living there alone, when we could house a family of estate-workers. Have you gone soft in the head, Freddie?' He climbed off the chair and stood up. 'We'll have him out for a start.'

He crossed the room away from the window. Frederick stood up and took a couple of steps after him. 'That's not possible. I promised the girl her father could stay.'

Rupert turned, still holding the papers in his hand. 'You promised her—why?'

Frederick made a throwaway motion with his hand. 'Because of what happened, I suppose. And because you can't just throw an old man out. It's been his home for a long time, and he's a good farmer. He knows the land. I like him. He's never missed a day, he's always polite and hard-working, and when everybody else walked out during the war, he stayed. He's loyal, and I think that's a very fine attribute and deserves consideration.'

'Consideration, consideration!' Rupert came towards him, repeating the words. 'Freddie, we can't afford to be charitable. I'll bet he knows that more than you do. That's not the way things work. We need that cottage.' He stopped the flow of words and regarded his brother. 'No,' he said thoughtfully. 'It's not that at all, is it, Freddie? It's that damn conscience of yours at work again. I suppose you've been oh-so-guilty all these years. She was a farm-girl, Freddie. She wanted it. No, don't look like that,' he said, 'I know. I sensed it. They all do, didn't you know that? They've got baser instincts than us. You're feeling guilty for nothing. And he's got to go. That's where we're losing money. Why the books don't balance up. Now I see.' He made a big red cross beside Jim Bennett's name. 'I've got a whole family of farm-workers who want to work. They can move into Oak Cottage.'

'And what about Bennett? Where's he going to go?'

Rupert looked up slowly. Yes, what would he do with Jim Bennett? His anger ground away at him. He hated the Bennetts. How dared they jeopardise *his* future? He would humiliate the old man. Far better than turning him off altogether. He would teach them a lesson, show them who held the power now. 'He can probably get a cottage in the village,' he said. 'I'll offer him a gardening job. It's not the end of the world.'

'Rupert, he's a farmer.' Frederick spread his hands in emphasis. 'He doesn't know anything else. He doesn't know about gardening! Rupert. Come on man. What would the church say about this. What about charity for once, eh?'

Rupert ignored him. 'I'm sorry, Freddie. I've got to think about Foxhall. It's my responsibility.' His eyes met Frederick's, an icy, guarded blue. Their meaning was quite clear. 'I want to make the thing work, and mistakes are not what I have in mind. I want more friends here, a better house and less farm-work.' He pointed at Frederick with his pen. '*You're* the one who said let's keep the land. So be it. But to do that we've got to be ruthless about making it pay for us, and that includes using our tied cottages fully. My mind is made up. The Lovelocks will have Oak Cottage from the end of the month.' He put the book down on the table. 'When you go down to the farm, tell Bennett I want to see him.'

SIXTEEN

The small plane was taking off. She had not seen the patch of soft sand at the end of the grass runway. As the wheels hit the sand the plane suddenly tipped and nosed over. Dickie was jerked violently in her seat as she tried to right the machine. It slewed round and lurched sideways, just missing the hedge.

As it came to a standstill, she breathed a sigh of relief. Now to inspect the damage. She undid her harness and climbed out. In the distance she saw Bill running towards her, Max alongside him, trying to keep pace.

She pulled off the helmet she wore to protect her ears against the roar of the wind and the motor and then removed her gloves. As she climbed out and down onto the wing she threw them onto the leather seat in the plane.

The metal propeller blades were badly bent. She ran her hand along the edge. All she needed were a hammer, a wrench and a large stone. She looked around her and into the ditch. Her early years surrounded by farm equipment had paid off. She saw a heavy stone. She dipped under the wing and went to get it.

It was early autumn and soon the barnstorming season would be over. Flying circuses did not operate in the winter. Already she was well accepted with the troupe and she had earned her place on the shop floor with the engineers.

Dickie had already tested for her pilot's A licence. She had decided she wanted to qualify as a ground engineer while she clocked up the necessary hundred hours flying for a B licence, which would allow her to fly for hire or reward.

She knew instinctively that the only way to be free was to be independent. She got up at five every morning before going out to do her stint as a wing-walker and she spent a couple of hours with the engineers, without pay. For months she had stripped engines down, decarbonised them and built them up again. At night, she had pored over technical manuals. She and Max had found a small clapboard house near the airfield. It was home, and he now attended his first school. After supper each night they studied together. Bill would visit. He had elected to teach her all he could.

She had fifteen lessons before she was allowed to go solo. She took to flying with a natural aptitude; she was spurred by the adventure and love of flying, but teamed it with her own practical nature and her need to learn. Meanwhile, she wormed her way into the group of mechanics who serviced the planes. The chief ground engineer, Bob, liked her enthusiasm and they had become good friends. She joined the rough-and-tumble of the shop floor, her cheerful interest and her willingness to do even the most arduous and dirtiest of jobs endearing her to the men, and breaking down most of the barriers.

She pulled her bag of tools from the plane, and selected the hammer and wrench. She took off her windbreaker and threw it on the grass. Underneath she wore green leather jodhpurs and a silk shirt. The distinctive colours matched her dark hair and green eyes. Dickie was unaware of the picture she made with her short dark bob and trim figure. She knelt on the grass and went to work on the plane.

'Mama!' Max ran up and slowed as he approached her. 'Uncle Bill bought me a fishing-rod!'

Dickie laid her tools on the ground and turned. Max proudly displayed the fine new rod. In his other hand he held a bucket of wriggling worms.

'We're going down to the river. We've got a picnic. You're coming, aren't you?'

The dark brows knitted together. The green eyes looked into the urgency of her son's face. 'When I've done this, yes, of course,' she said. 'A pilot has to learn to do her own repairs, Max.'

A look of disappointment crossed his face.

Behind him, Bill moved into her line of vision, blocking the brightness of the sun.

'You coming, Dickie? We've got a great picnic. All work and no play . . .' he said, teasingly. 'River's running high. Good day for fishing.'

'I'll be along,' she said. 'Just as soon as I've got this fixed. I promised Bob I'd help out tonight. I'm going for my C licence as ground engineer next week.'

'I know.' He hefted the picnic-basket higher on his arm. He threw the red tartan rug across it. 'Got a surprise for you, too. Uh-uh,' he said wagging a finger at her. 'Won't get it till you join us! See you down by the river! Come on, Max.'

Max gave his mother a last look. She was so busy these days. 'Come on, Mama. Just this once.'

Bill's eyes echoed the boy's words. She nodded and laughed at them, and climbed to her feet. 'All right. Just this once!' Her eyes met Bill's.

The three of them walked off towards the river.

Jim Bennett stood in the hallway turning his cap in his hands. He looked up and around him at the huge staircase, the chandelier, the vast empty hall, awed by the space and the silence.

The big door to the estate office opened to the sound of voices. Rupert stood there. He shook the man with him warmly by the hand.

'Friday, then. That suit you? We'll make up a quick team!'

The other man strode across the hall. Chalmers opened the front door and bowed. 'Good afternoon, sir.' He proffered the man's hat and cane. The man took them and strolled out into the sunshine, donning the hat as he went.

Chalmers closed the door. He came nimbly back down the steps and crossed the shining, chequered hall towards Rupert's office. He went in. Words were exchanged inside.

Jim waited. He felt as if he wanted to shrink away. He had never been so uncomfortable. He looked over his shoulder at all the closed doors behind him, leading off to countless rooms.

'Mr Redfield will see you now.'

Jim turned back quickly. He held his cap in one hand and went forward and into the room.

Rupert sat behind the desk. The afternoon sun touched the immaculate broad shoulders of his jacket. His yellow cap of hair was highlighted against the dark of his face. He held a pencil between his fingers.

'Ah, Bennett!'

Jim's first sensation was one of apprehension mixed with a total discomfort at being in these surroundings. He was absolutely ill at ease. Once again he twisted the cap between his hands, wishing he were somewhere else. Only dimly the thought rose in his head that this was the man who had raped his daughter, but it never came to the surface. The idea of a confrontation on the subject was as alien to him as this room itself. Here, he was no more than a speck on the carpet. Mr Rupert was the one who held sway over them all, here and in the village. And he was a man of the church. A man of the church wouldn't do the things Dickie had mentioned. He did not question what that thought made of the man or his daughter.

Rupert stood up. He went round his chair and looked out over the lawn. The afternoon sun glowed on the sweeping parkland, softening and warming it. The river idled by at the foot of the incline, reflecting the colours of the sky. It was the end of a warm, early-autumn day. The weather had held and the crop had been saved. A bird twittered close by. The window, open on its catch, shifted slightly in the breeze. The papers rustled on his desk. Rupert leaned his hands on the stone window-sill and breathed in. This was the best time of day at Foxhall.

He turned back into the room.

He cleared his throat.

'Bennett, I've called you here today for some bad news, I'm afraid. I need your cottage for the family I've hired to work the farm. As there's only one of you now,' he said, watching the man, 'you can no longer legitimately stay on. I'm sorry. You have until the end of the month.'

Jim was dumbfounded. He did not know what to say. His brain spun with the news and its implications. 'I've always worked hard, sir.'

'I know you have. But it's a cottage for a family. You can see the sense in what I'm saying. However hard you work,

Bennett, it's not the equivalent of three, say, a man and two sons, as for example, the Lovelocks, a family I have recently hired. I have no option. You're a sensible fellow. Come now, Bennett, you can see that.' He crossed his arms and leaned against the window.

Jim was horrified. The end of the month? Where would he go? What would he do? He would never find another job, not at his age. He had known Dickie's departure would come to this. His health was failing and he needed some sort of work to survive.

'Don't know as how I'm going to get another job now, sir. Not at my age.' He looked bewildered and hurt.

'You won't have to,' said Rupert.

Jim looked up hopefully.

'You can have a job as a gardener. I'm taking on new men. We're expanding the gardens, you see.' His eyes were as expressionless as his voice. 'How about that?'

'Gardener? I'm no gardener, Mr Redfield. I'm a farmer.' He lifted his head abruptly. His chest lifted too, and his eyes struck forcefully at him. 'Farm foreman. Always have been.'

Rupert saw the pride. 'Well, it's take it or leave it, Bennett.'

Jim thought hard. He had no idea how to get in touch with Dickie, no idea what to do. He had absolutely no choice.

'Very good.' He looked down. 'Thank you, sir.'

'Good.' He sat down at his desk. 'I'll sort out your wages with my brother. He can pay you. I'm sorry, Bennett. It's a pity, but there we are.' He looked over his books.

'Yes, pity, sir.'

He was dismissed. Rupert bent his head and began writing. Jim left the room. He was shown to the door by the butler, Chalmers, and it closed firmly behind him. For a moment he stood on the step and then he took a deep breath and started to walk away for home.

There was nowhere this side of the village to live. He would have to find a place on the far side, on the outskirts of Foxhall Green. It would take a long time to get in of a morning, and he would have to take the humiliation of a large drop in prestige. It would be quite a walk, at least four miles. Why hadn't Dickie written? He hadn't heard from her for such a long time. Had she forgotten him?

He walked slowly back across the fields to his home. He opened the door and let himself in and looked around. It was quiet and clean. This had been his home and Elsie's for twenty-five years, ever since they had come to Foxhall to work for old Mr Redfield. They had raised a family here. A family. Jim crossed the room to the old scrubbed oak table. He laid his head on his arms and he did not move.

Dickie lay back against the tree and watched Max playing by the river.

Her shoulders were thin but she held them erect and straight. Bill had never seen her stoop or bow to anyone or anything. She wore her flying gear well, her long legs encased in the leather jodhpurs and her silk shirt open at the throat. The wind stirred her dark hair and the expression of her mouth warmed as she watched Max play with his new fishing-rod. She had few feminine curves, yet she was feminine in a subtle way. She had a soft curve to her cheek, and a tiredness and gentleness around her mouth. Her hands were quite beautiful; calloused inside but pale and slim. She had pretty feet, a small frame and a straight nose with nostrils that flared in humour or anger, but of course, it was her eyes that held him the most. Those hooded eyes were a challenging pale green that was very forceful. In fact, the force shone out of her face and made it striking. She was formidable, though so tiny. And in her face was courage— and sexuality.

He knew that sexuality was now channelled into an energy that was given over to the boy and hard work. He could sense it but read it as power. Her energy for work was unlimited where, with a different life, she would have been a dutiful wife, a good mother and responsive in bed; a sensualist. He had seen her face when she had come down from flying, that exhilaration that made her look as though she had just made love, a wildness in her that she did not even know she possessed. It brought out her beauty. Her sexuality may never have been exploited but it was there. Bill was mystified by her apparent lack of need for a man. He was not immune to the challenge. He wanted to make love to her and bring that deep-rooted sexuality to the skin.

'Are you sure you want to be a pilot, Dickie?'

'Sure, I'm sure,' she said. She turned her head to look at him. 'Why?'

He narrowed his eyes as he surveyed her. 'Most women pilots are considered very unfeminine. Suffragettes. Rejecting the traditional woman's role of housewife and mother. You're more feminine than that.'

'Can you generalise? I thought all pilots were supposed to be different. That's what Joe told me, anyway.'

'How *was* Joe figuring in your life back in England?'

She leaned her head back. 'I told you. We hardly knew each other.'

Bill looked over at Max. He plucked a piece of grass and split it in two. 'What about Max's father? Were you in love with him?

Dickie looked quickly at him. The look that crossed her eyes was one of pain and warning. She turned away again. The look told him that she was not going to answer him.

Max cast his line, his small bottom perched importantly on the picnic-basket. Bill pulled at the grass.

'There's no man in your life, is there? There should be.'

She did not look at him. 'What makes you think there should be?'

'Because you're pretty and all pretty girls have a man chasing after them.'

'Not this one. I don't need that. I only want to fly and give Max more than I had.' Her eyes misted over, her expression far away. Bill wanted to know more, but she was silent.

'Why did you leave England?' he urged. 'Were you drummed out? It's a long way to come on your own with a kid.'

She lifted her chin and breathed in the fresh air. 'Nothing more than the need to live a better life. Did you think it was really something more?'

'Perhaps.' He grinned at her.

'You're too romantic, Bill.' There was a note of humour in her voice. She stretched her legs.

'And you're not? All flyers are romantic. Otherwise we would never try, and never survive.'

She looked at him properly then, with that strong look that he loved. 'What makes a good flyer, Bill? Tell me. Do you think I have it?' She pulled her legs up under her and sat sideways, looking into his face.

Bill folded his arms. He stretched his long legs out in front of him. 'Well, you need to be clever, alert, mechanically minded, sensitive to the controls and have the ability to push the aircraft to its structural limits and no further.' She thought of the blue sky above them and how it was hers now, and how much she loved flying. 'You need to be cautious in your pre-flight inspection and maintenance, able to patch the plane to get it airborne for a show. You need to be able to fly by the seat of your pants—'

'That was the expression Joe used . . .'

'. . . and yes, I do think you have it.'

Her eyes were brilliant, cast on him. 'And yet you try to persuade me to stop.'

'No.' He spoke casually. 'I'd just rather you didn't do something so dangerous, that's all.' His eyes, as he spoke the words, were quite revealing but she was not looking. 'I couldn't stop you, anyway. All the women flyers I've met are different and yet they're much the same, really. They're romantic, emotional, adventurous, looking for freedom from something, some oppression—or their past,' he added, his eyes flickering towards her profile as he saw her thoughts drift away. 'But they're also practical, cool, and self-controlled. Composed, you might say.'

'Contradictory,' she murmured.

'Yes. When something goes wrong up there you don't need to be woolly-headed and panic. I'd say, at the risk of offending you, that you need a masculine brain and feminine intuition. And you need to be fit.'

'So you admit we women have something?'

'Yes, I'd admit you have something.' His eyes were warm, showing his feelings. 'Dickie, you haven't done an extended flight yet. Up there in an open cockpit you're at the mercy of everything going. Rain, snow, hail, dust, and anything else in the sky. You have to look over the side to see where you're going sometimes. Make your own routes . . .' He reached into the pocket of his jacket. 'Here,' he said, opening a Pennsylvania Railroad folder. 'This is my map.' His voice softened. 'Used to belong to Joe.'

She studied it.

'Tell me something about Joe, Bill. How it happened . . .'

'Joe?' He leaned back against the tree, while she held the map in her hands. He looked up into the leaves above him. 'Well . . . let me see . . . Joe and I served together for a start, and we had the same plans. We were Dominion men. We both learned mechanical skills with the force and when the war broke out, we were attached to a fighter squadron of the RFC.'

'You were in England?' she said, surprised.

'Briefly.' He crossed his arms. 'Anyway, Joe and I decided we would set up back here and join the US Post Office Air Mail Service after we had done our bit with the barnstorming. The Post Office opened the Air Service in 1919 with De Havilland DH-4s. We both knew those. It would be easy, we thought. It was tough, though, in the early days. No instrument flying or weather reports. If a pilot got caught in clouds or fog and lost sight of the horizon, it was not long before he lost control and fell. Why, you couldn't tell if you were flying upside or downside up if you got stuck in fog,' he explained in an aside. 'Ham Lee barely escaped in fog off Staten Island. When the clouds were low, you see, you had to fly close to the ground, close enough to see it. The lower the clouds, the lower you flew, dodging buildings, jumping trees and telephone lines. Ham Lee almost rammed into a ship coming out of New York Harbour. That's how low they flew. That's where the railroad map came in.' He pointed to it in her hands but only gave it a cursory glance. 'They followed the railroads from town to town. In bad weather they damn near collided with oncoming locomotives.'

'Why didn't they wait for good weather?' she said.

'Because pilots were only paid when they flew. And because they were the type to take the crazy risks. Like Joe!' He grinned at the memory of his friend. 'As it turned out, he joined the Post Office ahead of me. That's where I heard the story of Ham Lee. Seems the official in charge, a guy called Otto Praeger, hardly knew a monoplane from a biplane. Pilots said that he would look out of the department window and if he could see the Capitol dome, he expected them to fly that day, whether in Washington, or New York. Well, one day in March 1919 when it was real blustery, a pilot named John Miller was sent north from Bustleton despite Weather Bureau warnings of forty-eight-mile-an-hour winds. At Trenton he ran into thick snow. Blundering into New York he just missed hitting the Woolworth Tower. Over Long Island his engine cut in and out three times!' He pulled his arms in tighter at the thought. 'Unable to see or even control his plane he finally crash-landed in a field at Great Neck. He was OK, he handed his mailbag to the local postmaster and came back to Philly by train. Well,' he said, spreading his hand open, 'in the end it was just crazy. There was fog one morning covering the Belmont racetrack, and one of the pilots, a guy called Bonehead Smith, suggested waiting until the weather lifted. Back came a wire from Praeger: "Fly by compass. Visibility not necessary." Smith refused. Ham Lee arrived, and he said no, too. Well, when Praeger was told that both pilots had refused to fly in zero visibility back came the wire again: "Discharge both pilots Lee and Smith." With that, all six pilots went on strike. For six days not a mailbag moved. Then a compromise was reached,' he said, smiling at the memory of the way Joe had told it. 'In future, the field manager would make the decision to fly. He would go up and see how things were and he would say yea or nay.' He closed his eyes briefly. 'I guess there were fewer weather arguments after that.' He reached over and picked up a biscuit from the plate. He took a bite. 'I can't forget that story of Ham's, though. Flying a few feet above the water, and that damn boat coming up the Narrows right at him. He had to pull up, and in blind fog. All he had was a compass that was spinning at every bump. I tell you,' he took another bite of the biscuit, 'my dream is to invent. Instruments that will help pilots in bad-weather conditions. Sometimes it's appalling. It's not surprising they die so easy . . .'

'You're trying to tell me that's what happened to Joe,' she said.

'Yup. He was flying at twelve hundred feet, I guess, in dense fog. The snow must have plastered his goggles. When human sensations fail, you're pretty well blind. Deprived of a horizon he must have lost the feel of his position in space. I reckon he banked, lost speed and fell.' He paused. 'His body was never recovered.' He fell into an uneasy silence. 'For Joe's sake, and for all pilots, that's why I want to invent all the things we need to make flying safer. At the moment it's fatally dangerous. Robby Robinson was killed—decapitated—when he hit some cables. There's a power-line across the Delaware river. You have to be in the middle to go under it. They're still flying that river, though. And Charlie Ames, he crashed in fog one hundred feet below a crestline near Bellefonte. Last year, I was doing some crop-spraying to underpin my barnstorming and I struck an overhead cable and somersaulted. I thought I'd had it. That's what made me start inventing. I fit a cable cutter to the forward fuselage of my plane after that. It could sever a cable without causing damage to the aircraft.'

Her sadness at Joe's death was overridden by the interest she felt at the possibilities of his inventions.

'What else have you invented?'

'What else?' He looked thoughtful. 'Let me see. Well, I had an idea for a mechanically retracting undercarriage to improve flight performance for high-speed aircraft, and a ground lighting-system by which a mail pilot could accurately plot his progress!' He smiled at the high-flown ideas. 'But what I actually ended up with was a mechanically rolling map which would turn automatically according to airspeed.' He lifted a finger in explanation and turned slightly towards her. 'It could only work on established and accurately measured routes, of course, as the map could not compensate for straying errors. It used airspeed as the only method of dictating the speed at which the map turned. In other words, if the rolling map showed Chicago to New York, then any straying from the route would cause the map to turn out of sequence with the actual land being overflown.'

She looked admiringly at him. 'Well, that sounds wonderful. Why didn't you use them commercially?' She opened her hand. 'And what about the first two—why didn't you develop them?'

'Why?' He looked amused. 'Same reason we all don't get around to doing the things we'd like to do. Money. I need money, and sponsorship, and until you're a name you don't get sponsorship, and you can't get to be a name without money. *C'est la vie.* The chicken and the egg.'

Dickie leaned back against the tree. Her mind was working fast. Bill obviously had a great mind, one that should be developed. His inventions could help the aircraft business enormously. He could help *her* enormously.

'You should be in business on your own, Bill, with ideas like that. Why stay working for Gerry Oswald, risking your life with stunts all day and laying off in the winter?'

'Easier said than done.'

'Still,' she went on, 'that's what I'm going to do.'

'Start a business?'

'Yes. Soon as I've saved some money.' She watched Max tugging at something in the water, his line taut. 'Why don't you come into business with me?'

'I'd love to,' he said simply. 'First, I'd like to know how you're going to get the money to start it. You need capital you know, for any sort of business. Have you got that?'

'No,' she said evenly. 'But I will have . . .'

'How?'

She stretched her arms behind her head. Max started to reel in at the edge of the bank, his legs braced sturdily.

'I'm going to enter some competitions,' she said, feeling his eyes upon her. 'There's real money in that.'

'And real danger.'

'Yes. Isn't there in everything worthwhile? Air races, that's what I'm aiming for. And after I win I'll sponsor you!' Her eyes were bright with humour as she turned her face to his.

Bill paused a moment as he cast his eyes over her face. He did not want her in danger, yet knew he could not stop her. He could only go along with her, caught in the tide of her certainty. Somehow he felt it was that certainty that would pull her through.

'How about pioneer flights?' he asked.

'No. That's not for me.' She loved the freedom and adventure. Though she was told hair-raising stories of danger, they enchanted rather than frightened her. She could go either of two ways: fame and pioneering a flight that had not yet been done by a woman, or building a business towards monetary strength. She chose the latter. She would make money and build that business somehow, getting that vital financial strength so that she could go home and take her revenge. It hardly left her mind. Air races brought in large rewards so she would enter them, but she was not romantically foolhardy enough to want to conquer speed or endurance records. She did not want to die; she wanted to live too much.

'How much money have you saved already?'

On the bank, Max reeled in the fish. It was tiny and wriggling, hooked on the end of his line. 'Mama! Mama! Look!'

He brought it back to her. Dickie looked at the poor, silver thing, shimmering and wriggling in the air. Bill saw her distaste. 'Well done, darling,' she said. 'About three hundred dollars,' she answered Bill.

'Here, fella, let me unhook it.' Deftly he took the end of the hook and carefully unhooked the fish. 'It's a beauty. Too small to keep though, eh?' he said to a heavily breathing Max. 'Shall we throw it back?'

'OK.' Max was ready to agree with his friend.

Bill went to the edge of the river and dropped the tiny creature into the water. He turned back towards Dickie.

'Remember our surprise?' he asked Max.

'Oh, yes!' Max forgot instantly any remorse he felt over the loss of the fish. His blue eyes burned eagerly.

'Come along!' Bill reached out his hand to pull Dickie to her feet.

She stood pulling down her blouse. 'Where to?'

'You'll see.'

He led her to the next field. Planes belonging to members of the club were parked there. At the near end there was a blue Canuck biplane, a Canadian-built version of the Curtiss Jenny.

'It's been in a slight crash,' he said. 'But I managed to get it for two hundred and forty dollars. I reckon another three hundred will lick it into shape. Then again, if I was to work on it, I could probably do it for, say, sixty . . .'

'Well, it's a beauty, Bill.' She went forward. She touched the crumpled wing, examining the damage. 'But why would you want another plane?'

'I don't.' He stood back, folding his arms. 'I bought it for you. You can pay me back.'

Max was grinning with pleasure at her face.

'For me! Oh, Bill, thank you.' She glowed, the transformation startling as always. She came across and kissed him. Bill's hands came up to hold her arms a moment longer.

'Happy business-hunting,' he said. He bent towards her

and whispered more quietly. 'And, by the way . . . that's a *son* you've got,' he said pointedly. 'You'd better get used to the fish!'

Frederick went to the stable. He took the old gelding, Fitzroy, out to the paddock. From there, he decided, he would visit Katherine. He had to talk to her.

They had an arrangement now, through her maid. Frederick waited in a cottage on her husband's estate.

She came hurrying through the trees towards him.

'Frederick. I was in the middle of entertaining your family.'

'I know. I had to talk to you.'

'What is it, my darling?'

But it was not for some time that he told her why he had come. Their hunger was so strong in them now because of the clandestine nature of their relationship that they clung to each other. Frederick led her in and over to the bed. Katherine lay back against the pillows.

He told her swiftly what had happened.

Katherine leaned up from the pillow. Her long black hair trailed and curled in a shining curve beneath her shoulder. The soft eyes looked into his. Her warm bosom was edged with the fine satin and lace of her gown. Frederick's fingers traced the lace. She found that she had difficulty concentrating.

'I hope that Bennett finds a cottage in the village,' he said. 'Unfortunately, he's got no family here now, and I can't do a thing to help him.'

'Perhaps I can help you, Frederick. Henry has a few cottages here on the estate. One of them is empty. I could make sure he gets it. I don't think we could offer him work, though. We're overstaffed as it is. Farmers are not exactly needed any more—even *we've* cut down on land. Rupert's right in that, at least. He could have the cottage, though it'll be a journey for him.'

'Katherine, thank you. You're such a fine woman. So good to me . . .' His fingers moved lightly on to her skin. 'I think Rupert suspects us, you know.'

'Let him.' She stroked the back of his neck. 'I don't really care what your brother thinks. He's too like Henry for words. He doesn't frighten me. Come here, Frederick. Hold me in your arms. I need you. Stop teasing me, I can't wait any more.'

Her eyes were dark with emotion. His light touch had feathered her nerve endings to flame. Frederick's hand stole in and touched her breast. She wanted him. Now he knew it. She smiled, her lips trembling with excitement.

Gently he pulled the gown from her shoulders and bent his head.

They lay together quietly. The room got darker, the sun was going down.

She stirred. 'I think I should be getting back to my guests. They must have wondered where I'd gone.'

'What did you tell them?'

'That I had a dire headache. I went upstairs to lie down and slipped down the back staircase with Mary, my maid. She's up there now guarding my door!'

Frederick smiled and kissed her one more time. Katherine rolled to the side of the bed and sat up, picking up her clothes from where they lay strewn on the floor. 'By the way, Freddie, you never did tell me why you allowed Rupert to throw Bennett off the land.'

'Well, you know Rupert,' Frederick said, sitting up. 'There was little I could do about it. He's also planning to sell off some of the land. I did all I could to persuade him otherwise.'

She turned towards him as she sat on the side of the bed. 'You'll stop him, of course?'

'Not if he's determined.'

'But he has no right to change Foxhall. It's yours.'

'Foxhall?' He looked bewildered. 'What made you think that?'

'Well, the will, of course!' She shrugged prettily. 'What else?'

'You know about the will?'

'Yes.' Katherine's soft eyes held him. 'Your father came up to see Henry the day after Rupert's wedding. He was in a dreadful state. Of course, Henry being Henry encouraged him. He said he should cut Rupert off without a penny. Alexander surprised us both. Quite coldly, he agreed. He was almost matter of fact about it. He said he had already done exactly that the very same morning.'

'So you know. Then you already knew about my . . . liaison without my telling you, simply through knowing about Rupert?'

'No.' She shook her head. 'Alexander never said a word about what it was exactly that Rupert had done. In a way, I had a feeling that that was almost mild in comparison to the way Rupert treated him with such contempt. It was his manner that angered your father enough to change the will. And never to change it back,' she added, as she turned to pick up her underclothes.

'Never to change it back?' Frederick echoed.

'Yes.' She smiled. 'Your father knew how you loved the land, Frederick. He watched you take care of it all through those war years. He knew what you suffered through not being allowed to join up. It was his way of saying thank you, as much as his anger at Rupert that made him take such a drastic step and bequeath it to you, while disinheriting his eldest son in your favour. And quite rightly, in my opinion.' Her voice warmed. 'You were his favourite son.'

Frederick felt his heart sink. He was very still.

At his silence she turned towards him, seeing his face. Something spoke to her and made her understand. 'Frederick?' Her eyes looked into his. 'Has Rupert got Foxhall?' she asked darkly.

'Yes.'

'How?' she breathed. 'How on earth did he get hold of it?'

'I signed it over to him. And everything else that should have been his.'

'Frederick, you didn't! Why, in God's name?'

'Because . . .' He spread his hands open. 'Because it was his by right.' His eyes searched emptily into the distance beyond her. 'And because he didn't betray me. When he had the row with Father, obviously he never told him my part in the whole thing, and for that I was grateful. He could so easily have done so, and Father would have been angry with us both. I thought once he had calmed down he would have changed the will back again to the way it should have been.'

'No!' she cried. 'You were so wrong. He had no intention

of changing it back. And as for your part, Rupert said nothing simply through his own arrogance. Not for you. You
know your brother. I'm sorry to say it, but he has no loyalty,
Frederick.' She paused, watching his face. 'Did he persuade
you, darling, with that charm of his?' she asked gently.

'No. Actually he didn't. The day afterwards I offered it
to him.'

'Off your own bat?'

'Yes, more or less. I'd had a talk with Caroline, and . . .'

'Caroline,' she murmured. 'I thought so. She is not
blameless, Freddie. She had her part to play in this.'

'I cannot believe that, Katherine. Not her. She was so
sweet about it.'

Katherine held her tongue. She was not a woman to condemn another bitterly. And he was a man obsessed, she
could see that. She thought of Caroline. That woman had
made a mistake, and this was her revenge on Frederick. He
would never believe that Caroline could possibly be that
manipulative; she was the woman he idolised and he was
blind to her. She had made a fool of him as women of her
hypocritical sort so often did. Yet Katherine loved him too
much to make him face the truth and to hurt him more. She
had come too late to help him. Frederick's strength would
have been Foxhall. Now Rupert ruled them all, as he had
always meant to.

'Well, whatever the truth is,' she said softly, 'the prin-
ciple is the same. Your father knew how little the land meant
to Rupert, how much it meant to you.' Her eyes were tragic,
and Frederick closed his against the look in them. Her words
came through to him with fatal clarity: 'Together they have
taken it from you. Frederick, it was yours, my love. Your
father *meant* you to have Foxhall . . .'

SEVENTEEN

Summer, 1923

Dickie's machine rose gracefully towards the sky and swiftly turned into the breeze. She shot up into the air to a great height, dropped sheer for a couple of hundred feet, turned her machine right over on its side, and then sent her nose diving straight downwards again. It appeared as if she were out of control, but she could do just what she liked with the aeroplane and just when it seemed that she had got perilously close to the ground she shot skywards again, shut off her power and came down with a wide sweeping circle. Within forty feet of the field she darted up and over the stand buildings. This was followed by roars of applause from the crowd.

Dickie lifted the nose of the tiny plane and banked right to speed out over the river. A fresh wind blew across the Potomac, and conditions were perfect, a cloudless day and unlimited visibility. The engine had not missed a beat and she relaxed, enthralled by the experience. Ahead stretched the ocean, sparkling under the sun. She knew that nothing could touch this; it was worth any price. She felt herself expand with power and vitality.

There was a beauty and exaltation about flying. Above the haze layer over New York with the sun behind her, alone in her open cockpit, was a new world. The upper surface of the haze stretched like a vast, endless desert to the horizon. She threaded her way through the light summer clouds that hung over the land, tiny patches of ground far below, and pushed her aircraft to its structural limits, revelling in the challenge and the power.

The plane's slipstream caught the top of her head and bullied and buffeted her. Up here, it was her world alone. With some regret she pushed the stick to the left and back and banked for her return to the field.

Air aces flew all manner of planes at the four-day meeting in Belmont Park, New York. They spun their planes earthwards only to pull out at the last minute, leaped from their planes in parachutes, freefalling to within peril of their lives and flew their tiny craft upside down.

Dickie came back in low over the ground. Ten laps of the ten-mile triangle were marked out by steel pylons. She rolled her machine vertically and pulled round the marker so tightly it seemed that she almost touched it. Her sheer nerve stole the show. The crowd was right behind her.

On the sixth lap though, with forty miles to go, her fast turns appeared to be her undoing. The fabric on the right wing of her plane tore like tissue paper and the linen swept away, torn fragments fluttering in the slipstream. The crowd watched in horror. Turning away from the course, she raced over the field and the spectators, searching for a spot to make an emergency landing. Then, all of a sudden the nose seemed to drop and the plane dived towards the earth.

The tiny machine seemed nothing more than paper. It rolled over and over, crumpling against the ground. Already the crowd was beginning to run towards her.

Back at the base, Bill took off and headed for Rattlesnake Mountains. From there he followed the river to Clearfield with little trouble. The weather was worsening but for the moment it did not seem too bad. The Post Office Air Mail Service had begun between New York and Cleveland the summer before and the pilots were expected to fly in all weathers. The cloud forced him to duck and dodge as he flew through the ridges and the squall was growing worse. By the time he reached the approach leading up to the air-mail base at Bellefonte in the centre of the mountains, the clouds were so impenetrable that he had to turn back. He hated to be thwarted; this was only his third run. Back at Clearfield again the sky seemed much clearer in the north so he took off again in that direction, not knowing that he was about to fly over some of the wildest country in Pennsylvania, with no fields or habitation for fifty miles around.

The engine stopped cold. The timing gear had failed. The moment before it had been roaring along; now there was an ominous silence. Quickly he tried all the knobs in the cockpit; there was no response at all. Down below, he saw a small clearing. Bill pulled the plane around and headed for it, diving in steep because of the lack of room. It was choked with brush, disguising a large ledge of rock. As he brought the plane in there was an almighty jarring sensation as the ledge slammed into the undercarriage. Bill's neck cracked like a bullwhip, the plane snapped in two and he was thrown out head first straight into the brush.

He rolled to a stop and groaned. He shook his head to clear it, then hesitated. He felt gingerly all along his legs for any broken bones. He was still holding the rubber grip from the control stick. Nothing was broken. The mail was the important thing.

He stood up and clambered back onto the wrecked De Havilland, pulled out the mail-bag and started down the hill on foot.

He knew there would be little reaction to his accident. He was just lucky to be alive. Engine failure and forced landings happened every day on the mail run. As long as pilots were not seriously hurt, no one bothered about them. At least he was doing the run, that was all that mattered. It was high pay—two hundred and fifty dollars a week—and plenty of leisure time, even if it might be a short life. Mail pilots were rarely crippled, they were usually killed outright. They worked two or three days a week, and were on reserve one of those days which meant keeping the field advised as to where they might be reached. That left him plenty of time to work on his experiments. Dickie encouraged him. Partnership with her was turning out to be a fine thing.

He trod heavily down the steep hill. Ahead of him there was a track and a farmer and his cart pulling steadily along. Bill shouted, and began to run as well as he was able with the heavy mail-bag. The man turned and stopped. Bill raised his arm, stumbled down the last few steps of the slope and onto the flat.

Once he had delivered the mail he would find transport back to the airfield. There would be another run waiting, returning to New York, that one far more hazardous. Night flights had begun.

The largest number of planes left over from the war were De

Havilland DH–4s. The Post Office took a hundred. At first, the planes had flown only by day, surrendering their mail each evening to be carried forward in the night by train, but the service had progressed quickly. By 1923, it had been ready for night flights.

For pilots like Bill, these flights were tough work, often in very rough weather. If the weather became impossible or the fuel ran out there was only one way left to safety: the pilot's parachute. Bill had already survived two such jumps, one in fog and one in a snowstorm.

The fatality rate among the mail pilots who crossed America was appalling, yet it was accepted. There was no alternative. In every weather condition, blistering heat over the deserts, or freezing blizzards over the highest mountains in the country, the biplanes droned their way through, and somehow they got the mail to its destination, though many crashed or simply vanished.

When fog overlaid the landing strip, the ground crews would tie balloons at the four corners of the field so that pilots could see them sticking up above the low white blanket. Flare pots were put out at night. Powerful lights were installed at landing fields between Chicago and Cheyenne, and a string of flashing beacons every twenty miles in between. With these lights, the Post Office could schedule flights that started out in New York and San Francisco on one day and then completed their journey on the following one.

By 1924, the entire three-thousand-mile route across the mountains, the deserts and the prairie had been lit. Night flying in the Rockies was no longer so hazardous, and if the weather was bad, the planes didn't fly. Night flying relied on the pilot's eyes to follow the lighted beacons across the country, and on an extra sense if something were to go wrong. It often did, and then that extra sense was essential. It was what kept them alive. Engines would seize up, magnetic compasses would stick, and carburettors would often overheat or freeze. Pilots like Bill saw that their only resort was to invent their own rude instruments.

Wesley Smith's determination made him a pioneer in instrument flying, or 'blind flying' as it was called. He took a half-empty whisky bottle, a 'spirit level' that he placed on his instrument panel. Then he found that the Air Mail's instrument mechanic had persuaded an old German glassmaker in Chicago to fashion a curved tube with a ball in it, like a carpenter's level. He fastened it to his front panel next to his altimeter—the makings of a turn indicator. He had already been using a clock on his panel to time his turns. With this latest gadget he could still get the mail through when nobody else did. He could fly in clouds, and that meant the start of passenger aviation. Pilots flew blind, by dead reckoning, navigating by fixing their position with the sun and the stars, with no other engineering training than the usual knowledge that most pilots picked up along the way. They were exposed to the elements and the blast of the slipstream, bombarded as well by torrential rains, winds and violent turbulence. But it was the sort of challenge that life was made of, they were there at the start of something new and stimulating. Nobody had tried it before and they were embarking on adventures more exciting and more perilous than anything else so far that century. The currents of the air were more volatile by far than those of the ocean. Even in the finest weather, engines would stall and the mail planes would simply drop out of the sky to alight in a country field or some other fatal landing site. And when the clouds piled up and the winds lashed, there was nothing to compare with it. For up there it was one man, and one man alone, against the elements.

It was during the long lonely night flight back to New York that Bill first started to devise his idea for an air-cooled engine. It would be lighter and the plane could fly further and carry passengers, perhaps, as well as mail. The idea spun through his head. Beneath him he kept a check on the bonfires that were lit along the cross-country trail so that pilots could steer for the next while keeping the last one in view behind the tail. The idea was germinating, and tomorrow was a day off.

Bill heard the plane arrive on the field outside the shed.

She stood at the door to the shed. She still wore her helmet but the straps were loosened. She leaned against the door jamb and surveyed him for a moment.

'How did it go?'

She stood up straight again, a smoky smile in her eyes. She pulled the wad of notes from the inside of her jacket and showed them to him.

'Holy Christ!'

She laughed and came across, handing him the money. She pulled off her helmet and ran a hand quickly through her hair, ruffling it free again. Bill counted the money. She sat down on an upturned orange crate at the side of the shed. 'I won my race. Told you I would.'

'One thousand five hundred!'

'It all adds up.'

The door of the shed stood open to the day. The sun was still shining warmly outside. The edge of it touched the green scarred leather of her jodhpurs.

'How did the crash go?' he asked her more cautiously.

'It was all right. Not something I'd want to do every day, but the director was pleased. Oh, I brought you a souvenir . . . . !'

She pulled a red beret from the other pocket of her leather flying jacket and threw it across to him. Bill caught it easily and held it, the question in his eyes. 'Lily Ventura's beret?'

'Yes. I had to wear it for the flight. It's what she wears in the picture.'

Bill turned it in his hands. Lily Ventura was one of the most famous of the silent-screen stars. Pert and pretty, she was taking the role of one of the pioneer aviatrices, a subject very much in vogue. Dickie had doubled for her in the crash stunt on the day of an air race. Lily was supposed to crawl from the wreckage, half dead. Dickie was supposed to survive.

'I'm glad I wasn't there to see it,' he said. 'Was it dangerous?'

'Oh!' She dismissed it with a wave of her hand as he had known she would. It had been dangerous. 'Where's Max?' she asked.

'Still at school.'

'Of course.' She stood up, pushing her hands into her pockets. 'Bill . . .'

'Help me with this, would you?' he interrupted.

'What?' She looked over at him.

'Here.' He handed her a packet of chewing-gum. 'Eat this.' She took it. 'Whatever for?'

'I'll show you. Come on.' He pulled some sticks free and started to chew them as he walked with her out to his plane. 'Eat,' he said as she walked beside him. Dickie put the gum in her mouth.

The cowling was back. Bill pointed inside.

'I couldn't think what was the matter with her,' he said. 'The engine was overheating, so I had to bring her down. A cracked induction pipe. I searched around for a replacement, but there wasn't one, so, I decided to use gum. There,' he said, 'that should be enough.' He pulled the gum from his mouth. 'How's yours?'

She handed him the ball of gum.

'Don't look so puzzled!' he said. He added them to a large wad of gum he had collected and stuck to the side of the plane. Then he leaned forward and spread the ball of putty-like material around the fractured pipe. On the ground he had laid the rest of his essentials. She watched as he covered the gum with a bandage of friction tape and finally sealed the bulging mass with coats of shellac.

'She'll be all right now,' he said. 'I'll just take her up for an airtest and then I'm going back to the base.' Bill was smiling and confident now. Dickie did not doubt that the home-made repair would hold. She had done similar herself already.

'Bill, how much money have we saved now? Enough to set up our own fixed-base operation?'

'Yes, I reckon.' He pulled down the cowling, and handed her the tool-box. 'Put this back in the shed for me, would you?'

She took it from him as he pulled on his jacket and helmet. The wind stirred her hair. She looked up into the sky. A frown touched her eyes.

'I think the weather's turning. Maybe it won't be so good for flying. Where've you got to deliver today?'

Bill looked up into the sky as he pulled on his gloves.

'Bellefonte to New York. Sky looks clear to me.'

'I'm a farmer, Bill. That cool wind stirring up, it's got rain in it. Can't you feel it? It'll be wet by the end of the day. Look, see that front?'

She pointed over to the horizon. Bill grinned and laid a hand on her shoulder. 'I've flown in worse. Gotta get the mail through or I don't get paid.'

'Bill,' she said quietly. 'That's what I've been meaning to talk to you about. I think we should leave here. Move somewhere else and set up business together. We've made enough now. You could leave the Post Office and get involved in your inventions. I could fly passengers.'

Bill nodded. 'Sure. Set up somewhere else, why not? Do you have anywhere in mind?'

'Yes.' She held the box of tools in her arms. 'As a matter of fact I do.'

Bill pushed the fingers of his gloves together. 'I thought you might!'

'California,' she said. 'That director today. He was talking about it. Hollywood and Los Angeles. The film business is starting to pick up there, and where there's people with money to spend on work and pleasure there's business for us. I started to think that today. The air's clear, it's near the sea, Max will enjoy it, and we could buy some flying-boats and fly down the coast. They're building huge film studios there, and I imagine they might need stunt-flying or just planes to take them to different locales around California. What do you think?'

'What do I think?' he echoed her. 'I think your mind's already made up. That's what I think!' He leaned against the plane's fuselage and smiled wryly down at her.

'Yes, it is really,' she said. 'I'm going to tell Max when he gets home from school.' She lost her defensive stance, and looked up at him in the silence that had fallen between them. Her eyes searched his. 'Are you going to come too?'

His eyes were deep as he looked down into hers. The flippancy had burned out, only the warmth remained. 'Do you want me to?'

'Yes, I want you to.'

His voice was soft. 'Then I'll come.'

January, 1925

A thick grey mist hung over Los Angeles airport and clung to the silver fabric of the Curtiss flying-boat. Dickie touched the switches.

'Switches off?'

'Switches off.'

'Gas on?'

'Gas on.'

The dawn was still.

'All clear?'

'All clear.'

On the first swing of the propeller, the engine coughed, crackled and then broke into a steady purr.

Inside the cabin, Lily Ventura and her *amour*, the director, John Swainson, held hands. It was deafeningly noisy and freezing cold, despite Los Angeles' near-perfect weather. This was a winter day. They were dressed in heavy coats, with cotton-wool plugs in their ears. Lily's hat was pulled down over her head not only to keep her warm but to disguise her from the curious—John Swainson was a married man and she was a famous lady now. She looked out of the window through the thin Celluloid, and wondered at the wisdom of their trip to Catalina. Her wicker chair was not fixed to the floor and visible parts of the structure projected into the cabin. This swaybacked old crate did not seem ready to get off the ground, let alone ferry them across to the island. One hand held tight to the hot-water bottle that she carried on her lap beneath the blanket, the other one to John. She comforted herself with the thought that that night they would be in each other's arms in a big, warm bed and free of his confounded nosy wife.

The flying-boat quickly skimmed the water and they were airborne. Dickie eased back on the control column. The weather was clearer above the sea fog that lay like a blanket over the land. They climbed steadily to a hundred feet and she set her heading.

The sea was totally obscured by cloud and fog, giving her little chance to assess the drift. The flying-boat carried only crude navigational instruments. However, just before the light failed, a small break in the overcast weather gave her a brief look at the breaking waves. She roughly calculated a new heading to compensate for the cross wind.

Lily settled back in her seat. She thought the intense cold was murderous. The plane had no cabin-heating system and the temperature inside seemed freezing to her, despite the Californian climate. Over her silk and wool underclothes she wore a shirt and trousers of oiled deerskin and outer garments of fur. She felt like a trapper.

Dickie watched the temperature control carefully. The engine temperature was low. If it could not be raised they would be in trouble. She climbed slightly. A storm picked up, and huge clouds were gathering on the horizon. She was not unduly concerned. They would soon be in Catalina, and her business was under way. Bill's strip map, mounted on rollers in a small box, unwound inch by inch as she went, successfully marking out the crossing.

They operated seven flying-boats. With his old military contacts, Bill had managed to buy them from the navy's war surplus stock at a bare third of the cost. Each of them had eleven wicker seats. She and Bill flew the coast, from Los Angeles up to San

Luis Obispo and further on to San Francisco, down the coast to San Diego, and out to the islands of Catalina and Clemente.

Bill and Dickie flew all day. Bill maintained the planes, sometimes working far into the night. They did formation-flying, joy-riding, cross-country flights, aerobatics and barnstorming. During the summer months they had taken up local joy-riders. Children had put their feet through wings or were sick after innumerable ices and lollipops while others tried to throw things out of the plane or stood up and waved their caps and handkerchiefs, blocking her view. Dickie simply counted up the money in her head, continuing to take the joy-rides out over the sea, hiring a local speedboat operator to drive as fast as possible, swerving about in the sea while her passengers were armed with flour bombs ready to hit him.

She took on any flying job at all. She transported people and cargo. In her sensitive hands the machine became an extension of the woman. The business grew and grew. The passengers liked her quiet, assured manner. She was never cocky or arrogant like many of the male flyers of the day. She was doing well, but she was thinking ahead.

At Dickie's insistence they published timetables and served coffee in the winter and cool drinks in the summer from their 'passenger terminal', a small hut at the edge of the beach. Each morning, promptly at nine, one boat took off from the Los Angeles waterfront for San Francisco and another for Catalina. Reservations were necessary at weekends in the summer, and even the seats were numbered. Dickie sensed the acquisitive nature of the California film and business people. They wanted their own seat; they wanted attention. They would have it. It was show business. She and Bill charged rates accordingly: two hundred dollars a round trip.

They had leased their piece of land above the beach. It had two weatherproof huts, one for repairs, and the other for the terminal. They kept a variety of planes, and contracted to fly people or goods, sometimes quite regularly, to an agreed-upon destination. Within a year of operation they had posted four signal towers along the way to keep watch and telephone reports of their aircraft's progress.

People who would not normally fly seemed ready to travel in a seaplane provided with a hull—it could always find a safe landing place on water. And those who would not travel at three thousand feet would fly in seaplanes ten or fifteen or even a hundred feet above the water.

Continuous performance of commercial flying day after day, however, required planes, pilots, mechanics and stock. If the company were to keep going steadily they needed a banker. Dickie knew they would soon have to approach Wells Fargo bank. She had just the young man in mind. He had already taken a few rides with her line and was a personal friend of John Swainson, the director. (She had produced a perfect stunt for John when he had needed it; now he patronised her line and recommended her to his friends. She looked after them well.) Wiley Fairfax was from a rich family and a banker. The time would come when she would need him.

In the hotel on Catalina Island she relaxed with her newspaper. Outside the squall was picking up with the coming night. Upstairs, Lily Ventura and John would be warm in their luxurious love nest.

Dickie put the paper aside and left the comfort of her chair. She went across to the storm window and gazed out across the sea. The black clouds gathered momentum. She was strong now, ready to move on.

Autumn, 1925

Dickie held Max in her arms, as they sat on the stoop of the house. It was a quiet moment, a beautiful evening. A burning sunset filled the sky, streaking deep gold across the horizon. The sea was as still as if it had been brushed with oil. There was the deep scent of sage in the air, the sea, and the warmth of the Santa Ana winds drifting in. It was magnificent country.

Max had been fishing with Bill all day. Proudly, he had brought home a batch of *bonito* hooked to the end of his rod. Together, he and Bill had cooked over a brick barbecue set up on the lawn beyond the house. Now, full and content, all three sat on the porch and watched the sunset each with their own private thoughts.

Max attended the state school and was receiving the fine education Dickie had wished for him. Their life was better than she had ever imagined it would be. Now, though, she thought of home, England. There had been no communication from home. It seemed like another life. Her father's silence worried her. She had sent him money on a regular basis, but had heard nothing. Maybe it was his embarrassment at his lack of learning, his inability to write, and a reluctance to ask Mrs Canter for help. She hoped that was all it was and decided to write to the lady herself. That would allay her fears.

The glow of the barbecue was dying. Max leaned more heavily against her. She patted his back. 'Time for bed, Max. I want to talk to Uncle Bill.'

Max yawned. He was exhausted from his day. He stood up, kissed her and climbed tiredly up the steps and onto the porch. 'Night, Mama, Uncle Bill.' The screen door opened and closed and he was gone.

'Business is going well, Bill,' she said. 'But something interesting caught my attention . . . Did you hear the news today?'

He looked up curiously, waiting to hear. 'Yeah?'

She stood up, walked down the steps and went over to join him beside the fire.

'Congressman Kelly has passed a bill to open the flying of airmail to private contractors.'

'Yes, so I gather.' He lay sideways on one elbow, his eyes on hers.

Her voice was steady. 'I think we should get involved.'

'Involved? How could we?'

'They've advertised for bids to fly the mail over eight feeder routes to supplement their own New York to San Francisco coast to coast service. We should make a bid.'

He sat up higher. 'We haven't got near enough money for that!'

'Not on our own, perhaps.' She eased herself down onto the ground. 'But if we were to go in with a couple of other people . . .'

'Who did you have in mind?'

She made a quick pout with her lips. 'Oh . . .' she shrugged her shoulders. 'I thought maybe John Swainson might be interested.'

'The movie director? Why should he be?'

'Money. Opportunities. Why else? He's a businessman, and an astute one. He might be very interested in being a partner. He knows how well we operate, after all. He'd put money behind me, I think.' She picked up his glass and drank from it. 'I feel like asking him.'

'Don't, Dickie,' he said. 'You might find he doesn't go for it at all. I think you're wrong there. He's a movie man, not an entrepreneur.'

'Well,' she argued, 'I think I'm right. And the other one is a friend of his, Wiley Fairfax of the Wells Fargo Bank. We'd have to get a bank involved to put up money for our bid, and he's very well connected. His father's a senior partner in a Wall Street investment house. I think he might join in.' She took a deep breath. 'Anyway, I think we should do the mail run. If not now, then keep an eye on it and do it as soon as we can. There's a big future in it'.

'Perhaps.' Bill looked deeply at her. 'But business isn't everything, is it, Dickie? Some time you just gotta stop and take a look at what's around you.' He lifted his arm and made a broad sweep indicating the panorama of the night and the sea in the distance. 'Let's just relax together,' he said. 'Dickie, I came out here with you, and you've done a great job. Mind you, I expected no less after that performance with Gerry that day at the fair!' he said, his eyes teasing slightly. 'But I do think I should know what's driving you. Isn't it time you told me?'

She knew it would come. Now she was silent. Bill was a good man and a patient one. She knew too how he felt about her; he did not hide his feelings very well.

She sat up cross-legged, resting her elbows on her knees. Her face was lit by the fire. 'All right, Bill,' she said finally. She looked swiftly towards the house. It was silent. 'I'll tell you . . .'

The retelling of the story brought it back. Again she heard the kitten's cry, saw herself run outside, felt the sun on her face as she opened the back door, saw him sitting there, and knew immediately he was dangerous. She remembered the way his eyes had looked when she had confronted him, told him to get off their land. She remembered, and knew that the change in his eyes had been fatal for her. She felt the horse barge her again, saw as if from a distance how she began to run for the fields to Sam and her father, running through the woods. Again she heard the dogs barking, felt the pounding of the hooves as the horse came up alongside her and he swept her up and over his saddle. The fire flickered before her, Bill's dark brown eyes were steeped in pain, full upon her face in absolute silence, but she saw none of it, only that vivid picture as clear as if it were being spun right in front of her. Her voice hushed slightly as she told the last part, that clearing in the woods, the sun on the leaves and the way she scrambled on the soft earth, how she did not escape them . . .

'*My God!*' he whispered. He stared into the fire as she finished and then at her as her eyes caught his. She thought he looked just like Sam at that moment.

He did not speak for a moment, his anger contained within him as he realised what they had done to her. He lifted his hand and rubbed his face. She was glad he did not immediately reach out for her. That would have been too easy, and she was imprisoned still by the story's retelling and made frigid with the pain of recall.

'Dickie,' he said softly at last. 'No words can tell you how I feel. It's a terrible, terrible story. But all the same, shouldn't you put it in the past where it belongs? It isn't healthy to dwell on hate, and brood. Is revenge your only motivation for yourself and Max?'

'It's not just that, Bill,' she said, breathing easier once she had broken the pattern of the story and spoken freely again. 'It drives me, of course. But I've told you about my brother, Sam. He was cannon fodder. Subjugated. He had to do what he was told and he died. I don't want to be subjugated.' The light eyes encompassed him, held him fiercely, like a cat's eyes in the fire's glow. 'Held under the thumb of people like the Redfields. Don't you see that?'

'I do see it.' He sat up, his eyes equally strong. 'But you're a healthy woman, a young woman.' His voice slowed. 'Dickie. You need love, and love from someone who ain't gonna hurt you . . .' He paused. 'I need it, too.'

'A lot of women want you, Bill.' Her voice was steady. She did not look at him. The silence built.

'Only one that I want . . .'

She heard the night sounds all around her, and she heard his words. They were provocative. The silhouettes of the cypress trees on the point darkened to black spears against the bay, the sunset flaming behind. The distant sea crashed in and sucked out again.

'Dickie,' he said softly. His voice was soothing. 'Little Max isn't the only one who needs holding to comfort him and love him. We all need it. We're human.'

'You've been good to him,' she said. 'Like a father.' His eyes were on her. 'If you'd rather go . . .'

'Go? Dickie . . . ! God, I *love* you,' he said. She looked up at him. His brow was furrowed, his normally open face tight with emotion. 'Come here,' he said. He lifted his arms. 'Come. Let me hold you.'

The words unlocked something in her. She felt it. She did need love, but not the way he needed her. She needed only herself, and Max, her son. They were two, as she had chosen. But she was a woman, with a woman's needs. Bill's arms were strong and his shoulder was broad. She was tempted. Her body had moved before she had considered the effect, for once uncalculated. He had spoken the right words to unlock her. Comfort. The right word. That was all it had taken.

His arms were strong, his sweater smelt warm and good, the skin of his neck against her face had a deep, clean sensuality to it. He did not move. He held her quietly, just pulling her head to rest it in against his shoulder. Gently, he stroked her forehead. She closed her eyes and let go.

She heard the fire crackle, felt his fingers in her hair. Felt them curve over her head and down into the nape of her neck, gently touching her, then massaging her expertly, freeing the tension. Her head tipped back in pleasure. The strong fingers stopped, cupped her head. He moved. Before she knew it, his lips touched hers, his body was pressed to hers and his arms were holding her.

His hands were touching her skin, sliding down beneath her blouse, travelling the warmth of her. Her eyes opened, their expression languid. She knew what was coming and now that the moment was here she wanted it. It was the right place and time at last.

Her hand stopped and held his.

'Max,' she warned.

Bill understood. 'Come on,' he said, lifting her to her feet. He took her hand and led her to the beach.

He was slow, taking his time. He laid her back on the rug he had brought and dexterously unbuttoned her blouse. His lips were against her throat and his hands gently caressed her. Dickie's head was arched back, feeling the sense of pleasure starting. Still the memories burned in her.

'Make love to me, Bill. Don't wait.'

She wanted him to do it, to take her fast, to wipe the slate clean and blot out the past. But he knew that was not the way. He took no notice of her impatience, just stroking her slowly against her desires, building her up to want him, and not just as a solution to a long-remembered pain.

His body was warm, like an animal. Hers was like silk. The discovery was mutual, the pleasure good. Naked they were well matched and strong. His hands touched her waist, slid over her hips and thighs. In wonder, she ran over the strength of his chest, the breadth of his shoulders and then down to touch him, shivering with her own fear. That fear made him growl with wanting her, beneath her hands he grew and she saw his eyes and knew her power, a woman's power. And the moment passed as he closed his eyes and pressed his lips to hers, sliding his body above her. Dickie's hands were tight on his shoulders, but he was gentle. Gentle at first and she felt the fear go, the pleasure start, heard him groaning his need of her, knew now how he could not stop. She looked into his face and saw his transport, how this act held him in a clutch all of its own so that he had to control himself to be gentle with her when he wanted to be fierce. She saw his strength and marvelled that he did not crush her, saw at last that this did not defile her in any way, saw how even here she controlled him. She felt the surge of him, and herself felt the little grains of pleasure rubbing inside her, running through her. It built. She saw the strain in him, the holding back, the fever that struck his brown eyes so that he was in another focus altogether. And then, then she felt it come to her, she heard distant moaning and knew it was her. She heard the surge of the sea, felt the roughness of his hair beneath her hands, felt the graze of his beard on her shoulder, the deep primal sound of his cries against her, knew how her own body started to move and move against his. The wind shivered over her skin. She sighed. He lifted away from her, his shoulders like a giant against the scudding sky; his hips plundered her. She felt the first wave ride through her and she rose to meet him with a cry. She saw his eyes, saw the surprise as her body took from him with joy, and knew what it was to be a woman.

Bill's arms held her. He had found the passionate woman he had known was there. Her hawk-like need of purpose had had to have some earth. He had been there. Now, he thought, she would be his and forget the past. He would father her boy; they would be a family. He loved her.

He slept under the stars.

How simple is man, thought Dickie. She lay awake and saw the peace in his face. He was already asleep. Bill had been good to her and the revelation that he had wrought in her she would not forget. It was a release of tension. But it did nothing to deter her from her chosen path. In fact it worked in reverse; it made her resolve even stronger. Now she knew for sure how they had taken away her early youth and destroyed it for their own illicit greed. They had used her and stolen from her. With Bill, for the first time, she was fulfilled. She was even stronger than before.

EIGHTEEN

Early summer. 1926

Wiley Fairfax was Wall Street's own child. He was the son of Winston Fairfax, a senior partner in the Wall Street investment house of Boyd, Home and Company. The family name traced back to colonial Maryland. Winston Fairfax had taken him to watch the first American air race from the Mineola field on Long Island, around the Statue of Liberty and back. Wiley was hooked. He had never had the desire to actually fly himself but he had learned a good deal about what it cost to keep planes airborne.

He was not surprised when he heard that Miss Bennett wanted an appointment with him. He had expected it for some time. He had not missed that sense of urgency in her, nor the tenacity with which she had built her small business out of nothing. He unwound his lanky frame from the chair and shook her hand.

With her was a tall, strong, young East Coast pilot.

Dickie introduced him. 'My partner, Bill Latimer.' She came straight to the point as she sat down. 'We're interested in bidding for one of the feeder routes to carry the mail across the States, Wiley.'

Wiley leaned back in his chair, ready to listen. 'I believe the routes are already in operation, aren't they?' he asked, pulling a sheaf of papers towards him. 'New York/Boston to Colonial, Chicago/St Louis to Robertson, Chicago and Dallas to National . . .'

'I know,' she said. 'We were too late, or rather, not big

215

enough, to take the first routes, but we are an established airline for the coast. We already run our passenger airline to San Francisco and San Diego. We thought of putting in a bid for the next batch of contract routes. I made enquiries. The Post Office are ready to throw open contract routes for bids for many other routes throughout the States.' She crossed her legs. 'Bill has carried mail for the Post Office on the East Coast. We both know what it's about, and it's very profitable. Colonial reckons to pull in a thousand dollars per trip. Still, they are looking for all the passengers they can get.'

'Don't Pacific Air and Western, Pop Hanshue's outfit, get Los Angeles' outward-bound mail, though?'

'Yes.' Her eyes were direct and businesslike. 'Western has Salt Lake City to Los Angeles, and Pacific has the mail up the coast to Seattle and Portland back to San Francisco and here in Los Angeles, but they've only got enough planes to carry the mail.' She pulled a map from her handbag and spread it on the desk. 'We thought of carrying the mail inland to Denver, Santa Fe, Palm Springs, Phoenix. We already fly down to San Diego, perhaps we could get that contract.'

'I see. How can I help?'

He looked at the young woman sitting across from him. She was smartly dressed in a black dress, belted at the hips; her legs in sheer silk stockings were elegant, and the pale green eyes under the brim of a black hat were startling. She interlaced her fingers and looked him in the eyes.

'This time we need to be ready. We need backing and we need strong partners. I've already approached John Swainson and he is interested. I told him I was coming to you. You have influence and you have contacts. We could use you, and you could use us. We, Bill and I, have the expertise. We've worked out the figures,' she said as Bill pushed the sheaf of papers across the table towards him. 'Together we could form a company that will corner this square of the California market. There's more interest in passenger flying here in California than in any other part of the country. And there are two more points I would like to mention . . .'

Wiley Fairfax was concentrating on the rows of figures. They were impressive. 'I see you've done your homework,' he said. 'Mail is more profitable than passengers, though, isn't it?'

'That's what I was coming to,' she said. She laid her hands on the arms of the chair. 'We know we can operate mail-planes successfully. Those are all the figures on mileage and pounds of mail carried.'

'You've taken your calculations as far as Kansas City,' he said. 'But what I'm concerned about are the dangers—the tremendous distances, the terrible winter weather I've heard so much about, the flying at night. The conditions are bad, especially over the mountains and the deserts where you're planning to go. If we're going to operate an airline, surely it's got to be carefully considered? Consistency is essential. If there are accidents, fatalities, it'll all come to nothing. You need to be secure. You've only flown the coast so far.'

Dickie smiled. She had heard him say 'we'. He was already interested. Now she just had to lay her trump card on him. 'The coast!' she said with a light in her pale eyes. 'The Pacific coast is one of the best places to learn. The coastal fog and the storms are legendary, as you well know. We've got two ideas. People will only fly if they are offered reliable planes. Bill and I flew to Hasbrouch Heights yesterday, just across the Hudson River from New York. There's a man there called Tony Fokker . . .' she said, looking at Bill.

'Tony Fokker?' said Wiley. 'I've heard that name.'

Bill nodded. 'Yes, he is getting quite a reputation. He designed the most advanced military flying machines for the Kaiser. After the war, he brought his experience to the States. He's designed a magnificent new aircraft. It's got a cantilevered construction, without struts and without exposed flying wires.' His hands described the machine in the air as he spoke. Dickie and Wiley watched him. 'The planes have spacious interiors, fabric-covered walls and upholstered seats. Tony Fokker understands the limitations of wartime engines. His argument is that two engines are more reliable than one, and three more than two by a factor of one half. The Fokker is a high-wing monoplane. And a trimotor. It's a superb machine. Comfortable, trim and appealing. The other thing I thought of was this . . .'

He stood up and walked across the elegant grey carpet. The room was large and very neat, one palm plant stood at the edge of Wiley's massive desk and behind him was a large picture window with a view out over the city. Bill looked briefly at the view and turned back into the room.

'. . . the Liberty engine, in the Boeing Model 40 for example, is very heavy. Now, an air-cooled engine could be made two hundred pounds lighter. That means, quite simply, that two hundred more pounds of mail could be carried. If we were to produce this engine we could put in a much better bid for mail across the country than anyone else.'

Wiley sat listening. He was a very astute young man and knew that listening achieved much more than talking. Bill Latimer's words made sense—if the thing worked.

'How about manufacturing this engine and putting it in a commercial plane?' he asked them. 'Then we could carry more passengers.'

Bill's voice was thoughtful. He pulled at his lip. 'Yes.' His voice was slow. 'We could do that.'

Wiley leaned on his hands. 'Tell me about the air-cooled engine. Technically.'

Bill returned and stood beside the desk. 'The air-cooled engine carries more power per pound than the liquid-cooled engine. By keeping planes light and small we could ensure the best use of the limited space available on board. The saving in weight is due to the absence of a radiator and coolant pump.'

He lifted his hands and described the motion. 'The radial engine—so called because the cylinders are arranged around a drive shaft attached to the propeller—is kept cool by the passage of air around the cylinders rather than by pumping liquid through the engine.'

There was a brief silence.

'Well,' said Dickie. 'Are you interested?'

'I'm interested,' he said. 'Yes. Let's talk a little about figures.'

'Of course.' She tapped the paperwork briefly. 'The desert trip, for instance. That round trip would bring us in a profit of one thousand one hundred and fifty dollars for the mail alone. With the new engine or the Fokker trimotor, we would also carry passengers. An airline cannot progress on passengers alone. We need the mail. We thought of putting in a bid for one of the less glamorous routes. We figured that way we might get it more easily. We will enter a bid of two dollars a pound for the first thousand miles and eighteen cents a pound for each additional hundred miles. That will be undercutting the other bids. We should win the contract.'

Wiley Fairfax thought for a moment. He had various friends in power, sons of presidents of some of the richest companies in California. The idea appealed to him.

He laid his arms on the desk and smiled. At Dickie. 'I'll see what I can do. I've got friends I'd like to talk to. And if John Swainson wants to come in, that sounds good to me. If it all works out, we'll draw up papers for a new company. Do you have any name in mind?'

The smile spread up her face. It lit her eyes. 'Coast Airlines.'

The storm engulfed her machine. The rain thundered down onto the wings of the aeroplane like millions of tiny pellets and visibility was so bad that the wing tips had disappeared from view and the coastline was completely blotted out. It was like flying from day into night, and in the semi-darkness the luminous instruments glowed an eerie green from the dashboard. The open cockpit was almost flooded and her tropical flying-suit wet through. And then the engine coughed and faltered, and suddenly died.

Dickie gave the machine full throttle but the plane did not respond. Silently it began to glide slowly towards the water. The altimeter swung from five thousand to four thousand five hundred then four thousand. Dickie immediately prepared for ditching in the sea. She undid her shoe-laces and flying-suit and grasped the hatchet she carried which might help her hack off a bit of wing to float on. As the plane neared the water, she tried the throttle again, but there was still no response.

Suddenly with a great roar, the engine caught. She took the plane up to six thousand feet and flew the next hour with fingers crossed and a prayer in her heart.

In rain and overcast conditions she approached the runway. The headlights from a car and a lorry were shining onto the soaking runway and marking the far corner of the aerodrome. Two mechanics with torches indicated the path across. Dickie brought the plane down, the headlights illuminating the cabin. She tore across the tiny space and managed to pull it to a halt yards from the end of the runway.

Bill jumped from the lorry and ran towards her, his coat pulled up over his head against the lashing of the rain and gale force winds. 'Dickie!' His voice was torn away by the wind.

Dickie grinned as she saw him.

She started to climb out, her clothes stuck to her legs.

'Are you all right?' he shouted as he neared her. Then he saw her face. 'God's sakes,' he said as he lifted her from the wing and into his arms. He kissed her wet face. 'You crazy woman, you enjoyed it!'

'Well, I won, didn't I?' She put her hands on his shoulders.

'You won something else, too.'

'Not the contract?'

'Yes. Wiley rang me just before I came to meet you.' He laughed at the pleasure in her bright green eyes. The rain streamed down her black hair and her face, spiking her eyelashes. 'They accepted our bid for Southern California and the desert route to Denver, everything.'

'Bill, that's wonderful. When do we sign?'

'As soon as we get you out of those wet things and into something more dignified.'

'Dignified, hell,' she said. Her hands gripped his shoulders, her eyes shining. 'Let's go.'

He ran with her into the passenger terminal at the airport. Behind them the ground staff quickly covered the cockpit of the plane.

Inside, he closed the door behind them. The silence was loud after the hissing of the rain and the howl of the wind. She looked at him. Her sunburned skin was wet and glowing, the green eyes burning with health and vitality. She went across to the washroom and emerged with a towel. She rubbed her short dark hair roughly.

'What else, Bill?' she asked. 'What about the finance for the trimotors?'

'Yes, we've got that too.' He was more subdued now.

'And the air-cooled engines?'

He shook his head. 'No. Too expensive.' He kicked lightly at the ground with his foot. 'We're just not big enough.'

'Oh, Bill . . .' She knew his disappointment.

'Well, we've got so much expenditure now. The planes, the crews, the maintenance forces, the managers. Setting up a separate unit for me to work on the designs was just not on, and far too costly. They said no to that, and we should go on with what we had—a sure thing.'

'I don't believe it,' she said, after a pause, her eyes flashing. 'We will get the money for you. *I* will.'

'It doesn't matter, Dickie. We've got everything else we wanted.'

'Yes,' she said, the smile catching at her mouth. 'We have.

And we'll make it work, Bill.' She shook her head. 'It's a shame about the engines though. What did Wiley say?'

He walked her to the back of the building and the car.

'He tried his damnedest, that's what he said. He believed in them.'

'Quite right too. So did I.' She turned her face to look up at him. 'Someone'll pip us at the post, Bill. I bet they're already thinking of it, working on it. You'll see. It was such a damn good idea of yours. Why don't these people have more imagination?

'Because they're bankers,' he said. 'They want facts, not speculation.' They reached the door. 'Dickie?'

'Yes?'

'Why did you fly in that storm? It was crazy.'

Her eyes surveyed his worried face. 'I needed to, Bill.' Her voice was soft but clear. 'Sometimes I just have the urge to challenge myself physically. Get out there and fight, force something out of myself.' Her eyes remembered the storm, drifting away in memory over the turbulent mountainous seas. 'It may have been crazy, you're right. But . . .' her eyes held his again, 'I just liked the feeling of being alone for a while.'

She could see the look in his eyes. Gently, she touched his face. 'Come on,' she said. 'Let's go and sign, partner.'

He pushed open the door. They walked out to the car.

January, 1928

Dickie flew down over the Arizona desert. Beneath her spread for miles were the brilliantly coloured sandstone rock formations. Reflecting the setting sun's warm rays, the rocks glowed deep orange under the limitless blue of the sky. The sightseeing party was going down to Santa Fe.

The new airline was quick to make money. In Los Angeles they flew from Glendale and in San Francisco from Oakland. However, the federal government had not as yet installed lights along the California route. Equally, the Weather Bureau were not particularly accurate in their forecasting. The fogs and storms along this stretch of the Pacific coast were legendary. Dickie bought up some old ship's searchlights and had them placed on the hills north of the airfield. The planes flew the route, keeping close to the coastline. She signed on the Post Office department's veteran pilots and mechanics to maintain the planes, and she and Bill flew the passengers themselves.

Slowly, the passengers started to come in, seduced by the novelty of the Fokker trimotor and by its comfortable ride. Tony Fokker had been right. They were reassured by the new design, the absence of wires and struts, the all-metal construction, the cantilevered wings and the strength of the machines themselves. The planes started to fill up. Often they would hand their pilots twenty- to fifty-dollar tips on landing, after discovering that the novelty of flying could now also be a pleasure.

By the late 1920s, their planes were also being equipped with blind-flying instruments—an airspeed indicator, an altimeter, the turn-and-bank indicator, a rate-of-climb indicator and an artificial horizon. All these instruments made flying possible when the light blended together at dusk and the natural horizon of sea and sky was lost.

Within a year's operation, Coast Airlines had become an airline with a reputation for safety, comfort and reliability.

Around Dickie now, the azure blue skies of New Mexico stretched for ever. The following day she would fly them up to Colorado, over mountain lakes and magnificent forests that were part of a vast recreational area, dotted with tiers of aspen trees and the jewel-like serenity of the still lakes, the mountains capped with snow.

Even though it was January, the flying conditions were perfect and Dickie took the opportunity to fly the passengers herself. Bill was flying the mail through to Denver. They would meet there for dinner.

She lifted the nose of the trimotor and checked her instruments. The horizon levelled out on her indicator. Flying was getting easier than in the old days. She allowed herself a small smile and got ready to drop over the mountains and into Santa Fe.

'Bill Boeing got the Chicago/San Francisco route.'

She looked up with interest. The small restaurant was intimate and warm. It was a weekend and the tables were almost all full.

'I knew he would,' she said. 'What did he offer?'

'He offered to carry the mail half-way across the United States for no more than the Post Office is paying others to tote mailbags between New York and Boston,' said Bill. 'A dollar fifty a pound for the first thousand miles and fifteen cents a pound for each additional hundred miles.'

'That's pretty good.' Dickie forked up a piece of chicken and started to eat it, doing mental arithmetic. 'How about the others?'

'Pop Hanshue was mad as hell. He offered two dollars twenty-four and twenty-four cents. He fully expected to win the job.'

'He would.' She seemed amused. 'But he was bidding for profits, not a manufacturing outlet. That was his mistake.'

'I suppose.' Bill looked at her. She seemed to be taking it remarkably calmly. 'He and the others protested bitterly that Boeing was going to ruin the whole private-contract system. Didn't matter, though. He got it.' Bill picked up his glass of wine and studied the deep red colour. 'He's going to build twenty-five planes. With the Pratt and Whitney Wasp engine, of course.'

'Of course.' She chewed her chicken thoughtfully.

'You don't seem a bit upset, Dickie.'

'I'm not.' She laid down her knife and fork. 'I told you some-one would come up with an air-cooled engine and make it work. And they did.' Her eyes lifted to his. 'Bill Boeing. And who better. He's enterprising and he's going to make it work. Now all we have to do is follow him.'

Bill frowned. 'How do you mean?'

'I already knew what you were going to tell me. So, I went out and bought some more Pratt and Whitney shares. I got a hundred and ten for twenty-two dollars. I also bought shares in Boeing's airline. I told Wiley I wanted some of the new company too. He's got an eye on the future, and so have I. I'll tell you another story. Wiley told me this.' She picked up her glass and held it between her hands. 'Mergers are in the air, Bill. Jim Melloy instructed Wiley to put in a bid for Patton Air's control-ling stock at two hundred and fifty dollars a share. Wiley ex-tended Patton his first credit, he knows him. Well, he's a bit desperate now. He's struggling to finance his line, as you know.' She turned the glass in her hands. 'Wiley pointed out that Mel-loy's scheme made no provisions for other stockholders and left the line's employees out on the street. So,' she tilted her head, 'he came to me today. He suggested that *we* buy all the Patton Air stock, voting and non-voting alike, and merge the two air-lines. I've offered two hundred bucks a share for the stock and

Wiley thinks Patton will accept, mainly because I've agreed to keep on all the employees on the payroll and to buy out all the other shareholders on the same terms or better. What do you think of that?'

'Fantastic. He's got the mail route we need.'

'Exactly. And that's the bait.' She drank her wine and replaced the glass on the table. Bill looked curious. 'We're not going to operate it though, Bill.'

'Whyever not?' He opened his hand out. 'It's what we've been after all along. A substantial mail route. Why, we could operate it far better than Patton ever could.'

'No,' she said. Her mouth was firm. 'Wiley warned me. It's time to pull out. People are building far too high, and it's bound to break. It's a good time to sell.' She looked down at the linen napkin across her lap. 'I told him I was already thinking of going home. I think we should sell everything, Bill, except our shares. We should merge with CNA, and let Wiley and John hold the reins until we come back. It's time to start up back home. There's a slump in England. I want to pick my time to return, and it's pretty soon. Within a year or so. We should start thinking of tying things up now.'

She remembered the report in the paper. The effect of the general strike of 1926 was still being felt. Work was practically non-existent in London with depressed economic conditions.

Bill was astonished. He stared at her and then looked away. He shook his head. His voice was naked when he spoke to her again. 'Dickie. I had no idea you wanted to return. I thought . . .'

'Oh, did you think I had forgotten?'

'I thought that was all in the past.'

'Definitely not.' She let her eyes search over his face. There were lines of tiredness and exhaustion in him. He worked too hard, in appalling weather conditions. He had borne the brunt of the mail runs; the winter times when blinding storms drove into the open cockpits and somehow the mail had to get through. He had taken the brunt of it so that she could carry the passengers in safer weather. It was time to stop. Time to start again: in England. 'I cannot wait to get home. If my guess is right,' she said, 'we will be considerably richer very shortly. Wiley is always ahead of the market.'

'Are CNA interested then?' he asked. He picked up his knife and fork and put them down again. Suddenly he had no appetite.

'Oh, they don't know yet!' She gave him a broad smile. 'We've got to tie up with Patton first. Then we'll let CNA know, making them think it's their idea of course, that we're up for grabs.' She ran a hand over her hair. 'Wiley's all for it.'

'Wiley,' he said. 'That man's all for you, not the airline.' He felt the jealousy bite in him. Dickie looked bland.

'Is he? Can't say I ever noticed.' She started to eat again, cutting into her chicken. 'If you're agreeable to all this, anyway, Bill, we'll have it all sewn up with the stockholders, and you and I will hang on to the majority shares and stock.'

'I'm agreeable, Dickie. There is something, though. Something you may have overlooked.'

'What's that?'

'Your son, Dickie, sweetheart.' He watched her eyes. 'If you're going back to England, don't you think you'd better go . . . as a married woman.' He kept his eyes steady on hers. 'You probably don't care about respectability, but . . . and I believe you . . . if you want to take back from them what they stole from you, then you need respectability, along with your ill-gotten gains,' he said lightly, his voice teasing. 'Miss Bennett should return Mrs Latimer and family. Don't you think?' he finished.

She paused for a moment, her eyes soft. 'Bill . . . are you asking me to marry you?'

'That's about the size of it.'

'You know I don't—'

He lifted his hand. 'You don't have to say it.' He reached across the small table and took her hand in his. 'I love you enough for both of us. Enough to want your happiness and for it to go right for you, with no mistakes. I'd like to take care of you, Dickie. And Max.'

'Dear Bill.' Her eyes were moist. 'You could be right, but you know my reluctance to marry.'

'Yes. You've let me know so often in no uncertain terms at the most inopportune times,' he said ruefully, referring to their night-time trysts away from home so that Max would not catch them. 'But at least it would have an advantage in that we could save money on travelling thousands of miles to be together. Max could at least see us legitimately together in one bed!' His eyelids drooped in humour over his dark eyes.

She smiled warmly and responded to his hand. 'I shan't hold you to any old-fashioned codes of fidelity, Bill. And I cannot make any guarantees. From time to time I'll have to go away, to be on my own and be myself. I'm not the stay at home sort. You wouldn't get one of those.'

'Oh, I know that.'

'And if it doesn't work, you will let me go?'

'Unhappily, yes, I would. But it will work, Dickie. I know you too well to pressurise you.' His eyes looked into hers.

She was silent for a moment, assessing him. 'Well,' she said, 'all right. You are right. It would help enormously. Thank you for understanding my needs, Bill.'

He bowed his head, his eyes closing momentarily.

'So you will.'

'Under those conditions, yes. I will.'

He lifted his glass. 'To us.'

'To us.' She lifted her glass and clinked it against his, her smile reflective, the green eyes dancing in the candlelight as they toasted their future. Then, after a moment's pause, she continued her meal. Bill watched her from behind his glass, still absorbed in the events that had taken place. Jealousy, he thought, it had such a destructive and yet an erotic aspect. Maybe it was an important aspect of love. It could be exciting, obsessive, in fact, to be the one who was left or rejected. She, Dickie, was always taking off, to Mexico or wherever, making decisions that included him only if he were to follow along. And follow he did, because quite simply he had no option. It was true that the one who turned away was always the winner. Just as it was so much harder to break with someone emotionally if they had left you—the very fact that they were able to take such a step made them more interesting. Jealousy added a whole halo of qualities to a love object. The mere fact that she might leave him in time, or go off with someone else, like Wiley, he thought angrily, could set him simmering. Falling in love with someone was largely a matter of luck, and his fate happened that day at Gerry Oswald's fair. Those green eyes and that determined little face demanding a ride. And look at her now. Across from him Dickie happily finished her meal. She had a new poise and dignity that had not been there before. Responsibility made her glow. He could not help smiling. He knew how much he loved her. He would follow her to the ends of the earth.

Autumn, 1928

Max zoomed his paper plane through the air. Up and down. Zoom.

'We're going to go to the desert, me and my dad, for the weekend. We shoot and sleep out.' Jake looked important with his news.

'You shoot?' Max stopped the plane for a moment.

He strolled alongside his friend, Jake. Jake's dad had a ranch in Pasadena. Jake swung his leg and kicked a stone on the sandy path. 'Yeah,' he said. 'You wanna come? I'm sure my dad would say it was OK. Shall we ask your mom?'

'OK, let's do it.' They turned up the road towards the house. It was white stucco with Spanish tile. It ran long and low behind a wall with a black wrought-iron fence. Plants grew profusely in beds beyond the wall and beneath the windows of the house. Max pushed open the gate and walked up the path. 'Let's go down the creek after we eat, OK? Bob says there's a big, fat trout just waiting to be caught.'

'Yeah.'

They charged into the kitchen like young animals. Max was growing up. At fourteen, he was a strong boy with dark unruly hair and piercing blue eyes. His health stood around him like an aura, glowing California health that showed an outdoor life.

Dickie came into the kitchen as they burst through the back door. 'Hi, Mama. Anything to eat? Wow, you look terrific.'

Dickie ruffled his hair. She was wearing a white silk dress and her dark hair was gleaming. Her skin was brown and healthy and she wore a thin gold bracelet and small gold earrings. She had lipstick on and her green eyes were luminous, deep pools against her tan. It was a change from the jodhpurs and flying gear. She looked beautiful. 'There's plenty of food in the fridge,' she said. 'Don't eat too much, you'll make yourself sick. Hello, Jake, how are you?'

'Fine, thank you, ma'am.' His eyes admired her. Max sure had a good-looking ma.

Max raided the fridge. He brought the plates of food over to the bar.

'You going out, Mama?'

'Yes.' She sat down on the high stool across the bar from him. Max put together his sandwich. She looked into his face. 'We're celebrating, Max. I've got some news for you.'

'News?' He looked up.

'Yes. Bill and I just pulled off a deal. We're rich now, Max. And so we're selling out and going back home. To England.' Max looked puzzled. America was home. He ate slowly. 'We're going to set up a new commercial airline there, together. You know I've always wanted to go back. Or rather, needed to.' Her eyes caught at Jake, pouring himself a glass of milk beside the fridge. Her look was significant. Max knew she had a reason to go back. He had come to know the name Redfield; her hatred for them had become his own. In some way that family had persecuted his mother, in a way that had affected his whole family. At last the time had come when he would be able to stand beside her. He felt that he hated them with a force that was equal to her own.

He turned to his friend. Jake was draining his glass of milk.

'Hey, Jake. Catch you later, huh?'

'Sure.' Jake got the message. 'I gotta be getting home. See you. Night, ma'am.' He lifted a hand to Dickie as he placed the empty glass on the counter. He winked at Max. 'Ask about the trip!'

Max nodded. 'Sure will. See you.'

The door closed behind him, and suddenly Max was all business, no longer a boy, paper planes and camping trips forgotten.

'Go on, Mama,' he said. He bit into his sandwich, his strong eyes now on her. 'Tell me.' He ate slowly and waited.

'There's been a slump over there,' she began, 'a general strike. Now's the time to return. People are looking for work, and we'll give it to them. We know enough about the airline business now to compete and compete well. And you'll be a part of it, just as soon as you've finished your schooling. We've learned the American way,' she said, her eyes brilliant as she looked at him. She was proud of her boy, bright and strong—a product of the American system. 'Remember what my old friend Joe said? "If you've got guts you can make it." No guts, no glory. Well, we're going to take that ideal back to England. We're going to make it work for us.' She paused. 'What do you think, do you think I'm right?'

Max looked at her. They were very close. She had always treated him as an equal, not as a child. And he, too, was fuelled by her revenge. He knew that somewhere, somehow, someone in England had hurt his mother very badly and whoever it was, he wanted to be her champion. He had protected his mother and

studied hard. There had been many fights in the school play-
ground over his parentage, and his Uncle Bill's presence in his
mother's house. They lived on the same street, but he thought
they should marry. He had once asked her and she had said,
'I'll never marry. There's only one man in my life and that's
you.' And then she had kissed him and left him to lie in the dark
with the memory of her words. He had listened to her footsteps
recede, the screen door bang shut and the sound of the garden
gate and her car starting up. She would be gone to take another
night flight.

It had all been for the two of them. He knew what was expected of him. She had been poor and had brought him here to
make a fortune. Now that fortune was made. He still remembered the sea crossing, the grey swell and the seedy rooms in
New York. Life was good now and she had made it so. Now it
was time to help her take her revenge.

And there was one other thing.

'Will I meet my father?' His voice was quiet.

In the hallway beyond the kitchen Bill stopped as he heard
the question.

Dickie hesitated. 'In time.'

'Is Uncle Bill coming with us?'

'Yes.' Bill heard her pause again. 'What would you think if I
told you we were getting married?'

Inside the kitchen, the blue eyes lifted to hers. Their intensity
was dramatic against the sunburned skin. Fleetingly, she thought
what a beautiful child he was. 'Are you?' he said.

'Yes.'

'That's fine by me. He's a nice man and he loves you.'

Bill put a hand to his mouth, his eyes warm with affection.
He heard Dickie laugh aloud with the same reaction to his simplicity. Her voice was fond.

'That's what I hoped you'd say. We're going to build a new
company in England, Bennett Airways.'

'I'll help you, Mother,' he said with a new formality and a
mouth full of sandwich. 'We'll do it together.'

'Thank you, Max. That's all I need to hear.'

Bill stole quietly away.

Spring, 1929

In late 1928, Boeing and Pratt and Whitney had merged to form
an aviation company. Interest in flying had been aroused by the
Lindbergh flight. The public wanted aviation stocks, and in 1929
the two entrepreneurs set up a new holding company known as
United Aircraft and Transport Company. Bill Boeing became
chairman. They bought up plane makers, a propeller company,
and an air-transport service that lacked airmail contracts but had
five years' experience in carrying passengers. Their corporation
combined many lesser firms by an exchange of stock from which
all profited, and his timing was deft. It was the crest of the Wall
Street stock boom. Just before they had formed the trust in November, 1928, the directors had voted a seventy-eight to one
stock split. Then when the combine was formed, they exchanged
these shares for two point two shares in the new company.

Anyone who had paid eighteen dollars for his original ninety
shares in Pratt and Whitney aircraft, and in 1926 paid another
twenty-two dollars for a hundred and ten shares more, had those
shares increased by the board's 1928 action to sixteen thousand
shares. After the exchange of these shares for the thirty-four
thousand, seven hundred and twenty shares of United Aircraft,
his forty dollars' total investment would have become worth
three million, three hundred and sixty-seven thousand, eight
hundred and forty dollars.

Dickie turned to Bill as the steamer pulled out of New York
harbour. 'Would you keep an eye on Max for me?'

She walked slowly to the stern. New York was bathed in the
glow of a beautiful sunset. She pulled her fur coat closer around
her throat. The tugs hooted. She watched America recede slowly
into the distance. Her memories haunted her.

She was a rich woman. She was going home.

BOOK TWO

1929–1948

BOOK TWO

1939–1945

NINETEEN

June, 1929

Mrs Canter handed out the change to the customer.

'There you are, dear. Sixpence change. Here's your stamps and your bag of sweets for the little one. Not a bad day, is it? Weather's on the turn.' She nodded her head, still smiling as the woman and her child left, and she looked into the face of the next customer. She was elegantly dressed, a newcomer to Foxhall Green. Mrs Canter's curiosity was aroused.

'Yes, madam. Can I help you?' She laid her broad hands on the worn counter.

The woman smiled. The pale green eyes were somehow familiar. So was the smile.

'Mrs Canter. Don't you recognise me?'

It dawned slowly on her. 'Well, Lord, look who it is. God love us if it isn't you, Dickie Bennett.' She surveyed the cool linen suit, the pearls, the immaculate cotton gloves and silk stockings, the neat cloche hat. 'My, you look different, dear, and . . . it can't be! Little Max!' The young man standing beside her was already taller than his mother. He had strong blue eyes and an air about him. 'I used to look after you,' she said, 'when you were so high!' She levelled her hand to the ground. 'Look at this. I must call Albert. *Albert . . . !*'

'Mrs Canter. Where is my dad?'

Mrs Canter wasn't listening. She looked out of the window and saw the gleaming green Lanchester parked at the side of the

233

wide high street. Bill lounged against it, arms folded. He was looking down the street.

'That your young man?' she asked. 'Handsome, isn't he? American?'

'He's my husband, Mrs Canter. I'm Mrs Latimer now.'

'Ooh, I say.' She nudged Dickie with her elbow. 'Lucky girl!'

'Mrs Canter. Where is my father?'

'Your father, dear?' She looked puzzled. 'No, well, I suppose you didn't know.' She looked a little disapproving, and embarrassed.

'Know what?' She had been to the cottage and found signs of another family living there.

Mrs Canter scratched at the counter, and dusted with her hand at an imaginary mark. 'The Redfields, pet. They threw him out. Gave Oak Cottage to a new family. Lovelocks, they're called. Two boys and a girl, work the land alongside their father. Nice family, they are. Though they complain a bit. You know, they say the roof's leaking and things needs mending, and that Rupert Redfield, he doesn't do nothing for them, and he's a man of the church too. They say charity starts at home, don't they, and . . .'

'Mrs Canter. What happened to Dad?'

'Oh, he still works there, pet. As a gardener.'

'A *gardener*!' Dickie breathed slow and hard to still the furious beat of her heart. Those dirty swine. And he had promised. Wouldn't she make them pay for this.

'Yes,' said Mrs Canter. 'And he has to walk right from the other side of the village. From Menderley way. Laburnum Cottage, it's called. Part of the Menderley estate. Sir Henry's place. Yes, the Redfields certainly don't consider loyalty. They're selling off their land, you see.'

'How long's this been going on?'

'Oh.' She shook her head and looked upwards. 'Let me see now . . . past few years, anyway. Shortly after you left.'

'Why didn't you tell me?'

Mrs Canter's eyes were round. 'Well now, how could I do that? I didn't know where to write to you. You never wrote, after all. Your poor dad . . .'

'Never wrote? Why, I even wrote to you! Didn't you get my letter?'

'No, dear. Ah, here he is . . . Albert . . . remember Dickie and young Max? Look at them,' she said proudly. 'Don't they look fine! Proper gentry!' She beamed at her son and then at them. 'Strange you didn't know,' she said. 'But then, as I say, we never got no letters, did we, Albert?' She nodded at her son for confirmation.

Albert had come through from the back room when he had heard the sound of something interesting. Now he wished he had stayed where he was. He stood in the dark doorway and stared at her. He would hardly have recognised her. He was shocked. He had never expected her back. He mumbled something in reply to his mother. His habitual sour grin disappeared. He looked cornered.

Dickie gave him a quick look. Max, to whom most of this was a dim memory, looked more curiously. Dickie turned back to Mrs Canter.

'How is my father? Is he all right?'

Mrs Canter shook her head. 'Not too good, love, I'm afraid. He's a sick man. Has been for some time.' She crossed towards Albert. 'No family to take care of him. Hasn't been easy.' She put a motherly arm around Albert who shifted uncomfortably. Dickie threw him another look.

'How do I find Laburnum Cottage?' She turned back to Mrs Canter.

'Go to the Menderley estate. Down Gates Lane, last cottage by the field at the end. You can't miss it.'

'Thank you, Mrs Canter. Excuse me now, I must go and find him. I'll come and see you later.'

'All right, pet. Bye-bye Max.'

Max opened the door for her and they walked out into the sunshine of the high street. Through the window Mrs Canter watched them talking in the sunshine with the athletic young man. Dickie was gesticulating and pointing up the street, away from the direction they were heading. They all climbed into the gleaming motor and the man started it up.

'Well, I never did,' said Mrs Canter, with real wonder in her voice. 'Little Dickie Bennett. Latimer now,' she added proudly. 'Practically a lady. Never thought she'd make it. Did you, Albert?' She watched them as the car reversed. It was gossip to set the village alight.

Albert said nothing. He did not move as he watched the car turn and drive back down the broad, sandy high street. On this he had to agree with his mother. He had never expected that she would return.

* * *

The birds chirped prettily in the aviary. The Italian garden was new. The red bricks and silvered stones were laid in aesthetic formation around neat flowerbeds. Beyond, through the privet hedge, was a perfect small square garden, in its centre a stone sundial. A small ditch had been dug for a gentle river to flow from the Thames through the garden and alongside the house. A curved stone bridge had been built beside the yew tree leading to the side door of the house.

Caroline opened the back door and came out. She was followed by Lucy, her maid, and Jessamy. She walked over the stone bridge and down onto the bricks at the edge of the Italian garden. She was carrying a trug over her arm. She crossed over to the aviary and curled her fingers over the wire, clucking to the birds.

She went to the first of the flowerbeds and started to deadhead the roses. It was a pastime that she enjoyed; Rupert had instructed the gardeners to leave the roses to her. It kept her occupied. Caroline was in a world of her own most of the time, but today she was happy. Charles was coming home from school soon and Jessamy had been released from Miss Ingram to join her mother in the garden.

Caroline handed the trug to Lucy. 'There you are, Lucy. It's too hot today. I think I'll sit in the shade of the cedar tree with Jessamy. Bring us our lemonade, would you?'

Caroline put her arm in Jessamy's and they walked down the side of the main garden to the wooden seat, the same wooden seat where she had once sat with Alexander. They sat down. Ahead of them the river flowed beyond the line of trees. A statue of a young girl with a waterjug stood beside the edge of the lawn between them and the river. Caroline's eyes rested on its lines for a moment.

Lucy came hurrying back with a tray of lemonade. She wore a plain black dress with a starched white apron and white cap. She was a willing and cheerful girl, more than ever in the good graces of her mistress. Caroline had discovered a penchant in Lucy for village gossip which she encouraged. It seemed that Lucy was very *au fait* with life; she kept her ear to the ground, and she was proud of the privilege Caroline had given her. Caroline was subsequently more in touch with what was going on below stairs than any of the Redfields before her. She enjoyed the gossip; it was light and simple coming from Lucy, and she made it amusing.

She laid the tray on the wooden table she had brought out, and poured their glasses of lemonade. It smelt fresh and wonderful. Jessamy reached for hers.

'Well, Lucy,' said Caroline as she took hers too from the proffered tray. 'And how are you today?'

'Oh, I'm that excited, my lady,' she said. 'There's real news 'in the village today.'

'Oh.' Caroline held Jessamy to her and leaned back in her chair. 'What's that?'

'Well.' Lucy stood up straight. 'Dickie Bennett's come back. And as fine as a lady she is, begging your pardon, my lady.'

Caroline smiled gently. 'And who is Dickie Bennett?'

Lucy's brown eyes were round. Her pretty face was bright with her news. 'She used to work here! In the kitchens! As scullery maid!' Her voice held a note of disbelief. 'Just before the war. Before your time, my lady. Well . . . she went away to America to seek her fortune—after her brother died in the war, that was awful sad—well, none of us in the village believed her like,' she said in her Welsh lilt. 'But back she is and dressed in fine clothes and jewellery and with her boy and a young American gentleman. He's handsome, her husband. She's a Mrs Latimer, now. It's the talk of the village, it is. They came in a beautiful car, like a jewel it was, all shining and sparkling in the sun.' Lucy's voice sang. 'Brand new. I saw it on my way to the post office. It's like a dream come true, it really is.'

Caroline sat up slightly. Her imagination was stirred. If it was really true, it was quite a story. 'How did she make all this money?' she said. She felt the interest grow in her.

'Well, that's it, see,' said Lucy. 'Nobody knows yet. It's a mystery. So far, anyway. We'll know soon enough, though. She's gone to see her father now. Old Jim Bennett. He used to live down Oak Cottage, poor man, until Mr Redfield . . .' Her voice trailed. She had said too much. Jim Bennett's dismissal had made Rupert Redfield a name to be hated in the kitchens and grounds. They all went in for their tea with Mrs Maitland, all the farming men, and Jim, Lucy thought, had always been a nice, kind man. She could have bitten her tongue, but perhaps Lady Caroline had missed it. Sometimes she drifted far away even as Lucy was talking.

This time, however, she was listening. 'My husband dismissed him, did he?' Caroline looked at the obviously embarrassed girl. 'Do you know why?'

'Excuse me my lady. I don't really.' She seemed to be hiding something.

'Tell me, Lucy. You do know, don't you?'

Lucy drew a breath. She had to tell her now. 'Well, as I see it my lady, it was like this. Jim Bennett and his son, Sam, used to work the land for Mr Redfield. Well, when Sam died in the war and you were short-handed like, Mr Frederick took it upon himself to let Dickie, Jim's daughter, work on the land beside her dad. Then, after the war, it seemed she wanted to go to America.' She swallowed briefly. 'She met this pilot, see, who told her America was paved with gold and she believed him,' she giggled. 'None of us others did, but Dickie did. She always was one with strong opinions and a mind of her own. So, up she got and took the boy with her—Max—her son. Jim stayed on as head farmer and he had a tied cottage to go with the job. Mr Frederick let him stay.' Now her eyelashes fluttered as she got to the embarrassing part. 'Talk is,' she said, looking down, 'that when Mr Rupert got to hear about it he got angry and threw him out of the cottage and offered him a job as a gardener. That's a real insult to a farmer, my lady, if you don't mind me saying so. But old Jim, he had no choice, mind. He's old and in bad health.'

'He took the job.'

'He did that. He's the one looks after your roses. You've probably seen him around. He's a quiet man, well liked hereabouts.'

Caroline's arm moved slightly on Jessamy's shoulder. She lifted the frill on the shoulder of Jessamy's dress and rubbed it gently between her fingers. 'And his daughter,' she said. 'This Dickie . . . she didn't keep in touch with her father?'

'Well, that's what no-one knows,' said Lucy confidentially. 'It's not like Dickie to have left her father with nothing. She was always a good lass to him. Something's not quite right, but we'll be hearing more, I 'spect. Apparently they're up seeing him now.' Her face brightened in a smile. 'Does me good to know the old man's got her back though. He loved her fierce, he did. Looked just like her ma, I hear. Same temper, too. Never let go of an idea, her ma didn't, till she died of tuberculosis,' she added in an aside. 'Nor did our Dickie. It's exciting, isn't it? The whole village is talking about it. She's so beautiful now. Like a lady.'

Her eyes gleamed with wonder. 'Shall I get you more lemonade my lady? Miss Jessamy?'

'No. Thank you,' said Caroline slowly. She pulled her arm away from Jessamy's shoulders. 'That'll be all. I think we'll join my husband and Mr Frederick for lunch. Please tell them to expect us. Come along, Jessamy. Let's go and change.'

Caroline turned her head as Chalmers, the butler, left the room. She lifted her glass of water. 'I heard an interesting story today, Rupert.'

'Oh, really, what was that?' He continued to eat, half listening.

Frederick looked down the length of the table at her. It was highly polished and laid with lace mats, crystal and heavy family silver. A huge drift of sweet peas sat in a silver and glass bowl in the centre of the table. Caroline wore a pale blue silk dress, pinned at the throat with his mother's cameo brooch. Her dark hair was swept into a cropped page-boy cut. It complemented her long neck and the clean line of her jaw. He heard the timbre of her voice lift with her news. He smiled expectantly at her.

'It seems that there's a great fuss downstairs over one of the village girls. She went away and now she's back, and, it seems, quite exquisitely dressed and driving around in a brand new motor car. They're all talking about her. I hear she used to work here,' she added.

'Oh, really.' Rupert chewed his food. He bent over the newspaper beside his plate, studying the racing form.

Frederick's expression was polite, still. 'What was her name?'

Caroline looked strained. Her hand went to her forehead, and the lovely brow creased in perplexity. 'I don't remember . . . something strange . . . oh, *details* . . . ' She shook her head dismissively, and brushed her hand across her forehead. 'She went to America, that was it. She thought the streets were paved with gold. It's like a fairy story,' she said, smiling again. 'No one believed her, and yet she did it. Her father used to work for you, Rupert. You must know him. He is . . . was . . . a farmer. You made him become a gardener.'

Rupert slowly stopped chewing. His eyes swept from the newspaper and up to hers. They were cold and searching. He said nothing. He looked accusingly at Caroline, and her hand touched the cameo at her neck in confusion. Frederick's eyes were on her too. 'Why, what have I said?' asked Caroline. 'Why do you two look at me like that?'

'Dickie,' the voice piped up. 'Dickie Bennett.' Jessamy pouted her news as she forked at her potato. 'I remember. Lucy says she's a grand lady.'

'Grand lady . . .' repeated Rupert, dismissively. 'Impossible.'

Frederick leaned his elbows on the table. He rubbed his lips to and fro against the finger of his hand. His eyes were distant.

'All dressed in beautiful clothes with a big car, her son and a handsome American man,' sang Jessamy. 'They've gone to see her father.' She tipped her head from side to side and pushed the food around her plate.

Rupert and Frederick were silent. Rupert chewed slowly again as he stared down the table. 'Jessamy, eat your food properly.'

'They probably won't stay here now if she's really got money,' said Caroline airily. 'She'll probably move her father away from the old ties and try to set up somewhere where she's not known. She could do very well for herself. It's a good story, isn't it? By the way, why did you turn him out of the cottage after Frederick let him stay?' she said, addressing Rupert. 'That doesn't seem very kind, Rupert.'

The words irritated him beyond reason. He turned on her. 'You shouldn't be listening to maid's gossip, Caroline. What on earth's the matter with you?'

Caroline opened her mouth and closed it again. Her eyes swept briefly over the table before her. She looked suitably chastened. Rupert bent again to his food. There was a heavy silence.

Frederick still said nothing. She was back.

The Lanchester pulled to a stop at the end of the overgrown lane. Beyond the farm buildings, there was a small cottage. Brambles grew alongside the gate, and the garden was raked over. A few flowers were growing round the edge of the cottage but the garden had obviously been put over to seed for vegetables.

Dickie stepped out of the car into the sunshine. She saw the garden. Her heart went out to him. He was trying to do his farming here in this feeble plot of land.

She took a deep breath. Her pain was in her eyes. Bill saw it. He came round the bonnet of the car. 'This is it?'

Max climbed out behind them and stood behind his mother, looking.

'This is it,' she said. 'Laburnum Cottage.' She saw the roughly painted sign on the gate. In the hope of visitors? Had her father really thought she had forgotten him?

Inside the cottage Jim heard the squeak of the garden gate. He put down the kettle he was boiling for his tea and went to the door. He squinted out against the brightness of the day. It had been raining and now the sun's glare was almost blinding.

He saw the woman standing at the garden gate. He saw the boy and the man standing tall alongside her. He looked a bit like Sam, the same rough, blond hair. She was wearing a hat but then she pulled it off. The sun gleamed on her dark hair.

Jim thought he was seeing a vision. He had longed for this moment so much, and now he was imagining things again. He shook his head, his old eyes blurred against the light.

The vision spoke. 'Dad!'

And then she was running up the garden path and it was real. Her arms were around him, her warmth comforting and filling those long years he had waited. 'Dad,' she said.

Jim closed his eyes and held her.

'How I've longed for this moment.'

'Me too, Dad.'

'Let me look at you,' he said. His eyes took in the expensive linen suit, the stockings and the elegant shoes. 'My Dickie,' he said in awe. 'You've got rich.'

The same green eyes looked into his. 'Yes.'

'And taller.'

She laughed. 'It's the shoes.' She lifted her foot.

He smiled. 'You look well, girl, so well.' His hands trembled on her arms. 'America must be a fine place. Oh,' he said, 'I've missed you, I can't tell you. It's so good to have you home.' He sniffed, and drew his hand across his eyes. His face showed all his simplicity of feeling.

Dickie tensed as she knew the hurt he felt. He looked old, his open-necked shirt showed the sinews of his neck, and his braces held up trousers that were baggy and loose. He had lost a lot of weight.

'Dad,' she said gently. 'Here's Max.' She turned and opened her hand to include her son.

Max stood behind her, fully grown at nearly fifteen years of

age. He moved forward and shook his grandfather's hand.
'Hello, sir.'

Jim took his hand slowly. 'My, my!' he said. 'What a fine
lad you are. And you've taken care of your mother? Good lad,
good lad.' He patted him on the shoulder, covering his emotion.
'Yes,' he said. 'A fine lad.' He looked him up and down.

Max stood silent, a small smile on his face at Jim's words,
but his thoughts were very different. This was his grandfather,
bowed by the hand of these Redfields. He was bitter with anger
that their first meeting should be tainted with the old man's
humiliation. He renewed his vow to himself. In time he would
make up for their troubles. Dickie watched them both. She saw
her father stare at the man who had followed them through the
gate.

'Oh, and Dad,' she said. 'This is my husband, Bill. Bill Latimer.'

'Your husband?' Jim swung to look at her and then back to
Bill. He held out his hand. 'Well, how do you do? This is a
surprise.'

Dickie stood beside her father, her hands laid gently on his
arm. 'Let's go on in, Dad. There's so much to tell you.'

There was only one room. Jim pottered around like a mother,
fussing over them, setting the table. Dickie's heart ached to see
how much he had changed. The years had been rough on him.
She could not speak at first.

She stood up. 'Sit down, Dad. I'll get the tea.'

'Oh, no. With all your fine things. You sit down.' He poured
the tea. 'I'm sorry I haven't much to offer you, pet. Sorry about
the chairs. Look, there's one here,' he said, as Max looked
around for a fourth chair. 'Not what you're used to, I'm afraid,'
he said to Bill.

'Dad. Stop apologising,' she said then. 'Everything's fine.
I'm still your daughter, Dickie. You're OK. That's all that matters. Now, sit down. Let me make some supper for us all. Where
are the vegetables?'

'No.' He caught hold of her arm, clearly embarrassed by their
finery and his simple life. She sat down with him.

Dickie could not understand it. Her worst fears had come
true. She was horrified, and angry. The Redfields had done this
to him. But what had happened to her letters, and the money?
'Eight years, Dad. Why didn't you tell me? You've been gardening up at Foxhall for *eight years*?'

'Yes.' He looked down at his hands. He turned them over and looked at the deep lines that working in the soil had wrought with time. 'Oh, it wasn't so bad once I got used to it.'

She knew how bad it would have been for him, a farmer all his life and proud of it. 'Why didn't you write, Dad?'

'To tell the truth I didn't know where to find you, lass.'

'But I wrote to you!' She leaned across the old table and clutched his arm. 'I told you where I was. I wrote to you every month or so, and sent you money. I can't understand it . . . Didn't you get the money?'

He shook his head and looked across at her. 'No, lass. I didn't.' He looked puzzled, his mouth thin. He was tired and worn, his body stooped over his chipped, white mug. His hand folded around it. It was gnarled and leathery from years of sun.

'How long have you lived here?' she said.

'Ever since Mr Rupert told me to go.'

Mr Rupert. Her eyes hardened as she heard that name.

'Dad,' she tried again. 'Did you get any of my letters at all?'

He wrinkled his forehead. 'I got one. When you was in New York. Said about you having trouble finding good work, and you was living with some Polish woman or something . . . here, let me get it . . . it's in my jacket . . .' He started to get up from the table.

She stayed him with her hand. 'No, don't, Dad.' Suddenly she had a suspicion. 'Who read that letter to you, was it Albert, or Mrs Canter?'

'Albert,' he replied straight away. 'Milly was too busy. She gave your letter to Albert and he read it to me. I wrote one back to you, lass. He wrote it for me. Did you get it?' He looked up hopefully.

'No. I didn't.' Her voice was slow.

'That's strange,' he said. 'Albert said he'd send it off all right. I went down the post office every day after that for the next few weeks hoping. Milly, she was that sorry for me. She used to say ''No letter today, Jim'', and then she just stopped saying it.'

'*Albert*,' she whispered.

'What you say, love?'

'I said Albert, Albert Canter. He kept the money.'

'I don't think so, love.' He turned his cup in his hands.

'That guy we saw at the store?' asked Bill.

Dickie looked across at him. 'Yes. I knew it. I thought he

looked shifty when we were in there. Now I know why. Just wait till I get hold of him.'

Jim put out a hand. 'Oh, no, now don't make a fuss, lass. It's the village. Let it go. You're back now. That's all that matters.'

'But you've suffered so much,' she argued. 'Not knowing where I was, whether I was coming back. All the time I thought you were fine.'

'Well, I am now,' he said. 'And happy to see you and my young grandson.' He smiled proudly. 'Fine lad, Dickie, fine lad. You've done him proud.' He looked fondly at Max.

Dickie stood up. 'I'm going to see Mrs Canter and Albert and fix this, Dad.'

'No.' The smile left his face and he grabbed her arm. 'Don't make trouble, pet.'

'Oh Dad,' she said. 'You haven't changed.'

'Did you think I would?' he said calmly. 'At my age?'

The silence filled the little room. Bill looked from one to the other. He put his mug down on the table.

'Well,' he said brightly. 'What next?'

'*Next*,' she murmured. 'Next I'm going to fix those Redfields. Dad,' she went on, 'did I hear that they're selling off some of Foxhall's land?'

'That's right,' he said. 'They're selling Home Farm and the two fields that run adjacent to Cobbold's Wood. You know that one we used to plant the potatoes in?' he asked her. 'There's a good twenty-five acres they're getting rid of down by the river too. Good land.'

Dickie paused for a moment. She leaned back in her chair, and her eyes were thoughtful. She tapped the table. 'How would you like to live at Home Farm, Dad?'

'Eh?'

'Would you like to have your own land to farm again?'

The old man's eyes gentled. 'Oh, I would that,' he said, pushing himself back into his chair. His fingers toyed with the handle of his tea mug. 'I would that.'

'Then you shall have it.' Her voice was very quiet.

Jim looked at her, not understanding.

'Dad,' she said. 'I'm going to buy it for you. I'll buy it in the company name, Latimer Holdings. We're going to set up with that name here.' She walked round the table and stood behind him, touching his shoulders. Her eyes gazed out of the window at the fields of the Menderley estate. 'I always loved that field

up by the wood. That's where I used to go with Sam.' She took
a deep breath. 'He'd never sell it to me, but he won't know until
it's too late. You could keep a few cows, plant some good crops,
get an old carthorse of your own. That meadow land was always
good by the river. Max could do some fishing.' She smiled
across at her son. 'How about it?'

Bill watched her. He knew how angry she was, how she was
holding it in because of her father. Behind his back, though, her
anger showed, her emotions radiating through her eyes. She
looked magnificent, one of those rare people who are revitalised
by responsibility. Crisis and difficulty sharpened her perceptions
and her capacity to take decisions. Bill had still said nothing,
but a slight etch of concern showed in his face.

Jim looked up at her, and laid his own hand on the slim one
that rested on his shoulder. Now he saw her look and was struck
by the change in her. They were all diminished by Dickie's
radiance of resolve; it was her strength.

'How you going to buy Home Farm, Dickie?' he asked her.
'Where are you going to get the money?'

'Dad,' she said. 'You still don't understand, do you?
We're rich. We had this company in America, flying the mail
and passengers down the coast. We sold out for a very high
price . . .' She saw puzzlement. 'Oh,' she said. 'I've got so
much to tell you that you don't know. All these years . . .'
She touched his leathery cheek. 'Still, the main thing as you
say is that I'm back, and I'm going to take care of you. We'll
get you Home Farm, Dad. You can teach Max farming.' She
looked across at her son. 'And Bill, Max and I will live in
the big house across the fields.'

'Not Greatley?' he said, startled.

'Yes, that's the one. I made enquiries on the way here. It's up
for sale. There's a bit of land with it too. It joins Home Farm.'
She glowed with her new ability. Just wait till they find out!'

Jim screwed round in his seat. He pulled her down beside
him and held her hands.

'Don't you want to move away, Dickie? I know that look in
your eye, girl. If you want more for the boy, wouldn't it be better
in a town where they don't know you? You could make a fresh
start. You know how they are; roots stick,' he said, his forehead
creasing as he tried to make her see. 'They know you started
humble. They'll never let you forget!'

'I know,' she said in a low voice. She held his hands herself. 'That's just why we're staying. I don't want them to forget. Ever.'

August, 1929

Charles was home for the school holidays. The family was complete. He and Jessamy were inseparable. He was fourteen and she was just thirteen and already quite beautiful: raven-haired with deep, dark blue eyes and she adored him. She laid all her adolescent emotions at Charles's feet. He did not abuse her trust; he felt the same protectiveness towards her and her fragility as he did to his mother. His sister was a Dresden doll to be protected and admired. For once, Foxhall rang with the sound of childish voices and laughter.

Charles linked arms with Jessamy as they came into the house. The sound of piano music drifted out from the drawing-room. Caroline was playing her favourite piece of Mozart. The two children strolled across the hall and into the room. Frederick was sitting by the fire, listening, and they sat down too, quietly so as not to disturb her.

The music filled the silence. Frederick looked over at her, then at the children. He knew he would never marry now. These were his family, as much family as he would ever have. He had chosen his path and he was reasonably content.

The sound of the front door opening and closing made him look up. Rupert's footsteps echoed across the hall. He pushed the door open at the end of the passage under the minstrels' gallery and came in. His cold blue eyes were bright from the darkness of the passageway. He looked agitated, but he did not speak. He walked across the room to the window, his hands clasped behind his back. The children sat straighter in their seats, as if on edge. Caroline's playing faltered slightly as her eyes swiftly caught sight of him. She continued playing, but the atmosphere had changed.

What a pity, Frederick thought, as he knocked out his pipe against the fireplace. Rupert's presence had altered them all. He wondered what he had come to say. Rupert stared out across the lawn, his shoulders stiff with tension.

The piece came to an end. The resonance died away.

Rupert turned from the window. 'Very nice, my dear. Very nice.' He clapped briefly and smiled into the middle distance.

Caroline bowed her head slightly and ruffled through the pages of her music book.

Rupert appeared to be deep in thought. Then he looked over at Charles. 'Well, Charles. How is school?'

'Fine, thank you, sir.'

He pushed his hands under his legs and put his knees together. Frederick, watching from beside the fireplace, thought he looked apprehensive.

Rupert nodded. 'I have your report.'

Charles looked up, questioningly. He said nothing.

'Academically it's . . . fair,' he said. 'It appears you're studious and disciplined.'

'Yes, sir.'

'Not much on sports, though, are you, Charles?'

'No, sir.'

'I was always very good at sports,' he accused.

'Yes, sir.' Jessamy's eyes were wide. She looked from her father to her brother and back again. Rupert stared at the ceiling, up beyond the gallery.

'A man should be good at sports, Charles. Will you try harder next term?'

'Yes, sir.'

'Polo,' he said. 'Cricket, bit of rugger. Got to have a good seat if you're going to get in a good regiment.'

Charles's eyes flew open. 'Regiment, sir? You mean, the army?'

Rupert eyed him. 'Of course I mean the army. What do you think I mean?'

Charles's hands came out from under his legs and rested on his knees. They were long, sensitive hands. He plucked at the material of his trousers. He was going to say what he had to say, but his father made him increasingly uncomfortable. He was aware of Jessamy's heavy silence beside him.

'I don't want to go into the army, sir.'

Caroline peered at him from over the music rest. She looked apprehensive now.

'Not going into the army! Whatever do you mean. Of course you're going into the army. Into my regiment,' said Rupert. He stared his son down. 'Are you going to tell me you have other ideas?'

Charles swallowed. 'Yes, sir. I'm not interested in fighting, sir.'

'Fighting? Who's talking about fighting? I'm talking about background!'

'Well, sir. My tutor told me I'd do well at Oxford. And I'll need to go if I'm to become a doctor, sir.' He looked as serious about his decision as only a boy of fourteen could.

'A doctor?' repeated Rupert. He glared at his son. 'A *doctor*?'

'Yes, sir.'

'I'll be damned!' Rupert glowered at his son. 'It's out of the question. You are a Redfield, and you will enter the army and then you will be going up to London to learn about banking. Time somebody showed an interest there,' he muttered to himself. He turned to the mantelpiece to reach for his pipe, the subject closed.

'Sir,' the voice piped up. 'My tutor says . . .'

'I don't give a damn what your tutor says!' Rupert rounded on him. 'Didn't you hear what I said?'

'Yes, sir.' The boy bent his head.

'Then understand that I don't want to hear any more on this subject. Is that clear?'

'Yes, sir.' Charles looked him square in the eye again.

Rupert frowned. He addressed himself once again to his pipe. In his chair by the fire, Frederick warmed to the boy. He stood up in the silence that followed.

He saw the light flush that had appeared on the boy's cheeks. His pride was damaged but not squashed by Rupert. Of course, such a profession was out of the question. There was no prestige, no money, it was for an entirely different order. Still, there was no harm in discussing it with the boy, letting him down a little more gently so to speak, explaining the issue to him.

He smiled down at Charles. 'It's a fine profession, Charles,' he began, 'but not for one of us. I expect in time you'll lose the idea and find that working at the bank and learning to run the estate for your father is much more in keeping with your ideas once you're ready to leave school.'

'Yes, sir.' His voice was polite, but totally unconvincing.

Frederick lit his pipe. 'Good for you, Charles.' The conversation was finished.

Charles took a breath. 'I'm sorry, Father,' he said suddenly, 'but there's more I want to say.' Rupert's head started to turn towards him as he launched into his speech. 'I've given this very careful thought and I'd like to go into general practice here in the country. I've already spoken to Dr Biddy and he thinks I have the right attitude. I'd like to help people, sir. There's nothing wrong surely with a Redfield helping the community,' he added with unarguable naïvety. 'We're a local family. Surely it's one of the best things I can do. Apart from being a farmer, that is.' As his young voice stopped talking, the silence in the room was deafening. Behind the piano, Caroline stood, her face white as she waited for Rupert's reaction.

It came quickly.

'You've spoken to Biddy?' he thundered. 'Just who do you think you are, young man? I'll have you know, in my house, my word is law. You have no opinions here. I'll have no more talk of this ridiculous rubbish. The sooner you go back to school the better. I shall speak to your headmaster and tell him to reprimand this tutor of yours. Filling your head with nonsense. Man should be sacked. Next term you will find yourself with a new tutor and a very different attitude or you will be severely punished. Now have I made myself clear?'

'Yes, sir.' Charles was now flushed with embarrassment, his pride cut to the quick. He had a fine relationship with his tutor, a kind and intelligent man whom he admired enormously. To be severed from him would be a harsh blow. He wished now he had not chosen to be arrogant and stand up to his father. It had worked in his disfavour. As for his chosen career, he was a strong boy and equally as obstinate as his father. His mind was made up. He would be a doctor.

Caroline eyed the scene. She gave a tight smile at her son, and came round from behind the piano. 'I hear you've sold some of the land today, darling,' she said. 'Is that true?'

Rupert brightened. His glowering expression faded. He looked over at Frederick who had encouraged his son. 'Yes, d'you hear that, Freddie? Sold them today. Home Farm and Greatley House. For cash! Buyer didn't even want to wait. He came with his solicitors, exchanged deeds, he gave me the cash right in my hand. How about that, eh?'

'The asking price?'

'Yes! and I'm thinking of selling them some more. Maybe Cobbold's Place.' He looked well pleased.

'Oh . . .' Frederick felt sad, as well he might have done. In the end he had capitulated to pressure from Rupert and agreed to sell some of the farms, but he had stipulated which ones. Home Farm was self contained, it was not exactly Foxhall, as it lay neatly the other side of Cobbold's Wood. It was on their side of the river but closer to the village. It was a fine property, though it was not truly Foxhall land. The best agricultural land lay to the west of the house. It was a compromise. He still had some acres left to farm. Greatley House had no land really to speak of, just orchards and lawns. Cobbold's Place was at the other side of the village. 'Who was the buyer?' he asked casually. He pushed the tobacco down in his pipe.

'A fellow called Latimer.'

Frederick stopped abruptly. His eyes snapped up. 'Did you say Latimer?'

'Yes.' Rupert caught his tone. 'Why? Do you know him?'

'Tall, blond chap? American?'

'Honestly don't know,' said Rupert looking away as he tried to remember. 'I would have remembered an American accent. No, I don't think so. Come to think of it, he said hardly anything. Solicitor did all the talking. Yes, he was tall and blond. Why?'

Frederick looked at the waiting family and then at Rupert. He gave him a warning look. 'Because he's *her* husband.'

'Whose husband?'

'You know . . .' His eyes held a significant light.

'You don't mean—?'

'Yes.' His voice was clipped.

'Good God,' he breathed. 'She tricked me.' He bit his lip thoughtfully. 'I know, we'll buy him out. Offer a higher price to get it back.'

'I don't think they'll sell, somehow.' Frederick eyed him.

Rupert fisted one hand into the other, angry now. 'Well, I'm going to get back at that woman if it's the last thing I do. I'm not selling any more. I'll put a stop to the sale straightaway. I'm not having some kitchen girl trying to outsmart me. I'll fight her with the Redfield name, that counts for something around here. I'll close doors in her upstart face. I've got enough friends—'

Frederick attended to his pipe. Strange that she should be the one to keep Rupert from selling off what he, Frederick, wanted to keep.

Caroline stared at the two of them.

'The kitchen maid,' she said, bewildered. 'Do you mean . . . that girl Lucy told me about . . . ?'

'Yes,' said Rupert through gritted teeth.

'She's bought Home Farm?' She started to come out from behind the piano.

'Yes, yes, *yes*!' said Rupert. 'But she'll wish she hadn't.'

'Why? What does it matter who buys it?' Caroline asked. The men hardly heard her.

Frederick puffed at his pipe. 'We've no right to be angry after—'

'Ah, she wanted it,' said Rupert vehemently. 'All those country girls want it.'

Frederick's eyes flicked towards Caroline.

'But she needn't think she's so clever,' Rupert went on, eyes blazing. 'She's fighting Redfields now, not some damn Yankees. I'll talk to Renfrew immediately. See if we can find some loophole in the contract. Caroline, come with me, I want to talk to you.'

With a furious sound, he strode from the room leaving silence behind him. Caroline walked across. 'What's this all about, Frederick?'

'Nothing.' Frederick nodded towards the door. 'You'd better go.'

Caroline gave him a brief look, then followed Rupert out.

'Sir?' said Charles in his clear voice. 'Why is he so angry about the kitchen maid?'

Frederick smiled at his perception. 'It's an old story, Charles, and not one for your ears. She fought back. And she's still fighting,' he said with something like admiration in his voice. He looked away down the gardens through the window. The stone maiden stood at the edge of the lawn in the evening sun. 'Your father hates anyone to fight back.'

Charles followed his gaze. 'Yes, I know, sir.'

Frederick looked at him fondly. He laid a hand on his shoulder. 'How did he produce anyone as decent as you, young Charles?' he said softly.

'I don't know, sir.' He had humour in his eyes. 'You tell me.'

'You know what, you're going to make a fine young man.'

'Thank you, sir.' He turned to his sister, sitting quietly on the sofa. 'Come along, Jess,' he called. 'Let's go and ride those new horses in the stable.'

Frederick watched them run. They were still children. It was easy to forget in the midst of their seriousness, though Charles had already outgrown Rupert. He was pure, something that Rupert could not conquer.

* * *

Bill looked over at her as he pulled the car to a halt.

'Dickie,' he said. 'Don't fill the boy with it.'

Her hand was on the door handle. Now she turned towards him. 'What do you mean?

'Your revenge, your motives,' he listed. 'He's very influenced by you.'

Her eyes searched his face briefly. 'Bill. My revenge is my own. I'm not expecting Max to take it for me. He's a child, anyway.'

Bill shook his head. 'He's a man, Dickie, sweetheart, and he's at the age where he's looking for wrongs to right. He wants to be your champion.'

'He *is* my champion.' She smiled. 'Don't worry about Max, Bill.'

'When are you going to tell him why you hate them so much? He's already asked me, you know.'

She looked startled. 'He has?'

'Uh-huh. Yesterday. After you bought the land and were talking about it to your dad.'

'What did you say?'

'I told him you'd tell him when you were ready.' He watched her face carefully. She seemed to have no idea what she was doing to the boy. She was so bent on gaining her advantage.

'That's exactly right.' She opened the door. 'I will tell him when I'm ready.' The green eyes warned him not to interfere further. 'I'll meet you at the top of the high street after I've dealt with Albert Canter.'

'Your father asked you to leave it be.' He put his hands on the steering wheel.

'I know,' she said flatly. 'I'll see you in half an hour.'

TWENTY

Mrs Canter heard the bell ring as the shop door opened. Hastily, she put down her half-eaten sandwich and raised her considerable bulk from the chair. 'Albert!' she called with a mouthful of food. 'See to the customer, would you, love . . .'

Albert came thundering down the wooden stairs from the room above. 'Oh, Ma,' he grumbled.

'Go on,' she said, under her breath. She slapped him on the back of his trousers. 'I'm eating me lunch, can't you see?'

Albert lounged down the passageway into the shop. He emerged through the dark doorway and stopped, looking at her.

'Hello, Albert.'

She was radiant. The black dress set off her colouring to perfection. A green jacket was slung over her shoulders. Her eyes were like those of a snake.

Albert licked his lips.

'What can I do for you, Dickie?'

'Mrs Latimer.' The eyes raked over him. 'Why did you steal my father's money, Albert?'

'Ooh, I never.' He moved back as though stung, his hands lifting. 'What a thing to say! I didn't take the money. Must have been someone else, not me . . .' He looked round for his mother. 'I'm not the only one as opens the post, you know.'

She laid her hands on the counter and stared him in the eyes. 'You little worm,' she said, her eyes like gimlets. 'Now I know it was you. No one else knew there was money in those letters. I bet you opened the first one and saw what it said, didn't you? I should turn you over to the police.'

Albert went white. 'I didn't do nothing,' he protested.

'Albert,' she said quite quietly. 'That was eight years of my father's life. Eight years when he could have been living in comfort, and I could have known about him losing his job. My father has suffered terribly because of your greed, and so will you . . .' She lifted the hatch and came round the back of the counter. 'Now, where did you put them?' She grabbed him by the shirt. 'You want me to tell your mother? The whole village?'

Albert's hands went up in protest. He swallowed. 'In the well,' he said. 'I put them . . . in the well,' he finished as she let him go.

'And the money. I suppose you spent it all?'

'Yes.'

'What on?'

'Drinkin'.'

'Drinking,' she echoed drily. Her heart fell. All those wasted years, and this miserable creature had spent her money on drinking.

'Show me where they are,' she demanded.

Albert put up his hands again to try and quieten her. He had never seen anyone so angry. He opened the side door.

'Where you going, Albie? Who was that in the shop?'

' Just old Mrs Grant, Ma,' he shouted. 'I'm just going up the garden . . .'

He led her through the undergrowth. There was the old well. She looked in. Way down in the darkness there was the white glimmer of papers, lying in a pile. Discarded, not even read. At that moment she hated him more than she hated the Redfields. She would gladly have thrown him down the well for the hurt that he had caused her father. She looked down at the letters and the pain welled up behind her eyes.

He felt her anger and stepped back, afraid.

'I should throw you down there, you little weasel.'

When she looked at him again, her eyes were piercing in the wan daylight.

'My father has asked me to do nothing, Albert, so I'm not going to prosecute you. But I want every penny back.' She stood up and faced him. 'You will work for my father willingly and for nothing until you earn it all. You will never say a word. Dad needs a farm hand. He's not young. You will get up every morning at five and go to the dairy. If I hear one word that you are not working well, I will go straight to the police. Do I make myself clear?'

'Yes,' he sulked. 'Very.'

'Good.' She walked down the hill away from him. Briefly she looked back. 'I shall tell my dad to expect you tomorrow morning. It should take you four years to pay back all you have cost us.'

'What shall I tell my ma?' he whined. 'She won't believe it.'

She stopped. 'Tell her a lie, Albert. You're good at that.'

At the top of the street, Bill watched her walk towards him. She was imperiously beautiful, with the inner glow of power that fed a certain sort of person. The determination in her walk showed that she had obviously had her confrontation with Albert: her eyes held the pale glitter of emeralds. There was a luminous quality about her now which would have been unimaginable ten years ago when she was plain Dickie Bennett from Foxhall Green.

He looked at the young man who was now sitting in the car beside him. Max was fit and lean, as athletic as most young American men who lived an outdoor life; bright, too, sharp as a whistle. He had most things worked out, even his mother, whom he patently adored. Bill knew he could not wait to find out what the Redfields had done to her, knew how he hated them without even knowing why, and he worried at her tactics. She had drawn her son close, and he dreaded to think what it might do to the boy, all ready to defend his mother's honour. The one who was close always took more revenge for pain inflicted on the loved one than the loved one did. They never forgot either and were always slower to forgive. He thought Dickie was making a mistake by letting it build the way she did.

She had reached them and climbed into the car. 'Let's go home now,' she said.

Bill reached forward and turned the starter motor.

Across the street, Frederick sat at the wheel of his car. He watched the green Lanchester pull out onto the street and drive slowly away towards the bridge at the bottom of the village.

He, too, had been watching her walk along the high street. He leaned his arms across the steering wheel, his blue eyes absorbed. He believed now that she would fight. Now that he had seen her. She had changed totally. He remembered how he had once gazed out across the garden and likened her beauty to that of the stone maiden. He had not known then how prophetic that had been.

September, 1929

Dickie sat in the drawing-room of Greatley House and looked out at the fields behind her. They stretched down to Home Farm in the valley one way, while in the other direction an endless cornfield waved gently under the skies, beyond which was the towpath which led to the river.

It was a cold, damp day, a late-summer day with endless rain. Outside in the gardens there was a beech tree, its branches heavily leaved, the black bark dampened by rain. In the orchard, the grass was thick and lush. England.

She thought of the strong heat and colour of southern California, the dust and energy of New York. Here she was back in England after all this time, in this elegant drawing-room, and with a maid of her own.

Dickie watched the girl, Joan, bring in the tea. She wore a spotless uniform and kept her eyes averted as she laid it out. It was with a sharp bolt through her consciousness that Dickie fully realised for the first time just how much she had achieved. It was like going back to a familiar mirror after a long time away. She had been so much in pursuit of her ideal that she had not even stopped to think. She had just been driven.

Now, at the sight of the starched apron and familiar black dress, she suddenly let herself feel the enjoyment of her achievements.

She stood up and went to the window, opened it and drew in the smell of English grass and woodland. It was beautiful. By the fireside sat Bill and Max, the men in her life. It had all changed. This was her land now.

'Dickie?'

She turned back into the room.

'Are you ready?' It was time for business.

'Yes,' she said. She joined them at the fire, leaning back into the comfort of the upholstered sofa.

'Now,' said Bill. 'To start. The converted wartime bombers used to establish many airlines during 1919 to 1923 are not available, either through attrition or because much better purpose-designed airliners are available. I think we should go for charter hire for international services on an unscheduled basis. We cannot start from scratch competing against the giants,' he said. 'So we'll start where we can, and catch up later.' He held the pencil between his fingers. 'All right?'

She nodded, not wanting to speak and break the chain of his thought. Bill had an instinct for early organisation. He had been doing his research and doing it thoroughly.

'Good,' he said. 'Now it seems freight carrying is important . . . to all airlines; and those entrusted to carry mail do very well. So we have various choices . . .' He pushed the papers apart in front of him. 'We could set up an operation for domestic unscheduled charter passenger flights, aerial photography and surveys. Max is interested in the photography side,' he said, nodding towards him. Dickie's eyes rested briefly on her son. 'Maybe some joy-riding, et cetera. We could make the occasional charter into Europe. Typically London to Rome, which is . . . er, eleven hours' flying. As you wish, Dickie, we could call it Bennett Air Tours for the charter company, and for the other—Bennett Aerial and General Transport Limited. We will all three be directors of each,' he said, eyeing the two of them. 'We already have Latimer Holdings, of course, the property company.'

'What about aircraft, Bill?'

'Aircraft, yes,' he moved the paper aside and looked at the next sheet. 'I think the Armstrong Whitworth Argosy is too big for us. Expensive to run, too, and anyway, they really only go to the major airlines like Imperial. They take twenty passengers. A similar Handley Page is around ten thousand, five hundred pounds, quite a lot if we are to run a few. Therefore, we really have the choice of smaller aircraft, though two stand out.' He spread his fingers. 'Having said that wartime bombers are not in the running, if money is short, we could go for a reconditioned wartime De Havilland DH-9. With the pilots and two passengers in tandem open cockpits, it could attain a hundred and fourteen miles per hour, with an endurance of four hours. That could do for domestic flights. The Armstrong Whitworth has a ninety-foot span and does a hundred and ten miles per hour. The DH-9 is forty-two feet, four and a half inches, length thirty feet, six inches. And the last possibility is the De Havilland DH-50.'

Dickie's eyes were on him as he went on. 'Let us say the five-seater De Havilland biplane. It is designed for routes with low traffic volume and irregular taxi work and accommodates four passengers in an internal cabin. Some of the seats are removable for freight carrying if we need them. They're actually hammock-type bench seats. The pilot sits in an open cockpit aft of the cabin and above. Typical speed of the DH-50 is a hundred and five cruising, range at cruising speed is three hundred and eighty miles or more. The wing span is forty-two feet, nine inches, and the length is twenty-nine feet, nine inches.' He sat back and scratched his cheek. 'Or for international services to Europe a German all-metal Junkers monoplane or similar would be the most modern, though expensive. They all have enclosed accommodation.'

She pulled her feet up under her. 'Where shall we set it up?'

'It'll have to be close to a populated area, possibly a holiday resort. Croydon's the main airport. But we could, of course, have our own land. I was thinking that. That's why I gave you the dimensions. There's plenty around here that we could use.'

'I think that's what we should do,' she said. 'Eventually we can set up at an existing airfield, say, Croydon. We could erect a hangar ourselves.'

Bill nodded. 'Yes.' He bent to the table again, and lifted a sheet of his illegible scrawl. 'We could do it quite cheaply. We can pilot the planes and administrate. Max will be flying too. We need trained mechanics and grease monkeys. We could hire a coupla extra pilots. We have to get certificates of airworthiness, level the runways and that sort of thing, but that's not too much effort. Is that what you'd like, Dickie?'

'I think so, yes. "Bennett Aerodrome"?'

'Sure. I'll check it out.'

'What about staff?'

'Staff will be no problem. There are so many people looking for work now. And everybody's up on working with aeroplanes after Lindbergh's flight. The war produced a lot of qualified RAF/RFC pilots and mechanics. I'm sure a lot of them have not been able to settle or could not get jobs since. If not,' he shrugged, 'well, we'll just steal them with better conditions and better pay, maybe a family allowance, company pride and involvement, percentages or incentive schemes. That's how we do it in the States, don't we?' He grinned at her. 'I know, we'll steal them from Imperial. I bet that appeals to you, Dickie.'

'Whatever we do, treat them well. That way we'll always get

loyalty,' she said. She leaned forward, and reached for her news-paper. 'Saw an interesting thing in the newspaper . . . where was it? Oh yes, here it is . . . they've replaced the old beacons with radio stations in the States. They can send out signals along narrow beams to the pilot and back. The beams are split. Along the left half the pilot can hear the letter A in Morse code and on the right he can hear an N. On the centre-line the two signals merge to give a steady note along which he can fly directly! They're also building paved runways to cope with the new in-strument-landing system. I think we should think about both these things, too,' she said. 'We'll get them here eventually.'

'Well, at that stage we'll just move the whole operation across to Croydon.'

'I agree. Is that all?'

'I think so for now.' He pulled together all his scraps of paper. 'I've set up a test run of the aircraft we might be interested in this afternoon. At Croydon.'

'Good.' She sat back contentedly. She had been right to sell out when she had. It was perfect timing. The Wall Street slump had come right after their departure, and here in England any-body with money was right on top as the Depression hit home. Life was always about perfect timing. Now they just had to set up the airline.

She pushed herself up from the seat and stretched. 'While you two have been organising our company, I've been taking a look at the air races. I'm going to drum up some business.'

July, 1930

The air race at Hanworth was already under way when Dickie and Bill arrived.

Most of the machines entered in the 1930 King's Cup were biplanes. They had to race round a circuit of seven hundred and fifty miles in a single day, beginning and ending at the field. The first machine was away at seven a.m. It was July 5th.

Winifred Brown climbed into her Avian with her fiancé, Mr V. H. Addams, acting as navigator.

Dickie stood with Bill and watched Miss Brown take off .

A year had passed, a year in which she had bought property, registered her companies and laid down the groundwork for the future. Now they had to advertise.

Throughout the morning, the spectators were entertained with flying displays, aerobatics and a parachute descent. It was like the old days. Bill took them up; he stalled the plane and let her drop, pulling the throttle back at the last moment to lift her up and away above the heads of the gasping crowd. He speared off into the blue sky, his white scarf trailing in the wind.

By ten thirty the first Moth, flying high over Staffordshire, was heading the field. Aeroplanes droned overhead in a long line. The crowd cheered lustily as Winifred Brown, a local girl, came in third.

In a flimsy silk summer dress Dickie treated the crowd to an exhibition of wing walking. She stood on the edge of the wing, suddenly losing her balance so that she fell backwards into the air. As the crowd screamed in horror, her plunging body was pulled up by a short rope. She climbed back up and held onto the wires as Bill looped the loop. In a dress that showed every line of her boyish figure, she gave the crowd thrill after thrill as Bill dived at them faking a crash. He took her up again, and Dickie did her _pièce de résistance_, learned in those early days out in Pittsburgh: the ironjaw spin. She had a special mouthpiece attached to the end of a rope which she gripped between her teeth as she dangled and twirled in the plane's slipstream.

The race went on. The machines began to close together, and by the time they reached Newcastle Winifred Brown was in the lead. On the ground, pilots and their aeroplanes waited impatiently at the petrol pumps and the organisers desperately tried to get each entry airborne within an exact forty minutes of arrival. The Avian was leading as they reached Hull.

Just after six p.m., a tiny speck could be seen in the distance. Dickie brought her machine down for the last time. As she climbed out and waved at the bunch of onlookers who had come up to stare at her, Bill walked up. Dickie pulled off her helmet, her face glowing and her teeth flashing in a smile. She had loved every exhilarating minute of it. Together, they turned to watch the speck in the sky become a dot, wondering whose machine it was.

Dickie walked to the edge of the field and looked up into the sky.

'I'm sure it's the Avian, look,' she said. The dot grew closer and the biplane was at last identifiable. Within minutes, she was landing. It was Winifred Brown, a _woman_, who flashed across the finishing line winning the Air Derby.

Bill saw Dickie back to their car.

'Don't you wish you'd entered, Dickie?'

'Entered?' She turned and looked up into his face. 'I entered, Bill. That was great advertising. Miss Brown won the competition and the purse, but I won the audience. They're our future, they saw our name painted on the side of the plane. They'll remember us.' She opened the door. 'Now we've just got to put our plans into action.'

TWENTY-ONE

'Lady Haslett?'

Katherine turned with a warm smile on her face. She was dressed in a long, black dress with a fashionably low back, the skirt cut revealingly over her hips. She wore long gloves with diamond bracelets at her wrists, and a black silk head-piece with a diamond clasp and a silk tassel trailing to the nape of her neck.

'Frederick.' She offered him her hand. 'How nice to see you.'

'Is Sir Henry here tonight?' Frederick's voice was polite.

'Somewhere around, yes.' Her eyes were for him, bright with love and memories.

'Would you care to dance?' He indicated the dance floor where the dancers spun by in a whirl of colour. The Redfields' London residence had been transformed for Jessamy's birthday party. Banks of flowers graced the marble pillars and the floor was waxed to a deep shine. Three bands played in the adjoining drawing-rooms and in the marquee in the garden.

'Thank you,' she said.

She let him escort her on to the floor, graciously inclining her head in greeting to the familiar faces. 'All of London is here tonight, Frederick,' she murmured as they reached the floor. 'Rupert has done well for his daughter.'

'Would you expect any less?' Frederick's hands touched her back. He received a quick smile in response as he guided her into his arms. 'Darling Katherine, you feel so good. I've missed you.'

Momentarily she relaxed to the persuasion of his arms. 'I know.' She pulled discreetly away.

Her eyes showed her love for him. 'It's been impossible with the Season to cope with. It's hectic. Freddie, don't hold me so close. I'm the mother of one of the débutantes. I'm supposed to be a chaperone!' Her eyes sparkled nonetheless.

He spun her round in his arms, laughing.

'You still want me?' she asked.

'Always.' He smiled down into her face.

'Even though I'm old and grey, old enough to be the mother of one of this year's eligible young ladies and you could be her suitor?' she said gaily. She did not mention love. The question was there in her eyes unspoken; he had never said it.

'Even though. And you, Katherine, will never be old and grey.' Her luxurious black hair was finely streaked at the temples and the clasp of diamonds in her hair set off her heart-shaped face to perfection. She was undoubtedly a fine and elegant woman. 'You will always be as beautiful as you are now,' he said.

Her answering smile held a trace of sadness. Over his shoulder her eyes took in the sight of her daughter and Frederick's nephew, Charles, standing together at the side of the dance floor.

'My daughter's beautiful,' she said affectionately. 'Don't you think so, Frederick?'

He turned to look across the room at Melanie Haslett. She stood against a tall white pillar decked with flowers. Her long ball gown was of warm pink taffeta ruched softly around her shoulders, the colour emphasising the freshness of her skin. Her dark hair was mellow brown waving around a heart-shaped face both sweet and strong in which the most striking feature was the thick-lashed smoke-dark eyes.

'She is beautiful, Katherine,' he said.

Melanie's eyes were filled with a sleepy amusement as she listened to Charles tell her a story. The corners of her soft mouth held a dance of humour. There was a sensuality about Melanie, much like her mother's, that had not yet flowered. Charles, bending possessively over her, seemed totally smitten, as if he alone could see beyond the naïvety and into the future where that sensual woman would blossom.

As he finished his story, Melanie laughed and her face came alive, sparkling with gaiety. She said something quickly to him, the sleepy eyes now mischievous and intelligent. Charles laughed too. It was obvious that the two of them were very easy in each other's company.

'Poor Charles,' said Katherine.

'Why do you say, poor Charles?'

'Because he loves her. And because she doesn't love him.'

Frederick looked at the two of them again as Charles led her onto the dance floor, her arm linked through his. 'They seem very close.'

'Close, yes,' she murmured. 'But Melanie sees Charles as a very dear friend and no more. She has, after all, grown up with him. Jessamy is her closest friend. To her, he is like a brother. Unfortunately, no more than that.' Her eyes were sad.

'I see.' Frederick nodded his head. 'But maybe he will persuade her otherwise. He has a very strong will, young Charles.'

'Persuade Melanie!' Katherine laughed softly. 'No one could influence her to do anything against her will. My daughter, Freddie, has a mind of her own.' Her eyes were smiling, but proud too, as she looked up at him. 'She's a very bright girl. Says she wants to do something with her life, not just waste it away playing hostess on some country estate. She's looking for more than the rest of us. It's not easy to satisfy Melanie. Some man's going to have to do an awful lot of running to catch her.'

'Good for her,' he said, his voice with a soft timbre to it. She heard the breathy note in his voice and glanced up. It was the quality of tone that was there in their love-making, when he spoke to her and urged her on to heights she had never before imagined. She felt the rush of love run through her, weakening her, so that she pressed against him.

He sensed her feelings and returned her gaze, the answering flame warm in his eyes. His loving smile bound her in; she adored him.

She gave herself to it for just a moment and then pulled away again. She made conversation quickly to overcome her weakness.

'Tell me, Freddie, how is Charles getting on?'

He turned her into the dance. 'He's going to medical school. It was what he wanted,' he added reflectively. 'I think life at home is a little hard on him. He's at an age when he's in competition with father. You know, the old stag and the young stag. And Rupert's always been competitive. He wants to beat Charles at everything.'

'I shouldn't think Rupert cares much for the role of the old making way for the new. He still thinks he's the dashing young man,' she murmured.

Frederick nodded. 'Indeed.'

'And Jessamy?' She returned a polite smile as an old couple swirled past them. 'How's she?'

Frederick shrugged expressively. 'That's another thing,' he said. 'Charles has always been her hero. They adored each other from an early age. Jessamy's a strange girl,' he frowned, 'an unknown quantity. She's remarkably beautiful, yet you're never quite sure what's going on underneath.'

'Sounds like her mother,' said Katherine, watching his face carefully.

Frederick did not appear to hear her. 'Anyway,' he went on, 'Charles being her hero doesn't help. Rupert lets his jealousy show. Men like my brother, philanderers I suppose you might call them, when they have daughters they seem to be claustro-phobically possessive, beautiful daughters, anyway. And the other thing is that Charles gets her love so easily, he's done nothing specific to get it. He's a fine lad, very bright and helpful, the kindest boy I've ever known, but Rupert thinks that love can only be won by fighting and chasing. He doesn't understand Charles, never has. And there's the rub.'

'I know what you mean,' she said, her lovely forehead creas-ing in a slight frown of worry. 'Henry's like that with Melanie.'

Frederick clicked his tongue. 'It's a problem,' he murmured. 'Still, it won't last. Charles will be away from home again soon.' The music was drawing to a close at the end of the dance. 'Can I get you something to drink, Katherine?'

'A glass of champagne, perhaps.'

He led her away from the dancers towards the French windows that opened out onto the balcony and the garden. He stole two glasses from a passing waiter and, handing one to her, guided her up the step, his fingers lightly touching her back again.

'Frederick,' she admonished softly, her eyes alight.

'You shouldn't wear such revealing dresses.'

'We must go no further,' she said, standing at the door. 'Here we are still circumspect.' She lifted her face to feel the soft breeze that blew in and stole over her. Outside the summer moon was heavy in the sky, and the Redfields' Belgravia house was white and magnificent bathed in its light. The scent of flowers was intoxicating.

'Mm,' she said her eyes half closing. 'It reminds me of that first hot summer we made love. Do you remember, Frederick?'

'How could I forget? You're the most sensual woman a man

could know, Katherine. How long has it been? And I still desire you just as much.' His eyes darkened. 'You've brought me alive, my love. I don't know what I would have done without you,' he said, his voice low and vibrant.

She was silent, her skin strumming with his words. Their desire was in their eyes as they looked at each other. She gave a little laugh eventually to cover her need of him and dropped her eyes in case anyone should see; her smile stayed in them, heating them darkly. Frederick was handsome, familiar and passionate, but always a gentleman—just. She loved that about him. She had always loved him and always would. But though he needed and wanted her, his heart was elsewhere. She lifted her eyes to him again, wondering, and at that moment she saw what was happening at the edge of the dance floor. Her expression changed.

'Oh God, Freddie, I think we have trouble coming. Rupert's drunk, he's about to make an absolute ass of himself with my daughter.' She buried her face in her glass, clasping the stem with both hands.

Charles was dancing with Melanie and, as the music slowed, Rupert stepped in and whirled her from his son's arms. He was a handsome man, with his shock of yellow hair, and though now thicker in the waist, he still drew women into submission with the deeply imperious and suggestive voice, the almost cruel laughter and the cutting blue eyes that honed in on them. He was still a man with charisma, one who expected it to work.

Frederick's eyes searched the onlookers for Caroline. She had already looked for him. Rupert wanted to challenge Charles, embarrassing them all. She looked helpless, and instinctively he wanted to move to her side. Then she looked away, regal in cream satin and feathers against her black hair and pale skin. She looked like a statue as she stood bravely with her mother, Lady Lancing, and pretended everything was just as she wanted it. Katherine had not missed the look that ran between them. Frederick tore his eyes away to Charles. He stood strained and empty in the middle of the dance floor. Melanie had been virtually torn from his arms.

Rupert turned her in his arms in a fast waltz. Her dress twisted around her legs showing the line of her body. In Rupert's arms, she seemed almost exposed as he held her in the dance. Rupert looked like a mauling bear beside her, his shoulders framing her with their breadth. He looked like a man in his mid-forties, trying to recapture his youth, his face a bit ravaged, his skin more florid, but he still had grace of movement and imagined himself attractive to her. Tight in his arms, Melanie's position was intolerable: he was her host. Her eyes searched the edge of the floor for help. They caught sight of Charles.

Charles could not make any other decision. He crossed into the mêlée of dancers.

'Father.' He touched him on the shoulder.

Rupert's heavy-lidded eyes opened wide. He saw his son.

'Go away, Charles.'

The dancers craned their necks around them. Rupert turned Melanie away. Charles went round to the other side.

'Father. I was dancing with Miss Haslett.'

On the periphery of the dance floor, Frederick looked away. 'God, poor Charles.'

Katherine touched his hand.

Rupert's expression was hard to decipher. His eyes looked a little glazed. 'Go and find someone else, Charles.'

'No, Father. Please, don't do this. You're making a spectacle of yourself.'

'*You're* making the spectacle, my boy.'

Rupert whirled her away. Melanie tried to move, but he held her fast, turning her in his arms, crushing the lace at her breasts with the cloth of his coat. His strong arms held her around the waist in a lover's clinch, not that of a formal dance. He took Charles with them into the centre of the dance floor with no partner, making Charles look stupid. Rupert's eyes were half-closed again. In his arms, Melanie looked white-faced and stiff. She had had enough. He was Charles's father and her host, but it no longer mattered.

Rupert swung her round, sliding his strong hands to her waist. Charles felt the nausea flood through him. Melanie wanted his protection. He wanted to hit his father. He fisted his hands and his eyes bit into his father's profile. He was so close . . . he grabbed his father's sleeve . . . Rupert's eyes opened slightly in some surprise. Quickly, Melanie acted.

'Mr Redfield,' she said firmly. 'I must ask you to let go of me.'

At her words, Rupert's hands slid from her waist. His expression was one of absolute understanding. 'Of course, my dear. If you'd *rather* dance with Charles, of course.' His voice was disarming, perfectly charming.

He opened his hands in submission, and walked away off the floor, leaving them standing there. As if they were the guilty ones.

Charles knew his father. He sighed deeply and looked into her eyes. 'I'm sorry, Melanie.'

He put out his arm to take her from the floor. Melanie gave a grateful smile and walked off the floor ahead of him. Charles followed, his expression hidden. Neither of them felt like dancing any more. Behind them the gap closed and the music played on.

Jessamy watched her brother gently lead her friend, Melanie, off the dance floor. She was all too aware of the tensions in her family. Her gaze swept quickly around. No one was watching, but their very normality showed more than anything how aware they were of what had happened. Her mother stood white and motionless with her grandmother seated beside her, watching the dance. On the other side of the room, Rupert strode out towards the billiard room, a cigar clamped between his teeth and looking remarkably pleased with himself. He had just shown the whole of London society that he could claim a girl from his adolescent son. He was still the better man. May the better man win! Rupert loved to fight, and he had achieved his aim. He had got through to Charles and made him react. In his mind, he had won.

Jessamy turned and left the room. Her movements were swift and she fled out onto the terrace. There was a perfect moon. The vine twisted over the stone balcony and down into the garden. It was a beautiful night and she, herself, was a vision in white, a sash around her waist and her dark hair tumbling in black curls to her shoulders. The full dress drifted in the breeze. Her party was ruined. Her emotions were too near the surface to cope with anything off-key; Jessamy was fragility itself, hypersensitive to a degree. She felt and noticed everything, and everything marked her. Her father terrified her, her mother irritated her, and her brother she idolised. No one seemed to understand what adolescent tortures she endured, no one except Charles, who had been sent away just when she needed him. Jessamy was searching desperately for an answer, for direction. She stared miserably into the garden.

'Jessamy?'

The voice was tentative. Jessamy's head shot up, startled. Her shoulders lifted defensively. She did not turn.

'Jessamy? I've been looking for you. Are you all right?'

She did not answer. He came across the terrace and leaned on the balcony beside her, looking worriedly into her face. As always, her beauty stirred him frighteningly. He was obsessed with it. Jessamy, in her own world, did not give him a glance. She stared out over the garden.

'Did you see all that?' she said.

The young man nodded. He had seen, though only because he was totally aware of her every movement, her every reaction. He tried to help. 'I don't think it was as bad as you felt, though, Jessamy. Only your family really noticed, because it was your . . . father. Nobody else did. Just family. That's what families are. Aware of each other more than most.' He smiled hopefully.

She turned to look at him then. '*You're* not family.'

'Er, no . . .' The 'but' was in his eyes as he looked at her again.

Jessamy knew what he was thinking. She felt it in his stare, his adoring eyes and mouth that opened slightly whenever he gazed at her. He had told her that she was adorable, beautiful, exquisite, and that he loved her. She knew he was about to do it again. John Hamblin was a handsome young man, fair-haired and tall, with an impeccable background and lineage. And he was rich. Of all the young men around her who clung to her like bees to honey, he was the nicest, the gentlest with her, but she did not feel a hint of the surging adoration she wanted to feel. Jessamy was alive with emotion, and nobody noticed. Maybe John sensed it, but that was all. Alone at night, when Charles had been away, she had borrowed books from the maids: cheap, trashy novelettes about tragic heroines and misbegotten love. She had read them avidly in her bedroom at night and stared out of the window over the lawns into the distance, dreaming, wondering when she, too, would feel all those turgid emotions racing through her. She would fall in love with a handsome lover who would brook no opposition from a possessive father. He would carry her away against all protests, and make her his. It was glorious. Jessamy's breast rose and fell in the moonlight.

John saw. His own mind was so cluttered with desire that he could not think rationally at all.

'Jessamy,' he said. 'I must ask you something. You know I admire you terrifically.' He did not want to frighten her; she was so elusive, you never knew what would make her suddenly break away and leave. He licked his lips. He hesitated, tried to reach out for her hand, get some response. She was motionless, gazing out again over the garden. Her profile was exquisite; John felt the lovelorn yearning creep over him again. In the moonlight on the terrace, on the night of her birthday party, was precisely the most romantic time to do this, if it was ever to be done. 'Jessamy,' he said all in a rush, 'I would be glad if you would do me the honour of becoming my wife.' He stood straight, at attention almost in his formality. He waited.

Jessamy had the mind of a child and she was spoilt. She had never been allowed to develop. In Rupert's house his word was law, and she had been over-protected. No one else had an opinion but her father, or was allowed one—except the one that he held. To do something of her own, something that required action or thought—or opinion—would be novel for her. Jessamy wanted love. She wanted the touch of a man. John was handsome and he was kind. She hesitated, wrestling with the problem in her mind.

John saw her hands twisting on the stone balustrade. Her mouth moved as if she were about to speak. She seemed troubled.

'Jessamy,' he said, 'I'd be kind to you. I'd buy you a big, beautiful house. Anything you want.' He moved closer. He touched the hand that did not resist him. His fingers moved bravely around hers, and he held his breath as she did not move away. 'Jessamy?' he queried softly. 'Please say yes. I'll do anything you want. Just say yes. I love you.'

He tenderly lifted her hand and kissed the pale, cool fingers. Desire raced through him like a knife tracing over his spine and poured into his body.

She wanted to know what it would be like. She wanted sex. The only way to get it was through marriage. She turned to him, her eyes gleaming with a febrile light.

'You'll have to ask my father.' Her own house. She would have her own opinion. Would he stand up to Rupert? That was what she wanted.

John's heart began to race. He clutched her hand, aware that his own was hot and damp. She was saying yes. He overlooked Rupert, all he wanted was her, and thus he had all it needed to stand up to Rupert—the adrenalin carried him along. 'I'll ask him now, if you mean it. Does this mean that you are saying yes, my darling Jessamy?'

'Maybe.' She was staring at him, trembling, waiting. 'Kiss

me now, John.' She was still as a statue, though her eyes burned in the shadow of her face.

John moved to her. His hands touched her slender, sashed waist. She was thinner than he thought, but soft and sweet. His mouth bent towards hers, upturned cool and full; her dark hair was wild and disordered, the curls twisted around her face. Her eyes were sultry now, as her lids half-closed over them. She was like a gypsy. John bent over her, felt the bitter-sweet joy of her body brushing up against him. His whole being lifted with the sensation. Their lips met. Tenderly. He came back down to earth again and clasped her passionately in his arms. His eyes closed in ecstasy.

Katherine and Frederick had moved onto the adjacent balcony. He was about to kiss her in the moonlight. Katherine's hand stopped him.

'No. Look.'

He turned to look. John and Jessamy were sealed as one, her white slender arms draped around the dark cloth of his dinner jacket.

'Aren't they lucky?' she whispered. 'It must be nice to be free and in love,' she said wistfully.

Frederick's arm was still around her waist. He looked back into her gentle face. The young couple had stirred the voyeur in him.

'We'll meet tomorrow at Foxhall,' he said, his voice husky with his need of her. 'In the woods down by the stream. We're going back for the weekend, all of us. You are too, aren't you?' She heard his need of her immediately. She responded warmly, pleased.

'Yes. Henry has a meeting with his committee.'

'Go riding. We'll meet in our place.'

'I will.'

As Bill walked into the drawing-room, Dickie came towards him.

'How was the flight?'

'It was fine. Went without a hitch.' He held her in his arms and kissed her. 'It's good to be home. The engineers are working on her right now, giving her a quick overhaul, but I think she gets full marks.'

The recent delivery of four De Havilland biplanes was a perfect addition to their fleet of aircraft. It had taken four years for Bennett Air to reach peak performance with flights across to Europe, and with their new acquisition they were assured of more success. Each biplane sat six passengers with a crew in the cabin at the nose. They were reliable and economical, suited to short routes like the maiden flight he had just taken across to France and back. They had a range of five hundred and forty-five miles, cruised at well over a hundred miles per hour, and did not need a paved runway. Even in poor weather conditions, the sturdy planes lifted off easily from the grass. Bill rubbed his hand through his hair.

'I need a drink,' he said. 'Hey, Max,' he added as the young man strolled through the door, 'how's it going?'

'Pretty good. Flight OK?'

'Great.'

Max smiled. 'Let me pour you one.' He crossed to the drinks tray. 'Mother told you about the Boeing?'

Dickie rubbed her hands briefly. 'No,' she said as Bill turned curiously towards her. 'I haven't had time yet.' Her eyes met his. 'Pour me one too, would you, Max?'

'The usual?'

'Yes, please.' She went to the fireplace and rang the bell. 'You ready for dinner, Bill?'

He flopped down in the sofa. 'I am, yes. Thanks,' he said as Max passed him the Scotch. 'What's this news?'

She came back and sat down beside him. She lounged gracefully, one trouser-clad leg over the other. 'You remember I mentioned hearing about the 247? The one that entered service last year?'

'Yes.' He frowned slightly, recalling the Boeing's details. Bill was a man for details. Capable of ten passengers, powered by two radial engines, each enclosed in a cowling developed a few years earlier by the National Advisory Committee on Aeronautics to reduce drag and thus enable a plane to fly faster at no increase in horsepower. It had a retractable undercarriage and could fly at nearly two hundred miles per hour.

'It's a revolutionary aeroplane, Bill. Something we should go for. If we're going to get ahead of our rivals, we've got to have the 247.'

'We've only just taken delivery of the De Havillands,' he said.

'We could use them too,' she said, using her hands to emphasise her speech. 'But the Boeing is exceptional. We'd be seriously in the competition here, then. We've been dragging our heels for three years doing charters and freight. I want to move with the big league now. The Boeing is our oyster. I'm not going to miss out again,' she said emphatically, remembering how they had missed out on the first routes across the States, and the air-cooled engine. 'I want you to go over and get us one.'

'Me?' He pushed his fingers to his chest. 'Dickie, sweetheart. What's wrong with Wiley and John? If you're really set on one of these, and I can't see why for the moment. Why, we haven't even got a paved runway. We'd probably have to move to Croydon.'

She brushed that away with a wave of her hand. 'The least of our problems. Our problem is this.' She reached over to the occasional table and picked up the cable. 'I cabled Wiley. He couldn't get hold of the Boeing, and I think he's got his mind on other things. His interests are too diversified. We need a member of the family over there,' she said, nodding to Max as he handed her her drink. He returned to stand by the fireplace, watching them both. 'We need someone with our interests at heart to get things moving, especially in the States. Why won't you go?'

He opened his hands wide. 'You know why, Dickie . . . I've got my hands full watching over the boys here, I'm the manager. I've got to keep on top of things, watch out for everything. And I've got routes booked for the next week or so, unless you're planning to bring in another pilot.'

'I'm flying too.'

'Well, I'm fully booked.'

'I could go.' The voice spoke quietly from the hearth.

'*You*, Max?' she said. They both looked up at him.

'I think it's a good time for me to go. Since the Spoils Conference there have been quite a few changes,' he said, referring to the conference that had followed the election of the Democratic administration in 1932, when independent airline operators had been accusing the postmaster-general of favouritism in awarding the contracts. Now the Black Investigation had turned up evidence that substantiated the claims, and President Roosevelt had cancelled all airmail contracts. 'The army's flying in the mail,' he went on, 'they're bound to mess it up. I think it's a good time for one of us to be there and get ready to pick up the pieces. New business, Mother. Just what you want. And, incidentally, tie in a new Boeing as well.' The bold blue eyes smiled down at her. 'I think I could do it for you.'

John left the balcony and ran down the steps into the drawing-room. He spotted Charles and Melanie.

'Do you know where your father is, Charles?'

Charles looked at him. John's eyes still held the almost fanatical light of absolute ecstasy, and his appearance was slightly dishevelled, in contrast with their cool and somewhat sombre demeanour. The party danced on behind them.

'Yes,' said Charles slowly. 'I think he's probably in his study, or playing billiards in the billiard-room. That's the direction he took anyway. Why, John, what's the matter?'

John could hardly pause to tell him. He slapped Charles on the shoulder. 'Good man,' he said. 'I've asked Jessamy to marry me.' He grinned wildly, the grin hovering at the corners of his mouth. 'She's accepted! We're going to be brothers!'

'Good gracious!' said Melanie. She looked towards the balcony for a sign of Jessamy. There was none. 'This is very sudden.'

Charles was left shocked by the news. Jessamy confided everything to him. With a last pat on the shoulder, John raced away, not even staying for the inevitable congratulations. 'But she doesn't love him,' Charles murmured in his wake. 'Why is she doing it?'

'If she doesn't love him,' said Melanie drily, 'she won't marry him.'

'I'm going to find her.' He moved slightly.

'Too late.' Melanie raised an eyebrow in the direction of the far set of French windows. Jessamy was hovering on the edge of the step, and then she brushed past the dancers in the same direction as John had taken.

'I don't believe it,' said Charles. 'Do you think it's simply because he's the right . . . type for her?'

'No.' Melanie shook her head. 'It's not enough, Charles. Love is enticing, and John adores her, I know that, but if it's not in the heart even the most provocative love in the world won't hold anyone.'

'Melanie?' He turned towards her.

'Shall we dance now, Charles?'

'No.' He held her hand firmly. 'There's something I have to say first.' He saw Melanie's expression tighten. 'Please, listen to me. I'm so very fond of you, you must know that. It's growing all the time. I could easily fall in love with you,' he said, his voice softening and his eyes on her downcast face. 'Dammit, I'm so sorry about my father, but I can't change that now. I do want to know how you feel for me, and whether I have any hope of winning your heart, Melly. I'm sorry to be so blunt but I've got to know.'

Melanie was a strong girl and her heart was warm, but she was a romantic; she would only pursue a relationship for love. She had to tell him honestly, though by the admission she might lose his valued company as a friend. She could not be selfish and prolong their attachment purely for her need of his friendship. She had to tell him the truth.

'Charles, dear, I'm very fond of you too, but I'm afraid that's all. I know I will never love you, except as a very dear and wonderful friend.' She saw his eyes drop so that she would not see the hurt. She took his hand. 'You've asked me to be honest with you,' she said as gently as she could. 'And that's the truth. I love you in quite the wrong way for you, but for my own selfish reasons I haven't wanted to lose your friendship, which I prize greatly.' She paused. 'I'm sorry, Charles.'

'I'm the one who should be sorry,' he said. 'I've embarrassed you, Melly. The last thing I wanted to do. It's entirely my fault. I thought you felt strongly for me.'

'I do,' she said, pressing his hand with her own. 'It's hard not to. You Redfields are a very provocative family. There's a power in all of you. You're strong.' She paused. 'But it's not for me.'

He lifted his eyes to hers.

'In my father?'

'What?' Her hand slipped from his.

'The power in my father,' he said. 'Does it affect you?'

She looked away and back. 'Yes. As a matter of fact it does. He does have something. Despite the way he acts, there is something about him.'

'What?'

'Now, Charles, do you really—'

He took her hand again. 'No, come on, Melly. Tell me. Since

we're being honest. Tell me what it is that makes women swarm around my father.'

Melanie drew a breath. At the archway to the room, the trio appeared out of the dimness of the shadows. Rupert was striding at the head of them, John a few paces behind, the triumphant look on his face as he turned and reached for Jessamy's hand saying more than words. They crossed the room towards Caroline in the corner. Melanie watched Rupert, a sadness in her for Charles, knowing how he'd had to ask.

'In your father, Charles, it's . . . a maleness. He's alive with it. You could scratch it off him with a knife.'

Charles's mouth tightened. 'And in Jessamy?'

'In Jessamy?' She looked at her friend, dwarfed by the two men each side of her. 'In Jessamy, it's an eccentricity. All the boys are after her. They sense something in her. I'm very fond of her, as you know, but it's that quality of . . . almost madness, an illusion, that you can't possess her, that is what makes her attractive. She's like a fairy, a will-o'-the-wisp.'

His eyes searched her face silently as she gazed over at his sister.

'And in me?'

She looked back at him, the big, blue eyes clear and caring. 'In you, Charles, it's *strength*. Strength of purpose. You're open and pure. Like your uncle, Frederick. You're good.' She held his hand. 'That's what angers your father. You can't fight good.'

Any reply that Charles might have given was stopped as Rupert drove through the crowd towards the bandstand, pulling the two young people behind him. Jessamy seemed thoroughly bemused as though she had been swept into something beyond her control. She had only meant to play, now it was a *fait accompli* under Rupert's control. It was too late to back down. She had never said yes. She had only said maybe.

Rupert reached the bandstand. They stopped playing.

The party hovered to a halt on the dance floor.

'Everybody . . . stop dancing and listen. I have an announcement to make. Tonight, John Hamblin has asked for the hand of my daughter, Jessamy, in marriage. I have accepted his proposal. And so has Jessamy!' he laughed. The room tittered. 'Please raise your glasses to my daughter and her future husband. Ladies and gentlemen . . . Jessamy and John!'

'Jessamy and John!'

John beamed. So did Rupert. Jessamy's eyes danced glassily

under the lights. John held her hand and kissed her for all to see. She drew away, shyly it appeared, and the room murmured understandingly. To Charles she looked like a frightened fawn. And when her eyes swept the crowd and found his, he was certain: they rested on him, begging for his intervention, for him to answer this one for her. Charles felt as though someone had put a knife through his heart. What could he do? Rupert's wedding was already under way: nothing could stop it now. John Hamblin was a marvellous catch.

Charles's eyes held hers. His poor sister, so defenceless just like her mother. They were impossible against Rupert's power. He remembered Melanie's words. She was right: *male . . . good.* The words rang separately in his head like huge bells. Flushed with success, like a great bear, his yellow hair swept back even higher off his forehead with age, Rupert smiled and toasted the couple. *Male.* And he, Charles, was *good.* The two jarred together like confronting waves.

With the disturbing pull of first love and youth, he only wanted what Melanie wanted, and what Melanie wanted was that raw power. For the first time he did not want to be understanding, he wanted the charisma of his father. For the first time he hated being thought of as good. He looked into his sister's bewildered eyes. Rupert had angered him before but now, in that moment, he felt it. For the first time he hated his father.

TWENTY-TWO

The rain had been falling all night and had cleared just before mid-morning. There was no wind and the day was still. The clouds were clearing fast and the sky was a brilliant blue, pristine clean and sharp, and the sun would burn later. It was one of those fresh days of summer that comes after sluggish weather.

The bells rang out for matins, loud across the stillness of the morning, across the fields and meadows beside the river.

On the opposite bank of the Thames, Dickie walked down the towpath past their cornfields. Their land. She stopped for a moment and looked out over the still corn, smelt its smell sweeter now that the rain had been and the sun was warming the earth, releasing its musky smell. A day like this was like a new day.

She was elegantly dressed. Today there were no jodhpurs and shirt, with jacket flung casually around her shoulders, today she was in a close-fitting pale grey shantung caught at the waist and ruched across the bodice with tiny flowers. The skirt was long, stopping with a flared hem just above her ankles. She wore gloves and on her head a small, tilted, grey-velvet hat with a delicate pink veil.

As far as she could see from this point, it was her land. Running down to the edge of the river and back over the rise. Beyond was Greatley House, chimneys catching the sunlight, a slice of white shining over the tips of the corn as it burrowed into the dip of the valley.

Max knew what she was feeling. He took his mother's arm in his, feeling the goodness of it with her. Bill stood, looking out over the river. He felt the warm sun on his face and dreamed

his own dreams, of the American Midwest and his own roots.
It was one of those mornings that made one feel good to be
alive.

The bells chimed insistently across the water at the foot of
the village.

Dickie turned her head and looked up into the face of her
son. Between them there was a silent communion.

'Come on,' he said.

They both knew what he meant. It was the first time they had
attended church as a family, facing the gossip of the village.
There was no doubt that the Redfields would be there too. Dickie
turned to go. Church was a strange place for the second of the
confrontations that she would have with them; her first had been
silent, stealing onto their land. So be it.

Max walked her down the towpath to the old red-brick bridge
that spanned the Thames and led onto the village green at the
bottom of the high street. The church nestled there beside the
water at the apex of the crossroads. She had sworn on that evening twenty years ago that she would not return without taking
revenge. Now she was returning.

They had decided to walk, as she had always done with her
family as a child. Max had her strength. He was a good foot
taller than she, his shoulders broad in a new grey suit, his hair
smoothed back and respectfully neat. Yet there was no mistaking the aura of the man. His was a harsh strength, overlaid with
a natural elegance. He seemed exceptionally cool and collected,
a man who would never show his hand to anyone and detached
to the point of indifference. His strength was something both
silent and tangible, with an intensity more powerful than any
show of emotion.

Bill followed a step behind as they crossed the grating, hearing it clang under their feet as they entered the church. And then
they were in the shuffling quiet and gloom, the organ gently
playing.

Jessamy knelt on her hassock and prayed. She knew she should
be praying to God for forgiveness for all those sins she had not
committed and wished she had, but through her gloved fingers
her eyes roamed restlessly over the backs of heads and shoulders
and up to the pulpit and the choir and the stained-glass window
of Jesus Christ in his mother's arms and the sunlight pouring

through the colours. She weighed her chin on the heels of her hands and let her mind wander. The only prayer she wanted was an answer to her prayers for love. Love of the sort that would carry her away, love that she could lose herself in. The bulge of her new diamond ring pulled at the material of her glove, a constant reminder of her engaged state. The marriage would take place here, in this church, in under a month. It was so quick. She gave a deep sigh and saw her brother look quickly at her. She pretended it was a sigh of contentment at her state and avoided his eyes. He knew, and yet they could not discuss it because if she let it out she would have to face too much about herself, and that she could not do.

Both families were there alongside her. The banns were to be read out today. John's family were in the pew behind. There was no escape. Bored, she stretched her fingers wider and looked over to the right-hand side of the church, watching the gathering and movement there. People were pushing and smiling and kneeling. Who really meant it? she wondered, and who was here for show? Her family was certainly not without sin. The sun's rays poured into the chancel, suddenly lighting the scene. The whole thing was a farce.

It was more the sense of tension rather than anything physical that made her start. Something had changed. She glanced quickly at her uncle, Frederick, beside her. He was as stiff as a statue. On the other side of John sat her father. For once he was in the congregation, not taking the service. Past her mother's glacial profile, she saw his face darken with anger. Eagerly, she looked for the source of it.

Across the aisle, Max escorted his mother into her place. It was sacrilege. There was a pecking order in the church that had been observed for generations. The most important families sat at the front, in priority. The Bennetts had simply moved forward and taken one of the first three pews in the church. The whispers started.

Jessamy saw him almost immediately. She saw the way he shepherded his mother into the narrow pew. She watched him kneel to pray, and the way he pulled at the cloth of his trousers with long, strong fingers. He had a fit, powerful body, and there was something about him, a sense of belonging as if no man could put him down. She knew who they were and their reputation. So these were the notorious Bennetts, the kitchen-maid and her son. He was handsome, daring somehow. Her nostrils flared as she smelt his power. It wasn't so much in the width of his broad shoulders, but more in the way he held himself: so sure.

She stayed praying a little longer. No harm in people thinking she was devout. Today, after all, she was on centre stage.

He sat back. She waited for him to look casually around as everyone else did. He did not. His face turned only briefly, a mild curiosity merely to assess his surroundings and commit them to memory. She saw him, though. His eyes were strong and his dark face intelligent. She could not see the colour of his eyes but she felt that they were piercing and had surely pierced her, missing nothing as they passed over her and down the line of rigid Redfields. She could not help but contrast him with the effete John who simpered over her. Here was a man who would never simper. He folded his arms loosely and stared ahead, his chin lifted, no longer looking around, his interest satiated.

The service began. It passed in a dream for Jessamy. She watched every movement. He lifted his hymn book. She saw the strength in his hands. He was cool and clean and elegant and underneath there was that powerful animal strength. He leaned to listen as his mother whispered something to him. He smiled, amused. Jessamy's heart turned over. He was so handsome. They were the Bennetts that her family hated, and didn't they just know they were there! In her pew she sensed the absolute tension. Yet the man and his mother were so cool and indifferent. She loved it all.

She sat back reluctantly. Now she could hardly see him. They stood to sing but Jessamy's mind was not on prayer or thanksgiving. John touched her arm gently alongside. She turned to look at him, and now his grin seemed sickly, his nose too big, his mouth too soft. It was almost time for the banns. Across the aisle the other one stood, taller than her father. She was sure his eyes would be blue. If only he could see her, might not their eyes meet? In her books, the lovers always did. Her family would be horrified if they knew what she was thinking, and that made it all the more enticing.

The service was interminable for her and yet wonderful. The feelings that were stirred in her were those that she had longed for. Her emotions were equally as melodramatic as those of her tragic heroines about whom she had read so avidly alone at Foxhall.

She hardly heard the banns. It was only when John took her

arm possessively that she was aware of the congratulatory smiles that were being bestowed on them. Jessamy looked around and smiled, dropped her eyes, and then lifted them again to look straight and bold across the aisle.

He was looking at her. His eyes were as strong as she imagined, and thorough. She could not read their expression but he had seen her. Her courage failed her and she looked away. She wanted him with a weakness that assailed her wonderfully. Maybe he did not want her yet; she had not seen a response in those deep eyes, but it did not matter. She knew he would. It was only a matter of time. Just in time. Her prayers had been answered.

As she left the church, her eyes were bright. Now she had something to live for. She hugged her secret to herself.

In the summer sunshine, John Hamblin stood beside her, eager for her, her new bright-eyed look enticing him even more. Perhaps she loved him after all. Her smile was febrile, her eyes wild. Maybe that was all it needed—the church banns to make her realise it was all coming true.

The others looking at her thought the same. She was a young girl in love. She accepted the congratulations, her mind trapped in a whirl of its own. Vaguely she knew that he was leaving with the small, elegant woman on his arm, and the other man on her other side. They passed the group of Redfields, neither fast nor slow, just moving on their way home.

He knew who she was now, thought Jessamy. The fact that he was ignoring her was just his way of being careful. He would find a way of getting to her now that he knew she wanted him. She had shown him in her look. Now it was up to him. The thrill coursed through her. He would be ardent, yet forceful. She smiled and shook another hand.

Dickie had risen early. It was a perfect day. Down at the airfield she warmed up the Tiger Moth. The dew was barely off the grass. It was crisp and fresh as she hurtled down the runway and lifted off over the trees. It was good to get back to real flying; the Tiger Moth was not an easy plane to fly. It had to be kept in balance. She needed to test herself from time to time.

She decided on a spin. She throttled back, feeling the exhilaration as she hurtled downwards, the earth whirling towards

her, before she finally levelled and throttled out, soaring up once
again into the bare, blue sky.

Max whistled for the dog. The young Labrador puppy came
bounding in his footsteps as he walked down to the airfield. He
strode through the long grass in his wellingtons, his jacket flung
over his shoulder.

He could hear one of the mechanics tinkering on the Dragon
outside the hangar. The sound carried over the field. He looked
up into the sky and saw the Tiger Moth that his mother had
bought for herself, diving into a spin. He watched for a moment.
She was an expert at aerobatics. And it was a perfect day for
flying. He might go up himself. First, there was a lot of paperwork to read through.

He strode into the single-storey building, and made his way
down the corridor to his office at the end. It looked out over the
airfield. He settled himself down to his papers in a good humour.

Footsteps echoed down the passageway. There was a knock
on the door.

Max looked across the pages of the balance sheets.

'Come in.'

'How's the empire building this morning?'

Max leaned back with a grin, his arms behind his head. He
stretched. 'Morning, Colin. Have a seat. I'm just adding up
some figures. Expansion plans.'

Colin Farlowe came in and sat astride the chair. 'Never stop,
d'you? Hello, little chap.' Max's Labrador ran up to be petted.
Colin was good with animals and they sensed it. 'Time to be
down haymaking,' he said to Max as he fondled the dog's ears.
'Thought I'd drop by and see if you're interested. We got some
good cider.'

'Too busy.' Max linked his arms behind his head again. His
shirt was open at the neck. He was a powerful-looking man in
his shirt-sleeves. 'How's the crop this year?'

'Pretty fair. Weather's been good to us.' His forehead creased
a little as he looked out of the window and up at the sky. The
Labrador jumped up, paws on his shoulders. He rubbed its head
affectionately.

Colin was a sunburned, flaxen-haired young man, equally as
strong and broad as Max, but his aspirations were very different.
Colin was mellow, with an easy humour, and Max's closest
friend in the village. Their backgrounds were similar, though

there the similarity ended. Colin's family were content to be farmers; they had built up their small farm and surrounding acres through hard, consistent labour, and were fanatically proud of the fact and of their son who now ran the farm, the only boy among five girls.

'Colin,' said Max thoughtfully. 'Are you planning to take over your father's farm?'

Colin looked up. 'Eventually, yes. Why?'

'You wouldn't consider, say, a chance to work in California?'

Colin grinned at him. 'Now why would I do that? Go all that way when I've got right what I need here in Foxhall Green? I suppose you'd like me to join with you?'

'I would, yes. I'm going out at the end of the week. I'm going to set things up out there. I'll need someone I can trust to run it once I've got it going.'

Colin shook his head. 'Not me, but thanks for asking. I'd get tired of working day and night like you. I'd rather be out in the fields. Paperwork? I've only my food to add up and the price of pig swill. I like animals more than people, Max. Besides, that flying's all too dangerous for a fellow like me!'

'It's a beautiful land, California.' Max raised an eyebrow, half smiled at him.

Colin did not weaken. He sat up and leaned his arms on the back of the chair. 'I'm sure. What are you doing there, anyway?'

Max looked over briefly at the world map on the wall. 'We're going to organise an airline in California. We left a finger in the pie with a couple of guys, a film director who owns vast pieces of Los Angeles, and an investment guy, a banker, who is the brains behind the operation over there. We had the option to go back into business with them at a future point. I'm going to take up the option,' he said as he turned back to Colin. He leaned his elbows on the desk. His black hair was unbrushed and ruffled. He looked well; the responsibility suited him. 'Planes are getting more advanced every day, and the Americans are always streets ahead. They've got a plane over there my mother wants, it's called a Boeing 247.' His forehead creased slightly. 'Way things are going we'll soon be flying passengers across the Atlantic.'

'Do you mean it?'

'Certainly.' He twisted a pencil between his fingers. 'Already the 247 can carry ten passengers and flies at nearly two hundred miles an hour. I'm going to try and get at least two. We can get to Germany in eleven hours. My idea is to set up a quick shuttle service over to Europe when I get back. Imagine if you could just walk on to a plane and walk off like a bus. We could beat the competition with cheaper flights.' He gave Colin a deep look. 'You *sure* you wouldn't like to be involved with something like this, Colin? We're well on the way to big money. It'd be good to have you there with me.'

'Not me, old man.' He shook his head again and sat up, his hands resting on his strong legs. 'Too happy with the farm. Walking out at dawn. Nothing like it. Which reminds me, Ma asked if you'd like to come by for dinner tonight. She's making steak and kidney.'

'No one makes it like your mother.'

'That's what she says!' Colin grinned. 'Better than anyone I know. Good food, straight off the farm. You watch something grow from nothing,' he pinched the air. 'Just a seed. It does something good to you to see nature take its course like that.' He looked long at Max. 'Ma says it's been too long since you've last been. She says to tell you she misses her second son.'

Max's smile lit his eyes. 'Your ma and I understand one another.

'Don't I know it!' said Colin ruefully. Colin's mother was the archetypal earth mother: round, robust, always smelling of cooking-apples and pastry, flour on her hands and apron, permanently in the kitchen, with, often as not, her family in there with her, sitting and arguing and laughing around the huge kitchen table. At Brook Farm it was always open house and no formality, no servants. Colin's mother did everything for her family herself. It was a noisy, jolly house, often untidy but always clean.

'I'd love to come,' said Max suddenly.

'Good.' Colin stood up. 'Let's go now, then. We could do a bit of haymaking, then stop off at the Horse and Hounds before going home. We could get there just in time to get the first smell of good home cooking. She's baking you an apple pie.' He winked. 'She said to leave that for the last, in case up till now you said no. She knows how you are for working!' He pointed at Max. 'Put your pen down, man, and come along. You could put your back into some good hard work. It's a weekend, for God's sake. Time to give that brain a rest!'

Max's mouth twisted wryly. Colin was right. He slapped down his pen and looked out at the day. It would be good to get out in the fields, and then relax with their family. They were noisy and basic and warm. Greatley was more quiet and formal, the servants taking care of them as the three of them worked to build Bennett Air. He always had a good time with the Farlowes. Colin's quintet of blonde healthy open-air sisters all adored him and fought over the privilege of sitting on each side of their brother's friend.

'You've talked me into it,' he said. 'I was going to go flying, but . . .' He stood up and stretched. He felt the pleasure of the day ahead seep into him, now that he had given way. The farm life was rooted in himself, something he could not throw off quite so easily. He had never had the womb-like security of a big, noisy family around him and it was something he needed.

He grabbed his old tweed jacket. 'Should I bring a tie?' He looked down at his wellingtons.

'Should you *what*?' Colin surveyed his own open-necked shirt and loose trousers tucked into boots. 'I'll lend you my tails! Come on.'

Max cuffed him playfully on the shoulder. He threw his jacket over his arm and preceded him from the room.

The sun was warmer now, with a burn in it. The air was fresh and the grass drying out in the warmth of the day.

The two men crossed the grass towards Colin's battered old farm van which was parked under the trees away from the heat of the day.

They talked easily, the Labrador bounding along around them, sniffing the grass.

'What about this plane then, the Boeing? Are you going to have to move?' Colin looked into Max's face.

'Move from here? No.' Max pointed over to the runway. 'It has a larger wing-span than the Dragon's though, so I think we're going to have to lengthen the runway. We'll take in that second field over there.' He stopped and indicated the far distant end of the runway. Down the length of the field, aeroplanes stood shoulder to shoulder waiting for use. It was an impressive sight. Mechanics and ground crew moved in and out of the two hangars erected beyond.

Colin took it all in. 'You've done well Max. You and your mother. I'll give you that.'

Max looked him in the eye. 'And we'll do better. Come on,' he said opening the passenger door. 'You've given me an appetite.'

Colin drove out of the field, bumping over every lump in the ground. They reached the farm gate and he slowed, looking out onto the narrow country road that had a dangerous bend just at that point.

He inched the vehicle forward and jarred to a halt. The dog fell against Max's feet.

'Christ, what a dangerous corner,' Colin swore as he ground on the brakes. The oncoming car swept by in front of them. At the wheel the pale face under the grey felt hat glanced their way. Colin grinned, 'Worth it for a face like that, though, eh?' He lifted his battered old trilby to the girl who had smiled shyly at them as she blurred past.

'What?' Max stroked the dog's head. He looked up and saw her. Her eyes swiftly met his, and the car was round the corner, climbing the hill.

'It's you she's smitten with though, old boy. Pity. What a beautiful girl.' He put the van back into gear and chugged out in the opposite direction. 'Do you know each other?'

'No.' Max remembered her very well. She disturbed him. There was something about her sensual beauty that he had found hard to forget.

Colin negotiated the corner. 'She's one of the Redfields. Jessamy, I think her name is. She knows you, all right!'

'Oh.'

Colin looked quickly over. Max's face was noncommittal. 'Uh-oh!' he said. 'You *do* know who she is. You dark horse! I've never seen you interested in a girl before! Well, well!'

'I'm not interested in her, Colin.'

The van rattled down the road. 'Of course you aren't. I wasn't born yesterday, Max.'

She drove back up the hill into the darkness of the trees that lined the lane up to Foxhall. The sun filtered through making a dazzling pattern on the leaves.

The days had passed since that Sunday. The marriage plans were well under way. She had spent countless hot hours being fitted for her dress in her bedroom while looking through the window over the tops of the trees of Cobbold's Wood.

There, beyond the crest of the second hill, was Greatley House. If the hill had not been there she would be able to see the house. She had driven by so often in the hope of meeting him. Would he come and save her, carrying her off at the last minute in his arms?

Foxhall was empty as she returned, bringing the car to a halt on the crunching gravel. She stepped out into the silence, alive with her memory. The birds twittered in the bushes and butterflies fluttered over the flowerbeds. Her skin tingled. She went into the quiet house. Frederick and Rupert were out hunting, and Charles was playing golf. Her mother must have been either lying down or in her garden. Jessamy ran lightly up the stairs to her room. She threw herself across her bed, and visualised his face, his deep blue eyes burning into her.

She had little choice but to agree to the general upheavals that were taking place at Foxhall on behalf of herself—the bride-to-be. With as yet no message from him, she could not declare her real love to her father, nor could she defy him. She remembered how she had smiled at him in the car, and how he had looked back at her. His eyes were hard, and she had seen his open-necked shirt and the tousled hair. She rolled over on the bed, holding herself with her arms. She prayed for a miracle.

Colin drove him home. It was a clear night, studded with stars. Greatley House stood like a white monolith in the moonlight. Colin pulled into the driveway.

It was cool and quiet as they stepped into the hall, an atmosphere of elegance around them; quite a contrast to the colourful chaos of the farmhouse kitchen, where Colin's sister, Ann, had pelted him with floury buns and then dived under the table in sudden adolescent embarrassment.

'Hello,' said Dickie, taking the small reading-glasses from her nose as they walked into the drawing room. 'Did you have a good dinner?'

'As always.' Max gave her a kiss and sank into a chair. He smelt warm and musky and he looked fit and healthy. The two young men were handsomely matched, the one dark, the other fair. He lifted the brandy decanter from the small table beside him and poured out two glasses. He handed one to Colin.

Dickie looked rested and relaxed. She was wearing her old green jodhpurs and white silk shirt. Her black hair was tied back from her head. She looked much younger than her thirty-four years. She put down her paperwork.

'So, Colin,' she said, 'you tore him away for the day, did

you? Good! He works too hard sometimes.' Her smile was af-
fectionate.

'You're one to talk,' said Max, lifting his brandy. He stretched
out in the chair.

'Yes, we had him relaxed for a while,' said Colin fondly.
'Though I think he was in a bit of a daze after the look that
Redfield girl gave him!' He laughed readily and drank. 'Can't
say I blame him!'

'Redfield girl?' The smile faded.

'So Colin says.' Max seemed uninterested. 'How did the test
go this afternoon?'

'Fine, you can fly her yourself in the morning.' Dickie seemed
thoughtful. Silence balanced unsteadily in the room.

'Well.' Colin broke it first. He put down his glass and slapped
his knees heartily. 'Gotta be getting back. We farmers have an
early start, you know.' He stood up, went over and slapped Max
good-naturedly on the back as he went to the door. 'See you,
old fellow. . . . good night, Mrs Latimer.'

He went forward to shake hands with her.

She stood up. 'I'll see you to the door.'

She followed him out into the passageway.

'Well, good night again, Mrs Latimer.' He opened the door.
She stood alongside it and looked up into his face.

'Which Redfield was it?' she said.

'Well, there's only one that would interest Max . . . Jessamy!'

'Rupert Redfield's daughter?'

'Yes.' He looked puzzled. 'Is anything wrong? I hope I
didn't . . .'

'No, no,' she smiled. 'Nothing. Good night, Colin.'

She closed the door slowly behind him. When she returned
to the drawing room there was a different expression on her face.

She had seen the looks that the girl had given Max that day
in church. She was beautiful and very provocative. It would not
be hard for Max to become interested were she to entice him
further. He was silent as she came back into the room. That
silence troubled her even more. She sat down slowly on the sofa.

'Where's Bill?' Max's voice was casual.

'He's not back from the field yet. Max?'

'Yes?'

'This Jessamy Redfield. Are you interested in her?'

'Not particularly.'

'She's very pretty.'

'Is she?' He studied the glass in his hands.

'Same colouring as you, darling.'

He raised an indifferent eyebrow.

She saw the warning signs. He was patently interested in the girl and he had no idea of what was involved. Dickie thought hard. She had never told him the truth. Bill had warned her the day would come. She had to stop him before it went any further.

She patted the silk pillow beside her and plumped it up, putting it behind her back. 'It's been a hard day. I think I'll join you for that drink. I'll stop early tonight.' Her smile was forced, her eyes brilliant as they rested on his. Max poured her a brandy and brought it across to her. 'After this, we're going for a drive, darling. There's something I've got to tell you.'

The cottage was much as she remembered it. She had not been back for many years now. There had been no reason. Lights burned softly in the windows, the family was at home. The warm summer night reminded her of so many things. She could hear sounds, smell the cooking; a cat dozed on the windowledge. She stopped the car in the lane and got out. Max followed. She walked slowly to the edge of rough grass and looked up the path to the front door. Despite everything, she felt very nostalgic. There were so many memories here. Sam. Her mother. Those hard, hard days when Max was a baby, the pain, the hate.

Max said not a word.

Dickie walked round to the back garden and stopped. She looked across the scrubby vegetable patch, now untended for some reason. The bushes seemed somehow smaller now, but there was still the clearing by the copse and the thickness of wood beyond.

She walked to the edge of the wood.

'When I was almost fourteen,' she began, 'we lived here. Dad and my brother, Sam, we worked for Alexander Redfield. One day, just like this, I was cooking lunch. I'd just left school, about to go into service. I heard the hunt coming closer and didn't take much notice . . .' She walked to the edge of the clearing and looked back at the cottage.

'. . . and then the Redfield brothers came here. Their hounds set on my kitten. Sam had given it to me for my birthday. I ran outside and there he was. Rupert Redfield on his horse. Cold, contemptuous and cruel. I could feel it and he challenged me. I only knew I was not going to give in. He barged me with his horse. I fell, but I stood my ground. I saw the other one by the gate, and somehow, I don't know how, I couldn't get back home and I was running. Running for my life. The more I ran the more I lost—my pride, my mind, my respect. My heart was pounding and I could hardly breathe. All I could hear was his laughter, echoing all around me. I stumbled and fell and he caught me, brought his whip down on me . . .' The expression in Max's eyes became lethal as her words drilled into him. '. . . I only remember that I had lost all but I wasn't going to scream. I wouldn't give them that. He threw me onto his horse, rode me into the woods and the next thing I knew he had thrown me down. I was winded. As I fought for my breath he started to unbutton his trousers.'

Max's face contorted with pain; he masked it with anger. He wanted her to stop, desperately, but knew she had to finish. He had to hear it all.

'. . . He raped me,' she said. 'Brutally, bestially. I remember his hair against the sun, white; and the sky above between the beech leaves. And the pain and the terrible degradation and bewilderment. He was heavy and I could hardly breathe. I thought I would faint. And then he stood away, and his brother was there . . .' Her voice hesitated, her eyes moving over the scene from the past. Her expression changed. 'He was different . . . but his motive was exactly the same. I was incapable of moving. He raped me, too,' she said steadily. 'And then they left me there, undressed and ashamed, alone in the wood. They rode back to the hunt. He was laughing.' She paused. Her voice changed. 'Then I ran. I ran to the fields to get help. Dad. And Sam.'

Max's voice was no louder than a breath. 'What did Grandad do?'

'Nothing. Nothing. He said we could do nothing. Because we were poor. Because we were underdogs.' Her eyes burned a furious green and she looked at him then. 'We had no power. And that's why, Max. That's what drove me to change that for ever.'

Her eyes looked into his for his understanding. He did not touch her. She did not want him to. She wanted to stand alone in her pain.

The anger and the hate had filled him as she told the story. Now she saw it there. This was his legacy.

He knew there would be more. He waited to hear what he knew was coming.

'You are the child of that union, Max. I thought I would hate you. But I have always loved you more than life. You are *my* son. Mine alone.'

His gaze travelled over the route the terrified young girl must have taken; his mother. He had wondered all these years why her hate had been intense enough to drive her to seek retribution in a country far from her own village and then return with enough power and money to fight a long-concealed wound. *One of the Redfields had fathered him.* He had always wondered who. Now he knew. He felt no love for the man, no desire to seek him out. Fed by her pain, and her words, his long-nurtured hatred for that family became a seething rage of revenge. They had defiled his proud mother whom he knew so well, her humour, her spirit, her absolute pride. Now he knew what it had cost her. The name Redfield burned in his brain. He hardly heard her final words such was his rage, and yet they were also printed perfectly on his mind.

'Now you see why I had to tell you. Jessamy is Rupert's daughter.'

TWENTY-THREE

'I don't think we can lend him bank money, Rupert.'

'Why ever not?' Rupert looked out at him from under his eyebrows. He tapped the report before him on his father's desk. 'It seems a profitable venture. The company was set up by his father, a respected businessman. Lorimar Properties and Meriton Investments have been doing well. What does he want? Half a million pounds, to start a chain of dresswear shops throughout the south of England. I think he knows what he is doing.'

Robert Hewdon-Vassar looked very uncomfortable. He paced the room, his portly body bristling with indignation. 'Rupert, the man's a fraud. He's already borrowed money and I don't think the properties were ever built. It's been transferred through a series of companies for his own personal use. That's massive fraud!'

Rupert raised an eyebrow. His voice was cold. 'And I think he's a man of great integrity and a respectable businessman. The trouble with you, Hewdon-Vassar, is that you chaps are all the same. You don't give anyone a chance.'

'A chance? Give a man like that a chance?' He challenged Rupert with his belligerent face. 'He's been leading us up the garden path. The money went to an offshore company owned by him. He's not used it for the purposes he said he would. You don't give a man like that a chance! It's simply foolhardy to lend him any more!'

Rupert appeared calm. 'The way he puts it,' he said, 'is that the Depression hurt him as it hurt all of us. He simply wants another go, and I think that he could make it this time if we helped him.' He rubbed his cheek and looked at the documents spread before him. 'The company is doing well, and the order book is full. They have three factories already in the south, at Portsmouth, Southampton and Bournemouth.'

'It's good money after bad.' Hewdon-Vassar weighed his hefty body into a chair in front of Rupert's desk, pointedly avoiding Rupert's eyes in his own arrogance. 'No, we mustn't do it. At least we'll have an investigation. We might be lending money to people who are known to be dishonest or would be dishonest if we don't carry out even the most elementary of enquiries. We'll have an independent enquiry,' he finished adamantly. 'Then we'll see.'

'No.'

'Look,' said Hewdon-Vassar. 'You never come to the bank. You don't know what you're talking about. Frankly, I forbid it. You're out of order.'

'I'm also chairman and majority shareholder.' His voice was as soft as a snake.

'I want a meeting of the board.' Robert Hewdon-Vassar's eyes were angry and self-righteous.

Rupert leaned back in his chair. He eyed him carefully. He nodded slightly as if a thought had come to him. 'Do you mean to say, Robert, that you have never done anything dishonest with bank money, not cut any corners that might in some way . . .' his eyes narrowed '. . . jeopardise the bank?'

'Absolutely not!' spluttered the man. 'What an idea! Me? Hoh!' He clutched the arms of the chair and looked pompously around the room.

Rupert nodded again. 'Interesting . . .' he said slowly. He waited for a beat. Then he moved forward and opened the right-hand drawer of his desk. He pulled out a sheaf of papers. 'Read these,' he ordered. He threw them across the desk at the other man.

Robert Hewdon-Vassar took the papers slowly. He did not have to read far. His florid face paled significantly.

'Where did you get this information?'

'This is my bank. Where do you think I got it?' He was still and cold. 'Oh,' he said as if it had suddenly dawned on him. 'I see. You thought that because I haven't been here that I don't know what goes on . . .' His voice changed. 'That was a mistake.'

He pulled the papers back towards him, patted them back together and replaced them in the drawer. He gave it a quick twist with a key, which he then dropped theatrically into his waistcoat pocket. 'Now,' he said in a businesslike tone. 'Draw up the pertinent contracts for me, would you? I don't want to keep my chap waiting. He could be invaluable to us in years to come. Run along now, there's a good chap.'

Hewdon-Vassar was too shocked to argue. He pulled himself from the chair and left the room without another word. Rupert smiled tightly, picked up the phone and dialled a number.

'Caversham? . . . Want to meet me for lunch at the club? . . . Good. I think you'll like what I have to tell you . . . yes . . . goodbye.'

He had gone into silent partnership with the man. There were advantages to the merchant-banking game as he had found out. He would spend the money on Jessamy's wedding present. Only a few days to go and they would marry into one of the richest families in England. Rupert smiled and lit a cigar. He would stay in London tonight and celebrate. He knew who with. He lifted the phone and rang home.

Frederick put down the telephone in the study. He looked at the farm papers on his desk. The figures were not good. It was hard to make a really decent profit with so little land. Despite selling off the acreage, their expenditure was alarming. The bills for champagne and wine and rich French food came his way: Rupert's London life and parties were astronomical, as was the extra building work that had taken place at Foxhall over the years. Now Jessamy's wedding. The bills were already beginning to drift in.

His thoughts returned to Sunday, to the service and the sound of the banns being read. Sunday. It had not been far from his mind since then.

He hardly recognised the woman who had stood in the church beside her son. How that had hurt him. That boy! Dark as she was, but with the Redfield eyes and elegance and the powerful build of the Bryn-Parrys. He had them combined in him for that air of controlled power that was inherent in a highly intelligent and potentially successful man. And he was only twenty or so. He had looked at him and their eyes had met as the young man's had swept with mild curiosity over the church. As they had met there had been no reaction. He was sure he did not know. That meant she had chosen not to tell him. So why would she return here and so obviously confront them unless she meant to use him in some way? Was he his? Frederick was overcome at the thought and was filled with a fresh onslaught of pain. Was that her purpose, to display the product of their guilt to them?

Frederick had not been able to keep his mind on the service. The hymns had gone on and the sermon had seemed interminable, all about sin. They had sinned. Appallingly. He had not bowed his head though his mind had bowed to the accusations raining from the pulpit, and the silent accusation from across the aisle.

She had never once looked at him, and yet he so wished she had. He wished he could change history. He felt the draw of her even now and wondered, though, whether he would have been able to resist her, once led by Rupert to her sacrifice, or whether he would have done any different. She was too powerful for him. He had longed again to feel those underwater eyes on him, to look into them as closely as he once had done. She did not look.

The boy had their eyes. The Redfield blue. Who else would notice? Or was it just him, too aware of his own guilt? He had looked covertly at Rupert, but his brother's countenance had remained the same, stolidly staring ahead, singing the praises of the Lord. Did he wonder who the boy resembled? Maybe he did not even think about it. Did he even know? They never discussed it. *Let sleeping dogs lie.* He heard the singing of the choir all over again. His mind drifted as he recalled the choir walking slowly out of church. She had faced him across the aisle . . .

Through the open window he heard another voice singing. He broke away from his thoughts and looked out. Caroline crossed the lawn, wielding her secateurs. She was singing in a high-pitched voice, and making her way towards the conservatory. She had her trug over her arm. Her step was light and carefree.

Frederick sighed aloud. He pushed his hand to the desk as he stood up. He had to go and tell her about Rupert's phone call.

The door of the conservatory stood open. The singing wafted out, gay and wordless, a little tuneless.

She was snipping off the dead heads of the flowers. Her thin body seemed boneless under the wrap of clothes. Her slender neck was still balanced by the short, dark, shining cap of hair and her narrow ankles glimmered under silvery, silk stockings.

She was in her own world, cocooned from Rupert, from them all.

'Caroline?'

The singing went on. 'There we are,' she crooned to the flowers. 'All so much prettier now!'

'Caroline!' he said more firmly. 'Rupert just called.'

'Oh, Frederick!' She turned brightly, her eyes pale blue crystals. 'I didn't see you there. What did you say, dear?'

'I said, Rupert called.' He folded his arms. 'He's not coming home for dinner.'

'Oh. That's a pity. Mrs Maitland was preparing something special. Oh, well, will you tell her for me?'

She snipped at a leaf, gathered it in her hand and dropped it into the trug. Her face hardly showed a glimmer of expression, but her pale lips tightened and her eyes were cooler still.

There was a time when he had felt at peace with her. He had thought that with her he could have sat for hours by a river bank or quietly somewhere and never have to speak, that their thoughts would be in communion. She would have lain there quietly like a fairy queen and he would have stroked her forehead gently. Strangely, he had never thought of sex with Caroline. She seemed too pure, above all that wrangling and coupling. She was to be adored, revered like a saint. He had closed his mind to her and Rupert. That must have been anathema to her. He had wanted to make up to her for that, to give her some gentleness to compensate.

'Of course I'll tell her, Caroline.' He stood back. 'It's a lovely day, would you like a walk? Perhaps a punt down the river like the children do?' he laughed.

He saw the shadow that crossed her face. That was the last thing he had promised her before she had agreed to marry Rupert. How careless of him; he did not know what to say. She snipped away at the leaves and was silent.

'I think I'll go and see how my birds are doing,' she said. She came towards him and handed him the trug.

He took it from her. 'Of course . . .'

'If you see Jessamy, will you send her to me?'

She wandered away from him.

'Yes,' he said.

She hummed her song again as she walked away towards the aviary. She was so hard to reach these days. He wished she would not be so alone. He wanted to share with her. Everybody was so separate in this house now. He was not sure what had happened. His only solace was Katherine.

Caroline's fingers reached over the wire and touched the soft breast of the bird. She shivered. The wedding was nearly here. She remembered her own wedding night. She must warn her daughter. She sang lightly; a song from her childhood.

August, 1933

It was a hot summer day, heavy and still; a day of deep humidity and slumber in the country. All the colours were bright, the grass almost too green, the sky very blue. The marquee on the lawn was erected, the ribbons on the guy-ropes fluttering in a light breeze. The windows of the house stood open, airing it for the guests that would arrive later in the day. The broad stone balcony was alive with action. Long tables were being erected with crisp white tablecloths and down the steps to the garden went maids and footmen carrying trays to and fro, to and fro, with food, champagne and glasses. The band was arriving, setting up their instruments to play in the drawing room that evening for the happy couple and their families and friends. Four hundred people were invited and the dining room was knee-deep in presents of crystal, silver and china. Rupert's present had already been given: the coach-house, the first home for John and Jessamy—close, if not under his roof. She was not leaving, after all.

Jessamy was in a panic. It was the eleventh hour and still he had not reached her. She looked out of her bedroom window. There were only hours to go before the ceremony. She could not stop it now. She did not have the strength to make such an announcement. She wanted to, but when she was with her father his force outweighed her and she lost all sense of identity.

There was only one way now.

She slipped out of the house down the back stairs and through the side door, over the little bridge. She ran quickly across the lawns to the field beyond, scrambling over the stone wall like a child and through the long grass down towards Cobbold's Wood. Once there, she slowed, breathing in the freedom and coolness of the wood. It was quiet, the birds occasionally chirping over her head. She had not been sure why she was doing this but now she knew it was an inner voice which impelled her. She had to see him face to face, to talk to him, while she was still free.

She knew he was helping with the harvesting. She had watched him the day before, in his open-necked shirt, the sleeves rolled above his elbows, working with his grandfather in the fields of Home Farm. She had parked her car down by the red-brick bridge, and crossed the towpath beneath the long corn-field. Today, a car had been out of the question. They would have stopped her.

A little out of breath, she saw the edge of the wood, the light breaking at the edge of the trees. She half ran, half walked. She was nearly there. She could hear the sound of the harvester and men's voices over the crest of the hill.

She came out of the wood on the opposite side. To her left the field ran down to the towpath. Here she was on the border-line of two fields. She stayed there for a moment, unseen. The men worked on the harvest down to her right. She leaned against a fence post beside the open gate and waited to get her breath back. There was nothing and no one here, only the silence of the wood behind her. She took off her hat and shook her hair free, brushing the glossy, black curls back with her fingers. She wore a frothy white dress, cut to show off her pale skin, and her slender neck and arms. Peach ribbons were threaded through the bodice. She wore her grandmother's pearls around her neck, a gift from Caroline. Her lips were lightly touched with rouge but her cheeks were as downy as a child's in the sunlight, and flushed a delicate pink with her excitement. Her blue eyes were dark and smoky.

'What are you doing here?'

The voice startled her. She whirled round. He was there, a gun over his shoulder. She had heard nothing.

Jessamy could only stare. Her eyes were wide.

'I asked what you were doing here? This is private land.'

She recovered.

'Looking for you.'

He looked down his nose at her, hefting his gun onto his shoulder. He was wearing the same shirt, open at the neck, trousers and boots. He said nothing. His eyes were cold and his mouth humourless. She shivered. He held her eyes with his own. She did not move.

'Why?' he said at last.

'Because . . . because,' she said, her voice softening, 'I

wanted you.' And then, emboldened by the cold smile that caught the edge of his mouth, and the lift of his eyebrow in query, 'I saw you in church. I've seen you since. Don't send me away. I needed to be near you, to tell you how I feel.' Her hands lifted. 'Ever since that day I've thought of you. I had to know whether you felt it too.'

'No.'

She moved forward as he turned away.

'Please . . .'

Max stood still and looked down at her. She came towards him slowly, her ankles touched by the corn stalks, the hot sun on her face warming her. His expression did not change. She moved to stand beneath him where she could smell him. Her senses rocked. His skin was lightly freckled from the sun and dark and his eyes were a cold, vibrant blue. He did not appear to blink, just to look down on her as if he dismissed her entirely, as if she was nothing. His mouth was full and well formed and his nostrils flared from a straight and elegant nose. His brows were dark and his hair waved thickly from his forehead. His power was a tactile thing that she wanted to feel under her fingers. His open shirt showed the muscles of his chest. She lifted her hand to touch it. It was damp. His eyes were a darker, fiercer blue. Braver, she ran her fingers down, her lips parting, her insides shaking and the perspiration of desire standing out along the line of her hair. She felt damp between her thighs and her skin sang with need for him. She willed him desperately to lift his hand and touch her, willed with all the force in her body.

The brightness of his eyes was shadowed by his brows, but she felt them piercing her, scoring her spine and breasts.

'Please . . .' she said.

'Please, what?'

'Please . . . touch me.'

He was still. He did not move. He did not make a sound. She could not stand it. Her skin jumped for his touch.

'All right. Have it your way.'

He pulled her to him and her head fell back. She thought he would kiss her but he did not and she found her eyes opening, dazed, as he threw his gun into the long grass and took her by the wrist to the edge of the haystack.

He threw her to the ground, and started to pull off his belt. Jessamy lifted herself up to her elbows instinctively, as if in protection. He stood astride her, his legs braced. She was a girl trained to obey, a girl of stifled desires and high sexuality. This was her fate; nothing could have taken her from it.

She started to unbutton her dress. She stopped, her eyes lifting up to him. He leaned forward and pulled the dress open, roughly feeling her breasts. She cried out, about to protest, the tears filling her eyes, and his eyes changed. He was not gentler, but she saw the desire, saw his eyes darken. He stripped off his shirt, his eyes on her. Then slowly, he bent and took off her dress, peeling it down so that she was exposed slowly and vulnerably. His fingers reached in, each side of her hips, and eased it down over her thighs, his fingers sliding along her skin. Her leg came over, hiding herself from him but he pushed her back. The hay scratched the skin of her back but she was mesmerised, hypnotised by the rich desire that showed in his face. His power now *was* hypnotic, his strength transmitted to his own immediate need. He wanted her. From that glorious moment she knew. He could not stop. She had him. It was wrong, but it was wonderful and she would not stop.

He persuaded her to lie still, his hands running the length of her thighs. Jessamy murmured with the pleasure of his featherlight touch, and moved by the sound of her cries, he shrugged himself out of his trousers and knelt before her, the sunlight along his broad back and shoulders. She saw how much he needed her, shadowed by the line of his body. There. He had soft dark hair on his body but his muscles were tight and brown as if he had worked with his shirt off in the sun. She had seen that body so often in the field by the planes, back in her room in memory, and now it was hers. She lay back, waiting.

He had what she had always wanted: that harsh strength overlaid by a natural elegance. Now the roughness and harshness showed. The clothes were gone; only the animal need remained. And his need was of her. At last the moment was here— at last.

His hands reached out for her, taking her swiftly underneath him as he laid his body full length on hers. His face was against hers and she thought he would kiss her, but again he did not. The rough beard was against her cheek, and she felt him push against her thighs, his hands lifting her legs around him as he pressed against her, his shoulders broad and glistening under her line of vision, so that now she could see the sky and the edge of the wood, the stubby cornfield alongside, and . . .

She cried out, muffled into the skin of his shoulder as he

entered her. And cried again. She threw her head from side to side wildly, her eyes wide and fearful. He was breaking her apart, tearing her, not stopping. Her hands reached for the iron of his arms.

'Please, please . . .'

It did not stop. His arms gave not an inch. They held her like bands of steel in their place, his head down beside hers, the black waves now brushing on her cheek, the relentless rhythm quickening and slowing and tearing, and tearing . . . and then warming and soothing. Suddenly she felt the glow spreading through her and her own body started slowly to respond, to pick up the rhythm and go with him, letting him ride them both to the edges of their senses with pleasure.

The sun bore down, hot and hotter, the hay scratched her back, their bodies slipped with sweat and slid against the earth and the bed of hay. She was dazed with it, her vision hazy and delicious, her mind spinning as she breathed erratically and moaned against him.

And then his rhythm changed, was faster, and he filled her more, urging her without words to understand, his rasping breath filling her ears as he strove to pick up and climb.

Jessamy suddenly rocked back on her spine as he exploded inside her, the heat searing and fanning out through all of her body. She screamed out violently as she contracted; his hand came over her mouth as he shouted his pleasure against her hair, and her screams of ecstasy were poured in against the cup of his palm. They slid from tension into a halt and subsiding relaxation.

Jessamy breathed long and deep, drawing him in. Her eyes were closed. Her slim arms slid around the width of his back, feeling him. Her man; he was hers.

He pulled out of her arms and stood up and away. Her eyes opened lazily, a soft smile on her face. She was drowsy and wanton, spreadeagled against her bed of hay. Her rejected hand slipped slowly to the ground beside her.

Max pulled himself into his trousers. Jessamy could not have looked more beautiful than she did at that moment. She would never forget this afternoon but nor would he forget her. It had been built on anger and hate, but hate had spiced the desire: he had wanted her too.

'Max. I'll cancel the wedding,' she said. 'There can be no other man for me now. Now I know I love you, nothing can keep us apart, not even my father.' With a sense of pure delight she knew she had found the man who could stand up to him.

His head snapped up at her words. His eyes were cold. He reached down for his shirt, his voice cursory.

'I'm leaving for America tomorrow. Your wedding will go ahead, Jessamy.'

Jessamy's eyes were wide with bewilderment. 'Take me with you. I'll be with you under any circumstances. I know for some reason our families don't like each other, but does it matter, if we do? I know it'll bring shame on me, but I don't care, Max. I love you. I want you. Oh, please . . .' She sat up, naked, and reached out her arms.

Max's expression was unreadable. He bent down for his gun.

'Are you going? Really?'

'Yes.'

'But you wanted me . . .'

'I wanted nothing. You came to me, remember. You had what you asked for.' He turned on her coldly, dismissing her pleas with his words. He shifted his gun over his shoulder.

'But . . . why?' she said slowly. She stretched out her fingers for her clothes. 'Is it that you're ashamed of me? I wouldn't want marriage, or anything,' she pleaded with her eyes on him, horrified by the coldness that emanated from him; she wanted to say anything to stop that, but what? What was wrong? 'Your mother didn't marry,' she said hopefully. 'Oh, I know people talk, but I don't mind . . .'

'Oh, you don't mind.'

'No.'

'Well, let me tell you something . . .'

Tell me, she said with her eyes. Whatever it is, however dreadful, I want to know why this is happening. She watched him gather himself.

'Your father,' he said, 'and your uncle . . . *raped* my mother. Cruelly and brutally. She was an innocent young girl, a village girl. So that didn't matter. She was nothing, just little better than an animal. And *your father* decided he would have her. He hunted her, through this wood,' he said, briefly thumbing over his shoulder, 'just like the foxes they love to chase. Running for her life. Scared out of her mind. On horseback, with the hounds too.' The blue eyes bored through her, his face bitterly cold. 'And your uncle Frederick the same. And then they left her without a backward glance and went off to join the rest of their merry friends and have a good time . . . *That was my mother . . .*'

She could not tear her eyes from his. She could not speak.

'And that was twenty years ago, Jessamy.'

Her mouth dropped open. The full horror and implication was coming through to her. *Those eyes.* She knew she'd seen them before. *That power.* God, no wonder she'd wanted him.

Her head dropped. She stared at the ground, her breath caught in her throat. Her eyes burned in her face. Oh, my God! She couldn't form the words, but his silence confirmed it.

She looked swiftly up at him again. Exactly the same colouring. The knowledge was in her eyes, answered in his. He lifted his gun onto his shoulder and walked away, over the crest of the hill towards home.

With a whimper she gathered her clothes to her and struggled into them. She brushed the hay from her legs with a cry. Half-dressed, she stumbled to her feet, the tears staining her cheeks. She ran for the wood and safety, home. Her eyes squeezed tight and briefly as she steadied herself against a tree, she felt the nausea swim over her. She had just made love to her brother.

TWENTY-FOUR

Dickie came down the stairs. She was dressed in her flying kit. The front door opened.

Max strode into the hall downstairs. He sensed her there before she spoke, poised, her hand on the rail. He stopped and looked up.

'Where have you been?' she said. 'We were expecting you in for lunch. Have you been with Dad?'

Max said nothing, but his feelings stood out in his face from the shadows of the hall beneath. Dickie was startled by that naked look. She said nothing, but her eyes were suddenly alert, trying to decipher what she saw there, something wrong.

The wedding bells began to peal out. Over the crest of the hill on the soft summer day they chimed on the breeze, proclaiming the wedding with joyous monotony.

Max's face held a world of expression. His blue eyes blazed with a mixture of emotions as he held his mother's look. A muscle worked in his jaw. He laid his hand on the newel post, his foot on the first step.

Dickie lifted her head and listened. She knew today was the day; she had heard the banns. Then she looked down into the face below hers. She saw the ruthlessness there, and the cold aching pain of knowledge. Her eyes ran over his clothes. She knew what he had done.

When he saw that she understood, he came up the stairs until he was alongside her. He looked down into her eyes, searching their depths for something. She did not know what. A narrow window at the crook of the stairs looked out over the fields, two

305

small stained-glass panes at the top throwing soft colours onto the bare wood of the stairs and across Dickie's shoulder.

Max turned and looked through the window. His thoughts seemed to be there as he listened to the pealing of the bells in the distance. His mouth was tight, his eyes inward.

Then he turned and laid his hand gently on her shoulder. It was a gesture of peace: now she could rest. Her revenge had been taken for her.

His touch broke her silence.

'Why, Max?'

'For you,' he said simply.

His hand slid from her shoulder as if it was too heavy as with a great weariness he climbed the stairs to the top. She did not turn. Bill was standing there. He had witnessed the scene. Max lifted his eyes briefly to his and went into his room without a further word. He closed the door.

Dickie had not moved. Her hand held the rail tight as she stood there facing the tiny window.

Bill turned to look at the closed door. There was bewilderment on his face. He came along the corridor towards her. He stood at the head of the stairs.

'What's going on, Dickie?'

Dickie stared out through the window. She did not trust herself to speak. She lifted her foot in the air as if she was about to walk down the stairs, but she did not move, just looked at the point of her shoe, then up and away. She shook her head. The bells pealed insistently. The sun came out from behind a white cloud. She sighed heavily.

Bill moved closer. 'What happened?' he said. He came down the stairs. 'What's the kid done?'

'Not such a kid, Bill. As you said, he's a man.' She looked lost for the first time. Her eyes lifted to gaze through the window. Outside the grass waved gently in the breeze. The green trees in the orchard dipped and swayed. 'I told him,' she said. 'I told him the truth of what happened.' Her eyes met Bill's as she turned her face over her shoulder. 'I wanted to stop him and the Redfield girl.'

'And?'

She turned back. She moistened her lips with the tip of her tongue. She was distant. 'He's been with her. Taken her virginity. He did it for me.' She hesitated. 'So that the Redfields would come second today.'

'Oh, *Dickie*. Didn't I say? Didn't I warn you? What have you done?'

She was tiny, standing there in the light of the stained glass, unmoving against the pale wood of the stairs. Standing alone, listening to the wedding bells. For the first time Max had shown his ruthlessness, won from her. It was true then that the one who fought on behalf of a loved one's pain always fought the harder, and the sacrifice was always dearer. Bill was a decent man; he did not like the way things had been going. He had always wanted to protect her, loving her. The pain had been carved out of her to make Max. He could not condone what was happening.

'He's young and vulnerable, Dickie. Alive with new feelings. He's not even twenty, for God's sake. It must have cost him a great deal to take revenge for you that way.' He looked back at the closed door. 'He must hate himself now,' he said, his voice soft and tense, knowing how the young man behind that silently closed door must be feeling, alone.

'Yes, I know,' she said. 'I tried to stop him.'

'But you had already started! What Max did today was inevitable. It was callous and cruel, and he did it for you, because you're his mother. He loves you and he did it for you. And what about the blood relationship? She might be his sister! What if there's a child?' he cried against her silence. He did not need her answer. Bill sighed. 'The girl loved him. I saw it in her face,' he finished more quietly. 'That day in church.'

'That poor girl,' she murmured. 'How he must have hurt her.' Her own memories came back, so clearly now. The betrayal of love, an adolescent love for Frederick Redfield destroyed. 'I only wanted revenge against Rupert Redfield and his brother.'

'Dickie,' he said, standing alongside her. 'Revenge is something you cannot isolate. It's like cancer. It spreads, sweetheart. You've got to stop this now. Are you listening? Stop your vendetta against the Redfields!'

'I can't, Bill,' she said, her voice almost hypnotised. 'I can't until I've got Foxhall, and they're ruined.' She turned to him. 'What Max did, he did for me. Because he understands. I wish I could change the way he did it, but I can't! I love him more than ever now. It must have cost him dreadfully to do it, but don't you see, Bill . . . more than ever now, and now for Max's sake too, I *have* to pursue it!'

'You would, anyway,' he said, his voice knowing and tired. 'I know you. You can't let go. Not until you nail that guy.'

Her silence confirmed his words.

'Dickie,' he said rationally, 'the day will come when I won't take your side. I won't be able to.'

She turned again and looked at him. She could not imagine such a day. Bill would always be there for her, had always been there. His loyalty was without question.

'You'll always be there, Bill.'

'No. I cannot justify revenge.'

'It's no longer that simple, Bill,' she said, her own voice tired and even now. 'I've waited too long for it to be simple revenge. I'm driven by it. It's a way of life now. It has to go on.' She turned and looked once more at Max's closed door. He was no longer a child that she could go to and draw into her arms for comfort. This time he was suffering for her. She felt as if a wedge had been driven into her. He had taken revenge for her, and now she must adhere to her vows even more for his sake. Bill was right, but she could not be deflected from her main purpose. For the first time she and Max must bear their pain apart. He was no longer a boy, he was a man. She remembered other wedding bells. She knew how much she loved her son and what a legacy she had borne him.

'You don't understand, Bill,' she said.

'And Max does.'

'Yes.'

She went down the stairs and out into the hot summer day.

Jessamy walked up the stairs of Foxhall, the long skirt of her mother's wedding dress trailing up the stairs behind her. She did not look back. The whole day had swum by as though she had been in a trance. She did not even notice that the bouquet of orange blossom was slipping from her fingers. John hastened up alongside her, and bent to catch it, placing it back in her hands, and pressing her fingers over it.

Ahead of her he climbed the last few stairs and went down the corridor. He opened the door to her room.

'Here we are, Jessie. Do you know just how beautiful you look? At last we're alone!' He stood back as she went in. 'I've been longing for this moment, haven't you?'

His love was in his eyes, and his desire. She was indeed

unbelievably lovely, the more so for the cool and regal way in which she carried herself. She went into the room. 'Can I come in?' he said. She did not answer. He thought she was too shy. He stepped in and closed the door.

At the foot of the stairs, Caroline still stood. She had watched them go up the stairs together. Her daughter was equally as lovely as herself. She remembered her own wedding day. The great hall had been thronged with guests, the summer day outside, the cool of the marble in the hall, the swishing of her skirts over its cool surface, the hot fear in her heart. And then Rupert . . . and his hands. She lifted her chin in a little intake of breath. She remembered it all. Quickly, she looked up the stairs to the empty landing. John was not Rupert. She breathed freely again. The dress had not brought her the happiness she had been seeking, but Rupert had wanted Jessamy to wear it. She looked around her. She needed a drink. Just as soon as she could she would slip away to her conservatory; there was a bottle there. She turned back to talk to her guests.

'Jessamy?'

John was coming across the room towards her. In his hand he held a long velvet box. 'I saved this for the moment we would be together.'

Her hands opened the box as if from a distance. The necklace of diamonds and rubies winked at her in the soft light that filtered into the young girl's bedroom. She no longer cared about anything.

'Let me put it on for you.'

John's warm fingers were spreading them around her neck, her own were touching the cold jewels into place. She caught sight of the Russian icon that Rupert had given her standing in the corner, a relic of her childhood, a room full of Rupert's gifts to his favourite child. John stood back to admire her. In his eyes was a different light. His voice came from a far distance.

'They belonged to my grandma,' he said proudly. 'Father said I could have them for you. He thinks you're a wonderful girl for me. Oh, Jessamy, I'm such a happy man!'

Her look was distant, but she was ethereally beautiful. He could wait no longer. He moved towards her, his arms held out to take her. He expected resistance. He met none. She was limp and cool.

Jessamy gave in to the kisses that rained upon her face now with all the fervour of her husband's pent-up need. Before their wedding she had surprised him with her passion, but then she had held it back from him. It had fed the fire ignited in him, and the last few weeks had been the longest of his life. Now she was his. In a few hours they would be man and wife in truth. His loins ached with his need for her.

He hardly knew what he was doing as he led her towards the bed, driven only by his need for her. Her clothes were laid out on the bed; the wedding guests were waiting downstairs. He carried her to the bed and lay beside her kissing her, her mouth, her eyes, her throat, her breast.

'Oh *yes*, Jessamy, Jessamy!'

He pushed the froth of lace from her shoulders, baring them to his mouth and hands. He pushed further. The wedding dress slid down over the swell of her breasts. Jessamy did not react. She did not resist.

In the midst of his fervour John realised the truth. Hadn't she wanted him on the eve of her party? Hadn't she shown him then how much? Maybe now this was her way of letting him be the man, her silence her way of showing she would not resist were he to . . . oh God, he could not wait. He took her hand and led it to the front of his trousers to feel his need so there could be no mistake. Jessamy was like a doll. She did not draw her hand away. She lay there on the bed, the yards of lace billowing all around her, her dark hair spread against the satin bedspread, the jewels flashing at her throat. Her dreamy, blue eyes were fastened on a distant point. John could not wait any longer.

He lifted the hem of her dress, pushing it to her thighs, murmuring her name and his desires. Jessamy heard nothing as his roaming hands touched her, felt her. It was like another coupling. She had no part of it. She saw his worried face, his agonised face looking into hers, felt his lips press against hers, heard him strain and groan as he pushed, felt it all over again. This time it was different. There was no ardour, no heat, no curiosity. John fell onto her on the bed crushing her wedding dress. He consummated their marriage, quickly and ardently. She hardly felt it. She did not care. John found no resistance or passion in his new wife. This time the man was gentle and did not hurt her. He held her afterwards, held her face in his hands, told her gently how much, how very much, he loved her. He did not leave her side. But it was too late. Her spirit never strong had been truly broken.

The seagulls flew up the field after the tractor, dipping and mewling as the ploughs cut fresh, new earth and grubs were exposed for them. The tractor climbed High Field towards the top, ploughing ready for the new crop.

Jim was feeling drowsy and tired. His head had been aching all day and he was getting old and weak. Farming the land held less pleasure for him than it used to. Soon he would give up. Twenty-five acres. It was too much for an old man. Albert Canter was gone. One day he had suddenly left the village and good riddance. Jim did not miss him. The lad had been surly and ill-mannered, though he had worked hard enough. Jim had no idea of Dickie's involvement—she had sworn Albert to secrecy—and he had been surprised, though not particularly dismayed when the youth had just upped and left one day without so much as a by-your-leave, exactly four years to the day since he had taken him on. But now, even with his grandson's help, Jim felt himself losing interest.

The tractor climbed the field and the motor puttered to a stop. Jim turned the ignition. He looked all around the dashboard.

'Damn!' he said, and climbed out of the cab.

He opened the engine housing and looked inside. New tractor, huh! He could see the loose wire from here. Dickie had bought it for him to please her old dad. Luckily, he understood machinery; he kept a set of tools in the cab. He went round, pulled them out and laid them on the grass before him. His bent fingers pushed rags and tins out of the way. Where was that spanner? Never there when you needed it. Probably that young Max had had it out. Young people, always the same, no respect for order. Jim smiled to himself. Max actually was a fine young man. Dickie was lucky to have him. It was all so much better now that they were back. She was always so tied up in business, though. She seemed to think that buying him a farm of his own and some land made enough sense. It didn't. He wanted a family around him. Twice a week up at Greatley didn't make up for every other night alone by his fireside. Oh, yes, he could go up there any time, she had said so, but you don't, do you, not unless you're asked. That young Dickie, she had no time for anything but business these days. She worked too hard. It was wrong.

Tonight, he would go up there. He would go up and tell her, he was her dad, he would ask them down to his house, not theirs, and they would have a good supper, a kitchen supper, not a grand one like she did now, but the old sort—gathered round the good smell of cooking. He chuckled aloud. That was what he wanted, that was all that was wrong, a bit of family life.

'Jim, look out . . . Jim—!'

Where was that damn spanner? Oh, there it was. Max didn't take it after all. Jim did not hear the warning cry.

'JIM! LOOK OUT!!'

He got to his knees with a groan of effort. And then he saw it, the great machine bearing down on him. He staggered backwards, wildly flailing his arms as he lost his balance.

The tractor crushed the tin box and rolled mercilessly onwards turning over and over until it reached the bottom of the field and lay still.

'Cheers!' Max clinked glasses with his mother and Bill.

'Good luck in California!'

They drank the champagne. Max was ready to leave.

Bill raised his glass again and then went over to sit down in the chair beside the fireplace. It was cream with a fine gold-and-green stripe in it. He sighed as he sank into its comfort. 'Ah! Wish I was going with you, kid. I miss the States. I could go along very easily.'

'And leave me to run the place on my own,' said Dickie. 'That's partnership! Besides, when I asked you, you said no,' she reminded him. 'And I'm very glad you did. Means we're going to find out just how well Max can do it.'

Bill laughed. 'Which is probably just what you wanted in the first place, knowing you! And anyway, you know full well I couldn't leave you if I wanted to.' His laugh was full of love.

Max looked at his mother. She smiled like a woman loved, but not like a woman who loved. She had missed out on that. His anger was kindled anew for what damage had been done to her. He knew how Bill loved her and was grateful.

'Hey,' he said. 'Where's Grandad? Wasn't he supposed to be joining us tonight?'

'Yes, he was.' Dickie paused. A frown crossed her brow. 'Bill, ring the farmhouse and see where he is. He ought to be here by now.'

'Sure thing.' Bill went to the phone. He dialled the number.
'Now, let us know as soon as you can, Max, what the situation
is on the Boeing. I'm leaving for Scotland in a couple of days,
and Bill's going too. Joan will take the message and call us.
Then we'll telegraph you back. Here's the people you should
see along with Wiley.' She handed him a typewritten list of
names from the seat beside her. 'I've packed all the rest of the
company information in your bag for you to read on the ship.'

'Mother,' he said gently. 'I'm going to handle it. You'll hear
from me within the month. Don't worry.'

'No reply,' said Bill. 'Must still be out.' He looked out of the
window. Dusk was falling.

'Can't still be ploughing,' said Dickie, pushing the edge of
the curtain aside with the tips of her fingers. 'It's dark.' She
frowned. 'Where can he be?'

Max put down his glass. 'I'll go and find him. He's probably
on his way over. Might have stopped at the pub.' He smiled. 'If
he has I'll join him. Be back soon.' He moved towards the door.

Joan opened the door before him. The young farm labourer
rushed in ahead of her. His face was white and his eyes like dark
pits of pain in his face. His mouth was working and his hands
clutched the air like a blind man.

'Oh, God!' he said. 'Miss Dickie!'

His voice was a wail.

Dickie was up in a flash. She knew the boy. She grasped his
arms. 'Eddie, what's wrong?'

His face was stricken as he looked into hers. His eyes darted
from one to the other.

'Oh, Miss Dickie, I'm so sorry! I was just passing your land.
I saw him. I tried to warn him, but he was just not hearing me
good. The tractor—it suddenly moved—the brakes can't ha' been
on proper. Your dad was bending down to fix it. Oh God. It
rolled over him—' Dickie's eyes closed tightly, her nails dug
into her palms. She gasped. *No. No, not Dad*.

'I—I'm sorry, ma'am.' He hung his head. 'He's dead.'

'Earth to earth, ashes to ashes . . .'

Her black chiffon scarf billowed in the breeze. No one stood
with her. Max and Bill stood the other side.

How easy it was to change history, and how hard. If only she
had realised he was hard of hearing: an old man's vanity, not

wanting to show he couldn't keep up. If only she had not bought the new tractor, if only she had made certain she had seen him every day, made him come to the house, instead of leaving it to him. The guilt washed over her. If only. It was always too late.

The funeral bells rang out in the village; so soon after the wedding bells. Jessamy was not there to hear them. She was away on honeymoon with her bridegroom. Everybody else did though. They knew who was being buried that day.

The bells drifted up as far as Foxhall. The family was eating lunch. Rupert raised his head slightly and listened. Frederick saw his look. He thought of the old man; he felt weighed by sadness for what they had done to him. He cupped his hand around his water glass and shook the bowl of it slightly, his eyes on the glassy light as his mind drifted. Rupert raised an eyebrow and carried on eating. Caroline was silent between them.

The event had already changed Dickie's life. Tragedy had struck again. His death was an awful blow for her. Her dad was the last of another generation, a generation that she revered, however much she had rejected its simplicity. It was a life of some sort of peace; at least a certainty of one's lot. The life she had chosen was a driven life. Only now she knew how much she needed that very same simplicity inherent in her father's presence to stabilise her own fighting spirit.

She threw her red rose gently in on top of the coffin. The first shovelfuls of earth hit the wood with a heavy, all too final sound. Now she was the first of a new generation; she felt the weight of responsibility heavy on her shoulders with each clod of the earth that was quickly covering her father's coffin.

Oh, Dad. He was a gentle man who never did anyone any wrong and had always tried to soften her. She had at least listened when he had told her not to be so hard, to be gentler. Now there was no one to tell her. Long ago, he had handed the responsibility to her; but she had never felt it till now.

Dickie looked up into the sky. The clouds scudded by. A storm was building up. She could hear his voice in the fields. On a day like this they would have been hurrying to get the work done before the storm broke. It all seemed so long ago.

It was finished. Dickie turned and walked out of the churchyard. One must never be defeated, Dad. She remembered how he had cried in her arms at Sam's death. She would not cry, not now. Head high, she started to walk home.

TWENTY-FIVE

May, 1934

The babies were born minutes apart. It was the only thing that distinguished them as twins; other than that they were different in every way.

The nurse held the little girl to her and tested the bottled milk on the inside of her wrist. The little mouth opened and wailed, demanding its feed; the dark hair brushed against the crook of her arm.

'There, there, it's coming. Wait a minute, now.'

She found the hungry mouth and pushed the teat in. The baby began to suck contentedly.

It struck Nanny Hopkins that this was just about the most beautiful, and demanding, little baby that she had ever taken care of. From the first moment that she had squalled her announcement of her arrival into the world she had had everybody dancing attendance on her. All that was, except her mother. Nanny Hopkins raised an eyebrow at that. How could she resist her? She was perfectly formed, not squashed and wrinkled like most early babies; her skin was soft olive with a brush of dark hair on a pretty head and those big, direct, blue eyes, even now so strong and unwavering. Nanny Hopkins disapproved of Mrs Hamblin. Sabrine Jessamy was everybody's favourite.

In the corner of the room, lying awake in his crib, Alexander was everything different. He was pale, weak and blond, as if his sister, so round and bonny, had drained all the

315

strength from him in their months in the womb together. He was long, narrow and quiet, his blue eyes watching, constantly watching, as if he would now observe everything the outside world had to offer in silence.

John opened the nursery door. Nanny Hopkins smiled approvingly as she stood back and admired her charge. Rupert sat on the white wooden chair with Sabrine on his knee. The big blue eyes were fixed on her grandfather, the little fingers reached up for him. She gurgled happily.

John came towards them slowly. There was something about his daughter. She appeared tactile and strong, seeming to want everyone to love her. Rupert obviously did. John was amazed to find his father-in-law in the nursery, what he considered his territory. It made him even more conscious of what he wanted to say.

He waited until Nanny Hopkins was out of earshot.

'Sir,' he said, sitting down opposite him. 'I wanted to say something to you . . .'

'Oh, yes, John, what's that?' He chucked Sabrine under the chin. She gurgled softly.

John looked down at his hands. He clasped them and turned them over awkwardly. 'Well, whereas it's very kind of you to give us the coach-house, and we'd love to use it when we're here, I think it would be better for us to move away from Foxhall.' He paused. 'Once Jessamy is better, of course.'

Rupert did not look at him. His voice remained quite even. John was surprised by that. 'Move away?' he asked mildly. 'Why?'

John looked at his son, kicking gently in his crib. He put his hand in and touched the tiny clasping hand.

'I think she needs to start a real family life, if you'll excuse me saying so, sir. She wants a home of her own.'

'You have a home here, John, for as long as you wish.'

'I'd like the home to be ours though,' John tried, wondering why his father-in-law was missing the point. 'My family has offered us a house in the Cotswolds, with a bit of land. We won't be far away. I think it would be good for her,' he finished lamely.

Rupert shrugged lightly. Nanny Hopkins returned to the room. She came towards them.

'If you wish, John,' he said, still looking down at the little girl. 'But I think you'll find that Jessamy prefers to stay here at Foxhall, among the people who love her.' Nanny Hopkins stood beside him, waiting to relieve him of her precious charge. 'This little girl's a Redfield, wouldn't you say, John? Just look at her. A real beauty!' He handed her back to the nurse, who gathered her into her arms. Rupert stood up. He patted John on the shoulder. 'See you at lunch, John.' He walked from the room.

John stared at the empty seat for a moment. He was totally confused. Only yesterday Jessamy had said she wanted to get away, and before their wedding she had told him she wanted a place of their own. The coach-house had only been temporary as far as he was concerned. He felt the oppression of living there. He was not nearly strong enough for the Redfields, and Jessamy was behaving so oddly. He wondered how long it would last. She had refused to see the children.

Jessamy turned in the bed and hugged the pillow to her. The birth had been worse than she could ever have imagined. Even now she recalled every detail.

'. . . I don't think it's all over yet, Mrs Hamblin . . .'

. . . the frightful pain that was unbearable . . .

She had screamed and screamed, and fought not to have to do it.

'Push,' someone had said. 'That's it, push.'

She didn't want to push. She couldn't stand the pain.

'Take it away,' she had said. 'I can't stand it.'

'There,' the voice had soothed. A cool sponge had touched her brow. 'You're doing very well. Just a little more. Baby's coming now.'

She had hated the baby. She didn't want it. They could take it away, give it away. Anything to relieve this terrible lurch of pain that grabbed at her insides and screwed and twisted like a giant hand. She poured with sweat and wished she could die, thought she would die. It was worse than she could bear.

It pushed against her will. She could not stop it. Nature had taken over and there was nothing she could do. She screamed as the pain dragged at her again, tearing her apart. Her face contorted with the effort of forcing the birth.

And suddenly there had been that release, the sliding weight pouring from her. But the scream that opened a moth-

er's love for the first time was not there for Jessamy; the cry
closed her. She could not bear to see the child.

'A little girl!'

And then those awful words: 'I don't think it's all over yet,
Mrs Hamblin.'

There had been two of them. She had had to do it all over
again. Was this Nature's way of punishing her? The second
had been easier, sliding through the already oiled entrance
into the world and onto the bed. They had lifted her shoulders
to see. The baby had been lifted and slapped, the piteous cry
wailing out like a mewling cat.

'And a boy! My, what a lucky girl you are!'

The babies had been taken away and Jessamy had sunk to
the pillows exhausted. The room had been dusky then with
the evening light, and the rose of sunset had filled the sky
outside Foxhall. She had borne her children in her old bedroom, not in the coach-house, by demand or request, it didn't
matter. She was here, by somebody's dictates, no longer her
own. Jessamy's life was a drift of obedience now. She had no
spirit to make her own decisions. Voices had murmured at
the far side of the room, and shadows had passed to and fro.
Someone had stroked her forehead again and pulled the bed-
clothes away. Clean sheets had been laid on her and a blanket. The nanny had brushed her hair.

'You look lovely, my dear,' she had said kindly. 'A lovely
mother with two beautiful children. Quite perfect they are,
and so different!' she said, as pleased as if it were an extra
bonus. 'Just you rest now and they'll be back soon to have
their first cuddle with their mama.'

And then the moment she had dreaded for so long had
come. The babies had been brought to her. John was with
them, a besotted expression on his face.

Jessamy had been tormented by the secret of their origin.
She looked out of the corners of her eyes at them. It was too
early to tell. Sabrine was dark like her and Alexander was
thinner, pale and blond, more sickly. It was too soon to see
who had fathered them. They both had the deep blue eyes
that all babies had. She turned away.

'Take them away.'

There was a sound of shock; a stillness of breath.

'But, Jessamy . . .' John said eventually. 'They're our children!'

'Take them away!' she had repeated. 'I don't want them. I want to be left alone!'

He had tried to reason with her. The nurse signalled him away. In the next room, Dr Biddy had counselled him.

'Mr Hamblin, don't worry. This is quite common in new mothers, especially one so young as Jessamy. The strain of having twins has been exhausting for her. It's only temporary, I'm sure. Just try to show her the support she needs and things will soon be fine. Wait and see. Good man.'

The offending babies had been taken away, and Jessamy left in peace. She was so unhappy; she felt as though her world was empty and she was useless and finished. Nothing meant anything to her any more. She had heard the voices at the door murmuring: 'Plenty of rest, that's all she needs. Keep the visitors to a minimum.'

'We will.'

And then they had left, the babies too. In her memory she saw their little faces, the pale one and the dark one. She would never be able to mother them. She thought she knew, with the truth of a mother's instinct, who their father was.

Alone, no one saw her cry herself to sleep. She could not help herself. She still loved him.

September, 1933

Wiley Fairfax had changed. He was no longer with Wells Fargo bank, but headed a huge corporate combine in Los Angeles. His early days with the bank had paid off: he had utilised to the full the knowledge and contacts gleaned then, along with his social connections, combining them to make him a real power. He was a sharp and utterly ruthless businessman, buying up weaker adversaries like a shark in a pool. His reputation was well known. Wiley was now in his late forties, greying at the temples, but as lean and elegant as he had been in the days when Dickie had first approached him at the bank. For him, the memory was a fond one.

He felt quite paternal towards the young man who now came through the open door at the far end of his luxurious office and walked the psychological distance across to his massive desk. For once, Wiley got up and came out from behind it to meet him halfway.

'Max.' He shook his hand, and clapped him on the shoulder. 'You look well. This is a nice surprise. I was just going to lunch. Will you join me?'

'I'd be happy to.'

Wiley's smile was genuine. He went round his desk, his dark brown eyes assessing the young man who now sat down across from him. He looked bright, strong too. He pressed the bell on his desk. A young woman appeared at the door opposite.

'Yes, Mr Fairfax.'

'Make that reservation two for lunch, Martha.'

'Very good, sir.'

He sat back, fingers clasped together. He studied Max again. 'How's your mother?'

'She's well. She sends you her regards.'

'Fine woman. Lucky man, Bill.'

A flicker crossed his face. Max noticed it. So, Wiley had wanted her too. They were too similar; they would have sparked like two pieces of tinder. But Max allowed himself a small smile inside. It was a useful piece of information.

'I'm here to build up Coast Airlines for her, Wiley.' He did not pause. 'She feels you've been too busy to give it . . . your proper attention.'

Wiley's eyes creased in the semblance of a smile. 'She's right. Quite right. I'm glad you're here, as a matter of fact.' He looked at the young man more closely, more cautious now. 'I've been building my own outfit, as you can see,' he said, indicating the penthouse suite around him. 'Coast Airlines is only one of my directorships, and it has remained small, I have to say that. Now you're back,' he went on smoothly, 'I'm sure you'll give it the attention it deserves.'

Max gave a quick, tight smile. His eyes remained cool. 'What about John? Has he other interests too?'

Wiley nodded slowly. 'He has indeed. Namely, another airline.'

'In competition?'

Wiley pursed his lips. 'Not strictly. His airline flies a different route, but it has meant that he has not given what he could have to Coast Airlines. To be honest with you, I don't really trust his motives. I'd wanted to talk to your mother about it, but . . .'

'You can talk to me.'

'I can see that.' Wiley tapped his teeth with the tips of his forefingers. 'Now, you've heard about what's happened with the mail.' He lifted his chin slightly. 'We can talk about John later.'

'Yes, I've heard.' He leaned his arm along the back of the chair. 'The word is that the army has failed to run the mail routes properly and they're being reopened for private use.'

'Except that all those airlines represented at the Spoils Conference of 1930 are not eligible. We were one of those.'

'I know. But the word is that we'll get the line. The government is deciding who qualifies for the new contracts, and Farley is interpreting this ruling to mean that none of the major airlines are to be excluded from a share in the airmail subsidy. I plan to make us a major airline.'

'I see. What are your plans?' Wiley's look was steady. He tapped the desk with a pencil.

'You're going to help me,' said Max, holding his look. 'We're going to buy up a few other outfits and merge them all under one new name, Coastline, Coastline Airways.' His face closed slightly. 'We'll get the contract.'

Wiley nodded. 'You're going to tell me how,' he said, mildly amused.

'In a moment.' Max stretched out his long legs. 'The other message that comes from my mother is that she wants me to get hold of a Boeing . . . 247. I gather you told her that that was not possible.'

Wiley's brow creased slightly. He shrugged and leaned forward over his desk. 'That's quite right. There were only so many made, and they've been snapped up. Coast Airlines simply wasn't a big enough venture to take one on.'

'Bennett Air is. That's what she wanted it for.'

'Yes, I know, but by the time she told me,' he explained, 'it *was* too late. You have to be on the spot.'

Max nodded his understanding.

'Mind you,' Wiley went on, 'there's talk of a new aeroplane from the Douglas stable. I've been keeping my ears open. Transcontinental and Western went to them when Boeing was unable to build all those wanted by airlines in the States, and so Douglas gained some early orders for the DC-1. I'm keeping an eye on it.'

Max's dark blue eyes narrowed with interest. Wiley saw. He was impressed with the young man. His silent detachment was powerful in one so young. He listened in an exceptionally collected way, never showing his hand emotionally. He would have made a good poker player, thought Wiley, and then smiled ruefully to himself. He probably was one already. When he had something to say it was concise and well thought-out. He was left in no doubt as to his ability and determination to succeed. He was his mother's son all right. The paternal feeling he had sensed on Max's arrival increased. He was proud of the boy.

Max interlaced his fingers. 'One of my plans is to undercut the major airlines with special deals. We'll talk about that later. First, I want to go for the mergers. Soon there are going to be international flights across the Atlantic. I want our airline to be one of the first. Tell me about John Swainson,' he said. 'Is he ready to be bought out?'

'Oh, for sure. At the right price!' Wiley shifted the pencil across the desk, the humour touching his eyes. 'He's only a small shareholder.'

'Does he know I'm back?'

'No.'

'Good. Well . . . let's offer him the right price. At the moment the airline is doing very little more than it has been doing since we left for England. It's been running along nicely but at no great profit. John knows you're involved in other things, I expect. He won't smell a rat. He'll sell right away—happily?'

'Yes. And put the money to good use in his own airline. He's hinted once or twice that he might be amenable to that.'

'Do it. Meet with him and see what he says. Then we'll make our next offer!' He smiled for the first time. 'This is where you come in . . .'

John Swainson was basically a lazy man. His interests now ran more to the girls that swarmed around Hollywood and the film world. His expenses ran high, and his alimony. The money that he had laid out on property was no more. He had sold much of it to finance his other interests. The aviation company, SunAir, the unimaginative films made for JSA Films Inc., and too many years of good life and drinking had blotted his prowess as a director.

SunAir was a big but sleepy company which was not producing for its shareholders quite the return on assets that it should. There was tension and division among the board of directors as John failed to pull his weight.

There was no hint of impropriety as John sold out his interest in Coast Airlines, and Wiley slipped in and bought a share stake in John's company, SunAir. John simply smiled to himself and realised what he had always known—he was the better businessman, Coast was going down the drain and he had done very profitably out of it. He did not notice as Wiley built himself a significant share stake in SunAir.

He knew when he heard that Wiley planned to launch a full takeover bid.

The reaction was as instant as a volcano. Wiley's reputation was foolproof and ruthless. He was a financier with real clout and know-how. The price of the shares soared.

The directors panicked. They knew Wiley's reputation. Anxious to preserve their own jobs and fearful of what might happen after such a takeover, they did a deal with him. Wiley's shares were bought out at a premium.

Wiley collected his fat cheque, and promised to leave the company alone for the next five or ten years. The directors had bought themselves time either to revive the company in the hope of deterring further marauders or to sink back into their previous lethargy—in John Swainson's case, the latter.

The unlucky shareholders who had seen the prices of their shares soar while Wiley was buying, watched those prices sink again—to a level lower than they were before the bid.

Wiley had acquired five per cent of the airline and said he wanted fifty point one per cent. If his bluff had been called, and if he had had to go through with the whole thing, he could have helped himself to the bits he wanted and sold off the rest. But the game was played. John Swainson had offered him a healthy price to go away. In theory, Wiley did and went away a loser, but in practice he was a good half-million dollars richer for the sale of his five per cent.

Max met Wiley in the bar of the small restaurant off the beach.

'What did I tell you?' he said as the waiter brought them the bottle of champagne.

Wiley drew the cheque from his pocket. 'It was a brilliant idea, Max. One I shall use again in the future. A simple way to make money. Here is your half.'

Max took the cheque from him, noting the figures. He tucked it into his wallet, and put the wallet back in his inside pocket. His eyes were smoky with satisfaction.

Wiley regarded him for a moment as he drank his champagne. The sea broke on the shore outside the storm windows with the sound of distant thunder. It was a fresh, sunny day.

'Tell me,' he said, holding the glass between his fingers. 'Didn't you feel sorry for him at all?'

'No.' Max shook his head. 'Sleepy companies get what they deserve. Surely that is the law of the City, or Wall Street for that matter.' His fingers touched the stem of his glass. 'And, besides, John Swainson deserved it. He let my mother down. She trusted him and he put all his energy into his own company in repayment of that trust. She understood from him that he would run Coast for her in her absence. She thought it was a good friendship, one that she could count on. She was wrong. That's all.'

Wiley felt a small chill run through him. The man was so young and so cold. *He* would not count on past friendship. Wiley himself was known to be ruthless as a shark, but he had at least acquired the habit over the years. Max was born to it.

'And now that you have your money,' he said, nodding at the cheque in Max's pocket, 'what's next?'

'Next?' Max echoed him. He looked out over the ocean. 'I'm going after West Counties Air tomorrow.'

Max came out onto the deck of the small beach cottage. It was seven a.m. The rented cottage sat just back from the beach on Beach Palisades Road in Santa Monica. Around him lived the stars of the screen, the Hollywood moguls with their extraordinary power, beautiful women, and, of course, men like himself—the young blood.

The beach was deserted. The air was fresh and still. There was a hot day ahead. Now the sand was damp from the night and the sea was calm, silvered like a lake. The occasional bird trilled in the trees beyond the beach house, and there was an early pastel sky, and not a soul in sight. They were probably all recovering from yet another late-night party. The empty beach was inviting. He had just tackled his first deal alone and enjoyed the feeling it gave him.

Max took deep lungfuls of air. He felt the need to stretch himself. He stepped down onto the sand and started to run.

TWENTY-SIX

Max held a glass of champagne and gazed into the flames of the fire that leapt up from the dug-out pit of the beach barbecue. His feet were bare and the sand was cool and silky beneath them.

He listened to the sea. It splashed in, the sunset touching the luminous crests of the waves. Beyond, the ocean was stroked into fine ripples by the soft Santa Ana winds. Voices murmured and chatted all around in the purple dusk, punctuated by laughter.

There was a rigid caste system in filmland society but at night they relaxed and gave beach parties like any other group of people. Tonight he had been invited. He was not particularly impressed by any of them; he had kept very much to himself since his arrival. He did not expect to enjoy the evening particularly.

He felt the champagne pour onto his shoulder before he saw the person who had done it. He jumped to his feet.

Oh, excuse me . . .

She came down on her knees beside him, mopping at his cream cotton shirt. 'I'm so very sorry. So clumsy of me!'

Her hair was the colour of rich toffee with curls of pure gold, waving artfully around the prettiest pair of hazel eyes he had ever seen. They were clear and laughing, her strong teeth showing in a wide mischievous smile. She had a short nose and a square face like a cat. She was beautifully tanned. 'But then, maybe I'm not so sorry after all!' The eyes under their flaring dark brows crinkled into dark lashed shadows as she laughed. 'What's your name?'

'Maxwell Bennett.'

'Cathy Riley.' She held out a slim hand. 'And I'm sorry about your shirt, really.'

'That's OK,' he said.

She sat down and tilted her head to one side. 'What are you doing here?'

He turned to look at her. Her expression was now both gentle and curious, and he noticed that her warm mouth was set in a permanently receptive smile. She latched long freckled arms around her bare knees.

'Well,' she went on lightly. 'You're not the usual type that attends Greta's parties.'

'And you are?' He raised an amused eyebrow.

'No.' Her smile lifted back into her eyes. 'I'm a country girl. From Oklahoma. My dad's got a farm back there.'

'That makes two of us. My family lives on a farm in England.' He was aware of the scent of her. The breeze blew a lock of golden-streaked hair across her face. She drew it back with long fingers, as he spoke.

'I'm out of my environment too,' she confided trustingly, suddenly serious. She looked around them, at the sea and the people on the sand. 'My family were pioneers. They were at the starting line when the American government gave anybody with a horse and wagon and any spirit the chance to acquire one hundred and sixty acres of American land free if they could make it work for them in the space of a year.'

'I presume they did.'

She smiled cheekily. 'Now they've struck oil!'

'So you decided to mix with the rich crowd?' His brow creased as he grinned at her.

'No,' she said, a little sensitively. 'I came to see Greta. She's my cousin, believe it or not.' They looked across at their hostess, Greta Rosenberg, flamboyant in a parrot-coloured silk kimono, a turban covering her blonde hair. She was tall and elegant, diamonds winking on her hands in the firelight and in animated conversation with a young industrialist. 'She may look a little . . . showy,' she murmured, 'but she's very strong. Ruby wouldn't know where he was without her. He adores her. He says every successful man needs a strong woman. Personally, I think family love is more important. What do you think, Max?'

Max looked into the crackling flames. 'I think both are important.'

'I've got a wonderful family,' she said. 'Six brothers and four sisters!' She laughed softly. 'We're bolstered by great family love. We do everything together. Dad taught us to be self-sufficient. We're all able to ride for days on horseback across the desert, setting up camp fires at night. I know the land. I like to live close to it,' she said distantly. 'I can survive for days in the wild. I know all the birds, the trees, which plants are edible, which things are dangerous.'

'Next time I go camping in the wild, remind me to take you along.' His eyes creased darkly as he looked at her. Her enthusiasm had brought a flush to her cheeks, and the hazel eyes were darker and warm. She was bare of make-up and yet natural and beautiful. She was refreshing and naïve, quite unabashed at sitting talking to a perfect stranger, her short shorts riding up high on her legs. He could see the curve of her breast as she leaned forward to poke at the fire with a stick.

'You couldn't do better,' she said, a teasing note in her voice. 'Dad says I'm the best guide in the whole of New Mexico. That's where we ride a lot,' she explained.

'I know it. We fly that way.'

'Yes.' Her voice was drowsy with pleasure. 'Camping out at night. Under the stars.'

'You don't want more?'

'I don't need more.'

Cathy was a free spirit. Her simplicity intrigued him. It was so opposite to his drive and competitive nature, but for some unknown reason she was the first person who had ever made him feel insecure. Maybe it was her obvious contentment, her absolute lack of need for anything more. And she laughed at him. No one had ever done that. Somehow she reminded him of Colin. She had the same ease. She had her own particular strength and he knew suddenly that he found it very attractive.

He wanted to move, finding himself quite uncomfortable.

'Would you like to walk for a while?' He started to stand.

'Sure.'

He put out his hand and drew her to her feet. She dusted the sand from the backs of her thighs. It drew attention to her legs. He looked. And looked up at her face. She tossed back her hair and laughed at him.

'I'll race you to the sea!'

She had already turned and was on her way down to the water's edge. He watched her go, a thoughtful look on his dark face. She was walking at the water's edge when he caught up with her.

She had slim hips, beautiful legs and the kind of walk he wanted to follow. Cathy had an athletic grace quite unlike any woman he had ever met before. She was totally at ease with her body and refreshing, a whole new world for him to discover.

He walked quietly alongside her, their feet splashing in the water. The moonlight lent a silver cast to the sea, and for the first time he felt relaxed with a woman as he listened to her easy laughter and found himself fitting in with her air of casual self-containment.

The sound of the crowd clapping at a tennis match was like the sound of sea crashing on the shingle and pulling back in the undertow. It caught his attention. He looked over towards the vast white house. There was a floodlit tennis court alongside, and in front, a huge swimming pool with a Venetian marble bridge over it. Tall, slender columns graced the front of the house and there were two double staircases down to the pool. An American flag fluttered proudly on a pole above the gracious colonial lines.

'That's Marion Davies,' she said, stopping to point. Max looked at the laughing girl with the fair, curly hair who had just come down onto the beach. She was surrounded by a circle of admirers.

'We're going to see her latest picture later tonight,' said Cathy. 'She's very good. A comedienne. But I think he has more to do with it than her talent. She's with Cosmopolitan Pictures, you see, and it's an affiliate of Warner's, a company formed by him as a showcase for her. She gets unbelievable publicity every time a picture comes out. Still, I think it's lovely that he loves her the way he does. She makes him very happy. Are you coming up to San Simeon this weekend?'

'San Simeon?' His voice was vague.

'Yes.' She fell in step beside him as he started to walk back towards the party. 'You don't know it?' she teased. 'I thought you said you knew the coast. It's William Hearst's castle. He's her lover.' Her voice was light-hearted and easy.

'Oh, *that* San Simeon.'

'Yes, *that* San Simeon! Well, are you?'

'No.'

'Why not?'

He left the water's edge and cut across the softness of the sand. The party guests moved like shadows around the little fires on the beach ahead of them. The laughter drifted over them.

'That sort of pomp and ceremony doesn't interest me too much,' he said. 'I'm surprised you're one of that crowd.'

'Oh, I'm not. There's no such thing as a crowd anyway. It's always different.'

'Why do you go, then?' He looked down at her profile, as sweet as a child's.

'For the riding. And the scenery. And I like Marion.'

She was full of surprises. She seemed so naïve and yet she knew as a friend one of the most notorious women on the coast.

'She looks like a party girl,' he said. 'You've just been telling me you're not a social butterfly.'

Her eyes were lit with a warm, mischievous light again as she looked up at him. They reached their fire. 'Maybe opposites attract!' she said smokily. She looked away before he could read her eyes fully or reply. 'Look, our fire's going out.'

He took his eyes away from her and bent down to the fire. He lifted the twigs and relaid them, poking at the embers.

'And I thought you said you were a country boy,' she said playfully. 'Don't you know how to build a beach fire. Haven't you done this before?' She lay on her stomach and blew at the embers. 'I thought you were the outdoor type.'

'Outdoors here is very different to outdoors in England,' he said, watching her. She had a perfect bottom. 'I was only born in the country. We were poor. We didn't have barbecues on the beach.'

'Oh, don't you sound sad!' The hazel eyes danced in the leaping firelight. She sat up. 'You don't have to be rich to have fun, you know.' She crossed her legs, the light glowing on her skin. 'The things I do are pretty simple, and they don't cost much money. Riding, travelling, being outside, swimming in the sea in summer and in the lakes and rivers around home. Now, that's fun. And having a barbecue after. You should relax a little, Max. Let your hair down.'

'Want to show me how?'

'Sure, I'll show you how.'

'How about this weekend then? I'll take you flying.'

Her eyes brightened. 'And I'll teach you to ride.'

'It's a deal.' She reached to shake his hand. 'Old man Hearst'll talk to you about flying. He has an interest in it. Howard Hughes too. He might be there!' Her tone was light and breezy. The touch of her hand had struck an inner chord in him. He held it a moment longer.

'Social climbing at San Simeon? I meant down here, in Los Angeles.' His voice was harsher than he meant.

'It's not social climbing, Max,' she said gently. 'You're a businessman. So are they.' Her words were simple. 'You might swap ideas, that's all.'

She was right. And now he knew: he had wanted to be alone with her. The realisation was dawning on him as she spoke again.

'What is it, Max?' The hazel eyes were clear with concern.

'Nothing,' he murmured. He remembered Jessamy lying in the field. How she looked. The picture was still clear in every detail.

Cathy looked at the intense blue eyes. 'Come with me, Max,' she said, interrupting his thoughts. Her voice was soft and persuasive. 'We'll have fun. We could camp out together, go to the hot springs at Big Sur, ride and swim and I'll even teach you how to make the best beach fire. Like an old pro. How's that for an offer?'

The tawny eyes held his. Suddenly she was no longer the tomboy, she was frail and very feminine, her words though flippant, holding a serious note. Her limbs were golden in the firelight.

He looked down into the languorous face. The memory faded. *She* was real.

'The best I've had,' he said.

The takeover took up only a small column in the *Los Angeles Times:*

>   The Bennett family extended their aviation interest yesterday when Maxwell Bennett, twenty-one-year-old son of aviatrice and businesswoman Mrs William Latimer, became West Counties Air chairman.
>   He resigned from the board of his mother's line, Coastline Airways, to acquire the controlling interest of West Counties—injecting $550,000 into an airline which faced bankruptcy earlier this year with a $1.5 million overdraft.

It means West Counties has completed one of airline's most remarkable economic recoveries and will begin business again with $200,000 in the bank and no outstanding debts.

The turnaround is largely down to the Bennett family whose financial strength helped them survive a winding up action and produce their revival package.

Max Bennett said last night: 'I love flying. There is no way you would get involved with a business like this unless you have an interest in it. I have certainly not come to West Counties on the basis of keeping the seat warm for my mother. The two airlines are entirely separate entities and will stay that way.'

Air travel is now very much a way of life for the family. The Latimers have opened a further company in England for the purpose of importing US spare parts and new inventions for English aircraft.

West Counties has paid off $305,000 to Wells Fargo Bank and $130,000 to unsecured creditors at 50 cents on the dollar.

Max put down the paper with satisfaction. The mail routes had reopened to private use. Wiley had put in their bid under the name of Coastline Airways. With their money behind the deal, there had been no question that they would win the bid after the May reshuffle. Their bid had been accepted. The newspaper report had been a good piece of public relations. Max was ready to run both West Counties Air and the newly named Coastline Airways behind the scenes. Later, when the publicity had died down he would move the two closer together, and one day they would all merge under the banner of Bennett Air.

He pencilled a cable to Dickie to tell her the news. He sat back at his desk and let his thoughts wander. They did not have far to travel: to Cathy, and the weekend ahead.

It had been a wet day. Now the wind had dropped and the rain had abated. It was still. The night air hung with silence.

They rode their horses into the stable soaked to the skin. The ranch at Big Sur was owned by a friend of Cathy's. Once again, he was surprised at the ease with which she treated her relationships. They had simply left San Simeon on the third day to wander up the coast together and find themselves another place to stay.

The endless mountain ranges ran for miles, right down to the coast. There, just above the cliffs were the stables and down a narrow pathway the rustic, wooden cabin that housed the hot tubs, hot sulphuric water harnessed straight from the ground.

They left the horses with the groom and went to the cabin. Their clothes were saturated and stiff, hard to pull off over chafed knees and damp buttocks, numb with cold.

They laughed at each other. Their eyes were hot.

Her eyes blazed a deeper tawny. And her cheeks were flushed. His eyes were glazed by her and very blue.

There was a spiky cypress tree up on the point, an emblazoned black silhouette against the dying sunset. The mist lay at the foot of the cliffs down to the sea. A rising moon paled over the ocean. The white, flying spray was filmy as it crashed and surged against the rocks, way beneath the deck of their mountain hideaway.

She held her towel to her and gradually dropped it. She stood before him in all her beauty. She looked frightened as if he might not like her, and yet brave. She was unbelievably beautiful. He felt a hand press his heart. His eyes looking at her showed all his feelings, her freedom, his containment, how they fed each other's needs.

'Oh, Cathy,' he whispered, and held her in his arms so still. He would never let her go. Never wanted this moment to end. He closed his eyes.

TWENTY-SEVEN

Summer, 1936

The cable from Max arrived shortly after his letter. Dickie sat outside the French windows and tore the form open.

She read quickly then lifted her head and scanned the horizon, thinking. The yellow of the cornfield met dark storm clouds on the horizon. The sun's rays parted the clouds and shone down. A clutch of dark green trees to her distant left showed the beginnings of the wood. The heavy light was metallic. They were in for a summer storm, the new wind now catching at the edges of the paper.

Bill walked out through the doors and stood looking down on her. A cream sweater was slung around his shoulders, his rough blond hair tousled as always.

'What's in the letter?' he said.

'News from Max,' she murmured. 'Here, read it.' She handed it up to him. 'He's coming home. Says he's bringing someone with him. A surprise, he says.'

Bill raised an eyebrow. 'A girl?'

'I think so, yes. He says he's appointed trusted people to the American operation, and that he feels it's time to return. There must be more to it than that, though. I can read between the lines.'

Bill scanned the pages. 'Oh, I don't think so. Sounds pretty cheerful to me. He's done very well for Coastline.'

'He has.' She stood up. 'And now we've got to do well for Bennett Air.' She held the cable out to him.

Bill read quickly.

'*Two* DC-3s? And an order for a third in a couple of years? That's going to cost the earth. We can only reasonably afford one.'

'No.' Dickie looked out across the field. 'There is another way.' She looked back towards him, the light green eyes intense. 'The civil war in Spain.'

'What about it?'

'I was approached earlier by a representative of the Republican Army.' Bill's eyes were alert. 'The war's been going a while now. They need help. He mentioned that they would not be averse to a little aid.'

'A little aid. Dickie, what are you talking about?'

'Flying in goods, arms, medical supplies. Things of that sort. The money talked about was high, high enough to buy two DC-3s and order a third!'

'You must be crazy. We can't start doing deals with them! Why, that's practically treason!'

Dickie gave him a long look. 'It's not, Bill.'

'Dickie, this is wrong.' His eyes pressed her to understand.

'Nothing's wrong, Bill. We're just going to jump ahead of the game a little. By getting our DC-3s, we'll steal a march on the competition. We want our transatlantic route as soon as possible. I know for a fact that the others haven't managed it yet. Imperial are the only ones capable of running them at the moment. We'll have to switch to Croydon, though, I think. I'm having difficulty getting the improved aerodrome facilities for the aircraft. I don't think we're going to be able to get the runway lengthened in time. So, I think we're going to have to go for putting our operation out of a major airport. Except for the domestic aircraft, of course.'

'Why can't we use some of Coastline's money, or West Counties?' He pushed his hands into the pockets of his trousers. He shrugged. 'Max has done well enough with those two over the last couple of years to cream a little off the top.'

'You know as well as I do that that's no way to run a company. You can't rob from Peter to pay Paul. You just don't want me to do this run.'

He rounded on her. 'Of course I don't.'

'Because it's wrong?'

'Because it's dangerous.'

She gave him a long look. 'OK. Now I know what you're

worried about. I've no time to build slowly, Bill. I want to be in at the beginning. I've missed out before, and I'm a fighter. Now I'm not supplying the Nationalists and Franco, after all. The government has already given a small number of aeroplanes from England to support the Republicans. Men had volunteered to go out there. I'm just going to do a little deal on the side with that general that called. The whole thing will be set up. I'll fly by night to Morocco—'

'That's where the Nationalists are set up!'

'Where they least expect us to be too! We'll drop our cargo and be home before you know it. The money will buy the second plane. That's all there is to it. We'll be up there where I want to be. Where we ought to be.'

The airline was now among the largest of the smaller airlines. They could not challenge the state airline's long-range routes to the Empire, to India and Africa, but they could compete for European destinations. With the DC-3 they could set up new routes to Europe, matching those of British European Airways. With the two DC-3s they could open flights to Frankfurt, and keep the Dragons for domestic flights and France, at the furthest.

'Dickie . . .'

'My mind is made up, Bill.'

'I can see that.' He leaned against the door jamb and his eyes, too, scanned the horizon. He pulled his hand from his pocket and looked casually at the palm. 'Well, when do you plan to go?'

There was a smile in her eyes as she turned quickly towards him. 'Tomorrow. I knew you'd understand. I won't be gone long.'

He looked up from under one eyebrow at her. *'We.'*

She looked quizzically at him.

'I'm going with you, Dickie.' He held her look, and paused. 'It could be dangerous. I don't want you to go alone. Do you have a route worked out?' The sun's rays left the cornfield. The dark clouds lumbered overhead, and the day was shadowed like evening. The wind picked up and caught at her dark hair. The skeins of hair snaked around her face. The green eyes narrowed slightly.

'Yes,' she said. 'Via Marseilles and down to Oran in Algeria. Then over the Atlas Mountains and drop into the desert the other side. We have to fly without lights. They'll put out a beacon for us. A fire.'

He felt the severity of it catch at him. 'And who will make the pick-up?'

'A group of tribesmen on horseback. Berbers.'

He saw the light in her eye. To her, it was adventure. He saw it differently. That was why he was going.

'*Berber* tribesmen?' he said, picturing the scene in his mind. 'It's as well I'm coming with you. Some of those guys are pretty hostile, you know, Dickie. Arab tribesmen. What if the wrong fellas just happened along while you were sitting there, alone with the plane and a whole pile of drugs?'

He could not dim the spark in her eyes. 'It's not going to happen, though, is it? You're coming with me.' The spark became a glow. 'But then I thought you might. I told him there'd be two of us.'

'Oh, you did.' The first drop of rain tapped him on the side of his neck. He looked up. 'Gonna be a storm.' He looked back at her. 'Better cable Max back, then, and tell him to put in the order, hadn't you?' His voice was deliberately casual.

'Pity we can't take the Moth. It'd be like the old days.'

'The Dragon's bigger. Depends how much we're carrying.'

'Couple of boxes.'

The rain started.

'Let's take the Moth.'

'We could sleep under the stars,' she suggested. 'Fly back in the morning.' The green eyes were provocative.

'Like the old days, Dickie. You're still my girl.' He pulled her into his arms. 'Come on inside.'

The girl was not at all what she had expected. Immediately she entered the room and crossed to shake hands with her and Dickie saw her son's face behind her, she knew what was happening. He had made a mistake.

Cathy went up to the spare bedroom to unpack. For propriety's sake she was staying at Greatley, though now Max owned Home Farm.

He turned to her.

'What do you think of Cathy?'

'She seems very nice,' she said carefully. She went to the sofa opposite the fireplace and sat down. 'Are you in love with her, or is that a silly question?' Her eyes did not leave his as she lifted her drink to her lips.

'Yes,' he said. 'In fact I've asked her to marry me.'

'I take it she hasn't accepted?' She crossed her legs.

'Not yet, no.' His eyes clouded. 'You know me Mother. I don't give up easily.'

They had lived together for two years, but he had never really held her. Cathy had stayed, but she did not need him. The ephemeral quality that had first attracted him was still there. He had thought the power of his love would be a persuasive force, but she had refused to marry him, not wanting the trappings of marriage, so she said.

'Is that why you brought her here?'

'Yes,' he said, 'as a matter of fact it is. I thought she should see me in my own environment. Cathy is a country girl.'

'Yes.' Dickie stared absently into the middle distance. 'And that's why you came back. I didn't think it was because the business didn't need you over there.' She straightened the skirt of her dress.

Max lifted a shoulder. He put his drink down on the mantel-piece. He noticed the old carriage clock was stuck at five o'clock. He reached underneath for the key, opened the case and started to wind it up. 'The business is fine, as a matter of fact, but love is a very powerful force, do you know that?' he said over his shoulder with all the arrogance of youth. 'I wouldn't have left the business if it had been shaky at all, but,' he turned the hands of the clock and waited for it to chime, checking his own watch, 'I might not have come back quite so soon if it hadn't been for Cathy.'

Dickie watched him.

'Yes,' she said eventually, looking into her glass. 'But love is a very different kettle of fish from business. It's not something you can force to your control.'

The clock whirred up to strike at six o'clock. 'How do you know?' he said. 'I didn't think you'd ever been in love.'

'Oh,' she said nonchalantly. 'You don't know everything.' She lifted her heels from the floor briefly. The clock started to chime.

'*Have* you been in love?'

'Along the way . . . yes.' She stood up and crossed to the desk, pulling at the edges of her sweater. 'Did you hear about our trip, darling? To Morocco? How we got the money for the second DC-3?' She re-sorted the papers on her desk with the tips of her fingers.

'Yes . . . *Mother*?'

'. . . It was touch and go . . .' Her voice was light, vague. 'Bill and I slept in the sand. It was very romantic. Quite like the old days in California. Do you remember?' She did not look at him.

'You're not telling me it was Bill?'

'No,' she said sadly. 'I'm not telling you it was Bill.' Now her eyes swept across the room before they finally reached him. 'Though I do feel love for him.'

'It's not the same thing.' The clock finished chiming.

'No,' she sighed. 'It's not the same thing. And anyway, it doesn't matter now. It was a good while ago.'

He thought she looked sad. The room was very quiet, only the gentle ticking of the clock. 'Do you still love him?'

'Oh . . . as they say,' she said lightly, 'true love never dies. The answer is yes. Now, go to bed and stop asking me questions. I'm tired and so are you. You've had a long journey, the two of you. You'll need sleep.'

He forgot the clock and came across to her. 'Who was it?'

She was no longer smiling. 'Sweetheart, it doesn't matter now. Go on. I'll do the clock. I'll see you in the morning. Good night. Kiss me.'

He bent down to kiss the smooth cheek. Dickie was still a very handsome woman. The subject was closed now; he knew her, knew she probably regretted her impulse. He went across to the door and opened it.

'Max?'

'Yes?' He looked back. She looked very tiny sitting on the large sofa in the middle of the long elegant drawing room.

'The floorboard creaks outside Cathy's room.'

After a while she got up and went across to the clock. She turned it slowly through the hours until eleven, listening to the soft Westminster chimes. Then she crossed to her desk where her mind had been for the past half-hour and pulled out a bunch of papers, a pressed flower, a newspaper cutting and an old brown photograph. Yes, she had loved him, but it had been a long time ago. The love was past rather than present, but it still hurt her. It was something different now; it was what drove her. Idolised perhaps was a better word than love. It was a strange memory.

She put the papers back in the slender middle drawer, the photo too, switched out the lights and went up to bed.

As she finished reading, she reached for the night light. She heard the distant creak of the floorboard. She smiled and plumped up the pillows, resting her face on the cool linen. She hoped he wouldn't get hurt.

TWENTY-EIGHT

August, 1939

'How on earth did he drum up so much power?'

Colin paced the room in Max's small office on the airfield.

'Because of apathy. That's the very thing I'm getting at.'

Max leaned his elbows on the desk and stared at his friend. He did not seem to understand. Colin had taken up a job with the Ministry of Agriculture, Fisheries and Food and had been lecturing all over Europe on new farming methods since Max's return to England three years before. The unrest over there had now caused his own return earlier that month. However, Colin still seemed bewildered by the events that had overtaken them all. Hitler's Luftwaffe filled the skies over Nazi Germany. It was the biggest, strongest, most efficient air force the world had ever seen. It marked a real problem for Europe, and for England. Max had a sense of foreboding stronger than anything he had experienced before.

'Hitler has armed Germany's navy, army and air force to a vastly greater extent than he was permitted to under the limitation of arms treaties which were placed on the Germans after the last war. He totally disregarded them, but because we've now moved eighteen to twenty years away from that war and the whole nature of people is to turn the other cheek the further they get from war—simply because they can't contemplate anything so awful again—we've let it ride.'

Colin looked at the wall map which still covered the whole of one wall of Max's office. Long windows ran across the other overlooking the airfield. 'I still don't believe though that we've got too much to worry about. I don't think he'll start anything, Max. Probably just wants to look tough, that's all.'

'Look tough? Colin! Where's your sense, man? Germany's already extended territorial claims through Europe. They've already marched into Austria with the usual cries and shouts of that's all they were going to do, and now this summer it's Czechoslovakia and we're next!'

'Chamberlain's signed with the French premier and Hitler in Berchtesgaten. That's something.'

Max stood up, frustrated now. 'That's bugger all, Colin.' He waved an arm. 'All that's doing is buying time.'

Colin kept still. 'I don't agree, Max. I think war won't come this time. No one wants those atrocities all over again.'

Max lifted an arm. 'Why are we arming so fast then? Tell me that? And why is France?' He fixed his eyes on Colin, leaning his hands on the desk. 'Any seeing, thinking person knows what's coming. Churchill's been very strong on the matter. He's been warning Europe since 1936 onwards. People simply don't want to know because they hate the bogeyman, but he's said if we allow this to go on and appease it's inevitable that we'll have war.' He stood up, pushing his hands into his pockets. 'I think Churchill knows what he's talking about.' He stared out of the window across the fields, the planes standing idle under the grey sky. 'Chamberlain waves a piece of paper saying "I've got a guarantee from Mr Hitler that they have no further territorial claims in Europe"!' He snorted derisively. 'It fools no one. All it's done is to enable us to get our factories into line and enable us to start producing aircraft like the Spitfire and the Hurricane, to be ready because now we have got very firm pacts with Poland so that in the event of a direct attack upon her, we actually have an understanding that we will come to her aid against an aggressor.' He looked up into the empty skies, and the sense of doom filled him. 'An appeasement policy always fails to put off an aggressor,' he said. 'An aggressor is an aggressor and if they have it in mind they will continue to attack. Like a burglar who plans to burgle a house. He will, if he has a mind to.' He shook his head. 'Appeasement is wrong.'

'I don't care,' Colin argued. 'We have to do something to try and calm the situation.' He palmed his hand upward and outward. 'And it's not because I'm a pacifist, so don't give me that, Max. If Chamberlain believed in Hitler, why shouldn't we?'

Max turned, a hard light in his blue eyes. 'Did he, though? I doubt it. You can't rationalise with a man like Hitler, Colin. Right through history you need strength to deter and only strong deterrents prevent the aggressor. Anyone who doesn't see that isn't seeing the thing through, they're being unrealistic. Non-aggression treaties don't work with a man like that. They might put the moment off, but if he wants us, he'll come after us. All this soft soaping's not going to work. Hitler'll march on Poland, wait and see.'

'Then we'll have to go in,' he said quietly.

'Yes. Then we'll have to go in.'

'Can anyone join this discussion?'

Both men turned together towards the door. They had the flavour of war in their eyes.

Cathy walked in, soft in her pink and green summer dress. 'Phew, don't you two look steamed up! I could hear you all the way down the hall! Hi!' she held out her hand. 'I'm Cathy.' She gave him the infectious grin. 'And you must be Colin.'

'Yes, of course, you two haven't met.' Max came round from behind his desk, the fire leaving his eyes, and stretching like a cat now that she was here. She had that effect on him. His face was proud as they shook hands.

The sudden and unexpected confrontation surprised them both. Max had spoken warmly about each to the other; they both knew quite a bit about the other, stories that had already made them attractive to each other, both so similar. The physical meeting shook them both. Their hands touched. Their eyes looked into each other's and smiled.

'Tonight,' said Max, coming round to claim her into his arms, 'we're having dinner *at home*! I've seen far too little of you lately. Everybody loves her,' he explained to Colin. 'Never get her to myself.'

She laughed, and held his arms with her slender hands. 'Right now I want you to take me for a long walk. I feel like going right along the river up to Greatley and over to the waterfall where you used to see the fat old trout!' Her eyes danced merrily. She swung the golden hair back over her shoulders. 'The highspots of Max's youth!' she teased them both.

Colin watched them. His eyes could hardly leave her.

'It's very beautiful country here. Don't forget your wellington boots though. It can get pretty muddy in places.'

'You're talking to the right girl. I left them outside. I walked over the fields from Greatley,' she said to Max, turning in his arms to face him again. 'It's a lovely walk.'

'You came over Colin's land then,' he said.

'Oh!' she said, tilting her head. 'Did I? It's very pretty.' She smiled only briefly at him. 'Well. Are we going?'

'Of course,' said Max, his hands to her waist persuading her away as he turned back to his desk. 'Just as soon as I . . . oh, damn!' The telephone rang urgently on his desk. He held her hand in his as he picked it up. 'Yes?'

Cathy tapped her foot and swung her leg to and fro. She did not look at Colin. Colin stared at the map, his hands in his pockets.

'What . . . ? Speak up, the line's bad.' Max sat on the corner of the desk, his leg dangling. He drew Cathy to him. She leaned against him, her eyes on her hands.

'Max, I'm afraid we've had an accident down here.' The engineer's voice was worried. 'We've smashed one of the engines in the hangar. We haven't got a replacement.'

'Damn. I knew we should have followed up a better line to get spares from the States. Do you know anywhere we can get one?'

The voice hesitated. 'Well, Royal Dutch Airlines is our only hope. They've got a fleet of DC-3s. They might help us out.'

'I doubt it.' Max's face was worried now. He needed a US plane in Europe flying the Pratt and Whitney twin Wasp radial engine. It was highly unlikely that Royal Dutch Airlines would let them have one of theirs. 'I think we'll have very difficult negotiations with them. Isn't there anyone closer to home?'

'Not that I know of.'

Max clicked his tongue. 'Just as things were going well. Isn't it always the way? An aeroplane out of commission just as we've got our routes going. Well, look, Pete, I'll be right down there. Just hold on till I get there, OK? I'll handle it.'

'All right, guv'nor.'

Max put down the phone slowly. His arm was still around

Cathy. He hung his head thoughtfully and pursed his lips. She looked at him.

'What's up?'

He shook his head. 'I'm going to have to go down to the hangar. In Croydon. One of our new planes has got smashed up. I'm going to have to go down and sort it out. There's no one else. Bill and Mother are both out of the country. Damn, what a nuisance . . . I'll be gone at least a few hours.'

She looked disappointed, but she smiled. 'Don't worry, Max. I'll entertain myself. I'm used to the country now, I might even get a ride somewhere.'

'Colin's got horses,' he said absently, not looking up. He was still deep in thought about the plane. Where to get that engine?

Cathy looked at Colin.

'Yes, we have,' he said. 'You could borrow a pair of jodhpurs, a shirt and riding boots from my sister, Ann. You're about her size.' His eyes ran over her.

'Thank you.' Her eyes were wide.

Max looked up. 'What? Oh, that's marvellous. Would you take care of her, Colin?'

He shrugged briefly. 'Of course.'

Max smiled and hugged her to him. 'There. I'm sorry, Cathy. But these things happen. I need to get on to these people though. Bill's import company is falling behind, and we can't allow mistakes. I'll have a huge workload to get through now. I might not even be finished until teatime. I wonder, Colin, would you . . . ?'

'It'll be my pleasure.'

'You could show Cathy the good places to ride. Leave the bits relating to my childhood, we'll catch up on those later!' he teased. 'Nice coincidence you dropped by.'

'Yes.' Colin looked at her. 'Well, shall we go?'

'My wellingtons await,' she said.

'I'll take you down to Brook Farm then, get the jodhpurs and the horses. Ann and May won't be riding today. They're both back at school.'

'Wonderful!' Max pulled her into his arms and kissed her. 'You look beautiful,' he whispered. 'Now, no going into the woods with my best friend!'

Her eyelashes fluttered and her cheeks flushed slightly. The golden hair fell across her face as she looked down. Max lifted her chin. He looked into her eyes. For a moment he hesitated. The engine could wait. No. He knew it couldn't. It was his responsibility. Still, something snagged at his heart. He couldn't place it. It passed, and he smiled as she did, a tight, forced smile. Disappointment?

'I'm sorry, darling,' he said. 'I'll make it up to you later.' He kissed her on the nose and patted her on the bottom. 'See you at tea. Colin, would you bring her back to Home Farm?'

'Certainly.' He gave her his slow, shy smile as he opened the door. Max picked up the phone again and was immediately involved in business as they went out together. He lifted his hand in a wave, and then turned back to the conversation.

They went round the corner of the building and started off across the field together. Max watched them through the window, while his mind stayed on the telephone conversation. They did not seem to be talking much. Cathy's head lifted to Colin, and he looked down into her face. His hands were shoved deep in his pockets and they were walking slowly. Colin pointed off to the left and they turned and went in that direction. Max put down the phone. She looked incongruous and lovable in her flowered summer dress and the heavy wellington boots. He frowned for a moment knowing how much he loved her, and that gentle giant beside her, Colin. He regretted that he had to work. For once, he wanted to play. He would love to have gone riding again with Cathy. He remembered Big Sur and the rainstorm. He had to force his concentration and his own disappointment back onto the problem at hand.

'Operator . . . yes, the number of Royal Dutch Airlines in Amsterdam . . .'

Max pulled the Lanchester into the garage at Home Farm. He came out, pulled the doors shut and wandered round the side of the house.

The lights were not on. She was not home yet. He had broken away from the office early to be with her. The last few weeks had been a torture, locked away in his office or down at Croydon airport preparing the way for international flights with their small fleet of DC-3s. Any day now they would fly to America in competition with the giants of aviation. It was a haul, and he missed Cathy.

He went round to the front of the house. The night was still and silent. The windows were flung wide and not a leaf stirred. Waiting hung in the air like a first night audience. The sky was a deep lilac and there was a mist of stars, the moon a luminous curve and the distant horizon over the dark fields still stained with the last streaks of sunset.

Max pulled a chair forward and sat down, looking out over his land. He lit a cigarette and stretched his legs out before him, drawing on the smoke. It was a beautiful night.

He heard the car draw into the driveway and smiled. She would be pleased to see him. The door slammed. He heard her feet running round the side of the house. He watched her, though she did not see him sitting in the shadows. She was not expecting him.

Her cheeks were flushed with the touch of summer, her eyes glowing, and she was laughing, obviously at something private that pleased her, her head held high and provocative, her walk sensual and fluid.

Max caught his breath, suddenly taken back to that day when he had seen her on the beach: that rich Californian colouring, the happy pagan laugh as her head was thrown back, tossing her thick, golden hair to trail down her bare brown back. She was glossy. That was what he remembered most about her. In that old pink and green sundress and wellington boots; the same she had worn on her first day when she had walked off with Colin. With a pang he realised just how long it was since he had seen that look on her face, just how much he loved her. He caught the look in a moment, a voyeur, and printed it on his mind like a relentless photograph.

He could smell her already, fresh and clean in his arms. He stood up, aching to hold her, though something stopped him.

'Cathy . . .'

With the sound of his voice, her expression changed. She swung round, her eyes startled.

'Max. I didn't see you there.'

He came towards her, and put his arms round her, happy now she was home again. He did not miss the tension in her shoulders, nor the way she twisted slightly as if to be free.

'Let's go inside,' she said.

He followed her into the house and went over towards the lamp.

'No, don't switch on the lights,' she said. 'Wait. There's something I have to tell you.'

She walked into the dark drawing room. He stood at the window by the door. When her voice came it was almost a part of the night it was so soft, like a continuation. It did not jar him at all.

Her back was to him.

'It's about me and Colin.'

Max felt the weight of his heart in his chest. He wanted her to stop. Cold fingers clutched at his throat and he couldn't speak, to ask her to stop. He stared out of the window at the trees and saw nothing. His fingers held the windowsill to steady himself. Life with Cathy flashed before his eyes; beautiful, wonderful moments as if it were before death. No, Cathy, no.

She knew Max had found the book of verse yesterday, the book she had been reading so deeply. She had come home with the shopping and sat in the car outside as the rain had started.

The book had drawn her into the past few hours. She remembered that Colin was beautiful, gentle. He had given her the book, signed it to her. She remembered many things and only then began to know what they meant to her. The rain had spotted the windscreen, grown stronger, blotting out the world. She had been miles away, dreaming.

Max had tapped on the glass. He had a raincoat over his head and his face had been frightened. She had never seen him frightened. It was that more than anything that brought her to reality. She had jumped guiltily and put the book under the seat and they had gone into the house. But she knew he had found it later. And today . . . today she had told Colin, seen his face. He felt it too. That was all she wanted to know.

She turned.

'Colin wanted to tell you,' she began. 'But I asked him not to.'

Max was filled with unseeing rage. Who was Colin to tell his girl what to say to him?

'. . . We love each other . . .'

He was shocked beyond speech.

'. . . we're going to be married.'

If he had been a woman he would have fainted. His head felt as though it were being crushed. It was the classic situation. His best friend and his girl. If it had not been so tragic it would have been laughable. His hands clutched the windowsill and he wanted to laugh. With horror, he felt the tears in his eyes, heard the choke in his throat. He could not see. He could not speak. He hung his head and tried to compose himself.

The soft hands touched his back. 'Max . . . I'm sorry . . . Max?'

He thrust her away. He had only one thought. To get out. To fly where she could not reach him.

He ran out to his car.

The storm threw the Moth from side to side, bounding it about like a ball. The blast from the stripstream almost blinded him, the torrential rains, wind and violent turbulence whipping into his face. His skin was numbed and frozen. He had known about the front coming in over the coast and flown right into it. It was madness; he did not care. He wanted the fight with the elements, he wanted to be wrenched physically to rid himself of this awful tearing pain in his heart. Death would not have been unwelcome. The weather was getting rougher. Beneath him the seas over the Channel were mountainous, swelling huge and black. The rain thundered down onto the wings of the little aircraft, and soon the coastline was blotted from sight. The pulsating roar of the plane filled his head. He shouted aloud. The cold rain lacerated his skin. His face was wet. The tears no longer mattered.

Dickie crossed the warm kitchen. It was clean and neat, not a thing out of place. She sat down at the breakfast table and switched on the radio. Big-band music swelled out of the Bakelite box. She was worried; she had been following the news. It was September 3rd, 1939. The previous day Germany had marched into Poland and attacked her, massacring her from the air as well in the *blitzkrieg*. Britain and France had said they would give them twenty-four hours to haul back to their frontiers because they were under an absolute and irrevocable pact with Poland to come to her rescue, and that was what they intended to do.

The blare of the music suddenly stopped. The silence seemed to last forever. Dickie looked at the radio. It was eleven o'clock. England had declared war on Germany.

Charles had just arrived at Foxhall Manor. He was stepping out of his car as he saw the small black Ford tearing up the gravel drive towards him.

'Charles!' The voice called to him, her hand waving as she pulled the car to a halt. Melanie's grey eyes were huge with concern. He straightened and walked over towards her. 'Have you heard the news. Oh, of course you have.' She climbed out of her car and kissed him quickly. 'We're at war. Isn't it terrible, Charles?'

'Yes.' He held her hands and looked down into the lovely face. The summer air was fresh and warm, the birds chirping in the trees around them; Melanie was deliciously pretty in a crisp summer dress. It was hard to imagine. He pulled her close into his arms.

'It's come at last,' she said, drawing away after a moment. 'Well, we've all been prepared for a while. We've done our drill with those wretched gas masks and air raid shelters for so long now, I never thought it would happen, did you?' she asked as he walked with her to the house. 'Mummy's at home getting the black-out curtains ready. We've even had to cover our headlights.' She turned briefly and pointed back at her car headlights. 'It's going to be hard on these country lanes.' She walked with him again, their arms around each other. 'I came over to visit Jessamy as soon as I heard. I know she'll be upset. John'll have to sign up right away. What about you, Charles? What are you planning to do?'

They stepped up towards the front door of the Manor. 'Well, I've finished medical school now, so I can work as a doctor. I thought . . .'

The door opened in front of them. Rupert stood belligerently on the threshold. He appeared to be bristling with delight.

'Ah, Charles. You've arrived. Thought I heard the car. And you too, Melanie,' he said, looking her up and down. 'Well, come in. You've heard the news, I take it. Ah, well, we'll get them. We got the buggers last time. Do it again. Come into the drawing room. We'll all have a drink to celebrate. Family's in there already. Your mother's waiting to see you, Charles. What are you going to do then, eh? Become a conscientious objector?' He laughed cruelly and eyed Melanie as if to bring her in on his little joke. 'Doesn't like fighting, you know!' He strode between them towards the open drawing room door.

'Actually no, Father,' he said quietly. 'I'd planned to join the RAF. As a doctor.'

'Not the army, eh?' said Rupert bitterly. 'You've always disappointed me, Charles. Well, I don't suppose I can expect that to change now.'

Melanie cast Charles a sympathetic glance in Rupert's wake.

'I think that's marvellous, Charles,' she said. Rupert had already advanced into the drawing-room ahead of them. She touched Charles's hand briefly. He was silent, his eyes flickering briefly over his father's back as he preceded them. By now, he was used to Rupert's jibes. It hurt Melanie, however, that a man as decent as Charles should ever have to bear the brunt of Rupert's unkindness. He had never forgiven Charles for going ahead with his plans to become a doctor. Charles's quick smile towards her showed that he was grateful for her understanding. 'Do you think your uncle Frederick will let me work on the land, Charles? I've always wanted to do something. I could be a big help here at Foxhall.'

'You'll be a friend to Jess, too,' he said warmly. 'Thanks for thinking of us. I'm sure Uncle Frederick will be delighted.'

They walked into the room together.

Jessamy was sitting white-faced beside the fire, her children, Sabrine and Alexander, playing with a jigsaw puzzle on the rug beside her feet. Caroline stood in front of one of the bay windows at the far end of the room, her back to them, slender as a reed, her dark hair coiled upon her head. Frederick was not to be seen. John leaned against the fireplace. It appeared he had been deep in conversation with Jessamy for now they both turned as if interrupted and looked towards the door.

Melanie quickly took in the atmosphere of the room. Charles saw the fear on his brother-in-law's face. Rupert had gone straight to the tray of drinks set out on the table behind the sofa. He was pouring a brandy for himself.

'Charles!' Jessamy was on her feet. 'Melanie! I don't want John to go. He'll never come back. I know it!'

John winced. Melanie went over to take her friend in her arms.

'Good to see you, John.' Charles took the man's hand in his own. It was clammy. The eyes looked into his for support.

'Frightful thing, Charles. I'm glad you're home.' The eyes looked across at Rupert, showing the pressure he had received from that quarter.

Rupert looked over at them all. His blue eyes were cold. He lifted his drink, his eyes on them as he came round the corner of the sofa.

'Wish I could go,' he said accusingly. 'Young men like you. I've seen what war does to a man. They'll make mincemeat of you, d'you know that?' He laughed roughly. 'Better pull your socks up. The party's over!'

TWENTY-NINE

Autumn, 1940

There was a soft autumn sun as the official car pulled into the area just in front of the Bennett Air hangar at Croydon airport.

Dickie walked out of the building dressed in her flying gear. She lifted her hand to shield her eyes from the sun and waited.

The air vice-marshal climbed out of the back seat and came across to her.

'Dickie.'

'How are you, John? I got the call from your office. What can I do for you?'

'To be frank, we need planes. RAF Fighter Command have Hurricanes and Spitfires in just enough numbers to inflict severe losses, and just enough production in the factories to make good our losses.' He walked towards the hangar with her. 'I'm going to have to requisition your planes.'

'How many?'

He came to a halt in front of the hangar. 'We need as many as we can get for transporting military personnel within Britain or freighting military goods, carrying spares between bases, shuttling engines, that sort of thing.' Parts were being built at many aircraft factories so that if a factory was knocked out only one part would be lost and it would not ruin the production line. They would then be assembled at one or two factories, all the parts being brought together. 'We will of course make good your losses. If any.'

'Thank you.' She looked up into the rafters of the empty hangar. 'What about pilots?'

'Yes. Absolutely. If we can get them, for ferrying purposes.'

Dickie's eyes narrowed slightly. 'Can I offer my services?'

'Well,' he looked at the ground. 'The ATA is looking for female pilots, but they're not taking on that many at the moment. There aren't very many to be had,' he added. 'It's early days yet.'

'Still, I'd like to.'

'In that case I'll arrange it.'

'Thank you.'

Her face held a decided expression. 'If you're using my planes, I can at least pilot them myself. I'll deliver them, and I'll fly them.'

'If that's the way you see it, we'd be grateful of course.' He looked back at his car. The driver stood by the bonnet, waiting. 'I have to get back. We'll be on to you.'

'Yes.' She paused. 'How is it going? My son's in the RAF, you know.'

'Yes, I know.' The taciturn face was strained with worry. 'It's been bad. Many of our airfields heavily bombed, especially Biggin Hill, Kenley and Tangmere. But we've got radar now, means the boys don't have to take off unless they know they're going to get to grips with the enemy. And we're getting the aircraft fit to fly again even when they're shot down. We're flying missions round the clock. The boys are determined and courageous. We'll defeat them, Dickie. I have no doubt. Well, goodbye, and good luck.'

'Goodbye, John. Good luck. And thanks for coming yourself.'

The air raid sirens howled their warning. The drone of aeroplanes filled the sky. Dickie and the other two pilots ran for the cover of the air raid shelter. The intensive bombing of London had begun.

Europe was collapsing under the weight of war. Hitler had staked his armed might on the *blitzkrieg* strategy—one of lightning war waged against his opponents one by one with massive blows, in which the terrifying Luftwaffe played a central role, its primary task to destroy enemy air power. Poland had collapsed after four weeks and the highly mobile Panzer divisions had pressed on through Europe, Holland's Air Force destroyed before it could leave the ground. Within the year, German armies had overrun practically the whole of Europe and were in control of the whole coastline from the southwest of France to the northern tip of Norway. Spearheading every offensive was the dreaded Luftwaffe, Germany's air arm. Their method of attack was simple yet devastating: first, the bombers flew in to destroy the enemy's planes and runways to stop them taking off and then the fighters and Stuka dive-bombers created havoc by bombing and machine-gunning the troops and supply columns. In the meantime, German land forces raced through the enemy's territory with massive armoured formations to secure victory. At Dunkirk, three hundred and thirty-eight thousand Allied troops miraculously escaped to England and the French government surrendered on June 25th. For Britain, a small lonely island facing the armed might of Nazi Europe, 1940 was the darkest year of the war.

The heavy bullet-shaped twin-engined Whitleys stood on the snow-covered runway fuelling up in the early-morning mist.

Max had been on operations the night before. He had got up at nine-thirty and gone to the operations room.

'Prepare to the best of your ability and stand by,' was the order. Max called all crews and bombed up ready to go, then stood by.

The squadron was airborne on time. Soon they were thundering through the sky, squat and steady like a swarm of menacing bees, in formation above the light clouds at dawn. The pattern of rolling fields in patchwork, way beneath, was shadowed and lit as the clouds passed over. England. They had strength in their hearts as they left the coast and worked their way across the Channel to meet the Luftwaffe. There was a good following wind as they crossed the coast of Europe.

Max had found something close to his heart. He had soon become a more experienced fighter than most and it had kept him alive. The sacrifice of Cathy had devastated him, making him a flying ace with a lack of fear for his own preservation. He had been in action over Belgium during the Battle of France and during the withdrawal from Dunkirk. His exploits had brought him his first rewards: the DFC and promotion to flight lieutenant. The tally of twenty swastikas marked on his plane indicated the number of German planes he had shot down.

The actual target was small and vital. Ahead of them they saw bombs streaming down ahead and on either side. It was twelve minutes of precision bombing. The weather was good. Underneath, dust and smoke and flying debris, which had been raised by the first bombers to go in, surged up into the air in constantly thickening clouds, blotting out the target indicators.

Max's bombing run was done at under two thousand feet and at that height the thump of the bomb bursts below was severe enough to shake the aircraft. Two or three hundred heavy guns were firing up around them over the German target, the light flak pouring forth. Max headed straight through the hail of flak, and up to the aiming point. He held straight and level to give the bomb-aimer the chance to do his job. The gunners knew they had to do the job and they were far more accurate on the bombing run than any other time. The bombs released, he held straight and level for another twenty seconds in order to have the aircraft steady with its camera lens pointing vertically downwards at the main point till the vital target photograph was obtained.

The German fighter was on his tail. It was their third trip without being caught. The gunner started firing to avoid a burst from a fighter before he caught on them. The German fighter wheeled down in a howl of flame.

The homeward run was easier. Flying light with a predominant westerly wind they approached the English coast at dawn.

April, 1942

The slim girl in blue slacks climbed out of the cockpit of the Lancaster bomber, and strolled across to the watchtower as if she had been delivering planes all her life.

She came in to get her delivery chit signed. A couple of RAF fighter pilots came in to collect a brace of Spitfires. They had witnessed her arrival.

'Women flying Lancasters.' He looked Dickie up and down. 'Might as well give up, old boy!'

Dickie watched them leave with a wry smile on her face. Their attitude was typical of the men who flew the planes. It was hard work. First, she had had to pass through the RAF's training school, and in between her actual ferrying jobs she had taken 'conversion' courses, gradually qualifying for piloting the different classes of aircraft. She was now Class Five, flying four-engined aircraft, which included the Flying Fortress, the Lancaster, Halifax and Liberator bombers. Her uniform was an extremely flattering one. The dark blue tailored tunic with gold stripes and wings worn with trousers for duty showed off her perfect figure to advantage, despite the fact that she was now over forty years old.

In the wet and freezing weather, they ferried the great machines on long flights to Scotland and the north of England. Often they had to break their journeys at RAF stations where the men greeted them with derision or cold-shouldered them.

A pilot was expected to fly all the aircraft. The 'ferry pilot's notes' encapsulated information about each aircraft's cockpit, speed and range, landing gear and other details. Before flying a new type, the pilot would read up and 'fly by the book'.

Dickie took her detail back out to the field again. She climbed into the big Albemarle and waited for her passenger.

The air vice-marshal was in a hurry to get to London. His car screeched to a halt on the Tarmac at Hamble ferry pool, and the officer was saluted quickly on board.

The big plane started to taxi down the runway.

Dickie turned to him. 'How are you since we last met, sir?'

He was shocked as he saw her small pretty face smiling at him from the cockpit. 'You? Flying one of these things?'

'Well,' she said, 'I expected to fly anything they gave to me. Wasn't that what the ATA was supposed to be all about?' She got ready for take off .

The air vice-marshal looked askance. 'Indeed, but not when the owner of the aircraft company blackmails the RAF into lending their planes as long as she can fly!'

'And you didn't expect to be my passenger, right?' She was cleared for take off. 'Hang on, sir. I haven't flown one of these things before,' she said as they hurtled down the wet runway ahead.

'You haven't *what*?'

But almost immediately the plane was airborne. Dickie waved the ferry pilot's notes in her small hand. 'It's all right, you're quite safe with me. I'm reading them as I go along. I'll have you there a damn sight quicker than anyone else.' .

The officer shifted more comfortably in his seat. He pulled at the cloth of his trousers just above the knees and moved his feet.

'That's very reassuring,' he muttered, folding his arms.

She looked quickly over at him, a smile on her face. 'As a matter of fact, I requested the flight.'

'Oh, you did? Perks of the job?'

'Not quite.' Her eyes met his. 'I wanted to ask if there was any news of my son, Max.'

The voice became more serious. 'You know better than to ask that.'

'Off the record?'

'Off the record, he's alive. Running a mission tonight.'

The weather was clear and beautiful. They set off before dark. It was a moonlit night. Two squadrons had been detailed out with two other Halifax squadrons to bomb from a high level in order to cause a diversion. The German navy was stationed in Trondheim, off the coast of Norway. They loaded up with five mines each weighing a thousand pounds.

They hit the coast at an angle and ran up to the chosen island, then turning northwest towards the target. The track, according to intelligence, was free from defences and should have given a good run in across the island. All was quiet.

Everything opened up on them. As they approached the first ship, the whole fleet was ready for them. The starboard wing was burning fiercely. They were down to two hundred feet and ready to release, but the bomb-aimer could not see the ship. There was a white haze beneath them; a man-made camouflage. A split second later, the ship's superstructure passed beneath but it was too late to let go. Max hoped to return for a second run, holding the plane in the air, but the flames on the wing were now mounting, the undercarriage had come down and the starboard flap had begun to trail. He pointed towards the ship's position and released the mines.

He turned east and tried to climb. There was no reaction.

Max half turned towards the boys behind him.

'Prepare to abandon aircraft!'

The flight engineer strove to put a ghastly smile on his face. 'This is it, fellows,' he said. 'We've had it now!'

Max turned towards him. 'Shut up, and don't be a fool!' he said harshly. His own face streamed with sweat from the heat, the muscles tense. He held fast to the controls. 'We're perfectly all right, we just might have to parachute, that's all.'

He held the plane's nose as high as he could, but the mountains that suddenly loomed up ahead rising to at least three thousand feet cut off their escape. He was forced to turn back west and give the order.

'Abandon aircraft. Jump. Jump.'

The small Mustang was flying alone when he had seen the Lancaster pull away from its formation. He saw that the two left engines were dead and the props feathered. He heard the Lancaster call him.

'I've got two engines out. Starboard wing's on fire,' came Max's voice. 'Can you see me?'

The Mustang pilot brought his craft right down close to the Lancaster. He pulled his flaps down so as to slow to Max's speed. A big hole gaped about three feet square on the bottom of the wing where the flames were burning inside and eating the skin away.

He called Max back. 'The aluminium is melting away on your wing. The flames are breaking through to the top.'

The bombers and fighters who made the long flights had developed a close teamwork. The fighter pilots guarded them jealously. This one he was powerless to help. The crew would have to parachute down to German territory and imprisonment.

Max called back. 'I'm going to have to bail out. Will you stand by and count us out?'

'Go ahead, I'll count.'

Inside the Lancaster, Max turned to the man next to him. 'Flight Engineer. Assist to the tail gunner.' The tail gunner was badly injured. Max had given the order and sat there alone, holding the wheel hard over to port with all his strength and with the port outer engine slightly throttled back in order to keep the aircraft on an even keel with full port rudder.

The flight engineer climbed back to assist.

The Mustang pilot counted the men out. He watched the seven-man crew parachute out of the stricken bomber.

Max called out to him. 'How many's that?'

'That's seven men out,' the Mustang pilot said.

'Fine. Thanks for the escort, chaps. See you after the war.' The Mustang pilot's reply crackled over the airwaves.

'OK,' he said holding his engines in check. 'Lots of luck to all of you.'

Max stayed as long as he could. It was getting hot in the cockpit and the flames were building up fiercely over the starboard wing. He was losing height far too rapidly and heading away from the mountains to the west and straight into trouble. The ground was coming up close. He held the wheel hard over to port, and eased himself out of his seat ready to jump just as the starboard wing collapsed.

Quickly, Max jumped through the hatch below him, pulling the ripcord the instant he was clear. It was lucky he did so. Above him, the bomber flipped over on a wing and went streaming down in flames. Max's parachute opened just as he struck the ground and he tumbled over and down into a copse of trees.

He tried to climb to his feet. The pain was agonising. Somehow he managed to drag the white silk of the parachute and the harness towards him, pushing it into the earth under the trees and covering it with leaves. It was a piece of evidence for the Germans to find. Around him, the country was sparsely dotted with trees. He tried to stand, clutching his arm which felt broken, and headed off, away from the direction of the crashed aircraft. Over the brow of the hill he heard voices that sounded German. The Lancaster bomber had crashed and they would be alerted by now. Vaguely, he wondered what had happened to the rest of his crew. He moved off as quickly as he could down the hill.

He entered a belt of trees. A torrent of water poured in a steep, banked river to his left. The banks were coated with ice and the river itself was running fast and dangerous. He slipped down the ice into the torrent and braced himself there, wading across with the help of overhanging branches. It was his best bet, the dogs used in the efforts to trace him would not go through this stream.

Once on the other side he climbed out and lay on the bank, exhausted by his efforts. The pain drove down his arm, and his right foot stabbed agonisingly every time he put it to the ground. He opened his escape kit. Inside was a small flat tin containing a silk handkerchief on which was printed a map of the area in which they were operating. The scale of the map was tiny, but invaluable to his navigational efforts. There was a tin of Horlicks tablets and a few barley sugars, and a small rubber bag. He put a tablet in his mouth, filled the bag with water from the stream.

He had his flying jacket on and fur-lined flying boots. As he had waded through the stream they had filled with water, which was now beginning to freeze. He would get frostbite before long. At least the pain was numbed. He studied the map and headed for the town and a railway line to the north. He had been walking for hours and was now tired and hungry.

The house was in the middle of a clearing. He looked around carefully and then hobbled across towards it. There was a light in the doorway. He knocked. There was no answer. No sign of life. He went into the hallway and called. There was still no answer. There were coats on the hooks in the hall and various caps. It did not look like German clothing. He went outside again and found a shed. Inside was a heavy fur sleigh rug. He dragged it to the floor, and into a warm corner. He was about to lie down.

Then everything went black.

Bad weather had hit Europe and blinding hail drove into the open cockpit. It was like a polar blizzard as the aircraft's forward speed whipped the air into her face. The windshield iced over, and her goggles became clogged, her face covered in an icy wet mask. She peered ahead, looking for a break in the weather, then ducked low in the cockpit as she approached the airfield.

Dickie was flying in to Eastleigh to deliver the Spitfire for repair. The flaps were down ready for her approach. The engine sputtered and almost failed as she brought it down gently onto the runway.

She coasted the plane in, smiling a wry smile of achievement as she brought the fractious machine to a halt in front of the hangars.

She saw the figure of Mary, one of the other pilots, coming out towards her. She was well wrapped up in boots, coat and fur hood. Mary's aversion to the cold was well known. She was waving frantically.

Probably thinks I'm half dead, thought Dickie, as she clambered out. It would take more than that. The war had been good to her in a way She had seen the future opportunity of buying up post-war unwanted military transport at very low cost, once it was all over. She had already alerted Bill to buy them at a future date. Here, she was sitting on the inside information.

Secretly, Bennett Air had bought land and made storage preparations. She would expand her own airline with these aircraft as well as making huge profits by taking the military hacks, fitting them out as airliners and selling them on to post-war customers. One day, the war would be over and she would be ahead of the game. Already, she had been promised a couple of Wellingtons in return for two of her own craft bombed while sitting idle on an airfield.

She climbed down onto the wing and started a fast walk, her legs stiff with cold. She saw Mary's face now. It was worried, even though she had seen she was all right. Dickie's heart caught in a vice of fear. There could only be one reason.

Mary's breath clouded the freezing air between them. Her gloved hand clutched at Dickie's arm.

'Dickie. Love, I don't know how to tell you. Max . . . he's missing, presumed killed.'

THIRTY

Cathy sat in the small draughty café on the station. On the table-top between them sat two untouched cups of tea. Colin's hand held hers.

'You'll be careful.'

'Of course I will, sweetheart.' He touched the wedding ring on her finger. From somewhere in the distance Vera Lynn started to sing: 'We'll meet again . . .'

Tears stood in the corners of her hazel eyes as she looked across at him. The sob stayed in her throat. She was trying hard to be brave for his sake. Her hat was tilted over her golden hair, now French-pleated and neat, and her legs encased in lisle stockings. She wore a fitted WAAF suit and heavy shoes. She was an Englishman's wife, part of the work-force.

The door of the railway station café clacked open and the sound of the approaching train could be heard. Cathy's eyes opened wide.

'I've got a lot to be careful for now, haven't I? There might even be a little one on the way. Imagine. All of us down at Brook Farm. It'll be noisier than ever.'

Cathy smiled, a touch of her old radiance. She squeezed his hand tighter.

'I'll be waiting every day to hear from you, Colin.'

The train pulled noisily into the station behind. The whistle blew, everybody started to call out their goodbyes.

'Write to me as much as you can,' he said.

'Every day.'

'I've got to go now.'

'Yes.'

He let go of her hand and leaned down to pick up his kit. He slung it on to his back and she pushed back her chair, scraping it on the concrete floor. She went round the table and into the arm that he held out for her. They walked slowly from the room.

Now she knew the heartache of saying goodbye. Her life had always been so lighthearted, even with Max—and with Colin. Cathy's free spirit was imprisoned in pain.

She held him tight as they kissed goodbye. Clouds of steam billowed round them on the cold and darkened railway station. The whistle blew. Doors clanged shut.

She felt him leave her.

'Please take care.'

'I will.'

He stepped up onto the train. He gave her that slow, shy smile: the one she had fallen in love with. She lifted her hand and blew him a kiss. The door shut. He pulled down the window. The steam hissed around them. The huge wheels began to turn.

'Goodbye, Cathy.' She started to walk with the train, half running.

'*Au revoir*, Colin. *Au revoir* . . . !' Not goodbye.

He was out of earshot. Smiling, waving. The dark tunnel eclipsed him. Cathy turned and the sob escaped her. She hurried out of the railway station and back to her car, the tears blinding her.

In the café, Vera Lynn sang mournfully to a close.

'. . . but I know we'll meet again some sunny day . . .'

The Whitley was coming in fast. Charles watched it from the field camp. It faltered and crashed suddenly, just about a mile away from the runway, some distance beyond the river.

Quickly, he climbed into his jeep and roared towards it, driving down to the river. The ground was frozen hard. Charles jumped out, waded through the river and up the far bank. The Whitley was blazing fiercely. He went straight to the wreckage and managed to pull one of the crew out and onto the bank. His face was horrifically burned and his eyelashes stuck together. It was as well because it meant he could not see his hands. They had been burned off to the bare bone back as far as the knuckles. It was a ghastly sight.

As Charles was trying to cope with him a sergeant air-crew member came running through the river. He was heading straight for the stricken Whitley.

Charles gently let the crew-man down to the ground. Then he ran to intercept the sergeant.

'God, man. What are you doing?' He held his arms.

The sergeant struggled fiercely with him, his eyes wild.

'I've got a mate in there, sir. God's sake, let me go.'

'You can't,' Charles said through gritted teeth. 'You can't. It's too late.' As he spoke, the tanks of the aircraft behind him burst. A sheet of flame leaped into the air. Charles and the sergeant were thrown to the ground.

The man beneath him cried out pitifully. The war had got to them all, even the bravest. Charles helped him up, put an arm round him. 'Come on, old chap. I'm sorry, but there was nothing you could have done. Come and help me with this one.'

The sergeant staggered helplessly over. Together they tried to lift the injured man.

'No!' he cried as they touched him. 'Leave me alone. Leave me to die!'

Charles bent down to one knee. 'What's your name, old fellow?'

The man swallowed fitfully. 'Flight Officer Jones, sir.'

'Well, Jones. It's quite all right, old man. You're safe now. We're taking you back to sick quarters.'

'No, no. I can't see. I'm blind. I want to die!'

'You're not blind. Your eyelashes are just stuck together. You'll be quite all right.' Charles's authoritative voice gave the man confidence. 'Now, come on, we'll just get you back.'

The airman tried bravely to pull himself together. Charles indicated silently to the sergeant to hold him by his wrist on the other side as they held him between them, otherwise he might touch his face with the bare bones of his fingers.

'We'll have to wade through the river,' instructed Charles. The man stumbled along between them, holding back his pain.

They reached the jeep and drove him along the bumpy track and out onto the airfield and back to sick quarters. He seemed well enough.

He died of shock two days later. It was a typical crash, but to Charles every death hurt. He could never get used to the atrocities of war.

* * *

Max came to. The faces were hostile. Inside him he was ready to run, but his limbs had probably stiffened in his sleep. He had no idea how quickly he could move. He lay there against the fur rug for a moment looking up into their faces and trying to assess his position.

He tried to explain first in English. He had no option. It was obvious who he was. At the very best they might be friends.

'I'm the airman whose plane came down over there,' he pointed back in the direction he had come. 'Please, could you let me have shelter? . . . and maybe some food? I need your help.'

There was no response. The three foreign faces stared blankly at him. They were all dressed in a similar fashion, worn country clothes; they were poor farmers, cloth caps on their heads, heavy mud-caked shoes on their feet. But they were strong. Max reckoned little on his chances of survival if he ran.

He tried the same sentence in French. There was no reaction. He tried to sit up, to test his legs. The butt of a rifle pushed him back to the floor.

Beyond the open doorway another of them came, pushing a man before him.

The man was recognisable.

'David!' Max's eyes lit up as he saw his wireless operator being herded in. The man's face was white and exhausted. The lacklustre look left his eyes as he recognised his senior officer.

'Sir, you survived!'

He was half pushed, falling to his side alongside Max.

Max spoke quickly to him in an undertone, keeping his voice as neutral and monotonous as he could.

'Get ready to run,' he said. 'I don't like the look of this. There are two of us now. When I give you the word to go, run as fast as you can towards the trees. All right?'

A grin broke out on the face of the man in front.

'It's all right,' he said in perfect English. 'We thought you might be German *provocateurs*. The police in the district are looking for you and we've been worried that the Germans might try to trick us, which would have cost us our lives or imprisonment. Come inside,' he bent to lift the grateful man from the floor. 'Let's see how badly you are hurt, and then you can have some food and we will talk about your escape.'

The kitchen was warm. Stew simmered on the stove. A young woman ladled out a bowlful for Max and his friend. The stew was excellent.

The other men sat round the table with them. They smoked their strong cigarettes continually.

The oldest pushed back his cap. He leaned his elbows on the table, gesticulating with his half-smoked cigarette.

'We will leave the house at eleven tonight. I will be your guide. I will walk one hundred yards ahead of the two of you, slowly, because of your foot,' he said, indicating Max's leg. 'If we run into trouble I will stop and light a match for my cigarette. That is the signal to get off the road and disappear as quickly as you can.'

It was just after eleven when they left. It was very dark. Their guide led them up a long, winding road through the trees and onto the crest of a hill. There were very few places to hide. Max moved as quickly as he could, David aiding him when he appeared to stumble. Soon they left the crest of the hill and started down the other side. The countryside was silent under the stars, only the distant sound of a dog barking. Their feet could be heard on the gravel of the road. Max felt very apprehensive. Ahead of them, their guide, Marc, ambled along, pushing his hand cart.

He led them to a small cottage just back from the road. Inside were a young man, his wife and baby. Quickly they ushered the two airmen into their own bed and kept guard while they slept. Marc left with a soft whistle.

Max and David slept for four hours. They were shaken awake just before dawn, by their host, with a finger over their lips.

The light was soft outside. They could see the country now lying under a morning mist, the trees rising like periscopes. In the distance, the hills were pale lilac against the sky.

The man and his wife spoke no English. They brought Max and David a breakfast of bread and cheese indicating that they should eat quickly.

They ate their food, and did not speak to each other. The order of the day seemed to be to keep as quiet as possible. Everything was being done in a hush and at speed.

The man was signalling from the back door. As they pushed back their chairs and went to him, he was looking left and right. He signalled again—to be quick. Right outside the back door the family cart was parked, piled high with farm produce. There

was a space left in the middle. The two airmen clambered in,
and lay down. The vegetables and sacks of potatoes were piled
back on top of them.

The woman climbed up on the seat of the cart, her baby in
her arms. She clicked her tongue to the horses. They jerked the
cart suddenly forward and the journey began.

For Max, it was agony. He was sure his wrist and ribs were
broken, and he was unable to move. Every stone in the road
jolted him unmercifully. He gritted his teeth. If he were to come
out of this alive it would be a miracle.

The cart rattled up over the crest of the road.

The hum of a motor car came towards them. The hum grew
louder. Over the far crest, a German staff car glittered in the
sunshine as it led the convoy. The woman's eyes flickered wide.
She held the baby closer, and urged the horses forward. There
was nowhere to go but onward.

The hum had become a roar. The German division snaked
over the crest and now the staff car came down the flat towards
them. The two officers looked with mild curiosity at the woman
and her cart as they passed her. Their eyes roamed briefly over
the farm vegetables piled in the cart. The car did not slow down
though their eyes returned to her. Her face was impassive. She
looked straight ahead and kept the casual pace of the horses
though the palms of her hands were damp with sweat. The baby
on her lap started to cry, feeling her tension.

She tried to soothe it, clucking gently; she had tried to be
invisible. Who knew what slight sound could make them suddenly decide to stop her, investigate her goods for their own
amusement or to humiliate her, or, worst of all, because they
were suspicious.

The horses clopped on. The cavalcade continued to pass.
Under the heavy weight of the sacks Max and John felt the
rumble of the cars and armoured trucks pass them. The sweat
poured from them. They closed their eyes and prayed. They did
not move a muscle. Their mouths were forced open by the strain.

It seemed interminable. Nobody spoke. The cold and curious
eyes of the soldiers watched the cart; another staff car passed
quickly, kicking up the dust to make it fly over the horses. The
offside horse started and threw up his head. The woman called
gently to him. The end of the division was in sight, the tramp
of the soldiers passing, their rifles slung over their shoulders.

The noise receded into the distance. The woman knocked her

fist lightly on the head of the cart. Max took a deep breath of relief.

The cart headed west towards the coast, turning off the main road half an hour later to lurch down a steep, pitted road to the edge of the sand dunes.

There she left them, with hurried goodbyes and a kiss on the cheek. The baby slept now in her arms; they looked as innocent as they had wished to look. Max's blue eyes spoke his gratitude, but her eyes were those of a hunted woman, a woman who had learned to hide all feelings, expressionless, gone from them already. Silently, she gathered her skirts back around her, the child in her lap, and settled onto her seat. She coaxed the horses forward. The cart lurched up the incline and back onto the high road. They clopped unhurriedly back the way they had come.

Max and David hid themselves under the fringe of seagrass that grew roughly over the dunes. They burrowed in and waited for the night.

It was almost madness. The patrols passed by on the road above. The sand shook and poured lightly onto their shoulders. It was growing dark at last.

The putter of the flying-boat's motor came out of the mist, washing in with the tide. Above, the country was silent again. Max and David crept out, looking all around. There was nothing.

Crouched over, they half ran towards the flying-boat. There were whispered calls in the mist. The pilot pulled them on board, the motor turning over, sounding like an armada of aeroplanes in the silence.

They were clapped on the back as they climbed in.

'Good to see you, fellas. Thought you were goners.'

'We're not out of this yet.'

The flying-boat turned and moved gracefully out to sea over the swell.

'Here we go. Last leg.'

The motor roared into life. They were skimming along the water, rising into the night. They lifted up above the waves, seeing them fall away beneath them as the plane banked and headed west for home.

Max turned to see the shoreline disappear behind them. There was not a movement in the blackness. No one had seen. They were safe. He grinned and put out his hand to David. He took it in a grip of joy.

* * *

She was waiting in her uniform at the hospital when they brought him in. The shock of seeing him again made her lift her head in surprise. Her green eyes flared briefly, but that was all.

She held herself straight and composed. She felt an impulse to throw her arms around him. Thank the Lord he was alive. She felt the thought through every fibre of her being. *Thank the Lord*.

They laid him in the bed and made him comfortable. The blue eyes were in pain, but the light was not gone from them.

She sat on the edge of the bed and held him quietly in her arms. Her son. The weight pressed on her heart as she knew what she had felt the past few weeks. She squeezed her eyes tight, just feeling him again, the tears pricking her lids as she was overcome. He felt so good. So *alive*. She took a deep breath to clear her pain.

Max patted her slim back. He looked up at her, his eyes smiling.

'Good to see you, Mama.' He used the endearment of old.

'You too, darling.'

They held their courage in their eyes, the strong mother and son. She smiled first. She bent to kiss him. Thank the Lord.

Charles Redfield made his rounds. Further up the ward, he bent to one of the men. His leg had been amputated above the knee, half of his face blown away. He was making good progress.

The sister handed him the report.

He took it from her. 'Who's the latest?'

'Flight Lieutenant Bennett. Burns to the hand, broken ribs and concussion, broken right fibula, and contusions, some frostbite to the right foot.'

'Bennett?' He looked across. Dickie bent towards him on the bed. 'Max Bennett?'

'That's right, Doctor. The one who took on the German air force single-handed!' Max's blood lust in the early days had been legendary. He was a hero for many, a courageous, invincible fighter. 'My nurses are drawing straws to see who will look after him!' she joked. 'He's a very brave man.'

'Yes,' murmured Charles, studying the report. 'I'm not his doctor, am I?'

'No, Doctor. Dr Hanson is taking over on that case, sir. He's only here temporarily. Being moved to another ward tonight. Pity,' she said, shaking her head.

Charles smiled down at her. 'Everyone loves a hero, don't they, Sister?'

'Isn't that what all good stories are made of ?'

Charles finished with his patient. He made his way down the long ward. By the time he reached the airman's bed, the woman had gone and he was asleep.

The nurse moved forward to wake him.

He stopped her, holding her arm.

'No, leave him, Sister. He needs his sleep. Dr Hanson will be along within the hour. He can look at him then.'

'Very good, Doctor.'

Charles was curious though. He walked over to look down at the sleeping man. Max was unconscious, fast asleep, his handsome face grained with weariness, a cut on his forehead, bruises around his eyes from exhaustion. His sleeping body looked strong and fit despite the bandages. His bare shoulders were muscular and broad, dark against the white pillows.

Charles thought of the last time he had seen him. He admired the man tremendously. He would like to have got to know him, become his friend. He tried to feel something; but he felt nothing. War had finally dulled his senses. In here, Max was just another wounded body.

THIRTY-ONE

June, 1944

The night sky was filled with the engines of a great army. Off the English coast they began to move through the Channel. The senior naval officer stood on his tiny flagdeck. The time was getting close. It was not zero hour yet, but zero hour minus. Astern, the assault craft had assembled, ready to set off for the beaches, the leaders only faintly visible through the dense light. The loud-hailer checked them in. Voices replied faintly out of the darkness. The naval commander looked at his watch. The night wind touched his skin. He lifted his microphone.

'Off you go then—and good luck to you.'

Hitler's invasion of Russia had taken the pressure off England. The Battle of the Atlantic had intensified. And then the Japanese had attacked the US fleet at Pearl Harbor and the United States entered the war. Yet the long slog still went on until General Montgomery's victory at Alamein. Now it was June, 1944; the war had raged in Europe for five long years. The whole might of the British forces was concentrated on the beaches of Normandy. It was D-Day; the start of their retaliation.

It was only a matter of minutes since he had stepped off the craft, and they had twice capsized in heavy seas. John Hamblin sat on the beach in his sodden clothes and looked around him. With first light, the landing craft had been lowered, and, as the light had broken and they could see around them, they had begun to become aware of the formidable character of the invasion fleet of which they were a part.

John had been in a barge due to pick up the brigadier of an assault group going in with the first assault wave. They had circled around opening fire on the beach which they could see quite plainly in the dim morning light.

The cruisers started banging away and soon the air had grown heavy with the smell of cordite. Looking along the beach they could see the explosions of their artillery creating a great cloud and fog of smoke. They picked up the brigadier in very rough seas and headed straight for their apportioned part of the beach, with the planes overhead giving them some cover.

The shells burst in the water along the beach. The wind was driving the sea in with long rollers. The Germans had prepared anti-invasion, anti-barge obstacles sticking out from the water— formidable prongs, many of them tipped with mines, so that as the landing barges swung and swayed on the rollers, they would come into contact with a mine and be sunk.

Their barge had come in and swung. A huge explosion shuddered the whole craft and water began pouring in. The ramp was lowered at once, and out of the barge they drove the bren-gun carrier into about five feet of water, somehow managing to get through it. John followed, wading ashore. The scene on the beach was depressing. He fell in in his appointed place and thought about Jessamy and the children. He had been forced into the war against his nature. He should have stayed at home and cared for her. He remembered Rupert's bristling delight as he held forth about the rigours of war and how he wished he could go too, a young man like John.

John climbed up onto a rock embankment and came to a piece of flat land where hundreds of men were digging slit trenches. At about a foot and a half they hit the water. There were violent shakes and tremors as the engineers set off demolitions, the troops throwing themselves to the ground. The water came to his armpits as he waded across the slough, the line of men moving upwards to reach the palisade above the beach. He held his rifle and equipment above his head. The water was warm and slimy at the bottom. A man lay at the top of the bank, dead. John looked up into the sky. There was no sign of aircraft, no enemy troops, just long stretches of empty roads shining with rain beyond the crest of the hill; deserted, dripping woods and damp fields. A static quiet reigned over the scene ahead.

The column of men stopped moving. John stepped out of line to look ahead. The reeds on the far bank were loaded with mines; they had been marked with bits of paper, and soldiers at the top were advising the men how to climb so as not to get hit.

There were bodies lying on the ground, some moving, some not. John made another step. A voice called out.

'Be careful, lad. The whole place is mined. Watch yourself.'

John stepped back quickly and looked towards the soldier who had spoken. He was lying on the bank with his foot blown off. He had made the same mistake some time earlier. The man looked drained but otherwise he was quite in control of himself.

'Are you all right?' John asked him. He was wary of walking towards him now he had had his warning.

'I'm all right. They'll be up here for me in a while. Once they've cleared the path.'

The man was right. John looked behind him down the hill. The pathway was completely jammed with men, the surrounding banks too heavily mined to cross.

'I could help you,' said John. 'This bit looks safe enough. Is it?' He pointed to the area between himself and the soldier.

'It is now,' the man said wryly.

John walked the few paces towards him. He bent down.

'I did first aid after a fashion back at home.'

He stripped a piece of material from the hem of the man's khaki shirt. He lifted his foot and bandaged him as best he could.

'It's not perfect, but it'll hold.'

The soldier's face was easier. 'Thanks, fella.'

John stood up, ready to go on his way. He was thinking of Sabrine. It was Charles who had shown him how to bandage before he had left for the war. He had practised on Sabrine, bandaging her finger after she had caught it on a splinter of wood. He loved his little daughter. She was beautiful and so . . .

'Watch out!'

The men flattened themselves to the ground. The glint of armoury had been spotted through the wood ahead.

John was a split second after them. As he threw himself downwards his eyes were those of a terrified man. The shells burst into his head and chest. John rolled into the slimy waters of the trench. He never felt a thing.

* * *

Secure along the banks of the Loire the Americans wheeled to the north, pushing ahead to Argentan to gather up the remaining German forces in Normandy.

The British forces moved northwards to the outskirts of Caen. The night raid was preceded by a heavy bombing attack.

Colin threw himself onto his stomach on the grass as the bomb screamed over his head. It burst behind him, throwing him forward. He waited for it to die down and then got to his feet and ran as fast as he could for the belt of trees.

Around him the bombs plunged into their targets. Flashes lit the sky. The moon rose over the valley through the haze, the dust and the smoke. The explosion of the bombs pressed his clothing against his body.

His unit had become dispersed, confused and lost in the dark under the surprise attack. To guide the ground forces, lines of tracer bullets were shot over their heads, stretching out like a string of lights sailing through the air. The tanks and the armoured carriers moved forward while the bombing was still on, groaning over the tufted mounds of the field alongside the wood. All around hundreds of guns grabbed the air itself, shaking it as if to tear it to shreds.

The darkness was lit up like day, the trees blown from their roots around him, the great tanks like dirty, prehistoric monsters pushing forward in the gloom, their guns booming, the light guns chattering around him. Colin held his gun at the ready. His face was smeared with dirt and his cheek was bloodied. He could not stay where he was. He decided to make a run for it, out across the open and up behind the tank. He made his break, rifle held like a charging rhino as he ran for the nearest tank.

The rat-a-tat-tat of the machine gun blasted straight at him. He was lifted from his feet like a rag doll, and thrown viciously against the ground again, winded and broken. He yelled aloud with the shock, and put his hand to his knee. The blood oozed like treacle over his palm. There was nothing below his knee. His eyes widened in horror. He screwed round to flee, some- how.

The second barrage lifted his body, twisting its shape to something unlike that of a man. He fell supine to the floor of the field, bent among the tree roots. His blood flowed gently into the earth.

* * *

Melanie and Frederick walked up the drive of Foxhall together. Throughout the war she had elected to work on the farm as a land-girl, alongside Frederick. She wore her trousers tucked into boots, and a man's shirt. She had no idea of the relationship between Frederick and her mother.

She pushed a strand of black hair back over the crown of her head. The dark grey eyes looked into his. Her cheeks were flushed softly pink from working in the fields all day.

'Have you heard from Charles recently, Mr Redfield?'

Frederick kept step with her. He headed for the front door. 'Yes. As a matter of fact he sent a letter only this morning. He should be home on leave any day.' The face looking up at his was like the early dawn, fresh as dew. She was truly a beautiful girl, her strength and sweetness shining out of her eyes, her mother's daughter. 'Are you fond of Charles, Melanie?'

She tipped her head to one side. 'Well, I can be frank with you. I am fond of him, but not in the way he would like.' She sighed. 'I'd love to be able to love him, he's such a good man, but . . .' She shook her head, and smiled ruefully at him. 'That's not the way it works out, is it?'

'I'm afraid not.'

'I write to him, though. He's not much of a letter-writer, unfortunately. Probably too busy.'

'Probably. You don't have a young man, then, to send love letters to?' he teased her. They reached the front door. He pushed off his mud-caked wellingtons on the grid. She did the same, pulling her heavy socks up to her knees.

'No, not yet! I'm all ready and waiting for him though when he comes along!' The dark grey eyes smouldered.

'He'll have to be a pretty fine young man.'

'I should say so. The very best!' She laughed happily, swinging her dark curtain of hair back over her shoulders. 'Maybe like you!' She looked very like her mother. Not for the first time in Melanie's close proximity, Frederick felt that he wanted to confide, to tell her of his love for her mother. Of course he could not. The moment passed once more.

Frederick pushed the front door open ahead of them and she preceded him into the large, cool hall.

She ran her hand up over her forehead, pushing back her hair. 'Phew . . . I'd love a drink, wouldn't you? Hello, Jessamy.'

Jessamy was coming slowly down the stairs. Her smile was gentle, a mere crease in the perfect smooth oval of her face. Her dark blue eyes were shadowed. She was slender and lovely. 'Hello Melly. How are you?'

Melanie put her hands on her hips. Her healthy outdoor complexion contrasted strongly with Jessamy's fey pallor. Melanie frowned. Jessamy always seemed troubled these days. She wished she would confide.

The knock came at the door.

Their heads all turned towards it.

Chalmers came across the hall from the dining room.

'I'll go, sir.'

He climbed the step to the front door and opened it. He exchanged a muttered word with the person outside and the door closed again.

'Who was it?' asked Frederick.

Chalmers looked scared. He held out the telegram in his hand. 'Telegram, sir.'

Melanie's hand flew to her chest. 'Charles?'

'For Miss Jessamy, ma'am.' His old eyes looked up to hers, standing on the last step of the curving staircase. Her hand held the rail a little tighter. She swayed slightly. Nobody moved as he crossed the hall towards her. He held out the form. Slowly, she took it.

She did not look at it.

'Melly, you tell me what it says.'

Melanie gave a hurried look at Frederick. She rubbed her palms on the thighs of her trousers as she went over. She gave Jessamy a quick glance and slit open the envelope. She read quickly.

'Oh, no . . .' Her voice was a whisper.

Frederick stepped quickly towards her. Jessamy did not move, her glacial face staring straight ahead.

'What is it, Melanie!' he urged. 'Read it out.'

She swallowed. 'We regret to inform you that Captain John Hamblin was killed on active duty . . . may God comfort you in your . . . *Jessamy!*'

With a cry, Jessamy slipped to the floor in a dead faint.

Piccadilly Circus was packed with people. Thousands of soldiers, sailors and airmen with their girls in paper hats thronged the area with a great bursting of balloons and whirling of rattles. They sang and danced in the middle of the crowded pavements, happily absorbed in enjoying themselves. Family parties drifted along the streets, linking arms with strangers and singing. It was May 8th, 1945, and the war was over. There was a special quality of joy, more a release from strain than triumphant exultation.

Crowds waited for hours in the sun, laughing and picnicking in the parks around Buckingham Palace. The palace balcony was draped in crimson and gold. The crowds waited for the Royal Family to appear through a window still covered with the brown boarding which had served as protection against the V-bombs.

At last the crowds were rewarded by the appearance over and over again of the King, in the uniform of admiral of the fleet, the Queen in delicate blue with a blue halo hat, Princess Elizabeth in her ATS uniform and Princess Margaret in a blue dress slightly darker than that of the queen. There were wild cheers and waves and attempts to sing the National Anthem which faltered into: 'For he's a jolly good fellow.'

The car made its way through the crowds towards the palace. The crowd recognised the man. There were tears on his cheeks as he drove through. Within a short while of the car whisking through the gates of the palace, the Royal Family appeared again and Churchill with them.

He did not wave. He had no cigar and he gave no V-sign. He stood on the balcony with his head slightly lowered and then made one deep, encompassing bow to the crowd. As the cheering broke out again and again, the King and Queen and the Princesses waved and blew kisses to the people below.

That evening in Whitehall, the crowds were crushed shoulder to shoulder round the fountains of Trafalgar Square while soldiers and sailors played a barrel organ further up outside the National Gallery with crowds dancing round them to 'Knees Up Mother Brown'.

Churchill's voice addressed the crowd once more.

'God bless you all,' he said. 'This is your victory—the victory of the cause of freedom in every land. In all our long history we have never seen a greater day than this.'

THIRTY-TWO

Dickie stood at the window. There was now iron grey at the temples of her dark hair. It was swept back from her face, highlighting the pale green eyes that had lost none of their brilliance.

It was late spring, a rare hot and sunny afternoon, just a slight cooling breeze disturbing the stillness. Above, a light plane trailed lazily back and forth. It spun and looped low over the distant fields.

Dickie watched it.

'We were right to stock up for the future, Bill, to make our preparations. I've got two men coming over this afternoon from Bayliss. We'll take them down to Heathrow. Potential customers. I think they'll be interested in the Dakotas.'

Behind her, Bill put down his paper with a light exhaling of breath. He pushed off the sofa and came across to her. He stood behind her for a moment, his hands on her shoulders.

'That Max?'

'Yes.' She watched him with the smile in her eyes. Then it dropped and she was more thoughtful.

'Boy sure likes to fly.'

'Mm.' She stroked her neck as she watched. 'I'd be glad too if he'd relax a bit more though. He drives himself pretty hard.'

'Probably got a lot to forget.' Bill's hands slipped from her shoulders. He walked across to the open walnut bureau to the left of the windows. 'These all the invitations?'

'What?' She turned towards him, her voice slightly absent.

'Oh, yes.' She raised a sardonic eyebrow. 'They all want to know us now!' She turned back to the window and watched the plane descending now for the airfield. 'Isn't it funny . . . *we're* still the same . . .'

The invitations had started to pour in once Max had returned home. Despite his lowly upbringing, the local hierarchy was prepared to overlook such shortcomings now. A war hero was a war hero, quite apart from the fact that this one was rich and eligible and the war had left many of the old families impoverished, their sons dead and gone. The villages had been emptied of the young men who used to attend the balls and tennis parties.

Dickie's early plans had paid off. She had known that the end of the war would mean many new pilots looking for work. She had bought her unwanted military transport at very low cost, including DC-3s and DC-4s. While she had not been able to progress her scheme to carry civilian passengers during the war, she had made plans to buy the military transport at a future date. Now they had opened up their airfield at Bower Hill. She had expanded her own airline with these aircraft and was about to make huge profits by taking the military hacks, fitting them out as airliners with all the trimmings and selling them on to post-war customers. Equally she had been well compensated for her losses: the RAF had given her a couple of Wellingtons and a Lancaster to replace her damaged planes. They had worked on the ex-military Dakotas, fitting them out in her own hangars. The sky was the limit now: Boeings, Viscounts, and Vanguards were readily available to those who had the money to buy them. Dickie had. Their transatlantic airline was ready to go.

The sky now empty, Dickie left the window and went to the desk. She leaned a hand on Bill's shoulder as he went through the letters.

'A tennis party at the Hasletts'. Are they the people who own Menderley? The place your father used to live?'

'Yes.' She reached over and picked up the elegant white card. She looked at it for a moment. 'Melanie Haslett,' she murmured. 'A very pretty girl.' She tapped the invitation between her fingers. 'You know,' she said in a louder voice as she stepped across the room towards the fireplace, 'they were very good to us. The Hasletts. They gave Dad a roof over his head when he had nowhere to go. She offered it, you know,' Dickie said, turning to look at him.

Bill screwed round on the Sheraton chair. 'Did she?'

'Yes.' She nodded. 'Dad told me.' She stared off into the middle distance. 'Lady Haslett. One of the few people in this village who has a heart.' Bill watched the workings of her mind. Dickie turned and propped the invitation up against the carriage clock on the mantelpiece. 'You know, now everybody's after us it does me good to make them wait, you know what I mean?'

'Yes!' He laughed.

'And so . . . when we accept, we do them a real honour.' She turned round and tapped the card. 'We're going to accept the Hasletts' tennis party.'

'Since when did you play tennis?'

'I don't. But Max does.'

Bill shook his head ruefully. He turned back to the desk. 'Max at a tennis party? I don't think so. You know he doesn't really go for that sort of thing.'

'I know.' She touched her thumb nail to her teeth. 'That's what we've got to try and change. He's got to get over that girl, Bill.'

'Cathy?'

'Yes.'

'She rang earlier . . . when you were out.'

'She didn't.' Her voice was hushed. 'What did she want?'

His eyes met hers. 'Colin's dead. She wanted to talk to Max.'

The years and the fighting had restored his confidence. He seemed more powerful than ever, slower in movement, but sharper in his mind. He was also a romantic figure. Jessamy had heard them all talking. They made him into a fantasy figure: what he might be like were he to lose that restrained control that made him appear so intense. To all of them he was very eligible, extremely male and very competent, his war-roughened face only adding to the magic.

As she saw him walk down the steps to the tennis court, Jessamy's heart skipped a beat. She looked around wildly, ready to collect her children and flee. Where were they? Her thin hands grasped the arms of the chair as she looked for them. She saw them, down on the bottom lawn.

Max stood at ease watching the foursome through the netting. It was a long rally, the girl at the other side really quite good, her figure too. The sound was hypnotic on the still summer air. A fresh wind blew up the hill, and up on the terrace of Menderley House the laughter floated down as the guests took tea and squash. The sky was perfectly blue and the sun was hot on his skin. It was a drowsy day. He felt its seductiveness. He turned back to the step to remove his pullover. Dickie stood with Bill at the top of the steps chatting to Lady Haslett.

Jessamy could hardly see through her fear. Her heart pounded wildly and she was in a clammy sweat. As he bent to the step she moved, half running forward round the side of the tennis courts and down the grassy slope to the lawn where the children played.

'Come on, we're going home.'

Sabrine glared at her. 'I don't want to go home.'

'We're going. Alexander!' She beckoned him from the croquet lawn. 'Come on!'

'Why?' Sabrine stared at her mother, the rage mounting inside her. She was a startling beauty: dark shining waves and vast midnight-blue eyes, almost violet in a tiny face so creamy smooth it was hard not to gaze at her perfection. She was absolutely aware of her beauty and her power, and her mother's fragility.

'No,' she said. She stamped her foot. 'I won't go.' She tossed her head, the blue eyes malicious and resentful. They could turn so quickly to melt hearts if she wanted. Now their full power was turned on her mother. 'You're mean. I'm staying.'

Jessamy panicked. She looked desperately around. The grassy slope behind her was empty. But she did not have much time.

Alexander was still playing croquet as though she did not exist. She had no authority at all. She felt a little cry escape her. In the distance, at the far end of the croquet lawn Nanny Hopkins strolled out of the apple orchard with one of the other nannies.

'Nanny!' Jessamy lifted an arm and signalled her frantically to her. In the distance, the woman's startled eyes saw her, stared, and then quickly apologising to the woman next to her, made her way around the croquet lawn towards her mistress.

She came hurrying up on heavy legs, her uniform rustling.

Jessamy grabbed her arm with an instant grip. 'Collect the children. We're going. You apologise to Sir Henry and Lady Haslett. Say I was ill or something.' She turned away towards the periphery of the grounds. A long laurel hedge ran around the lawns dividing them from the woods and fields beyond. It disappeared round the side of the house. 'I'm going round there,' she said. 'I'll meet you at the car.'

Nanny Hopkins saw the fear in the huge blue eyes, felt the trembling of her thin body through her hand. The woman was not well, and Nanny Hopkins had never grown used to her awkward temperament, nor the absence of love for her children. The poor things were very affected by it in their different ways. She thanked the Lord that at least she was able to remain at Foxhall and give them some stability, two beautiful children like that. Her manner showed nothing of her feelings. She had learned to act calmly for the sake of the children.

'Very good, Mrs Hamblin,' she said. She opened her hands to call the children. 'Come along, Sabrine . . . Alexander, stop your game now. We're going home.'

She touched Sabrine's shoulder. Sabrine thrust her shoulder away, her lips pouting, and her brows drawn together. She hated her crazy mother, absolutely hated her. She did it all on purpose to spoil their fun.

She kicked at the grass with her white sandal. 'I don't want to go home. We were having fun!' she complained.

'I know, dear.' Nanny touched her back gently. 'But I've got a surprise for you!' She saw the dawning interest in the angelic face. 'That new dress I was making, with all the frills and ribbons, the blue one . . . ?'

'Yes,' she pouted, but the anger was going. Sabrine loved anything new and decorative.

'Well, I finished it late last night. You can try it on when we get home. And wear it at your grandparents' party tomorrow night. Now, shall we go?'

The promise worked. The girl reluctantly moved towards the hill, but slowed as she passed her mother. The look she gave her was pure poison. Alexander, slender and pale, followed like a silent shadow in his sister's footsteps.

Up by the tennis court, Dickie had seen them, recognised them. As Katherine Haslett spoke to her, Dickie's eyes caught the scene, her green eyes curious as she sensed the tension. She saw Max walk slowly round towards the edge of the tennis court heading for the gate. Dickie stiffened slightly, hardly concentrating on what was being said to her. Beyond, the children started up the slope towards him. Katherine Haslett was finishing her sentence.

'Ah, yes,' said Dickie apologetically. 'Lady Haslett, would you excuse me? I have something I forgot to tell Max.' Releasing herself, she started down the steps.

Katherine watched her go. So that was the woman whom Frederick had known. Katherine thought she was beautiful, though distant. She looked down at her son, Max. He had Redfield eyes. She had seen him when they had first come into the hall at Menderley. She wondered briefly whose he was, but could not tell. Katherine felt a warmth to them both, born mostly out of sympathy for the knowledge she alone held. She sighed to herself. There were others to attend to. The most she could do to repeal their hurt was to integrate them here at her party. She turned away to greet the newcomers crossing the terrace towards her.

Max rounded the edge of the court. He stopped to watch the game. The children came past him. He gave them a cursory glance, that was all. He had no idea whose they were. They came on towards Dickie. Her eyes went to the girl who stood like a frightened fawn immobile at the edge of the long hedge. Her eyes stared upwards in her pale face, her hand to her lips as Max stood within her vision. He only had to look to the right, his profile was towards her.

Suddenly she looked up in Dickie's direction. The children ran up the steps and Dickie was momentarily distracted. Her eyes travelled quickly over the two children, looking. One dark and quite extraordinary, one nondescript and fair. The dark girl flicked her eyes at her as she went by, a sudden flash of deep blue, Redfield blue. The boy was not like him at all. Dickie's expression was written on her face as she looked back at the girl. The two women's eyes met. Over the distance the knowledge was there.

She seemed to catch her breath. She turned and headed for

the hedge. Dickie saw her son look towards her at the last moment. Dickie did not move. It was obvious the girl was strongly affected by him still.

At the movement Max's head turned. The shadow darted behind the hedge. A feeling snagged at him.

The ball bounced out of the court on the grass beside him. Max automatically bent to retrieve it. The girl was running towards him, her white piqué cotton dress flaring around her thighs.

'Thank you!' The dark grey eyes held his, the flushed cheeks complementing their colour. Her smile was hesitant and then wider. 'Aren't you Max Bennett?'

'Yes.' He held the ball in his hands and looked at her.

'Well, I'm Melanie Haslett. How do you do? I'm really glad you came!' She pushed her fingertips through the wire to shake his hand.

Max misunderstood, holding the ball towards her fingers. 'Oh!' she said, and then instinctively tried to grasp it. Of course it would not go through. She laughed, embarrassed. He laughed too and looked into her eyes. They were soft, yet strong and intelligent. She had lovely skin, fresh and natural, and her sable dark hair waved in light tendrils over her damp forehead. She was breathing quite heavily from her exertion at the end of the game. In the neat tennis dress she had an ideal figure, her long legs gently tanned from the sun.

Her eyes lit up slightly as he studied her.

'Can I have my ball?' Behind her, three faces stared at them, waiting for the game to continue.

'Melanie! Come on!'

'Oh, sorry!' he said and threw it over with the ease of a games player.

'Thanks!' Still her fingers curled on the wire. 'Do you want to play!' Her eyes danced as she looked into his face. She felt as if all her life was here; as if she never wanted him to turn away and had to keep him talking. It was an extraordinary and unexpected feeling for her. She was used to half the men in the country chasing after her. She had turned them all down. She had never felt quite as she did now. Everything literally faded away for her except him.

He looked up towards the far end of the tennis court.

'I see you've got a swimming pool. I was thinking of going for a swim.'

'What a good idea. Shall I join you? We're nearly finished with this set.'

He inclined his head. 'I'd love it, but there's only one problem . . . !'

'*Melanie!*'

She ignored them. 'What's that?'

'I've forgotten my swimming trunks. It might liven up the party a bit, but it would ruin your reputation.' The blue eyes were heavy-lidded with amusement.

'It might, but perhaps for now you'd better just borrow a pair!' The humour in her eyes matched his. 'In the bedroom at the top of the stairs on the left. It's my father's room. Top drawer of the little chest. He won't mind. I'll join you at the pool.'

He lifted his hand. 'I'll see you there.'

Jessamy stopped to catch her breath. Ahead of her was the gravel drive and the front of the house. The sound of the party had died away behind her. All she could hear now was her own panic breathing. She closed her eyes now in a moment of peace. She recalled his face in every detail, the slow and easy walk, his manner unchanged. He was more handsome than ever before. She felt sick with the realisation. He had looked suddenly as she had run; she had felt his eyes just touch her, felt their flame burn. She was certain that he must have recognised her and the terror had made her run headlong around the bush and past the wood. She knew how she felt; how she would always feel about him. She loved him still. It was like a curse.

Charles stood at the upstairs window of Menderley and looked down on the pool to the left of the terrace. He saw Melanie sitting on the edge in her black bathing-costume, swinging her legs gently in the water. She was laughing at something the man had said. Max stood in the pool, the water up to his shoulders, his hands clasping the bar at the side, and the black hair smoothed back over his proud head. His face was lifted to Melanie's. Their attraction was obvious. They looked very handsome together. For them, the world did not exist as they shared their laughter in the hot sunshine.

Charles turned away from the window in the guest bedroom and crossed to the bed to change into his trunks. He was not of the stuff of which heroes are made, unlike Max who had the whole village talking. Among the wounded on the field, Charles's calm, efficient manner had brought him many friends and gratitude, but no medals. Unlike Max once again, Charles's return had been unnoticed. Max, to give him his due, had been very modest, reticent about his achievements—it only served to make them admire the man more.

Charles pulled off his shirt and trousers and laid them on the bed. He did not hold any grudges against Max for what was obviously happening downstairs between him and Melanie. It was inevitable that sooner or later she would fall for somebody else. He had loved her faithfully since he was nineteen, an adolescent love which had diminished little with the passage of time, though now he knew he would never win her. Melanie had made it obvious she was waiting for a particular man. He pulled on his trunks and went back to the window. He felt somehow that the man could be Max. He had never seen her so absorbed. She kicked the water at him with her feet and then screamed with delight as he dived underwater, coming up to pull her into the pool with him. She went underwater and came up spluttering, her hands on his shoulders. She looked down into his face. He lay on his back and swam with her to the middle of the pool, his manner lazy. Melanie's feet kicked gently as they swam along.

Charles folded his arms and sighed, seeing her body lying along Max's broad frame. How he had longed for such a moment, and yet Max, not knowing such a desperate need of the girl he was holding, treated the whole episode with easy casualness. Charles had met other girls at medical college, had had other affairs during the war as they all did. Melanie's warm and lovely memory always printed itself on his consciousness at the moment of truth.

He admired Max, that was the truth of it. He had hero-worshipped him since he had been a teenager, seeing him as proof that any man could make good despite his background if he had belief in himself. He knew Max had to be a great chap. Those fighter pilots had been courageous beyond belief. He wondered again at the rivalry that existed between the two families. He, for one, was having nothing to do with it. He was ready to shake Max Bennett's hand and congratulate him on being a fine fellow.

He turned away from the window and collected his towel as he went out of the room. There was another reason he wanted to meet the man. He had heard the airline business was flourishing; they were looking for personnel. He knew exactly what he would do to heal the rift from the past: he would offer his services to the company. They could probably use somebody with medical experience. He did not see why he should tie himself to medicine just yet. His job with Dr Biddy did not come up until the spring, and perhaps until then he could become part of a flourishing and exciting new enterprise. And besides, he had always wanted to learn to fly.

Melanie knew about Cathy. You did not keep much quiet in a country village. She wondered how any woman could let Max go. She knew already with a fatalistic and quite glorious surge inside her that he was no ordinary man to her. She was acutely aware of him: his rough edges, his war-torn body, and sense of singular purpose. Her upbringing had been so different. Apart from the war, none of them had had to struggle. She had never met a man like him before. She was awed by this new feeling.

She felt herself lifted bodily out of the pool and into his arms, their wet bodies dripping with water. She was laughing, but as he held her in his arms, her laughter subsided and so did his. His penetrating blue eyes grew darker, deeper. And warmer. His smile was lazy. She felt it steal through her, felt its insinuation. Her own grey eyes looked into his.

It had all at once become very real. He wanted her. The hum of the party on the terrace faded away. All she saw were those eyes, their hungry need of her. The answering flame leaped inside her. She wanted to kiss her. Urgently. Desperately. Her eyes travelled down to his mouth and back, her eyes now naked with their knowledge. She saw the freckles on his dark skin, the high smooth cheekbones, the war scar on his forehead, the pale speckles in his radiant blue eyes. She saw the darkness in him and suddenly she knew. *She loved him.* He was the man she had waited for. She would have let him make love to her right then and there.

'Hello, you two!'

Melanie blinked herself back to reality. She felt Max let
her go with a sense of loss as she slipped slowly down to the
ground again.

'Oh, hello!' she said. 'Have you two met?' The unprepossessing man came around the corner of the pool towards him.
Max's smile was slightly forced. He, too, had been shocked
by that moment, knowing as he held her in his arms the
electricity that had been generated between them. The desire
for her had flooded him. He looked swiftly at her as she bent
towards the bench behind them for towels. The moment had
been broken. There would be others. His eyes met hers and
told her so as she handed him the towel. Her look was deep
and serious in response, then it was gone as she rubbed her
hair with the edge of the towel and looked towards the young
man who had joined them. He was medium height, his look
optimistic as if he recognised Max. Max did not know him.
He slung the towel around his shoulders; got ready to shake
his hand.

'Charles Redfield,' she said casually. 'Max Bennett.'

Max felt the steel slam down around him. The coldness
climbed into his eyes and sat there looking out. A Redfield.

The man's smile grew broader, his hand came out towards
him. 'Hello . . . I've been looking forward to meeting you,
Max.'

Max was silent. Pointedly he reached for the towel and
roughly dried his hair. His forehead creased in anger as he
kept his eyes on the man before him. Now he saw the resemblance; a family resemblance in the way he moved and
smiled.

'Charles is Rupert Redfield's son, Max,' she explained as
she rubbed vigorously at her legs.

Max saw only Redfield. This man could be his brother.
He felt nothing but pure dislike.

Charles's enthusiasm died slightly as he saw the rigidity in
the man, the pointedly ignored handshake. His own had
dropped to his side. 'Yes,' he said. 'My sister Jessamy's
somewhere around. Have you met her?' He looked around
for something to do to recover his composure.

Max did not move. Now he knew exactly who the shadow
had been at the side of the hedge. Jessamy. He had felt it
steal into him like a knife-blade in the dark. All the joy of
the afternoon had gone.

'Melanie!' the voice called from the terrace. Melanie looked up.

'Yes, Mother.'

Katherine smiled at the three of them. The young things were enjoying themselves. It was good to see them all together, as it should be. 'Come up here a moment, would you, darling? I want you to help me with something.'

'All right.' She threw the towel around her neck and looked quickly, heart-searchingly, at Max. 'I'll see you later?'

Max came back to the present with a lurch. He saw the marvellous grey eyes, remembered her warmth. She was nothing to do with this. Even at this moment he was able to divorce himself swiftly from the man before him and feel her again, her vibrations. He would see her again. Often. Very often.

His smile said so, though it could not warm the ice of his eyes so quickly. Melanie smiled in response, wondering at the air of coldness she had sensed. She looked from one to the other. 'I'll see you later, then,' she said. And was gone.

Max watched her bare legs running up the steps. His eyes did not want to leave her, but they did. He turned them back to Charles and their blue was colder than ever.

'We were in the RAF together,' said Charles. 'Do you know I was the doctor on duty the night they brought you in?' His smile was tight, remembering. 'I know you were a damn good flyer. They were always singing your praises back in Field Camp as they came down. I wanted to shake your hand.'

A muscle worked in Max's jaw. He held both ends of the white towel and stood straight, his chin slightly raised. His eyes were hooded like a snake. He looked remarkably like his mother when she was angry. He would not shake the man's hand. Ever.

'Get to the point.'

Charles looked startled. 'Well, there is no point, old man. Except that . . . well, I heard you were looking for staff around here, and I would be delighted to offer my services. In any category you care to name. I've always been fascinated by your progress, yours and your mother's, your achievements. I'd like to be a part of it.' He opened his hand and swatted at a fly that was bothering him. He grimaced briefly, and swatted again. 'Can't say I know much about flying, though I'd be willing to learn, but I could help out with medical advice, something like that. I'm signed to old Dr Biddy in the village for this time next year, so it'd only be temporary. What d'you say?' He smiled again.

'No.'

Charles looked puzzled. 'But I thought you wanted people. Aren't you advertising?'

'Not you.'

Charles's puzzled look disappeared. His voice was quiet now. His face cleared of friendship, but he did not look hostile. The two were very different. 'I see,' he said, looking down at his foot. 'Because of the family thing?' He looked up again.

Max did not answer him.

Charles scratched at the bridge of his nose. 'Look, old man. I don't know what happened with your family and mine, and I don't know that I really care but isn't it time to bury the hatchet? Whatever happened must have been a while ago and it can't have been that bad. These things often blow out of proportion.' He opened his hands wide. 'I know my father. He's a difficult man, he bears grudges, but that doesn't mean I do. And I can't see why you do. You're not like him, you're a good chap. I've just been through a godawful war, and so have you, and we've come out of it alive. Wouldn't it be better to turn the other cheek and shake hands, start anew? Come on, man, what do you say?'

He grinned hopefully and stuck out his hand again.

Max's look was hard. 'You're very naïve,' he said in a low voice. 'Not a quality I look for in my business, or my friends.' The lids dropped lower over his eyes. 'I would never employ you. Get that straight. I want nothing to do with you. The day you Redfields are lying in the gutter cannot come soon enough for me. Understand?'

'Yes.' He paused, his own manner cooler now. 'Fully.'

'Good. Excuse me.' Max turned abruptly away and headed for the steps. He climbed up on to the terrace speaking to no one. He strode into the house.

Charles looked back to where he had been standing, a thoughtful look on his face, the sun cresting his brown hair. He was upset, terribly upset. He was good and kind, stronger for the war. He sensed that Max was basically a decent fellow; his reputation had said he was very popular in the mess—

he had courage and yet compassion too. One got to know such things about a man. Max knew something he did not. It was obvious. He was in a mind now to find out what it was.

August, 1945

The lights of Home Farm were soft against the darkness.

Melanie climbed out of his bed. 'I have to go now, my darling. Otherwise the whole village is going to talk.'

Max pulled her back towards him. She laughed softly as he turned her round in his arms. She was beautiful, loving, warm, sweet, everything he wanted. 'You're greedy,' she said, her eyes overwhelming him with their love and laughter.

He looked into her face. He took a deep breath. She made him feel good. In the months that had passed since the party, she had become an essential part of his life. He lifted his hand and traced a finger over her face, across her lips. She opened her mouth and took his finger gently between her teeth. He ran the finger on down her chin to her throat. Her eyes smouldered like dark fire in the soft light.

'Max,' she said hungrily, 'how I love you.' Her voice was a sigh.

He pulled her down to him and kissed her forehead. He laid her head against his broad chest, his chin against the soft waves of her hair. Together they lay there. He looked towards the dark rectangle of the open window and stroked her bare smooth back.

She lay a while and then sat up again, reluctantly. The sheets were crumpled with the passion of their love-making, his shoulders dark and broad, his face magnificently proud, strong. She gazed at him. 'I have to *go*.'

She trailed her fingers across his chest, then reached to the rush-seated chair for her clothes strewn there in slow haste.

She sat on the side of the bed as she pulled on her under-clothes.

'Melanie?'

'Yes?' She turned. He leaned up on one elbow, tracing the line of her spine with his finger and marvelling at the texture. She arched her back. 'Don't do that.' Her laughter was soft and sensual. 'I'll never go.'

'I'm going to California soon.'

'Yes.' She looked at the blouse in her hands. She turned it through her fingers. 'I know,' she said.

'Would you like to come with me?'

She turned swiftly. His eyes were dark and warm. He smiled at her. Her heart caught as she looked at him. She did not see there what she wanted to see. She knew that in many ways he was a man on the rebound. She had spurned so many offers of marriage and now here she was ready to go to the ends of the earth, unmarried, with a man who didn't love her. For he didn't. Melanie was a romantic, but a realist too. Simply, she loved him and that was enough. It had to be enough, for the two of them. She did her best to soothe him, to heal him with her serenity. She knew her love was unreciprocated, which made it all the more poignant. Maybe he would love her in time; she believed that. His heart was still elsewhere, but time healed all wounds. She knew then that he was not asking her to marry him. Melanie was gentle, but she was equally strong and determined. If it was the only way she could be with him, she would go.

She thought all of that in the capture of a second. Her eyes marked his with their thoughts and the accompanying pain. He saw, and wished that it had been different. Melanie was the right girl to have been in love with, but as it happened, he was not. He loved her, it was hard not to. But it did not burn in him the way he needed. Yet, he did need her.

'Yes,' she said quietly. 'If that's what you'd like. You know I want to be with you.'

'Yes, I know.'

'Then, yes.' She smiled hard, bent forward and kissed him. He held her hand. She drew away, and hurriedly finished her dressing.

At the door she blew him a kiss.

'When will I see you again, Melly?'

'You know where I am,' she said simply. The door closed softly behind her.

Max tidied up the house, ready to go to bed. After Melanie left he went into the kitchen in his dressing-gown and put the glasses into the sink, the bottle of sherry back on the sideboard. She had come over ostensibly to go riding. He had expected . . . well, what had he expected? Not to go riding. To be fair, he had invited her to his house so that he could go to bed with her. He felt the strength of her love like balming ointment on his wounds.

He went across to the back door, open to the night air. The light from the kitchen flooded out across the grass. He saw the shadow by the wall. He did not have to speak to ask who it was. He sensed her immediately.

'I waited for her to go. Can I come in?'

Silently, he watched her as she came into the room. She had lost none of her beauty. In fact, it was more so. She was a little thinner, a little worn, but it added something poignant to her. Before she had been so emblazoned with health, now she was more finely drawn.

She turned towards him as she reached the pine kitchen table. The harsh ceiling light was not unkind to her. Cathy would always be beautiful. She wore a light cream raincoat, belted round her waist, and brogues; not wellingtons, he thought apropos of nothing.

'I saw your lights from the top of the hill. I came down.'

She looked into his face.

His eyes were guarded.

'What can I do for you, Cathy?' He pushed his hands into the pockets of his dark green paisley dressing-gown.

'Max,' she pleaded. 'There's no need to be so formal. I came to see you.' Her eyes, once laughing and bright, were haunted. 'Didn't your mother tell you? I've been waiting for your call.'

'Yes, I know.'

'You heard about Colin?'

'Yes.' He looked down. 'I'm sorry.'

She touched the table-top and looked down at her left hand, the wedding ring there. She pulled a face. 'We hardly knew each other. It was crazy, wasn't it?' Her eyes filled with tears. She held her emotions in check.

Max said nothing.

'Well,' she said, breathing heavily as she spoke the word. Her voice assumed a practical note. 'I've sold up the house and the furniture. The van comes tomorrow. I've booked my ticket back to the States. On your airline, I hasten to add!' she said with a laugh that echoed falsely. 'You do a good line in advertising. I could hardly resist.'

'Cathy, what did you come to say?'

'To ask if you still wanted me to stay.'

The silence was loud. Her words scored him in the back of his brain. There had been times when he would have longed to hear her say just that. Those times were gone now. He stared at the floor, his eyes catching on some invisible point.

When he spoke at last his voice came as if from far away, absorbed in itself.

'Once I had a dream.' His heart felt heavy. He stared at the solid kitchen units as if to find it, his eyes searching unfocused. 'A dream of you and me. And children.' His voice was slow. 'A dream that we would be walking down a street fifty years from now, hand in hand like those old couples you see. Perhaps I'm too romantic, but I'm all or nothing, Cathy. I couldn't drift along on a second-hand love. You didn't love me well. I loved enough for both of us. I wanted an ideal love. I wanted to worship you. To me, you had no faults. I wanted it like that. If you had them, I never saw them.'

'That's not healthy.' Her voice was a whisper as she heard the words dragged out of the depths of him. It seemed so painful for him to admit.

'Perhaps not,' he agreed. 'But it's my way. It's unrealistic, but my life is full of practical, realistic things. I'm a flyer, Cathy. I have that dual personality of practical and romantic. I need to love like that and no less. I need my woman to be perfect, beyond reproach. For a while I thought I'd found my dream. You sullied it. You betrayed me.'

Her eyes looked away and back. 'Would you give me a second chance?'

'Are you saying you made a mistake? That perhaps you loved me all along?'

'Perhaps.'

'At least you're honest enough to admit it. I could say yes to you, Cathy, you know what you meant to me. But I'm committed to someone else.' He knew as he said it and saw her eyes raise towards him, what he was going to say. 'I asked her to marry me and she accepted.'

She did not move a fraction. 'The girl who just left?'

'Yes.'

She felt as though someone had chipped her into stone.

'You love her?'

He could not lie. 'Enough.'

'But you said just now . . .'

'I know what I said,' he interrupted. 'But there is nothing

second-hand about Melanie. She's a fighter, beautiful and kind. And she loves me without question.'

'But you don't love her,' she argued.

'Not like I loved you, no, but look where it got me.'

'Max, please.' She moved towards him, leaving the stability of the table and out into the open, crossing the room a step or two, her hands outstretched in supplication. 'I want to try again,' she said, her voice yearning. 'Please. I think it could work.'

'No, Cathy,' he said with terrible slowness, watching her. 'It wouldn't. The dream is gone. I'm marrying Melanie within the month. We're going to go and live in California.'

'California?' She drew back, her face hurt. 'Back to the beach house?' It would be too cruel.

'No. I'm taking a ranch house in the hills.' He studied every detail of her lovely face. Saw how she reacted now that he was in a position of strength. He had never thought he would feel so cold with Cathy.

Her face had turned to the right and down. Now she brought it back up, a new look there. 'Max.' Her tone was flat. 'I'm going to be in California. I've decided to move up from the Midwest, to live there.' She held his eyes so that he would know her meaning. 'Can we see each other?'

He knew what she meant. The girl he had once wanted for his wife was offering to be his mistress. Revenge was bitter-sweet. He felt nothing, only pity. She lost his respect immediately, and respect was the thing he had built his love upon.

'No. I plan to be faithful to my wife. Cathy, I'm very tired. Would you mind?' He indicated the door. He hated her second betrayal, the worse one: a betrayal of his judgement.

She nodded. She squared her shoulders and pushed her hands into her pockets. She crossed the room to the back door.

Her hand was on the door. The wedding ring caught the light.

'Goodbye, Max.'

'Goodbye, Cathy.'

She paused a moment. His profile was to her, his expression closed against her.

The door shut softly.

Max lifted his eyes. He stared at it for a long, long time.

* * *

The family dinner was finishing. Charles sat back in his chair, turning his brandy glass between his fingers.

'Thank God the war has come to an end at last. I was certain those Japs would hold on till the bitter end. The kamikaze was such a frightening thing. One could never understand such a mentality.'

Frederick cut into his slice of Stilton. 'Yes, to die for your country that way. Suicide. How did they instil that into them?'

Charles chewed the last of his cheese. 'I don't know. It must be singular to the Japanese. You've seen those inscrutable eyes. They say in the war they did atrocious things and were unbelievably cruel and yet they never showed any expression. Their methods of torture were far worse than the Germans.'

Frederick leaned his arms on the table. 'What could be worse than what the Germans did? Abominable.' He shook his head and lifted his glass to his lips. He drank deeply.

Charles shrugged lightly. 'They operated without anaesthetic, marched those men till they fell by the wayside and then shot them without a second thought. They were butchers.' He sighed heavily. 'But it still seems appalling to kill them with an atomic bomb. It's total annihilation. Those cities were levelled to smoking rubble. Just the streets left. Devastated. I can't believe that anything like that should be accepted.'

Rupert pointed a strong finger at him. 'American soldiers at Saipan saw women hurl their children over the cliffs and then throw themselves down rather than be captured. When you face a people like that you have no alternative. They would have fought until all of them were dead, and we had had many more deaths too. The prisoners of war knew they were waiting to die. The Japs told them they were dead men. They're heathens. Nothing they understand but total annihilation.'

'But *two* bombs, Rupert.' Frederick looked at his brother. 'Did they have to use two?'

'Yes. To drum home the point.' Rupert sat back in his seat and stared at them.

Charles stared at his glass. 'There's an argument for it and one against. Let's hope it will make everybody realise that nuclear war is a terrible thing. Personally, I think all human life is precious.'

Frederick nodded. 'Trouble is, with human nature the way it is, there will always be those fanatics and those immovable people who will say that they have to have nuclear weapons. I have a fear that this is not the end of it at all, only the beginning.'

'I only hope you're wrong.' Rupert pushed back his chair. At the far end of the table the two women sat silently, Caroline at the head of the table, and Jessamy morose beside her. 'Have you two finished?' he asked.

Caroline looked up. 'What?' She had switched out at talk of the war. 'Oh, yes, I have.'

'All right then.'

He bowed his head and clasped his hands on the table before him. The family bent their heads in unison.

'For what we have received, may the Lord make us truly thankful . . . Amen . . .'

'Amen.'

Rupert pushed back his chair and walked through the door behind him which led to the small drawing room. The family followed. Rupert sat himself in the chair by the fireplace. He picked up his pipe from the hearth. 'And how did the day go at the Hasletts', Charles?'

Charles came over and sat down on the sofa at right angles to his father. 'As a matter of fact,' he declared, 'that's what I wanted to talk to you about.'

'Oh?' Rupert pushed the tobacco into his pipe.

'Well,' out of the corner of his eye he saw Caroline seat herself in the chair behind him, Frederick moving to sit opposite Rupert. Jessamy came to sit down beside her brother as he went on, 'I was up in the bedroom, and out of the window I saw Melanie Haslett in the pool with someone I wanted to meet. I went downstairs, greeted him in a friendly manner, mentioned that I was looking for a job and would he consider employing me, and he rounded on me like a rabid dog!' He looked around at the faces watching him.

'Huh!' Rupert sucked the flame from the match into his pipe. 'Who was it? Not that old fool, Whittington, with the stables, was it?'

'No.' He held a pause. Jessamy braced herself beside him. 'It was Max Bennett.'

Rupert's nostrils flared. His eyes spun towards Charles. 'What the hell did you go asking him for a job for?'

'Exactly for that very reason!' said Charles, flicking his hand at his father. 'Why does everybody either act struck dumb or furious every time one mentions the Bennetts?' His mild eyes were bright with the need to know as he looked first at his father, then at Frederick. Lastly, at Jessamy. He looked to her for confirmation. 'Don't you think it's time Jess and I knew what it was all about?'

'Charles, will you mind your own business?' Rupert glared angrily at the carpet, his pipe clenched in his hand.

'No. I, we, have a right to know. Mother, do you know what it's all about?'

'No, well, I . . .' She put a hand to her chest.

'Max Bennett is by reputation a charming, courageous and unbelievably brave pilot, the strong silent hero type. Everybody liked him in the service. He was very much admired. Yet I come home, he looks like he could kill me, and here his name is dirt.'

'God damn it, Charles, the man *is* dirt.' Rupert slammed his fist to the chair. 'Now, say no more about it.'

'Melanie Haslett didn't seem to think so.' He had their attention. Both Jessamy and Frederick looked towards him. 'No,' he said. 'I've never seen her like that. I think she fell in love with him.' He looked at them both again. 'Wouldn't surprise me at all if she were to marry him.' He looked harder at Jessamy. 'Didn't you see them together, Jessamy. No, you'd gone. By the way, where did you go?'

Jessamy's strangled cry surprised them all. She jumped up from the chair.

Charles grabbed at her arm. 'Jessamy?'

'Oh, for God's sake, leave me alone!'

She pushed him away violently and ran from the room. The sounds of her sobs receded up the stairs.

'What on earth is going on?'

'Well, you're so bloody tactless, Charles,' said Rupert, refilling his pipe. 'Obviously the girl's going to be upset. John killed so recently and everything. Don't want to go talking about people in love and wanting to get married in front of her. You're such an idiot.' He sucked his pipe. 'Fine doctor you're going to make. Won't have any patients left!' He leaned back into his chair with satisfaction and closed his eyes.

Charles sat slowly back in his chair. He was no nearer the truth.

Jessamy crossed the landing and pushed open her bedroom door. Upstairs from the nursery a face peered through the banisters, alerted by the noise. Sabrine watched her mother, saw her crying. Her lips went in and out, in and out, and she made a little smacking noise with her mouth, then, smiling, she danced back into the nursery in her nightdress. It was pretty and white with little blue flowers stitched across it.

She was a pearl of a child, with her lustrous dark hair and her huge, swimming, violet eyes and dusky skin. There was something about her eyes that looked so directly, and the manipulative smile in one so young. She pushed on Alexander's door and went in.

Alexander was pretending to be asleep. He had heard the noise too, and known it would alert his sister, and, wanting to vent her energy on someone or something, she would turn to him. She was always cruel, seldom sweet. Alexander shivered in his bed. No one would ever believe him against her. She was so beautiful and so angelic, and he, well, he was like a pale shadow beside her. He was pretty for a boy, but diminished by the ruddy good looks of his sister, whom everybody patently adored. There was nothing he could do.

He saw the sliver of light.

'Alexander? *Alexander?*'

He kept very still.

He heard the feet slip across the room. The breath was close to his ear. 'I know you're awake, Alexander. You don't fool me.' The hand came over and pinched him hard on the arm.

'Ow, Sabrine!' He clutched his arm. 'What do you want?' he said grumpily.

She sat on the bed, her eyes dancing. 'To play with you,' she sang.

'I want to sleep.'

'Want me to pinch you again?'

'No.' He rubbed the sore skin.

'Then move over.'

He moved reluctantly and she scrambled in beside him. He felt the twist of his skin again. 'Ow! I moved over . . . !'

'That's for not moving fast enough. Cuddle me, I'm cold, Alexander.'

Melanie woke from a disturbed sleep. The room was silent, the night black as the ace of spades. She pulled the sheet to her chin, instantly awake with thoughts of him. Max. She said the name to herself and stretched her legs in the bed. The stones clattered against the window.

She sat bolt upright.

'Melanie!'

She hurled herself out of bed, grabbing her dressing-gown. Barefoot, she ran to the window and looked out.

'Max!'

He stood below on the path that ran along the side of the house. He put a finger to his lips. 'Come down. I've got something to ask you.'

Her face was alight as she turned swiftly from the window and ran lightly to open the door, along the corridor, and down the back stairs. She opened the side door and looked up to the right, searching for him. He saw her, and strode towards her, taking her into his arms. She held him happily, her eyes gazing up into his.

'Couldn't you wait?'

He kissed the tip of her nose. 'Come with me!' He held her hand and drew her round to the front of the house. The small Georgian manor looked out over the fields below. The stone terrace was pale in the darkness of the summer night. She walked barefoot, her pale blue cotton négligé floating out behind her as he led her to the balcony.

'Sorry there's no moon, Melly,' he leaned against the balustrade and pulled her into his arms. She came willingly, leaning her body up against his legs, her arms looped around the strength of his waist. 'I don't mind,' she said, smiling.

He looked down into her face a full minute.

She was so secure, so straightforward. He felt at peace with her. She made him laugh, too. He had lied to Cathy. It had been necessary. If she had seen the chink in his armour he might not have had the strength to turn her away. Had she known—she did not. He took Melanie into his arms.

'Melly,' he said softly. 'Will you marry me?'

Her loving look was as warm as the summer night. 'You know I will.'

Their love affair was more autumnal now, a strong friendship mellowed over the years from the fire of their first love. Frederick pulled his horse to a stop under the boughs of the tree, reflecting on what she had just said.

He dismounted. So did she. They tied the horses to the fence and walked at the edge of the wood together.

'Well, he could be, Freddie,' she said again.

'No.' He couldn't be his son.

'Still, he's a fine young man. And Melly loves him. Things have changed a great deal, haven't they, Freddie? In the old days Henry wouldn't have entertained the notion of a village girl's son marrying his daughter. Now he's tickled pink. He thinks the world of Max. He's almost childishly delighted. The fact that she's twenty-eight and unmarried has caused endless rows, I can tell you. Melanie's pretty headstrong. And now she's fallen for a real man. She's always been stubborn, holding out for what she wanted.'

'She was right.' He held her hand.

She stepped beside him, slowly matching his stride. 'Yes. She's certainly no baby any more. She knows what she wants, and she wants him. Henry's happy, anyway.'

'He would be. A war hero. All those medals.'

She looked up, concerned. 'Don't you like him?'

'Oh, indeed. Though I don't know him. He gave Charles a real roasting. He came home, demanding to know about the family feud. Rupert put him off, of course.' He frowned, remembering Jessamy's reaction as he recalled the scene.

'Why did he do that? To Charles?'

'He asked him for a job. Max flayed him alive.'

They walked down the path deeper into the woods, now strewn with a carpet of russet autumn leaves. Katherine lifted her face, breathing in the damp and bracing smells of autumn. 'Yes,' she said slowly. 'That's the element that worries me. He's pretty ruthless.'

'Not with love though, surely? In business only?'

'I don't know.' Her voice was still worried. 'But at least he's strong, good and ambitious. And his mother's quite a character. And then, of course, I can't help feeling that it draws us closer.'

He stopped and looked down into her face. 'How?'

'If he's your son I would be proud for him to marry my daughter.'

'And if he's Rupert's?'

'He's still got your blood.' They turned and carried on walking again. 'He's inherited the fine qualities of leadership and strength tempered with intuition. Maybe she had a lot to do with that. They're very close. She's like a little tigress. Possessive, too. She chose Melanie, you know,' she said, her voice changing.

'Did she? How?' He smiled, amused and interested.

'When the invitation went out to her she responded almost immediately. She accepted ours. Somehow I knew her intent. Doesn't miss a trick. She staked out her claim as well as Melanie did.' She put her head to one side, and tightened her lips. 'But I'm going to give my blessing, even though I know Melanie loves him far more than he loves her. It's tragic really, isn't it? So many men wanted her, and yet . . . oh, well, it's one way to get future generations that will be ours!' Her brown eyes were warm as they gazed up into his face. 'Makes up for the children we never had, my darling.'

Frederick looked fondly at her, but with regret. He had never asked her to leave. Never, because he still loved another.

'Does he love someone else then?'

'I believe so.' She looked back at the path before them, their feet stepping out together. 'From what Melanie tells me. We're all sometime losers in the game of love. And then, again, maybe some men are destined to carry a torch for one woman all their lives. There's always one special one, isn't there, the one that is magic to your soul? You can love others, but there's always one you'll never forget.'

'Or two.'

She smiled and squeezed his hand. He was being kind, but she was grateful. They walked on in companionable silence.

He thought about her, Dickie, as they walked.

THIRTY-THREE

September, 1945

Dr Biddy had finished surgery for the day. He checked through the notes on his desk, putting them in order and pencilling in his comments.

In the outer office his receptionist, Mrs Alice Travers, was engaged in putting away the files. She pulled the drawer open in the cabinet and slotted in the buff folder.

The lace-curtained door behind her opened. Alice turned towards it. It was already dark outside. She did not recognise the man at first, his collar turned up against the rain.

'I'm sorry,' she said. 'Surgery's finished for the day . . . oh, hello, Dr Redfield. Sorry, I didn't recognise you!' She beamed an apologetic smile.

'That's all right, Mrs Travers.' He came in, turning his collar back down. The shoulders of his raincoat were stained dark with damp. 'Terrible night!' He turned towards the closed door. 'Dr Biddy in?'

'Yes. He's just finished with the last patient. You can go on in. Here, let me take it.' She reached maternally for the wet raincoat. 'I'll hang it by the radiator.'

'Thank you, Mrs Travers.' He rubbed his hands together and went to the door. He knocked.

'Yes?'

'Dr Biddy, are you busy?' He put his head round the door.

David Biddy looked up. His head was shiny and almost bald now, a few white strands across its surface. He wore his gold reading-glasses on the end of a somewhat bulbous nose. His face was wrinkled with the good humour and patience of years of learning. He was a small man. He sat in the old wooden chair and indicated the patient's chair beside his desk. 'No, not at all. Come along in Charles. Good to see you. How's the family? Keeping well?'

'They're all fine.' Charles eased himself into the seat and undid the bottom button of his waistcoat. 'Be better when we can get more things going, though. It's slow work picking up again after the last few years.'

'Indeed.' The old man nodded thoughtfully. He tapped the pile of folders in front of him. 'And the ailments are back. Strange how war puts paid to so many. Now it's peacetime and everybody's got aches and pains again!'

Charles smiled and sat down. He pulled a pack of cigarettes from his pocket, offered the packet to Dr Biddy's refusal, and then lit one. 'It's hard looking for a job, too. Any chance of my starting with you earlier?' He leaned over as he put the pack back in his side pocket.

Dr Biddy nodded. 'Yes, if you want to. Start now. As a matter of fact I've got more work than I thought I would, and I'm pretty tired these days.'

'Thank you.'

David Biddy studied him. 'Went for that job with Max Bennett, did you?' he said casually.

'Yes. And, do you know, he turned me down flat.' He looked upset. 'Any idea why? Everyone seems to keep mum on it as if there's some ghastly secret. I'm beginning to think there really is—more so than my father's usual dislike for someone just because they're jumped up, as he puts it.' He drew on the cigarette.

David pursed his lips and hung his head a little in thought. 'I don't know about that, Charles,' he said at last. 'But one thing I do know. If there's a family problem and you're prying—don't. You can start here by all means, you're what the village needs. But I'll remind you of one thing—lose that attitude of curiosity. It's all right to be interested, and hear what you're told, but no more. Village folk don't like you prying. Especially when you're the son of the lord of the manor, as it were. They like their old ways. They like *me*,' he said, tapping his chest and looking up at Charles from under white beetle brows. 'It's going to take some getting used to from both sides. And they might resent you at first, close up on you until they get to know you and trust you.' He leaned back, his calloused old hands clasped to the arms of the chair. He surveyed Charles in a straightforward manner. 'Don't push things like you do, Charles. That's a mistake in life and in practice, oh, and another thing,' he said, raising a hand and pointing at him. 'Your family files are strictly off limits. Taboo. You understand? And don't go looking. I'm going to put them in the safe!' he finished, a twinkle in his eyes. 'All right?'

Charles smiled with his eyes. 'All right!'

'Good. Now. Just another tip. Country practice is different from school. Or war, for that matter,' he added, looking quickly at the young man. 'When you come across an alcoholic, of which there are many, you don't say "Have you been drinking?", you say "It seems a lot of old bottles have been dumped in your rubbish.'' He cut his hand through the air. 'The oblique approach, you see. Or, if you want to approach a situation, maybe you talk about milking first, or their cattle stock or the price of corn this year, something like that. Whatever's appropriate, you'll get to know. Then you ease your way in,' he said, curving his hand through the air like a snake. 'You keen young lads barge your way in like a bull in a china shop. You've got to be easier than that. Slow. Country's slow. Understand that, Charles?'

'Yes.' He relaxed in the chair, looking forward to the challenge. 'I'll do my best for you, Dr Biddy. And thanks for the chance. I need a job, need to get going.'

'Yes, well, I'm sure you do.' He leaned forward, tapping the folders into alignment. 'And with country folk it's payment in kind too, don't forget that. Cheese, eggs, cream, raspberries, beautiful trout fresh from the stream. I know you can have it all, being a Redfield and not impoverished like the rest of us,' he teased lightly, 'but don't let them feel that. It's the way they let you gain their trust.' He sniffed and slapped his knees. 'Seventy per cent psychologist, that's what you'll be. Partners and families aren't interested, vicars are too busy or too remote above it all, really—so it's up to the doctor.' He pushed himself back into his chair and was silent for a moment, looking over at the other. 'You'll do fine, I'll see you here on Monday, then. Now,' he tipped his head towards him, slapping his hands to the side of the chair, 'come along next door and have a drink. Margaret's putting the dinner on. You want to stay?'

'Love to.'

'Good.' He stood up. 'Got a couple of calls to make first. You come on my rounds with me. Get to know the people right away. Let's go.'

The Imperial Airways DC-4 touched down at Los Angeles airport. You could smell the sea already, she thought, looking through the small window beside her, feel the air, warm and sweet. Life was secure and wonderful. Max held her hand.

'There's the coast.' He leaned across, pointing.

Beneath them lights glittered along the dusky shoreline; lone houses and cars beaming home, a string of street lights. The sun was low in the sky and the water was like molten gold.

'Look at the colour of the sky. And the water. It's beautiful,' she said. 'I know I'm going to love it.' She held his hand tighter. She knew she would love it, knew this was the start of a new life. The slim, gold wedding band glinted on her finger next to the blue fire of a single solitaire diamond. Their marriage had been quickly arranged because of Max's departure for the States. It had been select: family and close friends, and now their honeymoon was to be in California. The happiness welled up in her. There was something else too, a beautiful secret she hugged to herself until the moment was right.

'I've asked Wiley to have a car waiting. I'm going to drive you out to the house and then you'll really see how beautiful it is.' His voice was warm with enthusiasm as they circled and flew in catching the wind for touchdown.

He looked across at her and she saw his expression, sensing how much he loved this country. It revitalised him, unlike the sleepy English countryside. He wanted to be off the plane and away, living, working, whatever. Her smile was tender. She lifted his hand in hers and kissed it. He rubbed her face with his knuckles affectionately.

'We're nearly there!'

They drove along in an open car, a wide, white roadster with a grille like a shark's teeth. Melanie's hair was lifted by the breeze, dark as night, her grey eyes filled with warmth and love as she leaned her neck back against the cream leather upholstery. The warm evening air filled her and she sighed against its caress. They passed a beach club; the radio played a soft crooning ballad.

'Who's that?' she asked as the car turned to climb the hill away from the beach.

'On the radio? Bing Crosby. He's a famous singer over here. You'll meet him in time, I expect.'

As the car climbed the hill she could see down over the Malibu coastline again. The sea was dark and lustrous now, the sky like fire.

'I can't believe it, darling,' she said. 'It's like a different world. We'll be happy here.'

He lifted her hand and kissed it. 'I know. You'll soon feel at home. Americans are easy people to get to know.'

He turned for the bend and drove along the crest of the hill. 'I'm going to cement our holding over here, Melanie, and set up a head office in New York to liaise with the new London office now that the transatlantic flights are about to take off. We need to pull Coastline and Bennett Air together under one banner. We need a branch office in New York for the new line and the administration.'

He pulled the car to a stop in the driveway of the house. It was a low, wooden ranch house looking out over the sweep of the bay. Eucalyptus trees brushed the sky in front, and on the rocky point tall fir trees cut black and sharp outlines against the sunset from their promontory. The house was tucked into the edge of the cliff, protected from the wind, ready to take the sun on its deck in the day.

Max lifted her over the threshold and carried her through the wide cool rooms to the deck at the front. He let her down gently and she turned to put her hands lightly on the rail with a gasp. The view was breathtaking.

'Oh, Max!'

'It's one of the most beautiful views on the coast. I knew you'd like it.'

'I love it.'

A hummingbird danced among the bushes in the garden below the deck. There was a smell of sage and blossom. At one end of the deck a table stood with a bowl of flowers and a bottle of champagne in a bucket of ice.

She went across. Down below to the side of the house was a swimming pool laid carefully into the rocks to look like a rock pool. She shook her head in amazement. It was perfect.

The sky was studded with stars as he took her into his arms.

'Max, it's all I ever wanted. And you.'

He kissed her. 'Tomorrow I'm flying up the coast to Big Sur. Will you come with me? I bought a piece of land up there. I think you'd like to see it.' He held her. 'Will you fly with me?'

It was what she had hoped for. She knew that it had been a special place for him. Now he was going to share it with her. Now she could tell him her news.

She touched the collar of his shirt. 'For the moment, yes.'

'What do you mean?' He held her away slightly. 'Not always?'

'No . . . not always. You see, Max . . . I'm going to have a baby. Our baby. The doctor confirmed it.' She hesitated. 'Are you pleased?'

'I've never been happier, Melly.' He pulled her into his arms. 'Welcome home.' Her head against his shoulder, Melanie closed her eyes, the smile still on her face. No old love could touch them now.

September, 1947

Charles worked late. Every evening for the first year he had taken the files from the cabinet and sat down to study them after surgery was over. He was up to date on the villagers, many of whom he knew by sight. The information was surprising; the variety of hidden illnesses, imagined or real, endless. The second year had been easier; he knew what Dr Biddy had meant by then. There were many problems that necessitated an understanding hand to hold rather than any form of palliative, and an endless succession of colds and flu.

He sat back, tired. It was midnight by the wall clock. He had not realised how the time had gone by. It was silent too. The whole village was home by nine, and the curtains were drawn. He thought for a moment of the war, the scenes of horror he had experienced. He thought of now, when all was calm and ordinary. It seemed so long ago, almost like a dream—*almost*. He gazed around the small sparse room, whitewashed and hygienic, the examination bed, the basin, the instruments, his black bag on the floor beside him. He was a doctor now, and this was to be his territory, his role; helping those who needed help in any way he could. He thought briefly of Alexander starting public school that week. He had watched the boy. He was vulnerable and too pretty; he would be bullied mercilessly. He wished he could do something to make it easier for him, but he could not. He couldn't even help his own family. He looked around him with the thought, his arms latched behind his head. His eyes caught sight of the safe. Only yesterday he had seen where David Biddy kept the keys.

He remained looking at it. It was like a thorn under his flesh. He had to know. He had to find out, despite what David Biddy had said, to find out and put it into his own perspective of rationale. His arms came down to rest on the arms of the chair.

He opened the drawer of the desk slowly. He had made his decision. He knew what he was doing was wrong, but it was hard to stop himself. In there, in the wall safe, was the answer.

Like a man driven he searched the drawer, fully awake now. He moved the advertisements, the samples, the slips of papers and packets. He opened the next drawer, and the next. His hand pushed into the very back of the drawer. There was a hook there. He had found the keys.

The key turned easily in the lock. A car passed. Charles held still, his hand on the key. He waited, listening. The car passed the house and drove on into the dark. The lane was silent again. He opened the heavy door and looked inside.

The file on the Redfields was quite extensive. By the light of the lamp Charles began to read, and was soon engrossed. He did not even hear the car draw up outside.

Alexander Hamblin ran down the corridor towards the prefect's room. He knocked hesitantly on the door.

'Come in.'

He carried the plate of hot buttered toast in. 'I've brought your toast, Williamson.'

Alexander was Williamson's fag. The public-school fagging system demanded service from someone, and in an age-old ritual some were servants and some were their masters. The system bred cruelty and perversion in boys not mature enough to accept responsibility with grace. Alexander had always been weak, cast in his sister's shadow, he had always walked a step behind, glad to be unnoticed, used to being spurned and rejected by the precocious tyrant that was Sabrine. Life at public school was no different. It was only his first term and already he felt the deal of his fate.

Williamson leaned back in his chair and eyed the pretty boy.

'Ah, Hamblin. Come in. We've been expecting you.'

Alexander went towards him.

'. . . And shut the bloody door. Born in a barn, were you?'

'Have to teach him some manners for that, Bertie.'

'We will indeed. Come over here.'

The boy sitting beside the flickering flames of the fire was thin and cruel. His eyes warmed to the sight of the hesitant Alexander with his slender legs and arms and his pretty face. The word was that he was studious, an egghead. Prissy brain-boxes were always the worst. He was pretty to look at and pretty in his manners. And he was quiet and wary, showing the torment of his suffering. Charles had been right. He was ideal prey for bullies.

The elder boys were evil. He saw them all now. Like rats in the dark they were watching him. He smelt their excitement. They smelt his fear. There was nowhere he could go. Nothing he could do.

'Say after me "I must not bring burnt toast. I will kiss the feet of my master, Williamson." '

'The toast wasn't burnt . . .'

'Say it!'

'I must not bring burnt toast. I will kiss the feet of my master, Williamson.'

Williamson tipped the toast slowly onto the floor.

'Go on, then.'

Alexander got to his knees. The butter was seeping into the carpet. He leaned forward and kissed the proffered shoe.

'And the other one!' Someone sniggered.

Alexander tried to pretend he was not there. He leaned forward. There was a vile substance on the toe of the boot. Alexander knew what it was. He hesitated. The shoe came forward and kicked him in the mouth. Alexander felt sick and was close to crying. He fell back on his bottom and wiped his hand across his mouth.

Williamson kicked the toast around the room. 'Clean this mess up.' He sat back.

Alexander felt the whimper break from him. He was so ashamed, so frightened and lonely. He bent over and started to pick up the pieces of toast at their feet. They sat around in a circle above and watched him.

Somebody toed him on his grey flannel backside.

'What do you think?' The voice was a distant whisper.

'Yeah, go on, let's have a look.'

A hand pulled at his trousers.

'Stand up, Hamblin.'

Alexander clambered to his feet, the toast in his hand.

They stared at him. 'Take your trousers down.'

The fear bolted like a shock through him, over and above the ache that was already a part of him.

He drew his arms together protectively. 'No!' He looked for the door. One of the boys sauntered over and stood before it.

'We'll do it for you,' one threatened.

He undid the buttons, still holding onto his handful of toast. He pushed his trousers down his thighs. They slid to the floor.

A hand yanked at his pants. Pulled them to his knees.

'Well, would you look at that! The little bastard!'

Alexander stood there, shamed. He knew what they were staring at now. His penis was large, larger than the other boys'.

The laughter surrounded him like a storm. It beat against his head so that he wanted to lift his hand to his ears.

'Who would have thought it? With such a puny little frame, too!'

They laughed but it was unkind laughter, jealous laughter. He somehow knew it would happen. They came at him and he stumbled, caught round his ankles by his trousers. He fell against the fire, his hand reaching out to brace himself against the fireguard.

'Ow!' He cried out with the pain on his flesh.

'Ow! Ow!' they echoed. 'Little baby!'

Alexander scrambled to his feet, pulling up his trousers. They threw him across the chair and held him down. One of them beat him with his cane.

'That's for not telling us about your little secret,' he said.

Alexander grabbed at his clothes. They threw his tie around the room, his shoes, his jacket. He ran around after them, collecting it all. He ran for the door. They did not chase him. They were laughing too hard.

He raced down the corridor until he had put a safe distance between them. Then he dressed himself, buttoning his trousers again, retying his tie, and doing up his shoelaces. He smoothed his blond hair down again and sniffed unhappily as he tied the shoes. Life was miserable and there was no one who understood, no one who cared.

At home Sabrine had always held the upper hand, taken the

attention. He had no idea how to stand up for himself at school.
He had been ragged unmercifully, bullied, abused and teased
by the older boys. But this was the first time this had happened.
He could not sneak; he knew that would put him in a worse
position. Thirteen years of living in his sister's shadow had taught
him that. Thirteen years at her hands had not helped. She had
been precocious and impossible, always making him take the
blame for her misdemeanours, but, obsessed by her beauty and
persuasion like everybody else, he loved her. Now he took the
abuse as he had learned to take it. She had taught him how. Now
he made himself the masochist by never fighting back. He was
known as a weed and his life made unbearable, haunted by pain,
unhappiness, and loneliness. He did not have a single friend.
His father was dead, and his only friends were his uncle Charles
who was busy now with his practice, and uncle Frederick, who
was of a generation that did not question the system.

He stumbled down the corridor towards the chapel. He could
hear that the choir singing had already started. He was late.
Alexander had a perfect singing voice, high-pitched and a clear
treble. In surplice and ruff he had run the gamut of many ardent
older boys and learned to run away after choir practice. Now he
would be in trouble again.

The older boy barred his way.

'Where are you going in such a hurry, Hamblin?'

Alexander cringed. Smith major was one of the older boys in
the choir. He had a deep baritone, he was the best games player
in the school, and head of his house. He was a school hero. Now
of all people to catch him sneaking round corridors and missing
choir practice, Smith major was the worst. He worshipped him.

'I was on my way to choir practice, Smith major.'

'But choir practice has already started.'

'Yes, I know,' said Alexander miserably.

He looked pathetic and ragged, vulnerable. Smith stood above
him and watched him shake with apprehension. He had watched
him often over the last few weeks, had heard his voice in choir,
seen him in the changing rooms. He was pretty and pale, like a
girl. He looked down on the narrow shoulders and sensitive
hands, the soft, vulnerable mouth and the big unhappy eyes.

Smith put his hand on Alexander's shoulder. Alexander
jumped as though struck.

'Come to my room. I'll say you were fagging for me. Mine's
ill. They'll believe me, won't they?' he confided.

'Yes.' Anyone would believe Smith major, the school hero. 'Better to get out of the corridor before anyone else catches you, eh? Come along.'

'But what about choir practice? Aren't you . . .'

'No. I've got a lot of work to catch up on. They know about it. You could be helping me by making me some tea, couldn't you?'

'Yes.'

Alexander followed him as if in a dream. They reached the quadrangle and walked across together. The choir singing floated out across the quad. Alexander followed silently, treading in his tracks. They went under the archways the other side and through into the cold corridor beyond. They reached the room.

'Here we are.'

It was warm. And comforting. And Smith major had taken pity on him.

'Pop some toast on, Hamblin, old chap, and we'll have tea. Want to join me? Now, let me see,' he bent into a cupboard, 'what have we got here? Jam and biscuits. And a chocolate cake. How does that sound?'

'Splendid!' said Alexander. He sat down in front of the fire with a fork to toast the bread.

They sat down to tea. Smith major buttered his toast and offered him tea. It was sweet and soothing, the cups rattling in a homey way. Alexander was so grateful he was close to tears. He was rendered quite speechless, the kindness unbearable after all the misery.

'Now, tell me,' said the older boy, biting into his toast. 'What did they do to you, old chap? That nasty bunch.'

Alexander was silent. He did not want to sneak. The toast became a lump in his mouth. Was this a trap?

'Come on,' said Smith major. 'You can tell me. It won't be sneaking, you know, if that's what you're thinking. It'll be just between us, eh? We'll be friends.'

It was too much for Alexander. The truth came pouring out. 'They . . . they put dirt on their shoes and kicked me in the mouth. They threw the toast I made around the room, said it was burnt. It wasn't.'

'I'm sure it wasn't.' He buttered another piece and handed it to Alexander. 'What else?'

Alexander blinked and looked away. He was painfully embarrassed to recall the next episode.

'I'm your friend, remember, Hamblin. Come on.'

'They . . . pulled down my trousers. And laughed at me.'

'Why?'

'They said I was big and . . . I'd kept it a secret so I must be punished.'

'I see.'

'Then they pushed me against the fire, and they beat me. Over the chair.' He turned up his hand to show the burn.

The older boy looked serious. 'Well, we must put something on that, mustn't we?' He took the hand in his own, holding the fingers gently. 'Looks nasty, but we can take care of it.'

He went away across the room. Behind him, Alexander held his hand open and looked at it. It wasn't bad, really. He was lulled by the warmth of the fire, the crackling of the flames.

Smith major returned, a tube of ointment in his hand. He threaded his way between the worn chair and the sofa squashed in round the fire and sat down on the chair.

He carefully ran the ointment over Alexander's hand, gently rubbing it in. 'That should be all right.'

'Thank you.'

'Maybe we should have a look at your backside, old chap. Could be badly bruised. Slip your trousers down.'

Alexander hesitated.

'Come on, now,' he said. 'Don't you trust me yet? I'm not going to hurt you.'

Alexander knew he could not be foolish. Smith major was doing him an honour by being so kind. He pulled down his trousers and turned round, bending over slightly.

'Not bad.' The hands touched his hips. 'Just a little ointment there, though.'

It was not hard for the boy then to get closer, stroking the ointment carefully and then, his hands moving softly, starting to fondle him. At first Alexander tensed, trying to move away. But then the reality of his life outside that door returned to him. This was the first kindness he had ever known. The room was warm and Smith major had been his hero. He did not resist as the other boy grew braver. Alexander closed his eyes as Smith major pushed him to his knees.

After some time and his own satisfaction, Smith major told him to dress again. As he pulled himself into his trousers the voice promised him more comforts and a warm place to hide for as long as he wished.

'You'll be my fag from now on, Hamblin. You won't have to go back there any more. There'll be no more bullying for you. I need you now. No one will deny me. Come back in the morning.'

'Yes, Smith major.'

'Call me Boots. All my friends do. Good night, Alexander.'

Alexander ran down the corridor. He opened the door and went out into the cold night and the quad and across to his dormitory. He wished it was time for bed, the only place he was safe.

That night he cried silently into his pillow.

Charles read on. Frederick Redfield treated for depression, Jessamy coming in to see Dr Biddy after the birth of her children, talking to him. Jessamy sedated. His mother, Caroline, treated for alcoholism. Charles was devastated by the signals he was reading.

He went to the cabinet and pulled out the Bennett files. Somewhere in Frederick's report he had mentioned her name; Jessamy had mentioned Max. He searched for the notes on the birth of Dickie's illegitimate son. Village girls generally confided their lovers' names to the country doctors on the births of their love children. He looked in the appropriate place. Dr Biddy had not attended the birth. Father unknown. He looked quickly through Max's notes.

Charles read Frederick's report again. Psychological disturbance. He had confessed to his interfence with a village girl, his brother too. Charles put two and two together. Frederick's confession and Dickie's reticence both at the same time were too coincidental not to add together and make one. He closed the file with a sigh. The faces of the characters spun past in his mind's eye. He saw the likenesses. He remembered Max's anger. My God. He had no idea how closely they were related.

Now he knew it all, the beginning of the feud and the escalation. He felt the pain of his sister's hurt. He did not judge her, but equally he could say nothing. He was not supposed to know.

He heard the sound of the outer door opening. Hurriedly, he returned the file to the wall safe, locked it and pocketed the key. There was no time to return it to the drawer.

'Charles, you still here? Keen as mustard, eh?'

Dr Biddy came in and sat down.

He put his bag down with a sigh, exhausted. He ran a hand over his head. 'Freezing night. Mrs Dunbarton up at the farm decided to have her baby tonight. Little girl. Got a nip in that flask?'

Charles handed over the hip flask. 'Help yourself.'

David Biddy poured a little of the brandy into the cap. He threw it back. 'Firewater. Uh, that's better.' He shook his head, and screwed the cap back on.

'Well, time you went on home, young fellow-me-lad. Got to start again bright and early in the morning. Don't worry, I'll put the files away.' He bent over. 'Bennett, eh? Interesting family.'

He picked up the file and took it to the other room. Hastily, Charles slipped the key back on to its hook and closed the drawer. He ran his hands over his thighs, and came back out.

'Right. I'll be going on home, then. See you in the morning.' He took his trilby and coat from the rack.

'See you in the morning. Good night, Charles.' David Biddy was absorbed in putting the files away, and his own tiredness. He did not look round.

Charles walked out. It was a wet and windy night, the wind tugging at his clothes as he crossed the road to climb into his car. He started it up.

It seemed to him as he drove back up the hill to Foxhall, the gale whipping the trees around the banks each side of the road, that for every discovery he made about the dark side of human nature, he only became more determined to help and increase his faith in their basic goodness. His family skeletons were probably no more so than any other, but they were his.

He got home and climbed the stairs to his bedroom. The house was sleeping. David Biddy was right. Prying opened up a can of worms. He decided to take the two days' work at the hospital that David had suggested. He would be able to help the community even more.

Jessamy's bedroom door was half open. He knocked gently. 'Jess?'

There was no answer. He pushed the door open. The room was in darkness. A line of moonlight touched the white quilted bedspread. In the oak four-poster, Jessamy lay sleeping, softly as a child.

Charles stole across the room. He sat down quietly beside her, enjoying the peace of this room, the one she had had since childhood. They had been close then, had good times together.

Where had they drifted apart? Adulthood? He leaned over and stroked her hair. She had borne so much pain, alone. He wanted to share it with her, to let her know she was no longer isolated by it. Her hair was like silk, the lines around her mouth softer in sleep. Once again, she looked lovely.

'Jess? Jess, it's Charles.'

Jessamy stirred. The sleeping pills were too strong. Max's hands touched her again. She felt the heat of them on her skin.

'Max . . . ,' she murmured.

She moaned in her sleep.

Charles regretted his impulsive action. Maybe it was best left alone. The wounds were obviously still too raw for her.

He stroked the hair away from her face, and quietly lifted himself from the chair. His words could have changed her life but he did not know that, as he gently tiptoed from the room carrying with him a knowledge that she did not possess.

He went into his bedroom and pulled off his tie, throwing it over the back of the chair. He put his jacket over the chair and sat down to pull off his shoes.

Max and Jessamy. He could not picture it easily. It was quite obvious to him that she still loved the man. Poor Jessamy. He stood up and unbuttoned his shirt. It all fell into place now. His mind drifted back in time. Poor Max.

THIRTY-FOUR

October, 1948

'All right, darling.' He heard the note of disappointment in her voice. 'When will you be home?'

'In an hour or two.' He held the receiver closer to his ear. The party's noise drifted in as a door opened behind him.

'I wish I was with you.'

'You wouldn't. It's a bit of a bore. I'll be home soon.'

'We'll have supper on the deck. It's a lovely evening.' She looked out across the bay.

'How's Jim?'

She looked round at the boy. He played on the carpet. 'He's fine.' Melanie smiled fondly as she gazed over at her son.

'Let me say good night.'

'OK . . . Jim,' she held out the telephone. 'Come and say night-night to Daddy.'

The boy dropped his toy car and came running over. He grasped the phone. 'Hi, Daddy!'

'You behaving?'

'Yep. I'm wearing my new baseball cap.' He touched it proudly as he held the phone. 'It's great.'

'That's good. Now, off to bed. I'll be home soon.'

'Night-night, Daddy.'

Melanie stood by watching proudly. James Bennett, named for his grandfather, was a strong dark-haired boy, the image of his father, his body sturdy and his face softly tanned by the California sunshine, his hair streaked with golden lights. He was

spoilt by her and he loved her and took advantage of her. Max
was always remonstrating with her for more discipline, but it
was not in her nature. Jim, as they called him, was becoming
as headstrong as his mother, and untamed too. The California
lifestyle developed precocity. Jim was not immune, but he was
so delightful with it that she often gave in. Not tonight. She
wanted to get ready for a *diner à deux*.

She came off the phone. 'Into your room now and get ready
for bed.'

'Oh, Mummy!'

'Go on.'

He slouched off into the passageway beyond the huge sitting-
room. It was bare-floored, the furnishings done in slate blue and
cream. It was very restful, a long, low, white room, the deck
running the length of it, the huge windows overlooking the ocean
at the corner of the house.

Melanie laughed at his retreating bottom.

'He's very undisciplined,' she said.

'Oh, I don't think so. He's so appealing. You've brought up
a fine little boy. You're very lucky!'

Melanie came back and sat beside her friend, Terry. In the
three and a bit years they had lived out there on the coast she
had made friends with only a handful of people, the favourite
of which was Terry. Melanie did not find it easy to give of herself
to the open-hearted Californians who welcomed everyone to
their bosoms. She found her natural English selectiveness became even more predominant and it dissuaded her rather than
persuaded her. Max had become one for socialising far more
than she. Her life in the hills with her child and her close friends,
the intimate dinner parties and the flights up the coast to the
house at Big Sur were all she wanted. And the Californian
weather, which she adored. Terry was big, blonde and handsome, a voluptuous and statuesque woman married to a film
director. She put up with his infidelities, laughed at his jokes
and adored a man who was openly unfaithful to her. Melanie
loved her sense of humour. As she put it: 'One day he'll get
tired of those little pussycats, honey, and he'll come on home
to Mama!' Melanie could not think how she could be that phil-
osophical.

Melanie reached for her glass. She leaned back into the sofa
and tossed her dark hair over one sunburned shoulder. She was

dressed in brief red shorts and a striped suntop. She tucked one foot up underneath her.

'What's on your mind, honey?'

Melanie looked at her friend.

'What makes you think there's anything on my mind?'

Terry narrowed her eyes at her. 'You don't usually send Jim packing quite so easily. What gives?'

Melanie let out a big breath. 'Well, I just wanted to ask you something. Truthfully. I can ask you. I have to.' Her grey eyes were sensitive. 'Have you heard if Max has been with another woman? I have to ask, Terry,' she said, lifting a hand to stop any protests. 'And I trust you not to rub my nose in it. Everybody else would.'

'What makes you think it?'

Melanie shrugged slightly. 'Oh, I don't know. You know, he never loved me as I did him. And I remember saying once to an old friend of mine that love is very provocative but it doesn't hold someone who doesn't feel the same way.'

'Max loves you, Melly. I think more than he knows.' She sipped at her drink and watched her friend's beautiful face. It lit up now with hope.

'Do you think so, Terry? Oh, I do hope so.' She clicked her tongue. 'In the beginning I loved him so much, but he was in love with someone else. No way to start a marriage, I know, but when you love someone you think you can convince them to love you back, you know?'

'I know,' said Terry drily. 'But to answer your question. No, I've heard nothing. And I'm sure Frank would tell me, and revel in it were it true!' She raised a sarcastic eyebrow. 'He'd love to put the blame on someone else for once.' She laughed roughly. 'But let me tell you this, honey. It's not the first affair you have to worry about. It's the second. The first makes the break, but the children hold them. The first rubs the skin, the second opens the wound. It's the second affair you have to watch. If they don't leave you then, they're never going to. Then it's up to you.' She drained her glass. 'But in your case, honey,' she patted her on the knee, 'I don't think you've got a thing to worry about. You've got a faithful husband. A rarity in these parts, I can tell you!' She stood up. 'Well, I've got to be going. See if I can get home in time and catch the old bird at it. If I ever did, he'd never know what hit him! Bye-bye, darling. Come see me for tennis tomorrow morning, huh?'

'OK.' Melanie unwound off the sofa.

'Make it about ten. Give me time to sleep in a bit.' She kissed Melanie's cheek and walked towards the patio doors that slid open onto the deck. Melanie walked alongside her, out into the late afternoon air.

She kissed her at the step at the end of the deck and waved goodbye. Terry walked off towards the red convertible. Melanie turned back into the house.

The girl was beautiful, a stereotypical lovely California blonde. She came up to him at the party, a waiting smile in her eyes. Max was in demand with the glamorous set of movie stars who played equally romantic roles off screen. His own story was romantic enough: a legendary flying ace and a poor boy made good. He was the real thing and there were enough bored and beautiful women around ready to flock around him, were he interested.

The golden head leaned against his shoulder. She whispered in his ear. 'How you doing, stranger? Want to come for a swim?' She looked him in the eyes, her meaning clear. The playful smile hovered on her lips. 'We're all going skinny-dipping at Greta's.'

She swayed slightly as he looked at her, undulating her tanned and fabulous body. The white Grecian-style dress suited her very well, worn with a gold and turquoise heavy choker around her long neck like a slave collar. The green eyes taunted him, smouldered. She looked very like Cathy; a glamorised Cathy.

Max felt the temptation. It would have been hard not to. Then suddenly he remembered Melanie's voice, Jim's baby voice saying good night. The girl's brash manner grated on him rather than enticed him. She was long, tanned and silky. And totally unreal. One of many. Melanie was an original.

Max put down his glass. The girl's eyes still watched him. Ever since the phone call he had been thinking. Yet another party without Melanie. What was he trying to prove? That he was still free? That he only married her to spite Cathy? That it was not real love? What was love if it was not what he had with Melanie? A family?

The girl's arm wound round his neck and played with his ear. It was a practised art. 'Want some more champagne, darling?'

Max looked into the long green eyes. Green as a cat.

He unwound the arm. 'Not now, thank you. I'm leaving.'

'Oh, so soon,' she pouted. 'We haven't even got to know each other.' The lips pouted unhappily.

Max shook his head. What a fool he had been. She was so trusting, so loving. He had been wrong to hurt her; he was going to try at his marriage. This was wrong, all wrong. Out of gear. He wanted Melanie, her goodness and her trust. Suddenly he felt a great surge of relief. The pressure that had stayed with him for years lifted and he felt free.

'Goddamn,' he said, under his breath. 'What d'you know!' The girl had got to him. His eyes crinkled with humour. Melanie's love had worked at last.

He walked away from the girl towards his hostess. He was ready to make his apologies and leave. The first rumble threw the whole place into a panic. The girl behind him screamed in terror and ran to him to cling to his shoulders.

'Oh, God! Get me out of here! It's an earthquake!'

An earthquake! *Melanie!* He pried the girl's hands from his shoulders and ran for the door. The rumble built into a roar. Tables and vases and glass bookcases came crashing to the floor. The walls cracked and dust fired into the room, covering the guests with white chalk.

There was pandemonium. They ran in every direction like disordered ants. Max pushed his way through the hubbub to the front door where the guests were packed like sardines, trying to get out. They were yelling and shouting, the veneer of cool civilisation completely gone. The golden girl was right behind him, screaming her head off in hysteria.

Max stumbled on the rubble at the door and nearly fell. He picked himself up and elbowed his way through to a cloakroom by the door. He pushed open the broken window and launched himself out, scrambling to his feet again. Ahead of him the scene was total destruction as he ran for his car. The ground had opened up as if a prehistoric dinosaur was climbing from the bowels of the earth.

His car was up by the main gate. He had been one of the last to arrive. He ripped open the door, reversed wildly and screamed away out of the drive.

He headed for the hills.

Melanie saw Jim's face at the edge of the passageway.

'Mummy?'

'Darling. Go to bed!' She went towards the table to clear away the glasses. 'I'll be in in a minute. Daddy's coming home and you know how mad he gets if you're not in bed by eight. I'll come and bathe you. Now, go on.'

'But, Mummy. I heard a noise . . .'

'Now—' She straightened up. The rumble picked up from the distance. Melanie was instantly alert. The glasses on the table began to shake. 'My God, Jim! It's an earthquake! Quickly, darling!'

'Mummy!'

He ran into her outstretched arms. She grabbed him up and ran for the patio doors and outside. The roar broke out as they reached the doors. The walls heaved and cracked, the trees swaying on the hillside and then breaking in half with a terrible sound. Earth began to slide from under them. The whole house moved. Melanie was thrown to her knees, with Jim still in her arms. His little face was terrified. His arms clung tightly to her neck.

'It's all right, darling. Just hold tight to Mummy. Come on.' She climbed to her feet, her knees bleeding and the palms of her hands grazed by the fall. The house rocked around her. Walls came crashing down somewhere at the back of the house. She got him outside.

'My God!' The deck was sloping beneath their feet. Up on the hill behind, the earth and rubble were on the move in an avalanche. Huge cracks had opened up in the rock face.

Her grey eyes were wide with horror. She swallowed, looked back to her boy, calming herself. 'Come on,' she said. 'Quickly.'

'No, no,' he started to yell. 'My baseball cap!' On the edge of the deck lay his new baseball cap. Before she knew it, he had wriggled from her arms, falling to her feet.

'Jim! No!' Her hands stretched for him. The deck yawned into the abyss. Jim's foot slid through between the planks.

She turned and grabbed him.

His shoe was stuck between the boards.

'Mummy, it hurts!'

She felt the reverberation pass through her, the tremor building. My God, there was another one coming. Against time she pulled and pushed. It would not move. Short of cutting off his foot she could do nothing; there was no time left.

She gathered him into her arms. The deck broke free of the house and tilted wildly. She had made her decision. His trembling body was pressed against her breasts, his face in her neck as he had done as a baby. She did not look, but heard it come, her eyes closed as she held her child, her hand against the back of his neck, her arms around him, pressing him in against her to muffle the sound. She knelt in the stones, saw the hard-grained wood of the deck, felt the blue sky and the wind, the sun. The last time.

Goodbye, Max, my darling. I love you.

'Mummy, I'm scared.'

'Don't be scared, darling. Mummy's here. I'll always—'

THIRTY-FIVE

Charles walked into the surgery. The morning was cold and brisk.

'Good morning, Mrs Travers.'

'Morning, Dr Redfield. Cold today, isn't it?'

'Certainly is.' He handed her his coat and hat. 'Well, who have we got today?'

She handed him the notes. He took them and went on into his surgery, past the open door of the waiting room. Inside, the patients sat on upright chairs and all smiled at him. Charles smiled back. It was his practice now. Dr Biddy had retired the previous year, and Charles was well liked already, an accepted member of the community. It was to his credit; he was a man of immense sympathy and honour. His belief in human nature was absolute.

'Send the first patient in, would you, Mrs Travers?'

The girl came shyly into his office. She was very young, but she looked as worn and tired as an old woman. She sat down in the chair he offered, her bag on her lap, her knees pressed together. She was sharp with tension and fear.

'Now,' he said warmly. 'We haven't seen you before . . . Mrs Daniels. What seems to be the trouble?'

'I'm three months' pregnant, Doctor.'

Charles smiled. 'Congratulations!'

'No,' she said, 'no.' She looked down and fiddled with her skirt. Limp skeins of mouse-brown hair were loosened from her scarf. She looked frightened and ill. 'I don't want it. I want you to get rid of it for me.'

Charles looked at her carefully. 'You mean abort it.'

'No.' The weak grey eyes pleaded with him. 'It's dead already. I know it. My husband beats me, and, well,' she clutched a hand to her stomach, 'I know the child is dead.'

'Mrs Daniels. Abortions are illegal.'

'I know,' she said obstinately. 'But it's dead.'

Charles watched her for a moment. She was obviously distraught. She fingered her cotton dress and would not look at him now.

'Well,' he said as gently as he was able, 'first things first. Let's examine you and see. Up on the table, please, underwear off.'

The girl disappeared behind the screen. Charles felt very sorry for her. The poor creature was obviously in a desperate way. For a mother to want to rid herself of a child, a married mother as well, she had to be psychologically ill. He thought of Jessamy, and of Max's mother, Dickie, as he prepared himself for the examination. Two frightened women who went through with their pregnancies. He called out to her, 'Are you ready?'

'Yes.'

He went behind the screen. He made his examination with care and gentleness. 'Yes. You're definitely pregnant, but the cervix is still tightly closed, Mrs Daniels, so the child has not miscarried.' He patted her leg. 'Pop your clothes back on and then come and tell me all about it.'

'Now,' he said, laying his arms on the desk as she returned. 'What makes you think the baby has died?'

'A woman knows some things, Doctor.'

'I see.' He did not disbelieve her. He had heard of such cases. 'Well, there is no movement, but then I wouldn't be able to feel any at this stage. You are about ten weeks' pregnant, I would say. The baby wouldn't start moving until eighteen weeks, and we can't hear any heartbeat as yet. But, Mrs Daniels, I cannot abort it for you. It's against the law, there's no medical reason why it should be done. You're a married woman, and . . . .'

'The child is already dead, Dr Redfield. Why won't you believe me?' Her voice started to rise hysterically.

'Have you been to the hospital? I could consult with them.'

'No! They don't believe me either. I know it, though. And my husband beats me. Isn't that reason enough? He'll kill me, Doctor. He's already killed the baby!' She broke into uncon-

trolled sobbing. 'He hates it. I can't have it. He's already threatened to do me in. You've seen the bruises. It'll be me neck next.'

Charles sat by as she cried loudly, waiting for her sobs to
subside. He had seen the bruises. They were quite extensive on
her legs and arms. He wondered about the baby. Maybe it *was*
dead but then it would spontaneously abort. There was no reason to perform it. The hospital had obviously agreed. Yet the
woman was quite hysterical, unbalanced even. And terrified of
her bullying husband. Who knows what the man might do to
her were he to let her go home again, unaided? Charles pon-
dered the problem.

The sobs died again. 'He's beat the baby to death, Doctor. I
know,' she repeated again.

'Now, Mrs Daniels. Maybe you're just upset, that's why—'

'No. I feel *different*, that's it. You know.' She sniffed into her
handkerchief.

She could be imagining things, and for anyone to perform the
abortion would not only be unethical, it would be against the
law. Charles felt very deeply for the girl in her piteous state.
He knew what the high and mighty doctors at the hospital were
like. They never gave a thought to depression and mental despair. Also in his mind was his own sister, Jessamy, going
through her long pregnancy never knowing who the father was
and unable to seek help. Her lack of knowledge had affected her
badly: by the time she had had the children her mental balance
was gone. Also flitting through his mind was a picture of the
young village girl, helpless because she had been raped, helpless
because of society's dictates. Dr Biddy could have done nothing
for her. A village doctor knew everything and yet was powerless
to discuss it. He had to keep it all in his heart and mind. Charles
made a decision. He would help this girl somehow, for the sake
of others like her.

'Mrs Daniels,' he said. 'Do your parents live close by?'

She sniffed loudly and looked up at him. She was shaking
now with the relief of crying, her thin body tremulous. 'Yes.
They live down the road, in Foxhall Minster.'

'Are you close to them? Could you go and stay with them for
a few days?'

Her eyes were bleak. 'Yes. They hate Brian, my husband.
Said I never should have married him.'

'Good. Well, I just want you to relax. Now, you may be right.
I don't dispute that mothers know more than anyone else about

their babies,' he said, stretching out a hand to her. 'But equally, your depressed state and your husband's attacks may be leading you to imagine your baby is dead. I know,' he said against her protest, 'but, the baby may be fine.'

'I'm going to lose it, I know.'

'All right, but . . .'

'He'll kill it inside or outside the womb, I'm telling you. One more beating.' She shook and clutched her arms to herself. The words spilled out of her, burbling and monotonous. 'I can't be responsible for what will happen. As long as I've got that child he'll be after me . . . He thinks it's to blame for everything, no money, no food . . . He hates it and he hates me. Please, help me, get rid of it. I'm going to go crazy. I know . . . I know it's dying . . . You don't know him, he's like a Jekyll and Hyde. As long as it's alive he'll be after me. Everyone in the village thinks he's a charmer, but he's a brute. He thinks it's someone else's, that's what.'

'And it's not.'

'No.' She looked at him sideways. 'It's not.'

Charles scratched his face. She probably wouldn't tell him if it was.

'Go and stay with your mother,' he said, 'away from the husband for a few days. Try to calm yourself and then see how you feel. Here's my number.' He scribbled the number of Fox-hall on a piece of paper. 'Call me if you really feel the need,' he added, handing it over, hardly sure that what he was doing was right, but instinctively knowing it was something for her; a lifeline. 'I'll see you straight away. Maybe get you into the hospital. All right? But try this first. Stay with your parents for a week. Tell your husband your mother's ill, or something; any excuse, will you?'

'All right, Doctor.' She seemed flat and lifeless as she stuffed the paper into her bag. She stood up and walked from the room, weighed down by her agony.

Charles wrote up her notes. He looked at the next name on the pile. He sighed. It was hard work being a doctor. There were some things on which one had to make decisions with which no one would help. David Biddy had warned him—to trust his instincts. The hospital had already turned her down as naturally they would. Again David had been right: half of a country doctor's practice was the emotional and psychological side. Charles now had to make the decision as to whether that would be damaged by the continuation of the pregnancy. He would discuss it with one of the consultants, perhaps Mr Burrows, after surgery. The girl would have the weekend to relax with her mother. It would probably be all right, he told himself as he pulled the new notes towards him, but then, no. Something told him it would not.

He rang through for the next patient.

The old woman shuffled through the door. Charles stood up. He raised his voice.

'And how are we today, Mrs Field?'

'Oh, not so good, Doctor. Me liver's playing me up something awful.' She sat heavily in the chair.

She was a heavy drinker and smoker and would not admit it. Mrs Field was a moaner. She wasted time like nobody else did. He put on his professional smile and prepared himself. A doctor could never send anyone away. He tried to forget the unhappy face of the girl before him, but strangely it was printed on his mind. They all affected him. He was never immune. It would not fade.

The wheels of the car squealed on the corners as Max gunned it up the slope towards the house. The road was wrought open in places, but he thrust the car forward, twisting round the bulges and breaks in the road.

Ahead, he could see the police car already parked across the road. A red convertible was crushed against a tree. A tall blonde woman was being helped to her feet.

Max brought the car to a halt.

'Move that damn car!' he yelled.

The policeman came across. 'Now hold on one minute, buddy. You can't go up there. It's much too dangerous.' He put out a hand.

'God damn it!' shouted Max out of the window. 'My wife's up there!'

The woman looked at him. 'My God, Max! Melanie! I just left her at the house with Jimmy!' She looked wildly up the hill. The cracks ran in great zig-zags through the cliffs above. The road was bent out of shape, impassable. Where houses had once stood there were now mounds of smoking rubble.

Max gritted his teeth and leaped from the car, pushing past the policeman. He started running up the slope.

'Hey, you!' The policeman called after him. 'It's too dangerous. The whole place is about to collapse! Come back here!'

Terry stared at him, the blood coursing down her face.

'Go after him, you damn fool. He's going to need help!'

She pushed at his shoulder. The policeman gave her a quick
look, then looked away at the departing and desperate man. He
started to run up the slope.

Terry sat down on the road, her hand to her head. The ambulance was already on its way up the hill.

There was nothing left. It was like a bundle of matchsticks.
Max stopped as he reached the crest, the sight hitting him like
a hammer blow. Then he began to run again.

He reached the side of where the house used to stand. He
started to slide down the slope towards the front. Melanie must
have tried to escape by the deck.

The deck yawned hideously over the cliff. The roof of the
house had collapsed over part of it. His eyes searched vainly for
a sight of her and Jim. Carefully, he lifted himself onto the edge
of the deck.

He felt as if the skin had been peeled from his eyes. He saw
a leg sticking out from the mound of rubble. He crawled forward, and started to claw at the slates and stones that had tumbled from the roof onto their bodies. Little Jim. His tiny foot
came clear, tucked beneath his mother's body. Max pulled desperately at the stones, feeling the groaning of the timber beneath
him.

The policeman scrambled down the slope behind him.

'Is she OK? I'm coming up!'

'Stay down there!' Max shouted through his teeth. 'The deck's
giving way. It's only strong enough for me!'

He threw the stones over the edge. Melanie's body came free.
Her arms were streaked with blood, her hair matted with it. She
lay quiet and still. And lifeless. Beneath her, cradled protectively in her arms was their boy, his leg caught between the
boards. She still held his head to her breast, her mouth open as
if in pain, as Max pried the boy's foot from the broken boards.

It came free easily. Jim lay against her, his baby face as if
asleep. He gathered them into his arms.

'Oh, Melly, no!'

Her head fell back in his arms. He kissed her and held her,
the tears streaming. Her legs lay draped over his arm, Jim against

her breast, his temple gashed and covered with blood. He buried his face against them and wept.

From behind came the howl of the ambulance. There was the sound of feet scrambling down the slope. A hand reached out to draw him back. Max felt himself being pulled into waiting arms, Melanie and Jim sliding from him.

Jim's baseball cap fell from his hand as his body was recovered. His head lolled against his mother. Max bent down to the earth and retrieved it. He sat down slowly on the step, sobbing as he clutched the cap between his hands. Without a word, the policeman sat on the step and put his arm around the man's shoulders. He stayed there until the sobbing ceased.

The ambulance men had laid her down on the ground. The two men checked her over.

'I'm sorry, sir.' Their voices said it all.

Max knelt forward on the tarpaulin and gathered Melanie's broken body into his arms. He cradled her against him. The sunset filled the sky, the sunset that Melanie had loved. He knew then how much she meant to him, how much he had come to rely on her and love her for her sweetness, patience and loyalty. Now it was too late. Melanie was gone. The darkness drew in around him and he neither knew nor cared. The tears ran down his cheeks. The men left him alone. The boy lay on the tarpaulin between them.

The call came an hour after surgery. Her voice sounded desperate. Charles dressed himself hurriedly and went straight to her home.

The girl was in terrible pain. Her husband had beaten her up again and walked out. Her face was a mass of bruises. She was experiencing severe cramps and bleeding and she could not move.

Charles knew then that he had to save her life. There was no time to get her to the hospital.

An inner sense told him that it was dangerous, not only for him, but for her, but he did not heed it.

He listened for the baby's heartbeat. He could hear nothing, feel no movement. He examined her gently. She was almost certainly about to abort spontaneously. There simply was no choice. He could not turn her away; he had to help her.

He made her as comfortable as he possibly could and then

while the water was boiling he called both doctors in the adjoining villages. Both were engaged on the telephone.

'Damn,' he said. The hospital was too far away to get there in time. He lifted the telephone once again and called the ambulance.

'Get here quickly,' he said. 'She's aborting.'

He slammed down the telephone and went to work, making his preparations quickly, sterilising his instruments, gathering the boiling water and towels. They were alone in the small dirty cottage. There was no one else to see or to help. The girl might die if he did not act immediately.

He laid her out on the kitchen table, as hygienic a place as he could find, the bright bulb shining down on her from the ceiling.

It was over in minutes. He had worked fast. The foetus was dead. He could not have taken the chance of internal bleeding; he had been right to do what he had done. Charles breathed a sigh of relief.

He stood back, then washed his hands in the bowl and dried them. The girl had fallen into a deep drug-induced sleep. He was pleased to see a healthy flush return to her cheeks. Charles, the doctor, did not think about what this would mean when the next doctor examined the foetus. There was no one but him to say whether it had died before, or after, the operation. Charles thought of his patient: she would be all right now.

The ambulance clanged down the high street of Foxhall Green.

Up on the side of the hill there was a sudden quickening of interest. The policeman looked down into the boy's face. He pressed his ear to the tiny chest.

A hand was touching Max's shoulder. Gently, urgently. Max's face was buried in her, his arms holding the dips and swells, the curves that were Melanie. She still smelled good to him.

'Mr Bennett. Mr Bennett . . .'

He dragged himself back to the surface.

'Mr Bennett . . . your boy . . . *he's alive* . . .'

THIRTY-SIX

Frederick held her hand as they sat together on the bench.

'My poor Katherine. It's a tragic loss.'

She was very still. The weeks had passed now, dulling the pain, but not lessening the ache. She had so loved her daughter, her only child.

'We're moving away, Frederick. I came to tell you. Henry's selling Menderley. Neither of us can stand to live there now.'

He let her words sink in. Katherine had been there all his life. He felt the void of his future without her.

'Where to?'

She shrugged. 'Oh, I don't know.' She looked down at his hand, running a finger over it. 'Anywhere, far enough away from the memories. He says he can't stand it, he can hear her voice everywhere . . .' Her voice trailed off, the sob caught in her throat. 'Oh, Freddie. You can't imagine what it's like.'

'I can, my darling, I can.' He drew her head to his shoulder. 'You've got a grandchild though, you know.'

She sat up again, her eyes quickly looking towards the house. Even now it mattered if anyone saw them together. Frederick felt the pang of that look.

'I know,' she said, answering him. 'But Henry doesn't want to know him. He adored that girl. He takes it personally against Max. He says he'll ruin him one day.'

'But it's not his fault. I hear he rushed to save her.'

'Why wasn't he with her?' Her tear-filled eyes looked at him.

Frederick lifted his hand. 'We're not always at the side of the ones we love.'

She sniffed, clearing her head. Her eyes did not leave him.
'Like us, Freddie. We've been more apart than together.' She
paused. 'Why did you never ask me to leave him?' she said in
a small voice. 'Tell me, now I'm going. I would have, you know.'
'Yes.' He looked down at their hands. 'I know.'
'Then, why? Because of our ages?'
'No.' He held her hand tighter. 'Of course not.' He looked
away and back to the statue.
She looked too. And back to his face. 'It's all right. You don't
need to answer. I know the answer, Freddie. You loved some-
body else.'
His silence was answer enough. He did not want to hurt her,
but she knew the truth anyway. He did not love her enough to
break open a marriage for the two of them. Not that much; only
enough to be lifetime lovers. It seemed incongruous. Her eyes
said so as she looked finally at his face.
'It's the last time we'll see each other, Freddie.'
'You're going so soon?' He looked up quickly.
She nodded. 'I came to say so. We're leaving tomorrow.'
He held her hand to his lips. 'Katherine . . .'
She let him hold her hand for a moment. 'That's why I came
here to tell you. It's colder, easier.' Her eyes swept back to the
watching house. 'I can go more swiftly.' Her eyes kissed him as
she stood.
'Goodbye, Freddie.'
Frederick went back inside the house after a while. His heart
was heavy, his head full of thoughts of her, memories. He
crossed the hall towards the drawing room.
He did not see her at first. She turned from the window.
'Caroline! I didn't see you there.'
The blue eyes were alive. They looked into him as they had
not done in years. Frederick looked at her, feeling their message, and then his gaze swept towards the window. It had a clear
view of the bench. He looked back at her.
'You were watching us?'
She nodded. He crossed the room and joined her at the window, looking out at the empty bench. They were old now, strong
emotions spent. They felt the lack of demands that age had
brought to them and the close proximity of years. Still, he re-
tained a glow of fondness for her. Caroline in her fifties was an
elegant, silver-haired woman.
She stood by his side, looking out.

'I knew, you know. All along.'

'Did you?' He was surprised. He had thought her so wrapped up in her private world.

She nodded again. 'I used to see you ride off,' she smiled wanly. 'I knew where you were going. I must say, I was a little jealous.' She smiled again, but did not look at him. Her eyes caught at the memory.

He looked at her profile. Surely she did not mean she was jealous of Katherine? He did not know what to say. All these years? Had he been wrong? Had she wanted him?

'We all need someone,' she said at last. 'I was alone so much.'

'Did Rupert know?' he asked.

'Oh, no.' There was a soft laugh in her voice. 'With Rupert, it's all a front. He doesn't see what's under his very nose.' Her voice was pained. 'He convinces the parishioners, although even that's gone by the board now. He never convinced us though, did he?' She turned towards him. Her pale crystal eyes showed her hurt.

'Caroline,' he said, hurting too as he looked and saw, knowing she was showing him now the grief she had held back so proudly all this time. 'Why did you stay with him?'

Her eyes dropped and then rose again to his with terrible slowness. She seemed to hesitate, and then a sad smile crossed her lips.

'I don't know, Freddie. Perhaps it's our duty to stay as women . . . and mothers. Why didn't Katherine leave Henry?' She shrugged her slender shoulders, her eyes on the distant fields. 'At least she had a reason. I had none.' She looked at him then, her chin held high. Her eyes held his meaningfully. 'Perhaps I had nowhere to go.'

The years slipped away as she spoke. She remembered that sense of commitment to him, and then the dutiful daughter had married the other brother, the heir. The wedding night had destroyed her dreams. That was when she had chosen to be the Lady of the Manor. She had looked to Frederick, suddenly aware of his sensuality and his kindness but it had been too late. Not averse to using him then, for she had resented him for letting her go. She remembered that resentment one last time.

'You were too slow, Frederick,' she said. 'Too slow.'

The beauty that was Caroline was there for just a brief moment and then it was gone, the vague expression reappearing. As if she no longer saw him, she walked alone from the room.

Frederick sank to the sofa. He knew two things: exactly what she meant, and how right Katherine had been. Had he been free, would she, Caroline, have loved him all these years? Now it was too late and he had lost them both.

He held his head in his hands.

July, 1949

Oliver Lanyon's chambers were Elizabethan and ancient. His rooms were at the top of a flight of crooked wooden stairs. He was seated beyond a huge desk groaning with briefs tied in faded pink ribbon. The tiny room had an eave window looking out over a sloping roof to the square below. The heavy black door was so low that Charles had to bend his head. Yellowed paint was thick and glossy on walls braced with black beams. A threadbare rug was thrown in the middle of the stained oak floor and two hardback chairs faced his desk. An electric fire stood in one corner of the room, and a wig rested on a sideboard among a stack of paperwork.

Oliver looked him over. It was the day before the trial; they were meeting for the last time to go over the details once again. He looked at the sheaf of papers in his hand.

'Now we haven't much time,' he said. 'So we'll just go over the facts once more. You have been charged under the Offences Against the Person Act, 1861, section 58, with unlawfully procuring the abortion of this girl, Evie Daniels. Did you do that?'

Charles nodded. 'Yes, I did. But with the best of intentions. As you will see from my affidavit . . .'

'Yes, yes. Well, we will have to see what we can do about getting you off. But first, let me tell you what to expect. If the charge sticks, you will be struck off as a doctor. You will cease to be on the roll of doctors. The offence of procuring an abortion which is a specific offence is punishable with a maximum of five years' imprisonment. The chances are notwithstanding a good plea of mitigation and all the background concern for your patient, et cetera, et cetera, that you would probably receive a sentence of six months in prison minimum if found guilty. Clear so far?' He hitched his black gown higher on his shoulders and peered at Charles.

'Yes.'

'Now the prosecution has to prove beyond reasonable doubt

that the operation was not performed in good faith for preserving the life of the girl. You did not have to wait until the girl was in peril of immediate death, but it was your duty to perform the operation if, on reasonable grounds and with adequate knowledge, you were of the opinion that the probable consequence of the continuance of the pregnancy would be to make the patient a physical and mental wreck. Is that what you thought, Dr Redfield?'

'Yes. Well, as a matter of fact I thought the child was probably already dead as well.' His mind dwelt on Melanie. He was hardly concerned with what was happening to him. He had attended her funeral, her body flown home for an English burial. He had seen Max and their son standing at the side of the grave. He could not forget the man's face, nor the way Henry Haslett had spurned him as he passed him by. The man's voice droned on in front of him. *Melanie*.

'The case is to be held at what we call the Assize Courts, Central Criminal Court, Old Bailey and in front of a High Court judge in Number One Court in that building. All right, Dr Redfield, let's go down and see what we can make of you.' He stood up, grabbed his wig from the sideboard and ushered Charles out of the room.

They were all assembled outside the courtroom waiting for him.

He saw the girl with some surprise. She was standing beside John Moreland, his solicitor.

John Moreland was a pompous man and loved the prestige of being seen with a bright and pretty woman. It gave him a colourful dash. Sarah Harvey-Smith was far smarter than he gave her credit for.

Charles and Oliver walked down the wide hallway towards them. John Moreland raised his arm.

'Oliver. Glad you're here. Hello, Charles.' He put a bearlike arm around the counsel's shoulders. 'Christ, can you believe it, the case is running late. I've got to leave. Will you manage, old boy? Only formalities at first, of course. Mrs Harvey-Smith'll stay with the file of the case. If you need any information as to the circumstances she can give it to you.'

'That's perfectly all right, John.' He stood erect, his own file under his arm, his gown thrown back over his shoulders. 'I'm sure we'll manage without you.'

'Good man.' He clapped him on the shoulder. 'Charles,' he said turning, 'this is Sarah Harvey-Smith, my outdoor clerk.'

The girl exchanged a smile with him. Her blonde hair was pulled back off her face into a neat bun. She was slender and pretty and her eyes were very observant. Her smile was confident. Charles liked her immediately. He held out his hand.

'How do you do?'

'I have to be off somewhere else, old chap,' said the solicitor. 'Got a bit of a heavy schedule, I'm afraid. This case running late has screwed things up a bit. Not to worry though, Mrs Harvey-Smith will let me know exactly what happens. She'll take care of things until I get back. That all right with you?'

'Perfectly.' He hardly cared. At least the ordeal of the court case had been numbed by the tragic news about the girl he had loved for so long. Against his word now was the word of the sanctimonious hospital doctors who said that the child was definitely alive when they had examined its mother and that it could only have been killed during the abortion. Charles was in deep trouble.

He sat down on the bench, as the legal brains all discussed his case a foot away from him. His thoughts were of Melanie.

The girl bent down to look into his face. 'The case is being called, Dr Redfield,' she said with a kind smile. 'Shall we go?'

Charles preceded her into the courtroom.

'All rise.'

The case was going badly.

They had filed back in for the afternoon session. The girl had been the first witness. She had been led weeping into court, almost incoherent, a terrible blow for Charles. And the husband had stood in the witness box, distraught by the loss of his offspring, protesting his absolute love for his wife.

Oliver Lanyon stood before him.

'Dr Redfield, tell the court, please, in your own words, what happened after Mrs Daniels first came to see you.'

Charles stood in the dock. He rested his hands together in front of him.

'I consulted with Mr Burrows, a consultant at the Highfield Hospital. In cases of this sort no doctor would venture to act except after consulting some other member of the profession of high standing, so as to confirm his view that the circumstances were such that an operation ought to be performed and that the act was legal. I fully believe that now, and I did then. No members of the medical profession would ever lend themselves to the malpractices of professional abortionists. Our job is to save lives wherever possible.'

'Very commendable.' His counsel rocked on his heels. 'I accept that your evidence is a frank statement of what actually passed through your mind. And what did you decide, with Mr Burrows?'

Charles cleared his throat. 'That in view of the mental state of the girl, and the fact that she was severely bruised physically, and patently terrified of her husband, the abortion should go ahead.'

'Thank you, Dr Redfield. Your witness.'

Sir William Castlemore, KC came forward for the prosecution. His walk was slow and measured. He was a tall, elegant man, a ladies' man in many ways, and a performer.

He turned briefly to the assembled courtroom. Then he looked back to Charles, his manner friendly.

'Dr Redfield. Members of the jury. I would like you to take a look at the witness, Mrs Evie Daniels.' Everybody looked at her. By now, Evie Daniels, impressed by the novelty of a courtroom and the attention that she and her husband were receiving from not only the case but the publicity surrounding it, was recovering fast. She smiled tentatively and held her husband's hand. She had told the press she was staying with him now; she loved him, always had. They had the basic love of two people, whatever might or might not have happened. As the eyes of the court were turned upon them, she looked down shyly and saw the soft woven cornflower-blue wool of her new suit. She moved her legs, seeing how its elegance showed off their shape. In Brian's face was a look of proud admiration for his wife; her newly-blonde hair was puffed into a neat perm and fresh make-up, though a little garish, was painted onto her face and lips. A marcasite brooch was clipped to one lapel, and a frilled white cotton shirt framed her pert little face. It may have been true that on the witness stand she had become a little distraught, but it was with grief, not hysterics. She had wanted Brian to know that and had told him over a hot lunch across the street from the Old Bailey. She had not refrained from saying it in quite a loud voice as the press sat down at the next table and listened avidly.

William Castlemore looked satisfied with his client. His eyes took in the husband's possessive arm around her as he turned back towards the jury. His eyes were sharp as an eagle's. They were still looking at the radiant Evie Daniels.

Sir William addressed Charles. 'To me, Mrs Daniels looks the picture of health,' he began. 'But even if she were not—and as you have told us you consulted with your colleague, Mr Burrows, who provisionally agreed with your diagnosis, albeit on the telephone—why may I ask was this deed performed at Mrs Daniels's home, Dr Redfield, and not the hospital?'

'Mrs Daniels rang me at home. She was desperate. I went to her house. Her husband had beaten her up quite severely and she was incapable of moving. I telephoned for an ambulance and performed the operation.'

'You could surely have waited? At least until the ambulance came?'

'I did not think so. I used my judgement as I saw it at the time.'

Sir William smiled at him. 'Your judgement? Well, we've established what *your* judgement is, Dr Redfield. We have here a petition signed by the villagers of Foxhall Green and brought to the court.' He held up the list of names. 'All of these good men and women are standing outside the court, laying claim to the virtue of Dr Charles Redfield.' Charles wondered at his line of argument. So did the rest of the room. They listened intently. 'Character witnesses to his impeccable record both in civilian life and during the war,' he went on. 'We know how popular Dr Redfield is in his community. In his practice. And I do not doubt it . . .' Now he paused, and his voice became sibilant. 'But,' he said regretfully, 'it only serves to emphasise what I said earlier. He acted from compassion, a quality that is very much a part of his nature and not from the coldly detached view of the law, and that is what we are here to judge. Not whether Dr Redfield is a nice man. Did he act according to the law of the land? I think not. The law of the land holds human life to be sacred and the protection that the law gives to human life it extends also to the unborn child in the womb, and that must not be destroyed unless the destruction of that child is for the purpose of preserving the yet more precious life of the mother. Am I not right, Dr Redfield?'

'Yes and no, I . . .'

'I suggest to you, Dr Redfield, that there is a perfectly

clear line of distinction between danger to health and danger to life . . .'

'I cannot agree without qualifying it,' Charles argued. He would not be pushed into a defensive answer when compassion was involved. 'I cannot say just yes or no. I can say that there is a large group whose health may be damaged, but whose life almost certainly will not be sacrificed. There is another group at the other end whose life will definitely be in very great danger. There is a large body of material between those two extremes in which it is not really possible to say how far life will be in danger, but we find, of course, that the health is depressed to such an extent that life is shortened, such as in cardiac cases, so that you may say their life is in danger, because death might occur within measurable distance of the time of their labour. This is what I felt in this particular case.' He looked the man straight in the eye. '*And* I believed, rightly, that the foetus was already dead.'

The prosecutor tipped his head to one side and nodded. He lifted his black gown more comfortably onto his shoulders and seemed to think for a moment. He turned back to Charles.

'And yet Mr Freemantle, the hospital surgeon, has already told us that in his opinion the child was definitely alive when he examined the mother with his associates, and that it was only killed during the abortion. He told us that Mrs Daniels was merely a highly strung and imaginative girl, and those are no grounds to destroy the life of a child as yet unborn. Life, Dr Redfield, even in the womb, is held to be sacred. That is all.'

Charles winced. His heart sank. It seemed to be going so badly. He had performed the abortion with the best of intentions and the child had been dead. It was his word against everybody else's. His greatest mistake was not the actual performing of the operation but the fact that he did it alone, and there had been only himself and her to see what had happened. The dead foetus was endangering her life. There had been no time to lose. It was their word the jury had to believe and as a witness she was hopeless. She was incoherent, and terrified of admitting the truth in front of her husband.

He stepped down from the witness box. Beside John Moreland, Sarah sat watching him. She gave him a quick smile as he glanced in their direction. It helped.

* * *

Charles was sitting on the bench outside. He was thinking about it all, how it would turn out. The only good thing about it so far was that his good reputation had won him the allowance to be out on bail. He saw at that moment, walking into his field of vision, the solicitor's clerk, Sarah Harvey-Smith, coming towards him, her gown billowing out around her. He stood up, suddenly forgetting the dark thoughts that had preceded those that he felt now. He knew what he wanted in that moment.

'Hello!'

Sarah smiled. He remembered that smile. She was a strong and sympathetic woman whom he had begun to think of as a friend.

'Hello,' she said. 'Are you all alone?'

'Not now. Would you care to have lunch?'

The smile stayed in her eyes as she held the files to her chest. 'I'd love to. But we haven't long. There's a snack place across the street that we all use. Would that suit you?'

'Sounds fine to me.'

'Come along then. I'll show you.'

The lunch bar was crowded. They squeezed into a warm, smoky corner and sat down. Sarah settled herself into the seat, her files stowed away beside her. They ordered quickly—sandwiches and coffee. That they were together was more important.

The food arrived quickly. Sarah picked up her sandwich. 'Well, how are you bearing up?'

Her eyes were more than sympathetic. She could hardly hide her warmth for him. Neither of them had revealed their feelings to each other; it had not been the time or the place. But it had been there in so many looks and gestures.

'I'm fine. A lot of it is thanks to you,' he told her.

'Your truth will win through, Dr Redfield,' she said. 'I'm sure the jury knows that you did it with the best of intentions. I believe in you.'

'I'm glad. You seem to be the only one who does.' He gave a self-deprecating laugh. 'I wish I could have given you a chance to represent me.'

She stretched out a pair of neat legs, crossing them at the ankles. 'It'll never happen,' she said ruefully. 'In a male orientated world I am looked upon as merely a female, not as a potential lawyer. They'd never give me a big case were I even to qualify.'

'Really. I can't believe the odds are stacked up that highly against you, are they?' He was interested.

'Yes. There are so few women engaged in crime, and none concerned with criminal practice. There's only one female barrister,' she said looking at him with the clear brown eyes. 'Maybe one day. But the odds *are* against me. It's pretty rare for a woman even to be considered. Men aren't keen for us to hop on the bandwagon and show we could be as good as they are. The male bastions are well preserved!'

'Well, I would,' he said. She looked at him. 'Hire you,' he added, his eyes warming to her face so close to his. 'Next time I need someone.'

'Let's hope there won't be one!' She laughed lightly to cover her emotion. She realised that even in the midst of his own misfortune he was thinking of someone else. She had come down to comfort him, and he had ended up drawing the conversation to her. His caring nature wanted to give everybody an equal chance without judgement. It was that trait that had brought him into this situation. He did not think, like so many did, that there was one law for the rich and one for the poor. He did what he thought was right without judgement. She would have brought that out in court. She hoped Lanyon would too.

She looked at him to find him watching her with a peculiarly intent expression on his face. She must have looked startled, because he laughed as if she had caught him.

Sarah smiled broadly; it lit her eyes.

'That's better,' he said. 'I haven't seen you like that. Tell me,' he added after a pause in which his eyes had followed the lines of her happy face. 'John called you Mrs Harvey-Smith . . . Are you married?' His eyes had swept quickly over the finger of her left hand where no wedding ring was present.

Sarah stroked her fingers against each other. 'I was. I'm divorced.'

'Oh, I see. I'm sorry.'

'I'm also Jewish,' she said almost defiantly. 'By extraction.'

'Not choice?' he asked mildly.

'That too. Well, will you judge me?'

He laughed and leaned back in his seat. 'No! Should I?' He signalled for the bill.

Sarah toyed with her coffee, embarrassed now by her outburst. Of course he wouldn't have. 'Others have,' she said, her voice trailing away with the thought.

Charles leaned forward again. His eyes on her were warm, as were his hands as he took hers and held them, filling her with his confidence. 'Not me.'

She looked up to see the truth in his eyes. A quick and failed marriage had given her her Gentile name. Now she was working to make ends meet, for her own peace of mind, and for another small person.

'I have a daughter,' she said, suddenly wanting to confide everything in this very special man. 'Leah. Perhaps you would like to meet her.' Her eyes, glowing with need, met his.

The bill arrived. Charles withdrew his hands gently.

'I would,' he said, and smiled.

Sarah breathed deeply and leaned back against her chair. Her eyes studied him as he bent to write out the cheque. Now she believed he would be in her future and for the first time in years it looked wonderful.

'You look just like Max did at your age.'

Dickie laid a hand on Jim's head. The boy twisted away, and ran into the garden.

Dickie looked after him for a moment. Out on the lawn he picked up a small toy fork and started digging it relentlessly into the plot of earth that Max had given him as his garden. The earth flew everywhere, his motions erratic.

Dickie screwed round again in her chair. She looked at Max across the dining-room table. 'He's disturbed by it, isn't he, Max?'

'Yes.' Max watched him. 'But he's got to snap out of it. It's months ago now. We've got to make a new start. Without her.'

He was silent, staring at his hands as they lay before him on the polished oak. Dickie threw a look at Bill, sitting quietly at the other side of the table. The French windows were open to the summer breeze.

'Max,' she said quietly. 'You have to do something about it first.'

He looked up and met her eyes with silent hostility.

'The boy looks to you for guidance. Look at you,' she said, palming her hands open. 'You're so damn guilty, it's ridiculous, Max. There was nothing you could have done. Nothing you can do. You were blameless. Now, the best thing you can do is to get your life squared up again. Throw yourself back into the business, and eventually find a new mother for Jim. Yes,' she raised her hand, her eyes closing briefly, 'he needs a mother. It's no good you two living down here at Home Farm, isolated in the valley. You need a good family house, a nanny, and a wife. That's my recommendation.' She reached across the table and pulled some documents towards her. 'Now, the work I can do something about. The other you'll have to take care of yourself.' Her manner was brusque. 'You know we've been taking part in the Berlin airlift?'

Max raised his head again, the hostility dying and the bleak pain that had been there now since her death, reappearing. He nodded. 'Yes.'

'Well,' she said, pushing the documents towards him, 'it's given us the opportunity to make heavy use of our planes, plus enabling us to sell our remaining DC-3s and -4s. We've been doing very well by assisting the military in this crisis.' She tapped the paperwork. 'Read that. It's the latest breakdown on company finances. I think you'll find it impressive.' She checked her watch. 'Tomorrow I was going to do the run myself but I've changed my mind.' She nodded towards him. 'I want you to take the helm for a bit, Max. You are going to do it. They need all the help they can get, and we're going to be a part of it. You'll see what's involved when you read through those. All the supplies are provided, ready and waiting. All you've got to do is fly.'

She pushed back her chair, her eyes as watchful as a cat's. Max had started reading. He broke away and looked up at her.

'What about Jim?'

Jim was now occupied in stalking one of the farm cats. The cat turned and eyed him from the corner of the shed. She had kittens inside. She was ready to fight.

'We're spending a few days next week at the coast house in Bournemouth. Jim would enjoy the sea. We'll take him with us.' She looked at Bill. His face was whimsical. It was the first he had heard of a holiday.

'Sure,' he said. 'Great idea. Kid obviously likes playing in the sand. I'll take him fishing like I did when you were a boy.'

Max shrugged. 'OK. Then I'll do it.'

Dickie stood up. 'I thought you would. Take one or two of

the other pilots. As many as you need. Come round in the morning with Jim. Good night, Max.'

'Good night.' He kissed her cheek, shook Bill's hand.

They went out into the garden. 'Goodbye, Jim. See you in the morning.'

The boy hardly noticed them. He wanted them to go so that he could chase the black cat and see her kittens mewing.

'Jim, say goodbye to your grandmother.'

He sulked to attention. 'Goodbye, Granny.'

He held out his hand to her. Max stood behind him, his hands on his son's shoulders. Together, the two of them stood as Dickie and Bill made their way back across the fields. They turned, halfway up. Max had gone back inside the house; the little boy was back by the shed.

A worried look crossed Bill's face.

'Careful you don't push him too hard, Dickie. If he gets work under his skin again, the boy might suffer for it.'

Dickie started to climb again. 'Boy'll be OK. Work's good for Max. He needs to get over it all. He's got a lot to forget. They need to grow together. That's why he needs a mother for the child.'

Bill shook his head as he paced up the hill beside her. He remembered the many days that Max had disappeared after Melanie's death; the months when he had practically ignored Jim. Bill worried for the boy.

'He's hard on him,' he said.

Dickie kept on walking to the crest of the hill. 'He's his father.'

The judge leaned forward and stared at the room.

'Members of the jury,' he began. 'Now that you have heard all the evidence and the speeches of counsel, it becomes my duty to sum up the case to you and to give you the necessary directions in law, and then it will be for you to consider the facts in relation to the law as laid down by me, and, after consideration, to deliver your verdict. You no doubt are aware that under our system for the administration of justice, in a trial by jury it is for the judge to give directions to the jury upon matters of law, and it is for the jury to determine the facts. The jury, and the jury alone, are the judges of the facts in the case.

'The charge against Dr Redfield is the very grave charge un-

der the Offences Against the Person Act, 1861, section 58, that
he unlawfully procured the abortion of the girl who was the first
witness in the case. It is so grave a crime that the punishment
may be penal servitude for life. It is one of those crimes, like
murder, which may only be tried by the judges of the High
Court, and judging by the cases that come before the court, it
is a crime by no means uncommon. This is the second case at
these July sessions at this court where a charge of an offence
against the section has been preferred, and I mention that case
only to show you how different the case now before you is from
the type of case which usually comes before a criminal court.
In that case, a woman without any medical skill or any medical
qualifications did what is alleged against Dr Redfield here; she
unlawfully used an instrument for the purpose of procuring the
miscarriage of a pregnant girl . . .'

The voice droned on over the hush of the courtroom. Charles
drifted away into his own thoughts. Whatever they did to him,
he knew he had been right. The jury would have to decide,
twelve good men and true. He tried not to look at them. He was
unsure whether or not it would prejudice his case. He folded his
arms. Would that make them think he was too at ease? He sighed
inside himself. It sounded as if the old judge was really making
a meal of it, nailing him into place. He listened in again; he had
sensed the intonation change.

'. . . The case here is very different. A man of the highest
skill performs the operation. Whether it was legal or illegal you
will have to determine, but he performs the operation as an act
of charity, without fee or reward, and unquestionably believing
that he was doing the right thing, and that he ought, in the
performance of his duty as a member of a profession devoted to
the alleviation of human suffering, to do it. That is the case that
you have to try today . . .'

Behind Moreland's broad back, Sarah managed a careful
wink. The judge was directing the jury to acquit him. Charles's
hopes picked up. He listened more intently.

The speech came to an end.

'. . . The question that you have got to determine is whether
the Crown has proved to your satisfaction beyond reasonable
doubt that the act which Dr Redfield admittedly did was done
in good faith for the purpose only of preserving the life of the
girl. If the Crown has failed to satisfy you of that, Dr Redfield
is entitled, by the law of this land, to a verdict of acquittal. On

the other hand, if you are satisfied beyond all real doubt that Dr Redfield did not do it in good faith for the purpose only of preserving the life of the girl, your verdict should be a verdict of guilty.'

The jury shuffled out. It seemed an interminable age before they were called back to the court and their foreman stood up to address the room.

'Gentlemen of the jury, how do you find the defendant. Guilty or not guilty?'

The men did not hesitate. 'Guilty, Your Honour.'

Dickie fitted her glasses to her nose and examined the piece of material between her fingers.

The early-morning sunlight was easy on the fine wool. It was a soft check in lilac blue with a thread of green. She held it up against the artwork cards she had propped up on her desk. Against the original Bennett green for the cabin seats it was very pleasing. The new stewardesses' uniforms were in green with lilac trim and starched white pinafores over the top. They had a fresh appearance, one of cleanliness and efficiency, while the pinafores gave the impression of being there to serve.

Dickie replaced the cards on the desk top. She had chosen that green, now termed Bennett green, to remind her of that day in the meadow, when she had seen her first aeroplane: the Canuck biplane, the old Curtiss Jenny. She remembered now how Joe had stood there cleaning the machine ready for flight, and she, young and spontaneous, had climbed in and taken on the greatest thrill of her life. Dickie smiled. She remembered, too, how determined she had been, determined enough to risk the fates of herself and her little boy in a new land with new possibilities, and all to free herself from the shackles of servitude so that one day she would take her revenge on the Redfields from a position of strength.

She had waited, and that moment was now. Now it would begin. She was their equal financially, and socially—marrying into the Haslett family had made them acceptable and Melanie's death had done nothing to change that.

She absorbed her feelings for a moment. It might have been easier to forgive and forget as the years had gone by—years mellowed one, and years of success especially. The lean years hungering for revenge while scraping together a living had made her hate burn like a flame inside her. Bill would say to her that now the years had passed what did it matter, really?

It mattered very much.

The thud of the morning newspaper as it hit the mat in the hall was the sound she had been waiting for. Dickie turned and left the room. She bent to the floor and lifting the rolled newspaper, carried it back into the sitting room.

There, she opened it. The headlines proclaimed the news she was waiting for: LANDOWNER'S SON CONVICTED.

THIRTY-SEVEN

October, 1949

Charles walked out, his bag in his hand. The huge, double, studded doors closed tightly behind him. He heard the thud of the lock, the rattle of the keys. It had been three months. It seemed longer. He was free again.

He saw the car parked beside the road. She looked out and saw him. The smile was there in her eyes.

'Can I give you a lift, stranger?'

He walked over. He put down the bag and leaned his hands on the door. 'Which way are you going?'

'Same way as you!'

He kissed her. Her lips were warm and giving. He needed her so badly, her unquestioning straightforward love.

She smiled again as he drew away. Her voice was very soft.

'I love you.'

'I love you too.'

They held each others' gaze for a moment. 'Get in,' she said. 'Let's get out of this place.'

He went round and threw his bag in the back. He climbed in. She could smell the smell on him, the prison smell. 'Charles. I want to say something to you now that you might not like,' she said, looking at him, 'but I mean it, and have to say it, and you should not be proud and reject it.'

'What?' He held her hand.

'You're no longer a doctor with a practice. You're a man out of prison. Maybe your family will not stand by you.' She remembered his odious father with a protective pang inside her. 'I'm willing to move wherever you want to go and support you until you find your feet. I see no reason why you should kow-tow to your father. I have a little money. I'm behind you all the way. I'd like to help you rebuild your future.'

Charles did not know what to say. His heart was in his eyes, his voice roughened by emotion as he spoke.

'Sarah, you're the sweetest, most wonderful woman a man could have. I shall never forget your offer. I don't reject it out of hand . . . but there is no need for it. I have plenty of money. We can live quite happily. I want *you* to be my family . . .' He paused, looking into her lovely, kind face. 'Sarah, will you do me the honour of becoming my wife?' The tears started into his eyes.

She saw them. Felt her own responding.

'Of course I will. Yes . . . *yes* . . .'

He kissed her.

'That was the hard part,' he said with a sigh of relief and a catch of humour in his voice. His eyes were warm for her. 'The family's going to be easy after that.'

'You're going to be a farmer? Right here in Foxhall Green? Charles, you never cease to amaze me.'

Rupert slammed down his paper and crossed the room. The morning sun filtered in through the long windows of the drawing room and softened the warm polished boards and the colours in the furnishings. It was a mellow, softly textured room, contrasting perfectly with the fine wood carvings. 'After what you've done to us? Every single rag paper in the country made a meal of us. You did countless damage. What do you think my reputation's going to be like in the village with a jailbird for a son? They look up to me to be a pillar of the community. I'll bet the church is full this Sunday, and not for the right reasons either.'

'Rupert,' Frederick said, crossing the room towards Charles. 'Charles did what he thought was right. That's all that matters, really.' He looked at Charles, standing in the window alcove. He looked thin but not defeated by any means. He had always been good on inner fibre. Frederick smiled at him.

'It is *not* all that matters,' said Rupert. 'He's disgraced the family name. I know what these villagers are like, Frederick.

Don't forget I mix with them more than you do. They're ready to condemn. Gossipmongers, all of them. Waiting for hellfire and the Lord's condemnation. All ready to point the finger at their neighbours. Especially us,' he said, rounding on the two of them. 'They'll think he got off lightly because he's one of us, and not one of them. After all, he only got three months. They'll think we bribed the judge.'

'The judge *was* on my side, Father,' Charles interrupted.

'I would have done if I could,' Rupert carried on, ignoring him. 'Every ghoul's going to come out of the closet now. Write us vitriolic letters, I've no doubt.'

Alexander and Sabrine came into the room. They had been riding. They both looked startled. Sabrine was elegant in her jodhpurs with an earthy sensuality about her.

'Hello, Alexander,' said Charles, remembering. 'How's school?'

'All right.' Alexander's reply was noncommittal. He skulked behind his sister.

'Don't stare, Sabrine,' said Rupert gruffly. 'What did you expect? Striped pyjamas and a ball and chain? Shake hands, then go and get changed for dinner.'

She came across. 'Are you back for good now?' Alexander followed, silent and slight in stature. Charles shook his hand and knew he'd been right. Alexander was a bundle of nerves. Sabrine idled, one hip stuck out. She surveyed him with tilted head.

'No,' Charles answered her, his mind on Alexander. 'But I'll be in the village,' he said for the boy's sake, his eyes on him.

'Good.' She smiled, showing even teeth. 'We've missed you. Life's pretty dull around here.' She gave him a long look. 'Who was that who dropped you off here? We saw her from the hill.'

'That was Sarah.' He looked out of the window at the empty driveway. 'And that's the other thing I wanted to tell all of you. We, Sarah and I, are going to be married. I would have told you with her here but she had to attend to something in the village.'

'Congratulations, Charles!' Frederick shook his hand.

Rupert turned, a frown on his face. 'That clerk girl of Moreland's?'

'Yes.' Charles did not rise to the bait. 'I have introduced her to you on more than one occasion.'

'Well, she's certainly not marrying you for your money, any-way,' said his father, turning back towards the fireplace. 'But I want you both out of the village. I don't want the scandal here again.'

'Sorry, Father. We're staying. We're going to buy a house here.'

'You will not. I don't want everybody talking.' Rupert gave him a level look. 'You've already disgraced us enough. You'll move away.'

'No.'

'You've got no money.' Rupert raised an eyebrow at him. 'Thought about that? I'm not going to help you.'

Charles drew in a breath. 'Grandfather's trust.' He looked back at Frederick. 'Plus the money that Uncle Frederick secured in trust for us when we were children.' He looked quickly again at Frederick. Frederick smiled. At least he had salvaged something from his brief inheritance. 'I'm eligible for that now. This year. I won't need any more.'

'Grandfather's trust.' Rupert was irritated; he had wanted to push his nose in it for blackening the family reputation. It was disgraceful.

'Yes,' Charles went on. 'That's where Sarah is at the moment. Finalising the details. We're buying Home Farm.'

He saw all their faces swing towards him. There was shock and pleasure mixed. He looked at his uncle Frederick.

'I thought you'd be pleased. We're buying it back into the family. As it were,' he added sardonically.

Frederick took a step towards him. His hands lifted. 'Well, Charles. This is great news. But how did you manage it? Would they sell to you?'

Charles made a face. 'It's on the open market. I don't see why not. They won't have much use for it now, because . . .'

'Home Farm,' repeated Rupert with delight. 'Bastard's leaving. I knew the pressure would get to them in the end. Upstarts. They could never win, not against us.'

'. . . because I think they've a mind to buy Longbarrow.'

Dickie admired the view from the window of the master bedroom. The house was perfection: thirty rooms of elegant and spacious proportions, the long windows graceful and airy, opening out onto parkland all around. There was an established nursery at the top of the house and servants' quarters below, as well as stabling for six horses and garaging for three cars.

The formal lines of the house were deceptive—it had an air of light informality ingrained into it. Despite its intimidating size, it lent itself to being a family home. George, Earl of Lancing might once have complained about the cost of raising three daughters, but he had kept his family estate intact. There were one thousand acres of meadowland, downs, woodlands and fields, and a mile of trout fishing along the banks of the Thames. The house, where it lay in the palm of the hills, could be seen for miles around. It was as white and fluted and columned as a wedding cake. Longbarrow was magnificent.

'It's a perfectly beautiful estate, Lord Lancing,' said Dickie, rapt pleasure in her voice. 'I'm very interested.'

George Lancing looked at her admiringly. In mid-life, Dickie was a beautiful woman, erect and slender as a boy, her black hair winged with grey and her emerald eyes intensified. She wore her jodhpurs and open-necked shirt with a simplicity of style that he found very attractive. She had made no song and dance about coming over here and trying to impress him. He had heard a lot about this enterprising and dynamic woman, and her equally impressive son, and had looked forward to meeting her. He was not disappointed. George had always had an eye for a pretty girl and this one had a sexuality about her that could have made the right man happy all his life. He had a feeling it was still there, unchallenged and challenging.

What was more, she seemed to him to have a sense of family caring about her. She would be good to the house. It would grow with her and her son's children. George did not want to sell, but he was old and his daughters had all married men who had their own estates. He had no heir to inherit. He and Matilda needed a smaller place to spend the rest of their days in; a place big enough for the children to visit and stay, but not those endless empty rooms. Only the *nouveau riche* could afford those big estates nowadays; it was almost *passé* to own one. Longbarrow needed love and laughter. It needed to be a family home again.

He had made his decision almost as soon as she had climbed the long open staircase beside him. She was the rightful owner now.

'I'm inclined to sell to you, Mrs Latimer,' he said. 'The house would be in good hands, I can see that.'

'Thank you,' she said. The green eyes held his forcefully. She wanted this house more than she could recall wanting anything in her life. It was hers, she lived and breathed it, and it responded to her. Longbarrow had been waiting for her. That was how she felt. It was an uplifting feeling. Still, he had not said yes definitely.

'We'll talk later,' he said. 'I'll get the deeds out for you to have a look at. And I must square it with Matilda, my wife. It's part of her too, you understand.'

'Of course.' She directed all her energy at him. She wanted it.

'I think we'll probably find ourselves in agreement in the end, somehow,' he said.

She looked towards him hearing the note in his voice. The blue eyes twinkled. She let out her breath more easily now, surprised to find as she did so how she had been holding it in. It was as important as that to her. His eyes caught hers, and he smiled too. He understood how the house had affected her; that meant she was right for it. She allowed herself then to imagine waking up to this view of the valley in the early morning.

'We'll take good care of it for you,' she said, almost without thinking of her words.

He joined her at the window. There was warmth in his eyes now as he too looked out.

'I know you will.'

Sarah came slowly down the stairs of the White Horse Hotel. It was the only hotel in Foxhall Green, the place they had chosen to live while waiting for their marriage and the purchase of Home Farm. The offer had been accepted in Sarah's name, a precaution on Charles's part. He remembered his last meeting with Max Bennett. Sarah had handled the purchase. He had had no doubt, however, that the sharp Bennetts had known the identity of the purchaser and did not care, now they had bigger fish to catch. There had been only one proviso: the two fields that crested the hill behind Cobbold's Wood were not for sale.

Now Sarah had received a message from the porter that Mr Rupert Redfield would like a meeting with her. She had dressed carefully, brushed her hair and come downstairs.

He was waiting in the lounge. It was empty. He turned as he saw her.

'Ah!' he said. 'I've ordered coffee.'

She walked towards him slowly, her face puzzled. 'Charles is not here, Mr Redfield. And I don't want any coffee.'

'The coffee doesn't matter and I know about Charles. It's you I want to talk to.' He seemed quite pleasant, though the alien blue eyes were as cold as ever. 'Please sit down.'

She did.

'I'll come straight to the point,' he said, sitting down before her. He laid his cane on the low table between them. 'How much do you want?'

'What?'

'To leave my son alone.' The cold eyes watched her like a snake.

'You are not serious, are you, Mr Redfield?'

'Quite serious.' He smiled confidentially. 'Interested?'

Sarah crossed her legs. She smoothed down her grey tailored skirt and linked her hands together. She rested her elbows on the arms of her chair and looked directly at him.

'Now why would you offer me money to leave him alone?'

The tray of coffee arrived as he was about so speak. He looked up at the waitress, his expression moved somewhere else as he impatiently waited for her to leave. She laid out the cups with precision, handled the white china jugs with care. Eventually she rustled away.

Rupert leaned forward.

'Because,' he said, 'he can live this thing down and make a better marriage than this. In time, the village will forget and so will everybody else and he could marry well. We are the village family. People look up to us here. Charles should marry in his league, quite frankly, Mrs Harvey-Smith; it's better, and I'm sure you know that. The less background problems there are, the more the marriage is likely to work. You understand what I'm talking about, of course.'

Sarah nodded slowly. 'You think he's only marrying me because I was sorry for him at a time he needed it, and he's misunderstood his feelings. A bit like patients feel about nurses in a hospital. That I can only get him because he's down at the moment, is that right? A girl of my . . . class, would normally not have a hope in hell,' she said bluntly. 'That's what you're saying, is it?'

'Something along these lines, yes. Girls of our class don't work, Mrs Harvey-Smith. They marry and have children. They have no aspirations to anything more, indeed, neither do they need it. They are quite content.' His eyes were like flints. 'Now, what do you say? You're a smart girl. Should go far. What about five thousand pounds and a word in the ear of Moreland, the senior partner? I know how much you want to become a solicitor. Charles has told me.' His eyes glittered into a smile.

'Do you know something, Mr Redfield,' she said with wonder in her voice, 'you're even worse than he thinks. And you're quite wrong. I love Charles, and he loves me, genuinely, hard as it might be for you to understand. Now, if you hoped by coming here with your cruel words that you would destroy me, you are quite wrong. I'm not one of your sort of women, you're quite right, kow-towing to your appalling behaviour, and thank God for your son that I am not. I don't need your money, and nor does he. We may not have much, but as they say, we have each other. It's a pity you didn't find such a strength in your own life.'

'Strong words, Mrs Harvey-Smith,' he said heavily, his eyes drilling into her now. 'I hope you don't have to eat them when time goes by and he realises he might have made a mistake. I'm not giving him a penny, and Redfields are not used to penny-pinching. He's always been supported. I don't want my son marrying you, Mrs Harvey-Smith. You're not good enough for him, but I cannot stop you. I can only warn you that you will be ruining his life. If you truly love him, as you say, you will desist from this line of action.'

Sarah found herself glued rigidly to the chair. She was shocked by him. Still, she found the strength to make her thrust. 'Do you know something else?' she said evenly. 'You can't hurt him any more. You always have. But now he's going to have his own family, his own children and a wife who loves him and a new start. As it happens, this whole thing has been the best thing that could have happened. Through the ghastly turmoil of it all he has seen the light, and he would have moved out of Foxhall anyway, and away from you. We've already bought Home Farm together, Mr Redfield. This time, he's ahead of you.'

'Or *you* are,' Rupert said silkily. 'Is that what you're trying to tell me?' He pressed his fingers together and leaned them against his mouth. His eyes were almost caressing in their heat.

'No . . . yes. It doesn't matter,' she said, caught under the skin at last. 'We are one in our decisions.'

Rupert pushed himself to the edge of his seat. 'Take care that you don't make too many. A pushy woman is very unattractive.'

'Is that all?'

'It would seem so.'

'Then excuse me.' She stood up and walked from the room. She climbed the stairs rapidly and went straight down the corridor to her room. She closed the door and crossed to the window. She looked out, her eyes seeing nothing. Her mouth was open. She was surprised to find herself trembling. She let out a little cry of pain. The tears welled up. She pulled her handkerchief from her pocket and dashed it across her eyes. She sniffed. The man was despicable. She took another deep breath to release her tension, pulled sharply on the hem of her tailored suit jacket and turned back into the room. Jesus, what a bastard. He would not get her, though. He had picked the wrong girl to fight with this time.

THIRTY-EIGHT

George Lancing watched the man on horseback making his way up the drive.

'Well, Matilda. He's arrived.'

His wife put aside her tapestry and came over to the window.

Her elegance was still very apparent, though she was a great deal thinner and very much older—in her eighties. She held a matriarchal look in her bearing.

'Hmm. Thought he'd come in the new Rolls. To impress us. Still,' she drew away from the window, 'I'll leave you two together. I don't want to spoil your fun.' The blue crystal eyes caught at his. 'I'll be in the kitchen garden when it's over.'

George was waiting alone when the butler opened the drawing room door.

Rupert strode in. 'I've just come to pay a visit, George.'

George Lancing came towards him, round the back of the sofa. Longbarrow's drawing room was pale grey and peach. It stretched forever, the soft light glowing through the huge windows at the far end. A rosewood baby grand piano stood in the window. Once upon a time Caroline had played for all of them, in family days.

'Nice of you to come, Rupert,' He stretched out his hand. He was ramrod straight still, an old soldier. 'Have you brought Caroline?' he asked, knowing the answer. He had, after all, watched him ride up alone, but he wanted his barbs to stick.

'No,' said Rupert quickly. 'She's at home. She was . . . not feeling like the journey, you know. I came on horseback. Now

460

'George,' he said, his manner more businesslike. 'I want to talk to you, man to man.'

George's expression was curious, receptive. 'Yes?'

'I've heard that you're selling Longbarrow. I'd like to buy it. Keep it in the family.' He was certain of his success; financially, his underhanded dealings at the bank had netted him a substantial private income. He smiled fondly. 'Caroline has told me how much she loved it here as a child, and I—'

'I'm sorry, Rupert.' His look was level. 'It's already sold.'

'Sold? Or the sale going through?'

'Well . . . not exactly sold yet, but . . .'

'How much is she paying for it?'

The old man's eyes held a glint of malicious humour. 'You know who's buying it, then?'

Rupert looked away. He slapped his gloves together. 'I've heard, yes, but it's irrelevant.' He looked back. 'How much?'

'Fifty thousand was my asking price.'

'I'll give you sixty.'

George Lancing pursed his lips. He looked carefully at Rupert. He had actually never seen him so—angry? Out of control? He must really dislike this woman. But why?

'This is all very intriguing, Rupert,' he said slowly. 'I really didn't know you were so interested in Longbarrow. You never have been in the past. I might say,' he said as he turned away, tapping the sofa with his fingers, 'that you have very rarely even visited Longbarrow, much as we would have liked to have seen our daughter and the children.'

Behind his back, Rupert's eyes darkened with irritation.

'. . . And then of course, there is Foxhall,' the old man went on. 'What about that? Do you plan to sell your family home too, just to buy Longbarrow?' He turned again, his old face wreathed in puzzlement.

'I'm going to leave Foxhall to my children.'

'Commendable.'

Rupert pursued his advantage. 'Longbarrow is, if I may say so, a more beautiful house than Foxhall, richer land altogether. And Caroline has always told me how she would love to return here. I'd like to buy Longbarrow for her. Wouldn't it please you, George, to keep it in the family—have your daughter living here?'

'Oh, yes . . .'

Rupert's eyes warmed to his victory.

'. . . if it were for the right motives.' George walked towards the piano, and stroked its deeply polished surface. 'But, you see, Rupert, I am inclined to think that you only want Longbarrow because Mrs Latimer wants it. And you've never really cared what my daughter wanted, now have you?'

He turned to meet the other man's eyes. Rupert tried to conceal his anger. 'On the contrary. I am very fond of Caroline.'

'I'm sorry, Rupert. My mind is made up. I'm selling to Mrs Latimer. I know her plans for it and I approve. She will turn it into the grand old house it used to be, and I can't afford such an overhaul myself. I'd be happy to let her take care of it.' He looked round at the room.

'George. That woman's an upstart. A nobody.' Rupert thrust his hands in the air, the fury lacing through him.

George was quiet in contrast. 'Oh, is that how you see her? To my mind, she's a very enterprising woman. There's a lot to be said for her. She has taste and style and great energy. She will make Longbarrow live again. Matilda and I have loved this old house and we want to see it go to someone who will love it equally. I believe she will.'

George looked hard at Rupert now, the old blue eyes stern. The man had never been good to his daughter. He had never forgiven himself for giving her to a man like Rupert. Her life must have been full of hurt. He would do his best now to assuage that guilt. He would not pander to the man's whims; he would show him that he did not get everything he desired at a flick of his fingers.

Rupert drew in his breath.

'And you don't believe that I would?'

George played his ace. 'You don't have the resources, Rupert. She's much richer than you are.'

The thrust hit its mark. Rupert paled visibly.

'I see. If you change your mind . . .'

'I won't. Good day, Rupert.'

Dickie came out of the bathroom as the telephone began to ring in the adjoining bedroom.

'It's all right. I'll answer it.' She went towards the table beside the bed as Bill came into the room from the landing. 'Yes?' she said as she sat down on the bed. She tied her dressing-gown as she balanced the telephone against her ear. 'Oh . . . hello, Lord

Lancing . . .' She chuckled warmly. '. . . all right then . . . *George!*'

Bill came in slowly and stood by the window. The midday sun filled the room, drenching the soft peach carpet and the peach candlewick bedspread with warmth. Dickie lay back on the pillows as he watched. He could see the slow smile start on her face, illuminating the green eyes. He listened to her punctuate the conversation with murmurs of agreement. She stretched, bending one leg at the knee so that the dressing-gown fell away. His eyes travelled along it to the thigh, seeing the skin there still damp from her bath. Her legs were superb, well balanced and slender, as was her body. She saw him watching and smiled. Now her eyes were on him; glowing with pleasure, absorbing.

'Yes,' she was saying. 'That's wonderful . . . we'll be there tomorrow . . . goodbye, George.'

Her eyes did not leave his as she put down the telephone slowly.

'We've got it,' she breathed, her voice husky with wonder. 'We've got Longbarrow.'

Bill came and sat down on the bed beside her. 'That's marvellous, sweetheart.'

'Yes.' It was almost a purr. She stretched luxuriously. She was never more sensual, thought Bill, than when she had got something she wanted.

'How did you swing it?'

'What?' she said innocently.

His eyes softened with humour. 'I thought you said Rupert Redfield was after it.'

'He was.' Now her eyes filled with the light of battle. 'There was no contest. George and I got on pretty well; he knows I'll care for the house. Besides, the two of them are not exactly the greatest of friends. Do you know he told him I was far richer than he was!'

'That must have hurt him!'

She smiled delightedly and tucked her hands behind her neck. 'Yes!'

'Well, I've been saving something for this news. Stay there. I'll be right back.' Bill left the bed and went out of the room.

She heard his footsteps going down the stairs. She did not move. She was to be mistress of Longbarrow—that glorious house. Now she gave her imagination full rein. She saw the sweeping lawns soft with dew in the early morning, the sun rising over the hills beyond the valley, taking the horses out over their land first thing in the morning before breakfast. Longbarrow would draw them all together again. Max's involvement in the Berlin airlift had restored some of his shaken confidence following Melanie's death, but Dickie knew he would never be quite the same again. Still, he was a strong man and he was already picking up the pieces of his shattered life. She had spoken to him before his current New York trip suggesting her plans and he had agreed wholeheartedly. Home Farm held no fond memories for either of them. Contrary to Charles Redfield's worries, Dickie had fully expected one of the Redfields to try and purchase it. They had proved their point once before and now they were proving it again—Home Farm was a pawn in her chess game. She was selling it, not only for a vast profit accrued over the years, but also way above market value knowing full well that the Redfields would scramble to buy it back into the family, and away from her. She intended to keep Greatley and the two fields that adjoined the house to Home Farm on the lee side of Cobbold's Wood. That did hold fond memories. She could still walk to the crest of the hill and look down over the valley as she had done so long ago. She knew, too, that the purchase of Home Farm paled beside the effect that her ownership of Longbarrow would have on Rupert Redfield. She smiled at that thought. Two birds with one stone—she wanted Longbarrow herself. Home Farm had been no place for a small boy, isolated as it was in the valley. Now Jim would have a proper upbringing, Max would marry again, they would be one family under one roof as she had always imagined, and the house would someday be full of children. Bill would watch over them all, the fond father figure as he had always been. He had supported her through all of this, through all of her wishes. It would have been so very hard without him. And most of all, he had never stopped loving her.

She heard his footsteps on the stairs. He came into the room carrying the chilled bottle of Bollinger and two glasses. He sat down again beside her and popped the cork. The frothy liquid poured into the two glasses as he held them by the stems. He passed one to her and put the champagne back on the table. 'To you, my sweetheart, and to Longbarrow.'

They clinked their glasses and drank. Her eyes were lit with warm affection. 'Bill . . . ?' she said suddenly.

He looked into her eyes and saw their message. He knew her need. It was his too. Her skin at the v-neck of her silk dressing-gown was a warm gold and invited his touch. A pulse beat in her throat. Gently he ran his fingers down the lapel of the garment and pushed it aside to cup her breast in his hand. She gasped at his touch and he bent to take her into his mouth. Dickie's breath caught in her throat, and her head tipped back against the pillow, her eyes closing. His fingers found the belt at her waist and deftly slipped it apart, the garment falling away from her. His mouth travelled downwards, caressing her until her cries moved him so that he could no longer contain himself.

Swiftly he undressed and lay beside her, feeling the pleasure course through him as once again he took her beloved body into his arms. He did not wait any longer. He moved over her, taking her immediately, her cries building and her body cleaving to his. He was drowned in her; her breathing, her movements, intoxicated him. His throat burned with the harsh brush of his breath as the ecstasy filled him. His hands swept over her narrow buttocks to hold her there, against him. He thrust more firmly, her silky legs latched to his. He spoke the words she liked against her ear, rough words, encouraging, alternatively loving. He knew his woman. He felt her ready for him and closed in on her. Together they drew one another to the climax, their bodies pressed upon each other, as the explosion rent them both.

He held her in his arms without moving for a moment, just feeling the warmth of her flood into him.

'I love you, Dickie,' he said. 'You're such a woman.'

Her eyes sought his. 'And I love you too, Bill.'

He smiled at her. The love wasn't like his, but it was hers, and it was enough.

'Come on,' he said. 'Let's get dressed and take a walk. It's a beautiful day. We could go over towards Longbarrow. You can see it from the top of Sam's hill.'

Sam's hill. That's what they called it now. When they sold Home Farm they would keep those two fields that ran from the river up past Cobbold's Wood. She remembered now how as children, she and Sam had seen the house, palest peach in the glow of the early morning sunrise at the edge of the valley, right over by the horizon. Now it was to be hers.

She climbed out of bed.

* * *

In the shadows on the lee side of the wood the grass was still wet with October rain.

They strolled together towards the edge of the copse. Beyond, the brook that ran through Cobbold's Wood trickled out into the open past a clump of reeds and into the mother river. They would cross a small wooden bridge and make their way up to the crest of the field and Sam's hill.

Bill's arm was round her shoulders. He looked into the wood as they passed by.

'Dickie, hold on a minute.' He stopped, turning her. 'I bet there are some great conkers in there. Jim'd like them, wouldn't he? I always liked conker fights when I was little.'

'He's a bit small,' she said doubtfully.

'Still,' Bill was not put off, 'I think I'll get him a few, all the same. You coming in?'

'I think I'll just walk on to the bridge. Why don't you catch up with me?'

'OK.' He stepped through the long clutches of damp grass, pushed aside the brittle branches of the autumn trees and made his way in.

Dickie walked on slowly. A fallen branch lay in the long grass across her path. She bent and lifted it up, stripping the twigs from it. It would make a good walking stick. Her footsteps took her out of the shadows and into the sunlight. She came round the edge of the copse.

She saw him immediately. His face was more ruddy, his thick hair now white with age, but the arrogant stance had not changed as he stood beside his horse at the edge of the stream.

The snapping of the stick was like a pistol shot in the thin air. The startled horse reared up its head. His hands moved swiftly to steady it, his eyes moving instantly to find her. Hunter's eyes. She felt them again as if more than thirty years had not gone between, and the anger rose in her. The gate behind him was still open. He had come from the direction of Longbarrow and stopped by the brook as he would have done in the old days. Those days were gone; everything was different now. This time, Rupert Redfield was on her land.

Her eyes held his, the knowledge there. With satisfaction she saw the humiliation that touched his look of anger, anger because of defeat at her hands. And that was when she moved towards him.

His eyes wavered. He held the horse tighter, watchful now

and alert. She had surprised him. Dickie walked on, closer, her eyes trained on him. The horse danced skittishly, revealing his tension. He quieted it under his breath.

At the bank of the stream, she stopped. Then in one quick but graceful motion bent to the flowing water. She lowered her eyes and saw his reflection in the water. And it was at that moment that she felt a sense of complete serenity. He could do nothing to her now. A light wind skimmed the surface; and much as his image wavered and lost focus, she felt the strength of her pain from that day so long ago begin at last to lose its power. Very deliberately she cupped her hands into the cool water. The sound was soft.

She stood, the wind stirring her hair, and drank, meeting his eyes with a look almost of compassion.

Her eyes did not leave his as she dried her hands slowly on her sleeves. Her face held the softest of smiles. He began to feel cornered.

There was a movement, a crashing of branches in the wood. The man's head turned swiftly to the sound. He muttered something inaudible under his breath, grasped the reins of his horse and mounted swiftly. He gave her a last look as he jerked the animal's head roughly away and then she understood completely. She had frightened Rupert Redfield.

The horse wheeled round. With a scattering of mud he galloped away, scorning the open gate to take the fence at a canter and up the opposite hill for home.

She was still standing there as Bill came around the edge of the wood, his pockets bulging with conkers. His face seemed happy and boyish. The conkers were more for him than Jimmy.

He saw her expression. She seemed far away, as though something had affected her strongly.

'Are you all right, Dickie?' he asked.

She lifted her face to the sun and smiled.

'Never better.' She took his arm.

About the Author

PAMELA TOWNLEY was born in 1947 on an isolated Shropshire
farm in the Longmyd hills. A former model, she is now a full-
time author; her books include THE IMAGE, ROGAN'S
MOOR and WINTER JASMINE.